The Coming of the Demons

Gwenyth Hood

WILLIAM MORROW AND COMPANY, INC.

New York   1982

Library of Congress Cataloging in Publication Data

Hood, Gwenyth.
    The coming of the demons.

    I. Title.
PS3558.O54C6   813'.54   81-11263
ISBN 0-688-00776-7   AACR2

Printed in the United States of America

First Edition

1 2 3 4 5 6 7 8 9 10

BOOK DESIGN BY MICHAEL MAUCERI

Acknowledgments

I wish to thank those people whose kindness and encouragement have helped me to the creation of my first published novel: First, Maria Guarnaschelli, who took this story into her heart when it was still in its awkward adolescence and helped me to bring out the best in it; and Lois Wallace and Zibby Oneal, who befriended me and spent much effort working with me. My patient roommate, Valerie Hutchinson, acted as my faithful first audience, informal critic, and sometimes my proofreader. John Aldridge, Barbara Lazarus, Katherine Lever and Tom Wilson all supported and encouraged me. Finally, I wish to thank my parents, who gave me life and love and many other gifts too precious to be named or counted.

Antonio:

And I'll be sworn 'tis true: travellers ne'er did lie,
Though fools at home condemn'em.

Gonzalo:

If in Naples
I should report this now, would they believe me?

—THE TEMPEST, Act III, Scene 3

1

The planet's sun shone brightly on the dusty and crowded marketplace of the port city the natives called Naples. The sun often shone brightly on Naples, and the marketplace was usually dusty and crowded, but noon seldom offered a spectacle to the curious marketgoers such as it did today. It was the twenty-ninth day of the month they called October, in the year (reckoned from the birth of the founder of their religion) twelve hundred and sixty-eight. On this day a claimant to the throne of Sicily and Southern Italy was to have his head struck from his shoulders with an ax, the customary form of execution this culture accorded to an individual of noble birth, provided no one was extraordinarily angry with him, and he had not fallen so far afoul of their High Priest (or Pope, as they called him) to deserve burning at the stake.

King Charles had come in person to witness the execution, for it was barely legal with his presence and would certainly have been illegal without it. Formal execution of persons of royal blood was not an established custom in this culture. Life imprisonment or clandestine assassination would have been more usual and far easier, but King Charles was a stubborn and determined man. As a Frenchman invited into Italy by the Pope, he had no hereditary claim to the Sicilian throne. However, no one was to be allowed to believe he doubted the legitimacy of his authority or his actions on that account.

So King Charles (*Carlo* to the Italians) sat on his splendid horse in the midst of the marketplace, his armor and his mount's bridle and saddle glistening with jewels and silken ribbons. Beneath the shadow cast by his royal pomp stood the prisoner, a slender boy about sixteen with red hair and an alert look. He was the sole survivor of the dynasty Charles had displaced, and his name was Conradin.

Conradin's dynasty had been well-beloved in Naples. Some of his kinsmen had been strong and brilliant kings. So, because the boy was young, fair and innocent, because he was handsome, and because King Charles's determined legal proceedings had seemed unroyal and perhaps even villainous to many people, the streets were clogged with men and women of all classes. The air fairly vibrated with unspoken pleas and protests. As Abbot Sinibaldo later wrote to a friend in Milan, "Many of the people were in tears because they loved the boy's grandfather, Federico II, and his uncle Manfred. And even I myself, who hate the whole race and their Empire, pitied his youth and his mother's sorrow. Yet the Lord of Heaven is a righteous God, who visits the sins of the fathers upon their children unto the third and fourth generation." Sinibaldo remarked later on, "I let my heart be softened too soon, for I ought to have known Satan would not consent to let his favorite family become extinct so soon." The Satan he referred to here was the greatest of the demons, the enemy of God and of Mankind, hence, according to the Pope, the natural friend of the Hohenstaufen dynasty of which Conradin was the last legitimate survivor.

Conradin stopped abruptly before the scaffold he was to mount and whipped off his leather glove, royally adorned with jewels since King Charles had not dared be so petty as to deprive his captive of all marks of rank. He held it high, his face filled with spirit. "People of Naples, this I throw forth among you, that you may find me a champion to avenge the wrongs against my house!" As a French guard hurried to intercept it, Conradin suddenly hurled the gauntlet high over the heads of the closest bystanders, to the side of the square where the fewest of Charles's Frenchmen stood. The glove sped, its jewels glittering in the sunlight, and came down at the very edge of the crowd among a group of tradesmen. There was a confused bustle as someone seized and hid it while others whirled around him to shield what was happening from King Charles's view. Most of the crowd remained silent, though King Charles sensed that the youth's words had sunk deeply into the people's hearts. He gnashed his teeth. An attempt to deprive his rival of some brave last words would be beneath his own royal dignity. He would simply have to put up with this as best he could.

Two of Charles's French soldiers approached Conradin, since they feared he would not submit quietly. But disdaining to be touched by low-born hands, Conradin stepped calmly between them, mounted the scaffold and knelt down. "O Mother, what a cup of sorrow do I pour for you," he said, laying his head on the block.

Until that moment public opinion had been divided between King Charles, his French followers and his priestly allies, who did not object to what was happening, and friends of the Hohenstaufen dynasty, who did. What followed was completely unsatisfactory from everyone's point of view.

"Lo!" wrote Abbot Sinibaldo. "Suddenly there rose a great cry among the people, as from the very Heavens there came a flash of light so mighty all were blinded. With it came a crash of thunder so loud earth's foundations seemed to shake. The animals were driven wild by the sight and the sound. King Charles's knights were thrown to the ground by their horses, which bellowed, plunged and galloped off as though Satan himself pursued them. The common people cowered to the ground and covered their eyes and ears. When the noise ceased, I raised my head and beheld three strangers standing upon the scaffold where the prisoner was. In form they were like men, but they were dressed from head to foot in silver armor, including strange helmets on their heads with visors of clear material like glass, so their faces could clearly be seen. I wondered greatly what they would do, but they stood still and said nothing."

And while these strangers paused, more people began to raise themselves from the ground. No one was subsequently in any doubt about the meaning of the apparition, but interpretations of it varied drastically.

Some of the common people were certain the silver-clad strangers were messengers sent by God to prevent the blasphemous execution of a youth of royal blood. Those who had no breach of faith with the Hohenstaufen dynasty with which to reproach themselves broke into loud cheers. Others, who suddenly recollected they had in some way failed in their duty to the young king, began to beat their breasts and mourn. The executioner, in particular, was filled with terror and threw himself down at Abbot Sinibaldo's feet, begging forgiveness, which he believed the priest could grant in the name of God.

Abbot Sinibaldo had quite another interpretation of the event, so he ignored the supplicant. As he put it, "Satan can make himself appear even as an angel of light." Clearly it was Satan's business, not God's, to preserve the Hohenstaufen dynasty. Therefore the strangers must have been sent by him. Almost two thirds of King Charles's knights came to the same conclusion, and without waiting another moment, they took to their heels and fled.

Yet a third opinion arose in the minds of people of both sympathies: the great Hohenstaufen, Emperor Federico II, Conradin's grandfather, who had always been suspected of consorting with sorcerers and demon-conjurers, had obviously sent three of his necromancers to the aid of his heir. The Emperor's death, of course, had been announced, and a magnificent tomb had been built for him in Palermo, but wise people knew this was all a trick on his part to gain time. They knew for certain he was actually hiding with his court in a cave underneath some mountain, waiting for the right moment to emerge with all his forces and overthrow the Church's plans.

In fact, the only person present who seemed to doubt that the strangers, whether they were from God or from Satan, good or evil, had come to rescue King Conradin, was Conradin himself. The youth had recoiled from the light in terror like everyone else, and surveyed the scene with as much consternation as any supporter of King Charles. As soon as he regained possession of himself, he began to inch away from them.

This was the first thing King Charles noticed as he raised himself from the ground where his horse had thrown him. "Get back!" he called commandingly to his prisoner. The young Hohenstaufen stiffened, glanced briefly in Charles's direction, turned again to stare at the apparitions in silver armor, and took two or three more steps backward.

Raising himself fully to his feet, Charles sought his knights. Few remained, and those who did stood at the edge of the crowd, motionless and speechless. Charles realized he would have to deal with the interlopers himself.

This was difficult, since he had no idea who or what they were. Their appearance gave him no inspiration, for they were neither beautiful enough to require reverence, nor so appallingly ugly as certainly to be demons. When he looked inward to test his conscience, the question still remained unanswered, because he could neither wholly exonerate himself nor completely condemn himself for his treatment of Conradin. He took a step toward them and spoke with royal dignity. "Who are you, and from whence have you come? If from God, you need not have come in this manner; I would have obeyed you willingly and at once if you had made it known that the Heavenly King did not desire the Hohenstaufen's death. If you come from the devil, do you imagine you will be allowed to hinder me, the chosen instrument of God and His Holy Church?"

One of the intruders finally tried to speak, but neither the French nor the Italians could understand his words. "From his helmet came a sound like the roar of a ferocious beast," wrote Sinibaldo, "and there was a great crackle as if a forest were burning. Everyone drew back in terror, but lo! God was with King Charles, and his heart did not fail."

When the apparition failed to produce coherent language, Charles was absolved of all suspicion of its divine provenance. With amazing courage, he drew his sword, an act which none of his followers had dared attempt, and rushed upon the demons or sorcerers. These made no effort at resistance. Their armor, which had looked so imposing from a distance, did not protect them at all from his keen blade. "When he smote the foremost," wrote Sinibaldo, "his sword pierced right through armor to skin and bone, slicing off the arm completely at the shoulder so that the sorcerer cried out with pain and all were nearly deafened, for his voice was as loud as a thousand men's."

But while his comrade screamed in agony, another sorcerer drew forth, as Sinibaldo described it, "a bent rod which shone like silver and shot forth a ray of light so hot that when it struck King Charles on the neck, he fell to the ground like a corpse and has since had no power of movement."

Shamed by their lord's example, and heartened by the discovery that the strangers were of flesh and blood, vulnerable to the bite of steel, a great crowd of Charles's vassals rushed at the sorcerers from all sides. It did them little good. As the instrument flashed, man after man of the natives sank to the ground in a living but completely helpless heap. Meanwhile, another "roar full of crackles" was heard to issue from the helmet of the wounded sorcerer, as if he were trying to speak. None of the natives could understand his words.

But those words are fully and authentically imprinted on the Peleziterean memory to this day. Any qualified Peleziterean may request this section of the archives from the central computer and hear Agni yi-Induran cry out, in a voice rising and falling with his pain, repeating itself as if unable to remember what it had just said, "Archon, can you hear me? Can you hear me?" Agni yi-Induran's transmitter was damaged,

13

and he apparently could not hear the Peleziterea's acknowledgment. "The hatcherbrats have mutinied. And this planet is inhabited. Can you hear me? Very inhabited! Jori Hatcherbrat has my energet. The Prime Directive is at stake. Do you hear me? Do you hear me?" And those were the last words of a young man in whom the Archon had placed great hope.

2

In the outer reaches of the planet's solar system, where the Peleziterea was traveling, an emergency meeting of the High Council was rapidly summoned. The massive design of the Council room was a grim reminder of the colony's decline. Attrition, illness, and civil war had left less than one-third the number of members prescribed in the Consitution available to serve. So the six fragile elders now assembled were dwarfed by the majestic grey arches and the domes above them.

They were accustomed to this of course, and in any case would have been too absorbed in the business at hand to dwell on it. The Archon, or Sevenfold, had just entered a proposal for dealing with the sudden threat to the Prime Directive. The five sub-Archons, or Sixfold, who composed the rest of the Council were considering it. His plan appeared to them all as difficult and impractical. Yet it was high-minded and seemed to be exactly what the Constitution required in such cases. Therefore, none of them wanted to be the first to protest or offer a counter-proposal.

Nibbana Parzes, her bloodless cheeks appearing whiter because of her bright red synthetic eyes and hair, stared down at the table. It had been more than three generations since a Lawchild in her family had been born with healthy natural hair or eyes. The Peleziterean ruling class was badly inbred and riddled with genetic defects. Consequently, flamboyant and unnatural "accessories," as they were called, had become the style and the custom among them, an indispensable symbol of rank and status. Rho Smide, sitting beside Nibbana, had gold eyes and violet hair, while the eyes and hair of the others were all shades of red, green, orange and violet. So strong was the pressure for "cosmic" shades that even members of the much healthier yi-Induran coalition, who did not need them, had ordered contact lenses and wigs in a variety of colors for wear on ceremonial occasions.

The only eccentric was the Archon, Benrik Eridani himself. Five years before, on attaining the age of fifty standard years, he had suddenly discarded his matching lavender accessories and ordered eyes in natural brown and hair in old man's grey. This provoked a scandal that was still fresh.

Finally Jimmik Centauri, the medical sub-Archon, shook his synthetic green mane and challenged the Archon. "Sevenfold, you *certainly* appear fond of high-sounding rhetoric."

An indefinite expression glimmered around the Archon's mouth, probably reflecting relief that the discussion had at any rate begun at last. "I am sorry, Sixfold, if the manner in which I presented my proposal was objectionable. Please feel free to state it in your own terms, if you think it necessary."

"Thank you! " resumed Jimmik Centauri, laying both hands flat before him. Five pairs of eyes turned toward him, one brown, one red, one violet, and two gold. "Here is our situation: Agni yi-Induran, accompanied by two hatcherbrats, was sent to explore the third planet from the alpha star." The star whose system the Pelezitereans were presently exploring for habitable planets was always designated the alpha star. "He was to determine whether or not the planet was inhabited, and if not, whether it was habitable for us. The message you have just relayed to us states clearly the planet is inhabited. We may further infer that the planet is so temptingly habitable for us that the two hatcherbrats conspired against Fivefold Agni yi-Induran, with whom they have hitherto been on good terms (and why should they not be? Yi-Indurans and hatcherbrats have so much in common), and caused his death in some manner. Subsequently, they have either destroyed their transmitters or deactivated them. It would therefore appear they are bent on losing themselves among the people of this planet and making themselves both at home and important, which is, of course, what anyone but a yi-Induran would expect of a hatcherbrat."

Jimmik paused. The Archon said softly, "This is no time for innuendoes, Sixfold. But since you allude to the matter, recall it was you who insisted we send Agni with two hatcherbrats instead of with Natheless yi-Induran, who wished to accompany her brother."

"I pointed out she was too young," returned Jimmik Centauri shortly. "But to continue: As you correctly suggest, the Constitution our ancestors adopted a thousand years ago clearly and strictly enjoins us in these cases to form an expedition for tracking down the rebellious hatcherbrats and completely removing them and any potentially dangerous instruments they have with them. When we have rescued the threatened civilization from any kind of interference, we must leave them and return to the skies, even though we expose ourselves to every danger imaginable in the process, including that of contracting diseases which would wipe out our own colony.

"I maintain, however, we should stop and think a moment, which is more than our ancestors had time to do when they fled Urith. The most our hatcherbrats can do in a case like this is use our energets to subjugate an ignorant populace and build an empire which might last their lifetime but would certainly dissolve with their death. They have neither the knowledge nor training to build on or even to duplicate the tools we supplied them. So they can really communicate our knowledge to no one."

Several of the Sixfold stirred uneasily. No arguments could have more effectively driven them to support the Archon's position. Nibbana Parzes spoke up with strong feeling. "Our energets have lasted centuries. Just one of them, passed down from generation to generation in the hands of a repressive dynasty of rulers, could for all practical purposes stagnate a civilization permanently.

"And if it didn't happen that way," said Rho Smide, his concern for the Constitution dragging him into the argument despite his usual reluctance, "one of them could easily lie hidden for eons without impairment and be rediscovered at a time when the planet's science was far enough developed to learn from it. It could give their people a thousand years' boost along the road to self-destruction."

"So," said Jimmik Centauri almost flippantly, "if all civilizations eventually self-destruct, what's a thousand years one way or the other?"

The council members looked doubtfully at one another. The Archon answered, "As with all questions of life and death, Jimmik, it does not matter at all—unless *we* are responsible."

The Sixfold faced Jimmik Centauri, silent reproval in their eyes. The atmosphere of opposition only stirred his antagonism more deeply. Blood flowed into his cheeks, making them nearly as red as his artificial eyes.

17

"What I would like to know is why we of the High Council are too dense to take a lesson from the hatcherbrats. It is absurdly obvious there is a delightfully habitable planet in this star system. Its civilization is so inferior to ours that if we settled there we would probably be worshiped as gods. At the same time, does anyone here really doubt our science would be a great gift to the native inhabitants? Whatever culture we might develop there would be vastly superior to whatever they have now."

Five intensely colored pairs of eyes continued to focus upon Jimmik Centauri. The shockwaves his words generated in the communal consciousness did not immediately translate into anything visible. Finally, the Archon answered quietly, "Sixfold Centauri, it seems to me you have chosen a highly unsuitable moment to question the Prime Directive. Had you raised your doubts before, we might have had the leisure to discuss them with you. But as the situation stands . . ."

"Who would have bothered?" retorted Jimmik. The question never made a real difference before."

There was another pause. "Do any of the other members of the Council feel similarly?" said the Archon. "Do you presently wish to debate the validity of the Prime Directive?"

There was a shifting and shuffling sound as the Sixfold stirred in their chairs or altered their positions slightly. Then Nibbana Parzes spoke. "I do not believe anyone besides Sixfold Jimmik has any doubts about the Prime Directive. But if the Lawchild wishes it, why should we not devote a few minutes to discussion?"

Samlai Wyce, a quiet woman who had not spoken before, suddenly broke out. "The fundamental question is, does anyone have the right to take over civilizations, however primitive, and instruct their inhabitants about how to live?" She paused for effect, as though planning to pile several more rhetorical questions on top of that one. But Jimmik Centauri did not give her the chance.

"No one, ever, I suppose you mean to imply," he snapped.

Samlai shook her orange locks in irritation. "That's *not* what I intended to say, Lawchild Jimmik. I *was* going to suggest that only those who know everything and have a perfect civilization might have the right to take over other people's civilizations and replace them with their own. And I ask you, are we that people?" Perhaps unconsciously, she brought her hands up against her cheeks, near her artificial eyes.

"I believe Samlai is right," added the Archon gently. "As a people, we Pelezitereans have accomplished much. We obviously can manipulate matter and energy to a much greater extent than the planetary natives we are discussing. The fact remains, however, there are unresolved tensions in our culture. In a sense we carry with us the problem we ran away from when we left our own planet. We who are in this room right now grew up in the aftermath of a vicious civil war. And more subtle, insidious problems seem to be sapping the physical and mental vigor of our young people. In short, we run the danger of creating a new Urith on any planet we colonize. That is why, in fairness, our ancestors decided, when we left Urith, that we would never land on a planet with a less developed culture than our own. We were to find an uninhabited planet and settle there, if indeed we ever settled anywhere."

Centauri broke in. "Our problems are at least of a higher level than those of pre-atomic barbarians. I can't see what's wrong with raising every culture at least to our stage of development."

"But you don't create a culture with such an attitude," said Nibbana pointedly. "People solve problems by searching painstakingly for answers. When people like Karsma Megala on Urith impose their own solutions on others, certain they are right, they generate nothing but disruption. The people Karsma Megala imprisoned, tortured and killed were some of the finest and brightest Urithian culture ever produced." When she completed her analogy, she looked to the Archon, who braced himself mentally. He knew that while she meant what she said, she had said it only to render him more receptive to whatever position of her own she was preparing to advance.

Centauri continued rather cynically. "Of course the best and the brightest barbarians will be on our side."

"That's just what Karsma Megala thought," said Nibbana. "And he wanted to be worshiped as a god too."

Rho Smide shifted his position restlessly. "I think we have spent long enough on this. There was never really any question of actually defying the Prime Directive in principle. The question is whether we can afford the sacrifice the Constitution requires of us at this point to keep a violation from occurring."

"Which would put our very survival in jeopardy," added Mellis Holl, the other quiet member.

"That's well said," responded the Archon, "and sacrifice is the right word. The basic fact is our Founders felt so strongly about the oppression from which they had fled, they believed they and we would have no right to continue existing if they or we caused another civilization to be oppressed as they were. This is why they called this particular ordinance the Prime Directive. And why we are supposed to put it before everything, including our own survival. Consequently, those hatcherbrats must be removed."

At this point Nibbana straightened and assumed a somewhat combative expression. "Yet I must state, Benrik Eridani, it is one thing to respect other people's rights, another to place the survival of strangers' culture before our very own survival."

The Archon's expression did not change. "You are right, of course, Nibbana Parzes. But that is exactly what the Constitution calls for."

"It is simply not normal human behavior," continued Nibbana tenaciously.

"Are you suggesting our Founders were abnormal?"

"They were very idealistic," returned Nibbana, with the kind of indulgent smile one might reserve for overenthusiastic ancestors.

Jimmik Centauri guffawed. "That's abnormal enough!"

Nibbana went on. "It must be suggested they weren't too practical." And now the other three murmured in agreement. The Archon searched all their faces in order before he spoke again.

"Is that what you all think?" he asked finally.

"Yes," said Nibbana's voice loudly. Three other voices more or less echoed hers, softly, somewhat reluctantly. Jimmik Centauri said nothing.

"Well," said the Archon slowly, "I hope you will not mind if I disagree with you all. An action is only really impractical when it is not worth its cost. Our estimates of a fair cost are based entirely on our perceptions of the value of the thing to be won."

Nibbana nodded knowingly. "Of course, Archon, you are trying to employ the old shame strategy, trying to make me back away from admitting I value my own survival and that of my friends more than strangers'. You should know better, Benrik Eridani. I'm not a child and I can't be frightened so easily. Give me one good reason why our own survival is worth less than anyone else's."

The other Sixfold, with the exception of Jimmik Centauri, who seemed to have lost interest in the discussion entirely, shifted uneasily with sympathy for Nibbana's words. The Archon seemed intrigued by her uncharacteristic openness. "Well, Nibbana, that's a fair question. Let me try to respond. First of all, I think you're mistaken to assume our survival aboard the Peleziterea is something assured, something we can only lose by sending another expedition down to that planet. As a matter of fact, we are presently at a lower ebb than we have ever been in the thousand years since we left Urith. The last civil war among us wiped out much of the good breeding stock among our people. Now, according to our computer predictions, we were supposed to rear a fairly strong younger generation. And we have indeed reared more Lawchildren in the last twenty-five years than our eugenics department originally required. But something has gone wrong. A large proportion of these new young people, instead of assuming adult responsibilities, have chosen to behave as hatcherbrats, lazing in the gardens most of the day, dulling their minds on drugs and interminably discussing their intuitions. A smaller proportion, but one that contains some of the most earnest and vigorous young people, have developed a strange religious organization centering around the God-myth. You yourself, Lawchild Nibbana, in your official capacity, have been more disturbed about these than about the others. If we're to re-place all our high officials successfully, we're going to have to alter the attitudes of many of these Lawchildren. Thus far, however, our success has been quite limited. As a result, you cannot argue our survival is· as-sured. Even assuming we lose no more lives after Agni yi-Induran, we're still in grave danger of dying out from inbreeding and attrition in the next generation."

Nibbana answered impatiently. "Don't you see that's exactly why we shouldn't risk any more lives?"

"Is it?" said Benrik. "For what reasons are we in such a distressing state, Nibbana Parzes?"

"Why ask me about the causes?"

"Why not? You're the head of the Personality department."

"We have no idea why this is happening now. What makes you believe it might have anything to do with Personality?"

"If it doesn't? What is the cause, then? An infectious disease? A sudden mass genetic mutation?"

"It would save time," said Nibbana mildly, "if you would stop trying to lead me to your answer. Tell us yourself what you think it is."

The Archon glanced around the table. "It appears to me like a kind of despair, a disgust with this culture."

"I see," said Nibbana, "You are arguing since we are all really in despair anyway, the only sensible thing for us to do is commit mass suicide."

The Archon looked up, ruefully. "Actually I was trying to suggest something more complicated."

"What, then? We're all waiting," said Nibbana.

The Archon paused. "This really isn't an easy argument. Let me con-sider. My main point is that life itself is much like happiness—a very complicated phenomenon we do not fully understand. Doctors in the

Medical department know quite a lot about life, yet no one has been able to figure out why some apparently healthy people drop dead at young ages while some weak, sickly people, full of genetic flaws and in need of constant therapy, live to be old and lead productive lives. People who directly pursue the bare name of life, like those who directly pursue the bare name of happiness, are not always, or even often, the ones who find it. An example comes to mind. Years ago, when we were all apprentices, a group of three scout ships, exploring a binary star system, ventured too close to the denser star and were captured by its gravity. Facing this emergency, one of the pilots, Frofor yi-Induran, experimented with combinations of powers that had never been tried before and speeds which were believed fatal. He escaped with his crew, also leading a second scout ship, which dared to follow him, to safety. The third pilot was afraid to risk new methods. He continued to struggle for his life by conventional means. He was drawn closer and closer to the star, and finally immolated along with his ship and entire crew. So, you see, willingness to risk death sometimes leads to life."

"That's a special case, Archon," demurred Nibbana. "Anyone captured by a star's gravity ought to know that doing nothing means death, so that anything offering the slightest hope of escape ought to be tried. Our death is not certain if we do nothing in this case, and I can see no possible advantage from any attempt to intervene on that planet."

The Archon rested lightly on the table. "There is the point. We cannot foresee everything. Remember, Frofor yi-Induran had been reprimanded many times as an adolescent for being too adventuresome and wandering too far from the colony, for trying too many experiments. Yet, precisely because he was used to pitting himself against natural forces for the sheer joy of it, because he risked his life when there was no necessity, he was able to save himself and others when they found themselves in unavoidable peril. In the same way we might discover or learn something on this planet that will help us, or simply develop skills in members of the landing party which will be useful for the life of the colony as a whole later on."

Moved, but not completely convinced, the Sixfold looked doubtfully at each other. "I still don't think we should do it," said Nibbana coolly.

Benrik stood up slowly. "I have no desire to oppose the entire Council. And I suppose there is no reason for further discussion. I hope you do not think I will attempt to force my convictions upon you if there is so little concern in the Council for the Prime Directive." His voice was sad. "I will, however, immediately resign from my position as Archon of the Pelezitereans and attempt to organize the expedition the Constitution requires from the private sector."

Nibbana stood "And suppose the High Council forbade your expedition?"

Benrik Eridani's eyes set. But he answered in a gentle voice, "Would you forbid Lawchildren to leave the ship when hatcherbrats have already done so? I fear that is unconstitutional. Do you want another civil war, Lawchild Nibbana?"

Nibbana sank back into her chair. The Archon turned to leave the room. "Wait!" Nibbana blurted. "Don't leave, Lawchild Benrik! We can predict exactly what will happen if you arrange things from the Eridani Bubble. You'll involve your son Alrik and his fiancée Natheless yi-Induran, and with them, all the rest of the Haven company, which contains the most energetic and promising young people we have right now. The less support the expedition has, the riskier it will be, and if we lose the Haven company, we are all certainly ruined."

Benrik bowed his head. "I am truly sorry, Nibbana Parzes. I fear your analysis may well be correct."

"Come back then, take your seat once more, and remain as Archon," she replied. "If you are so determined to put our survival in jeopardy, the least we can do is organize it with the central government's support so no plan offering hope of success will be overlooked."

The Archon glanced around the room. "Is what I hear the desire of the High Council, or only of Nibbana Parzes?"

Three more chairs were pushed back, as the Sixfold rose to their feet. "You have heard the will of the Council," said Rho Smide, Samlai Wyce and Mellis Holl. Only Jimmik Centauri remained seated, watching. "How theatrical," he commented. "Playing the part of the Founders in too many Apprenticeship plays has ruined you for life, Benrik."

"What is your vote then, Sixfold Centauri?" demanded Nibbana.

"Why, who could dispute your judgment?" he answered.

"Do you stand with the others then?"

"I do," said Jimmik sweetly. "Can we all be seated now?"

The other sub-Archons settled in their chairs, relieved that the question that related so closely to the Prime Directive had been settled in a way that placed so little responsibility for it on their shoulders. Benrik returned slowly to the head of the table and repossessed his chair. "Our next task is to choose the landing party," he said. His eyes went around the table, silently scrutinizing every member of the council. The others assented inaudibly.

3

As the planet's sun appeared to move along its lengthy arc toward the planet's western horizon (though actually, of course, the planet itself was rotating), Naples remained in confusion. The demon-sorcerers had taken refuge in a church facing the square, carrying their bleeding and unconscious companion with them. And the marketplace was full of the prostrate bodies of those they had paralyzed. King Charles had immediately been carried back to his palace by those in his retinue who had neither fled nor attacked the apparition. Most of the other people were carried away as soon as their friends, relatives or other merciful people could recover from their terror and sneak back into the square to help them. Among the first to begin such work were the monks who had come with Abbot Sinibaldo to visit the city.

No one knew anything about what had become of Conradin. Some had seen him leap down from the scaffold and into the crowd, where way was quickly made for him. No one dared touch him for fear of demons.

Yet there was one man who would not have feared striking the boy-King down beneath his horse's hooves, if he had been there to see him flee. But as luck, fate or providence would have it, his terrified horse had carried him more than a mile from the marketplace before he could regain control of his own destiny. And it was not easy to make his way back to the marketplace against the tide of the stampeding populace. When, cursing and swearing, Cardinal Ughetto found himself once more before the now-empty scaffold, the sight of it bewildered him. The whole square around him seemed to be littered with corpses, not one of them headless or apparently wounded. Neither King Charles nor his intended victim was anywhere in sight. "Where is Conradin? Where is Conradin?" bellowed Ughetto. He had learned his hatred for the Hohenstaufen dynasty in the bitter wars that had racked Northern Italy during the previous generation.

To his further amazement, Ughetto was answered by groans and curses from the supposed corpses. "Where is Conradin?" mimicked one. "Gone to Hell for all I know! Go to the Devil and ask him!"

"Why ask people who are lying helpless here on the ground?" returned another more reasonably. "Seek him yourself, since you still have your legs!"

"Beelzebub!" roared Ughetto (one of his least offensive oaths, but he was trying to concentrate on other matters) as he spurred his horse across the marketplace. He shouted for his retainers. "Pietro! Roffredo! Filippo!" Ughetto was distraught at the idea all his men-at-arms might be lying useless among the paralyzed in the square. But a shout answered him, and Filippo emerged from the alley behind a nearby building. He was limping badly and leaning for support against a horse whose richly adorned bridle he was grasping.

"Filippo!" cried the Cardinal, and then he noticed the rubies set in the horse's bridle. "That's the King's destrier!"

"Yes, my lord," agreed Filippo lamely. "My own mount threw me and galloped off. Most everyone else grabbed the first horse they could lay hands on and rode off through the gates. I'm afraid mine was no exception, so I decided I would likewise have to borrow. I didn't notice the royal trappings until this moment."

"Fool!" cried the Cardinal. "Do you not see, Conradin might be escaping the city in that way this very instant?"

Filippo gaped at his master. "But, Your Eminence, what need would he have for horses when demons came to rescue him?"

"What are you talking about?" demanded the Cardinal angrily.

Filippo solemnly indicated the paralyzed with a sweep of his hand. "The demons who cast the spell on all these people came to free him."

"Don't talk nonsense!" snapped Ughetto. "I'm easily the wickedest man in the whole of Italy, if not the whole of Christendom, and Satan never sent a demon to help me out of my difficulties! Why would he aid this half-wit stripling, barely weaned from his mother's milk, who babbles chivalrous nonsense about right, wrong and revenge at the very edge of his grave?"

"But, *Signore*, if you had seen—"

"Silence! Whatever happened was a charlatan's trick and we'll expose it shortly. Now take that horse, ride like a fury to the port and see that no ships leave Naples!"

"The King's horse?" cried Filippo in alarm.

"A greater King needs it today!" cried Ughetto. "Be off!"

Filippo mounted with difficulty because of his injured leg, but galloped away quickly enough.

Ughetto rode on, shouting and calling, ordering anyone he could find to go to guard the several city gates. As he reached the street before the King's palace, he sighted one of Abbot Sinibaldo's monks walking between two French foot soldiers.

"Brother Ambrogio!" called Ughetto, reining in his horse. "Go and gather your brothers. Send them to the city's poor and simple people who love the Hohenstaufen. Have them proclaim high and low that Conradin is accursed before God. Anyone who aids his escape in any way shall be damned beyond the least hope of pardon!"

The monk glanced up at the horseman from beneath his hood. He bowed humbly. "Your Eminence, Father Abbot has commanded my brothers and me to care for the injured and console their families as best we can. If Your Eminence desires to change our orders, you will perhaps find the Abbot Sinibaldo passing somewhere between the marketplace and the hospital."

"Do you think your abbot will thank you for denying immediate help in this time of dire emergency?" cried the Cardinal. "Hasten at once to do what I say!"

Brother Ambrogio kept his head bowed. "Pardon me, Your Eminence, if I dare not disobey my father abbot."

"What ails you?" demanded the furious Ughetto. "The poor and the wounded you have always with you. If Conradin is not recaptured, the Church will soon be stripped of all her property and authority."

The monk responded in a low voice, but his words were perhaps not as guarded as they should have been. "That will not happen if God does not will it."

Now really enraged, Ughetto rode his horse forward until it stood almost on top of the trembling monk. The French foot soldiers backed off in alarm. "What impudence!" cried Ughetto, staring down at the bowed head. "So you must mouth platitudes at me, as if I couldn't produce a thousand for myself."

Ambrogio's lips moved in silent prayer.

"And now you pray for deliverance from me, as if I were a demon?" screamed Ughetto, really transported.

The monk was adamant. "I am reciting the *Miserere*, Your Eminence. Is that forbidden?"

"Go and do as I have said."

"I dare do nothing but what my Father Abbot has commanded," reiterated Ambrogio.

Ughetto knew his purposes had little chance of prevailing with the indomitable Abbot Sinibaldo, so he raised his sword menacingly. "The Devil take your father abbot! Obey me!"

The monk stood unmoving. Finally he said, "No, Your Eminence. I dare not obey you. I must follow the orders of the man I am bound to obey."

"Then watch for your head!" cried the outraged Cardinal, bringing the flat of his sword down hard on Ambrogio. The monk sank to his knees, a stream of bright blood running from his forehead down over his face. The foot soldiers cried out in horror, and one advanced to steady the monk.

"God damn you all," screamed Ughetto. He was just turning his horse's head to gallop away when someone called out from in front of the palace gates. Unnoticed by Ughetto, the great bronze doors had slowly swung open, and amid a cluster of bejeweled but bedraggled courtiers, King Charles was carried out seated in a chair. The two foot soldiers fell to their knees before him and Cardinal Ughetto turned to salute him.

The King rested back against the chair, motionless. His face expressed weariness and disgust at his inability to move. His limp body was wrapped in the royal purple, and it was hard to believe for all its bulk and brawn it was useless. Still, he could speak, and at his word his attendants set his chair down on the pavement. He looked at the bleeding monk and then at the infuriated Cardinal. "What is this?" he asked at last. "What does it mean, Your Eminence, when a Prince of the Church strikes an unarmed monk? If I had seen a layman do that, I'd have had his hand cut off."

Ughetto glowered. "It angers me when I see lazy, good-for-nothing monks who care too little either for Your Majesty or the Holy Church to do a good work."

King Charles looked at Ambrogio and asked, "What do you say, monk?"

But Ambrogio's head was still reeling from the blow, and he did not quite know where he was or who was speaking. Dimly he was aware of a voice addressing him, and he inquired of the soldier who supported him, "What does he say?" His vision cleared for a moment, and he saw the King's purple robes. "Your Majesty!" he cried, bowing his head again.

Charles grimaced exasperatedly and addressed one of his foot soldiers. "Oliver, what happened here?"

The larger of the two soldiers, the one supporting Ambrogio, spoke haltingly. "Sire—if it please you—this monk is a good monk, and he has been going back and forth tending the wounded and praying over them, and my brother Humphrey—he was injured today, Sire, trying to defend you, and the sorcerer struck him down and then he was trampled by a horse and his leg was broken, and this monk tended him and set his leg and was coming with us to tend other soldiers—we thought it was a good idea, Sire, since you had given no orders and we were sure we could do nothing to seize Conradin. But this noble Cardinal wanted the monk to preach to the people and tell them they would be damned if they aided Conradin, and he refused, saying he could only do as his Father Abbot ordered, and I don't know which of them is right, because I'm only a simple man."

The monk was no longer leaning on the Frenchman, and from this the King judged he was ready to answer for himself. "What do you say, monk?" he demanded again.

Ambrogio spoke. "If it please Your Majesty," he said, "neither I nor any of my brothers are preaching friars, but we do have some experience tending the sick, which is what our Father Abbot commanded us to do. Cardinal Ughetto would have us preach damnation against Conradin's supporters when not a soul in Naples does not already know Conradin is an enemy of the Church and has been excommunicated. I dared not, on my own authority, forsake my Father Abbot's commands for Cardinal Ughetto's, for it seemed to me the people of Naples do not love demons, and they are very frightened already and do not need to be frightened more."

The King lay still a moment, though his cheeks tightened as he instinctively tried to gesture with his hand and found he could not. At last he nodded in Oliver's direction. "Take the monk in and bandage his head."

"Yes, Sire!" cried Oliver. Relieved, the foot soldiers lifted Ambrogio to his feet and led him away.

28

King Charles next spoke to Ughetto. "Our Holy Father—the Pope— called me into Italy to drive out the wicked Hohenstaufens who would have stripped the Church of all its rights. I have done everything Christian arms and valor can do against the powers of darkness. Twice I routed the scions of the Hohenstaufen dynasty, that race of vipers. Manfred I slew at Benevento, and Conradin I captured after Tagliacozzo. I would have destroyed the whole house forever, if it had not been for these demons who intervened today. Arms and valor cannot drive off demons, Your Eminence. Only Christian holiness can do that. Why were these demons allowed to attack today, Your Eminence? Is the Church no longer holy?"

"You speak blasphemy," growled Ughetto.

"Indeed?" He smiled sourly. "So did Frederick II. Will you now invite Conradin back to protect the Church from me?"

The Cardinal had to ponder, to try different tactics. At last he said sullenly, "You sound like an old woman, babbling of demons. They are charlatans, and you'll soon have the pleasure of seeing them burn."

The King returned bitterly. "Is it an illusion, then, that I can no longer move my limbs?"

Ughetto clenched his fists in fury. "What other explanation could there be?" he cried.

"That this is demonry or witchcraft," returned King Charles icily.

"And what help do you hope for, outside the Church?" demanded the Cardinal.

"I don't know whether the Church can help me," retorted the King, "unless I can find a priest who is really holy."

"You speak heresy," said Ughetto sharply. "It is Patarine heresy to believe the efficacy of the sacraments depends on the character of an individual priest."

"Can you heal me then?" inquired Charles skeptically. "If you exorcise the demon, will I be able to walk again?"

"I would not try, after the discourteous way you have spoken to me," retorted the Cardinal, and turning his horse, he galloped off.

King Charles had not had much hope, at least not in Ughetto, and he chuckled acidly as the Cardinal vanished. "I think I would like to speak to this Abbot Sinibaldo," he said.

Inside the palace Oliver and Geoffrey led Ambrogio to the armory. "We are not so skilled as you with the wounded, good brother, but I think I can bind a cloth around your head to stop the bleeding," said Oliver.

"May God reward you," murmured Ambrogio. His head still ached from the blow, though he was able to see clearly again. They guided him to a bench, where he sank down. Oliver took a strip of linen cloth from a chest near the wall and began to wind it around Ambrogio's head. Geoffrey watched. A sudden thought struck him, and he became most agitated. "Oliver," he cried, "we are late relieving Gautier and Pierre from their watch at the dungeon. What if they've been attacked? If these demons rescued Conradin, why wouldn't they rescue his cousins as well? We're lost!"

Oliver had finished the bandaging. "God's wounds!" he cried. Recollecting the monk's presence, he caught himself. "I beg your pardon, brother!" Ambrogio saw Oliver's rough features turn red with embarrassment.

"Do you feel shame at swearing in front of me, only a fleshly man?" asked Ambrogio. "Yet God is listening all the time. Did you say you guard the dungeon of King Manfred's children?"

"We did guard them," said Oliver, shuddering. "But with these demons at work, who can say? Why have we been so thoughtless?" he added. "The demons have probably already been at them."

"God forgive us," said Geoffrey, crossing himself.

Ambrogio was startled, but the pain in his head forced him to rise slowly rather than quickly. "What do you mean, the demons have been at them? Did the children foretell Conradin's rescue?"

Both Frenchmen faced each other with a nervous laugh. "They don't foretell anything," said Oliver. "Two won't speak at all, and the third only raves. The demons have deranged their minds."

Ambrogio relaxed slowly. "Perhaps you need not fear. There is a great difference between people who are tormented by demons and those who cooperate willingly with them." Ambrogio suspected that whatever powers had freed Conradin wanted political tools and would have no use for witless children. However, saying so would be setting himself up as an expert in demonology, a role to which he did not aspire.

But the soldiers' thoughts were running in a different direction. "Brother Ambrogio, will you come with us?" asked Geoffrey somewhat shakily.

"Why, what can I do?" asked Ambrogio, but his heart held a desire, born partly of pity and partly of curiosity, to see the unfortunate heirs of vanquished King Manfred.

"The more of us there are, the better it will be," returned Oliver, in the same trembling tone.

"Then I will come," said Ambrogio simply.

As Geoffrey and Oliver led him toward the dungeon, Ambrogio ventured to say, "I doubt anything has changed there." But he could not tell whether his words reassured them.

4

Natheless yi-Induran felt uneasy as she approached the Council room. She had been there only twice before. Once, when she was eight, she and Agni had been formally condoled for the death of their parents. Again, at the age of twelve, she had gone there to swear allegiance to the Constitution and receive official recognition as a Lawchild. She had been expecting to go there again within a year to exchange formal marriage promises with Alrik Eridani. But being summoned there suddenly without explanation was unexpected, and boded no good. She had been startled when her Aunt Varuna had sent the message to her office at Haven, where she had been working on a Contact theorem. Natheless's first thought was that something must have happened to her brother; but then, she wondered, would not the Council have sent the news to her directly, summoning her for condolences later, when she had recovered self-possession? Unless there was actually a chance someone could go to Agni's help?

With a tightness in her throat Natheless spoke her name into the receiver, and the metal door before her slid open. "Come forward, Fourfold Lawchild Natheless yi-Induran," said the Archon. Only after she had crossed many feet of empty floor, passed five massive, empty chairs, bowed to the Archon and looked up, did she see her name in large letters across the computer data screen near the ceiling. She firmly gripped the back of the nearest chair to steady herself.

The Archon's eyes were fixed on her. Always benevolent, often kindly, they now focused all their energy on her. And he was the friendliest one in the room. Nibbana Parzes' gaze contained a definite note of censure or disapproval. The other women looked more or less similar. Jimmik Centauri stared at the ceiling beside the computer as though the whole matter bored him. And Rho Smide was eying her with something like hatred. A tinge of anger worked its way into Natheless's apprehension. What had she done to deserve this? Just because yi-Indurans were dispatched on all the dangerous missions, being the only Lawchildren in anything resembling a state of robust health, did that justify blaming them every time something went wrong? She frowned at Rho, but hastily relented when she remembered he no longer possessed the facial muscles with which to return such a gesture. She flushed as she grew conscious of her natural eyes and hair. On her other trips to the Council room she had worn her cosmic accessories. It was easy to forget the prejudices of the High Families when you were used to spending most of your time at Haven.

Sixfold Rho spoke, frowning with his mouth while his face above his nose remained as immobile as a corpse's. "You are only seventeen standard years of age, Lawchild Natheless."

This did not go far in explaining why a juvenile with no governmental rank should be summoned before the High Council and scrutinized in this way. Natheless bowed her head to the technical sub-Archon. "It is true that I am only seventeen, Lawchild Rho. People can only be one age at any given time. I am sorry if I am excessively young for the purposes of the High Council."

"Your name," said Rho Smide, "has been submitted because you are precocious in some matters. In fact, you are registered with Personality as a prodigy. However, prodigies as a group have been found to be unstable, and there are some reservations on your own Personality dossier."

Natheless agreed. "That is true."

The Council had been expecting more of a statement, perhaps protest. There was some shuffling and a loud guffaw from Jimmik Centauri. Rho Smide continued in a self-consciously even tone, "If you would comment on the reservations, Lawchild Natheless."

Natheless's resistance grew in proportion to their efforts to probe the sore spot in her consciousness. "Why would I comment, Honored Council?" she said. "It is the function of the Personality division to observe and guide the development of Lawchildren, to classify them, and to record their findings in regular dossiers including reservations when they see fit. I have not studied Personality Theory, and do not fully understand why there should be reservations on my dossier."

An exasperated sigh escaped from Nibbana. Natheless went on without heeding her, "I have continued to behave in what seems to me a reasonable and natural manner, which is *my* function. The reservations are entirely theoretical. And I certainly have been guilty of no delinquency."

"We would appreciate it, however," said Rho Smide, "if you would describe the causes for the reservations."

In spite of her growing anger, Natheless spoke calmly. "Really, Honored Council, I do not wish to seem uncooperative, but privacy in these matters is guaranteed in the Constitution. Only in cases where the security of the Peleziterea is in peril, does the Constitution allow Personality dossiers to be laid before the Council. It does not require Lawchildren to give accounts of their own inner lives, unless they wish to dispute Personality's verdicts. And I am perfectly willing to let you believe whatever Personality says about me." *If you're foolish enough to want to,* Natheless thought to herself.

Nibbana responded to the challenge. "Though the full particulars of your case, as Personality sees it, have already been laid before the Council, Lawchild Natheless, it is important for us to have your view. Rest assured we have sufficient reason for asking. As for privacy, it is true you cannot be compelled to answer. But if you have nothing to be ashamed of, why would you refuse to answer?"

Natheless bowed her head to Lawchild Nibbana. "If you're not ashamed to ask this of me, I am not ashamed to answer. Personality is disturbed because my brother, Agni yi-Induran, and I continue to hold ceremonies in honor of the myth called God which is told to our children, even though we were officially Undeceived at the age of ten like everyone else."

The Council clearly wanted to hear more, but Natheless had stopped. The Archon prodded gently, "That describes the naked fact, Lawchild Natheless. We need to know the reason for the fact."

"Do you believe this god is anything more than a myth?" demanded Rho Smide.

Natheless spoke with a kind of quiet concentration. "What is a myth?" she asked distantly. "If the Pelezitereans saw no truth in this one, why would they have taught it to their children at all? Yet they seem to believe it was not an exact enough representation of reality for adults to accept literally. So they created the ceremony called an Undeception, which all children undergo at the age of ten. In it parents confront their children and explain that God was only a myth, and also explain why they had been taught to believe in him in the first place. That way, Personality says, psychological attitudes considered advantageous, such as a hopeful view of life and the universe and also general considerateness toward other people, could be inculcated without the disadvantages of an unscientific outlook. That was the rationale, wasn't it?

"Every now and again, however, something goes wrong. It so happens our parents—Agni's and mine—were killed while exploring a star system for the colony, about fourteen days before the Undeception ceremony for Agni's age group. So when Agni attended the Undeception, his parents were not present to administer the blow properly, to tell him what he believed was not false, but only true in a sense different from what he must now leave behind. They were not there to tell him any of this. Therefore, Agni flatly refused to believe the Undeception. It seemed to insist that his parents had misled him and deliberately lied. Every belief in the goodness of the Universe and the immortality of love which had given him joy and comfort was total nonsense." As she recalled this, a mixture of love, anger and pain welled up in Natheless's heart. Something had surely happened to Agni. It could be their only reason for summoning her. Was the Council now checking on their common psychological maladjustment in order to bring evidence against him? But Agni would not have done anything wrong, and the High Council would not likely take the word of a hatcherbrat against him. It was bewildering in every way. Why didn't they tell her what was going on? Natheless felt tears coming to her eyes as she went on. "Naturally Agni ran directly to me (which, of course, he was not supposed to do, since I was only eight), and told me the dastardly lie about our parents they were trying to make him believe. I was as appalled as he was, and outraged and frightened, too. I stood steadfastly with him against everyone who tried to slander our parents. And to punish us for our stubbornness (so it seemed to us), Personality removed us from our Aunt Varuna's care and transferred us to the Personality Center in the Central Bubble. It separated us from one another, scolded us, threatened us, and exhorted us, all the while repeating that everything we thought we knew and everything we had ever cared about was nonsense." And where was Agni now? Natheless doubted anyone listening could miss the tremor in her voice. "After we had been there about a month, in various states of withdrawal, meaning that we were increasingly reluctant to eat or speak to anyone, Aunt Varuna succeeded in locating someone in the Personality division with an unusual amount of compassion and ingenuity. He managed to concoct some theory to the effect that our refusal to disbelieve the God-Myth was a benign neurosis designed to protect us from the shock of bereavement. It would disappear spontaneously when there was no longer any need for it, provided we were left alone. Personality accepted that—with reservations—and allowed us to return to the yi-Induran Bubble." Natheless paused for breath, and to get better control of herself.

Nibbana Parzes spoke. "All this has been laid before the Council. The Council has agreed Personality did not handle the case at all well and ought to act differently if such circumstances should arise in the future. However, what concerns us now is that you and Agni have continued to hold ceremonies in honor of this childhood myth right up to the present. You can no longer be in any doubt, it is our custom to teach this myth to young children only, and for particular reasons, so why do you continue with it?"

Natheless bowed, though her face was warm with feeling. She spoke carefully. "No law forbids it, Lawchild Nibbana. I have never understood why a thing that gives us joy and comfort should be so upsetting to you."

Nibbana's expression remained unchanged. "Urith was destroyed because of quarrels over a myth called God," she said.

"If you believe I have such violent tendencies, why don't you lock me up and have done with it?" retorted Natheless, a little more sharply than was courteous.

Having evoked something resembling delusions of persecution from Natheless, Nibbana Parzes sat back, a little pleased with herself. At last Natheless understood what was happening. Obviously she was being considered for some position. And Nibbana was trying to make her disqualify herself. Natheless resolved she would not lose her temper again.

Nibbana's next approach was to speak softly, with obvious gentleness, to make the yi-Induran girl sound more petulant by contrast. "Why be so defensive, Lawchild Natheless? We are not accusing you of illegal actions or of immorality. We are making a sympathetic inquiry into your personal adjustment, more for your own sake than anyone else's, so you will not be assigned duties too hard for you. The question is not whether you should cease conducting ceremonies that give you comfort, but rather why you, at the age of seventeen, still need the comfort of a childhood myth others have outgrown by the age of ten."

Had they summoned her merely to inform her she acted like a baby?

Natheless felt desolation pressing on her from within her skull, and carefully waited for it to dissipate before replying. "It would seem in some respects I grow more slowly than others" she said, very calmly.

"And yet," said Nibbana magnanimously, "your intelligence is not in question."

"Just your sanity," said Jimmik Centauri, jumping into the discussion from pure love of mischief. Jimmik Centauri was like that. He fired his verbal missiles so openly you could easily spot them coming, and duck. The idea that he might really have intended to hurt her by his remark suddenly struck Natheless as enormously funny. She had to bring her hand over her mouth to stifle her laughter. Nibbana was vexed to see her finely spun web rudely shattered by such a clumsy blow.

Natheless caught her breath and sought to regain her self-control. Samlai Wyce, who was nearest, indicated the chair beside her and said, "Sit down, Lawchild Natheless. I fear this meeting is difficult for you."

Natheless sank gratefully into the chair. "Is there anything else you need to know?" she asked.

"Only the answer to the question I am asking. Why do you need this myth?"

"I have told you before. You never understood then, so why am I supposed to believe you would understand now?"

"Perhaps," said Nibbana, "the others will understand."

Natheless stared at the grey floor, which was decorated at fixed points with yellow stars. "Very well. I will explain once more." She looked up at Nibbana, who had closed her eyes as if to concentrate better, or perhaps to restrain herself from speaking out and interrupting. Jimmik Centauri was staring at the ceiling again. Rho Smide, Samlai Wyce and Mellis Holl were regarding her with a mixture of sympathy and doubt, perhaps more doubt than sympathy. Only the Archon looked right at her, attentive with the promise of trying to understand what she said. She directed her words to him. "When we discussed the God-Myth before," said Natheless, "I asked the officials in Personality many questions. They are far better at labeling my questions unhealthy than giving me answers. 'If there is no God,' I ask, 'what is the point of life? What does anything we do matter? Why are we supposed to go on living?' And Personality says, 'That question has no answer. You do not require an answer. You are supposed to feel the love of life instinctively, feel it coursing through your veins and consciousness.' Well, I do not. Perhaps there is something wrong with my veins. It seems to me life is half boredom, one quarter pain and one quarter embarrassment. What little pleasure there is comes and goes before you can enjoy it; and, frankly, unless this life leads to something better, I see no reason to bother with it. Only God can make something better out of this messed-up Universe. That is why I want to believe in him. 'Man will change the Universe,' you say. 'Man will create the perfect society.' Well, of course I can't prove that Man won't. But I don't see how you can continue to believe in it after what happened on Urith, and after what has happened on this colony ship, when we left Urith with such hopes of building a good society. I don't begrudge you your belief. Go ahead and believe it, if you can. But I can't." Natheless stared down at the table. The Archon's gentle voice floated across to her.

"You think it more reasonable to believe in a God whom you haven't seen than in human beings whom you have seen?"

Natheless nodded. "Yes. Since I haven't seen God, I haven't seen him fail. I have seen man fail, before my eyes, often."

Rho Smide let out a snort. "In a crazy sort of way, it makes sense!"

Nibbana spoke drily. "As you say, Lawchild Rho, in a crazy sort of way. To prefer the nonexistent over the existent because it doesn't disappoint you is a dangerously neurotic attitude."

"There, you declare me neurotic," said Natheless. "How can I argue with you? My feelings seem normal to myself because they are the only feelings I have ever had. Naturally I assume everyone has feelings like them. And when you say you don't, Lawchild Nibbana, you appear crazy to me. I can't believe you are telling the truth. I can't believe you can be satisfied with what happens in this colony among people. I can't believe you haven't noticed that other people never understand you, that they acknowledge your presence only to inform you you're in the way. They're too absorbed in personal concerns to thank you even when you have gone out of your way to help them. If you haven't noticed, and if you can persuade yourself that other people love you as much as you want to be loved, then perhaps people are enough for you. But I think you need a God who sees and knows everything, never tires and is always available for consultation and is never embarrassed about anything you might be having trouble with."

"You are much too perfectionistic," said Nibbana. "At seventeen you still are looking for the perfect parent. Why, you are almost at the point of becoming a parent yourself!"

Natheless addressed the Personality sub-Archon. "You've said that many times, Lawchild Nibbana. You say my desires are unrealistic and unattainable. For all I know, you could be right. As I say, I have never been anyone but myself, so I cannot compare myself to someone you would consider normal. So I cannot argue. All I can ask is, when you have proved my desires are abnormal, what have you accomplished? They are still my desires, and I can't imagine wanting anything else."

Rho Smide broke in. "Lawchild Natheless," he said, "you confuse me. I understood from Personality's report that you really believe in this God-Myth. But you've been speaking as though you knew you were making it up. Would you clarify this point, please?"

Natheless paused briefly again and said, "What is a myth really? It is a story that captures something important about reality. What is Science? It is supposed to describe reality. But I am not deeply interested in the reality the Science we teach describes. It doesn't much affect me whether the Universe arose by accident from the division of nothingness into matter and anti-matter. I don't care whether life arose upon a planet through the evolution of atoms into molecules of increasing complexity and the subsequent evolution of simple organisms into more complex ones. I do not deny those ideas, I simply don't care about them. I have no arguments to raise against them, but studying them bores me to tears. They are empty and lonely. I prefer the God-Myth, in which the Universe was created deliberately by a loving being who had a definite plan for it, which he will bring to fulfillment. Because the God-Myth means so much to me, I have based my life around it. It influences the way I think of my work, my home and other people. It influences my hopes for the colony. Your Science, even though I do not dispute the truth of it, has no influence on me once I am outside the apprentice situation where I must learn about it. Am I aware I am inventing and consciously elaborating the God-Myth? How could I not know it? Do I believe in it? Yes, I believe in it, as much as I believe in anything, perhaps more so."

"Beliefs such as yours," hissed Nibbana, "caused all the trouble on Urith, and all the civil wars that have racked this colony."

"And so," the Archon interposed gently, "did excessive fear of them."

Natheless said, "Lawchild Nibbana, when food is scarce, people fight over it. You could stop the fight by starving both sides to death, but would that represent a real answer?"

"I don't feel starved," said Nibbana.

"And I do," said Natheless.

"It seems to me," continued the Personality sub-Archon, "your appeal to the supernatural is a defense against love and an excuse to withhold it from other people—who you claim have failed you."

Desolation pressed on Natheless again, and a heavy weight settled around her heart. She tried to resist it, pondering how to defend herself against this new and unexpected attack. Suddenly, with a sense of relief, it came to her that the question was unfair. No one had a right to expect her to answer it. She returned her gaze to the bloodless face of the older woman and said, "When are you going to tell me what has happened to Agni?"

Nibbana and the other Sixfold suddenly straightened in their chairs. The Archon spoke sorrowfully. "How much have you guessed, Natheless?"

"It must be something quite serious for you to put me through all this."

"He did nothing wrong. We are not entirely certain what happened. We received a message from him several hours ago clearly indicating he was in distress. Then his message was cut off. He spoke of the hatcherbrats acting treacherously. The computer declares he is dead. We are sorry."

The brightly colored eyes of the Sixfold and the grey walls of the room were yanked from Natheless's vision. All she could see was the endless black vacuum of space, full of death and loneliness, the loneliness she had known was coming, the emptiness she had tried to prevent by petitioning for permission to accompany her brother. Now it was over, too late, gone beyond hope, lost forever, done, ended, finished, nonexistent, nonsense—just like the God-Myth.

"Are you all right?" said Samlai Wyce's voice. Natheless became aware of her surroundings again. She had bowed her head over the table and was shedding tears involuntarily. With an effort she straightened herself and tried to look at the Council. "You have known this for hours, and you did not tell me! You could not even spare me half an hour for tears before you summoned me to ask these pointless questions!" Her voice broke and she bowed her head again.

The Archon waited a moment before speaking. "We hoped to obtain information from you first and tell you later. Our need was pressing. If you are overcome now, you may retire. But there is more we must know. Agni said the planet was inhabited and that the hatcherbrats meant to violate the Prime Directive. The computer tells us you are head of the Contact department in the yi-Induran Bubble."

Natheless reacted. "Am I now to voyage down to that planet where my brother died?"

"You can't be required to go down there," said Nibbana. "Not if you are mentally unstable."

"I'm not mentally unstable! You just don't have room for the way I've stabilized. I can distinguish the colors of the spectrum as well as any of you. Besides, this is what the Contact department was organized for in the first place, why the Central Bubble supported it for seventy-five generations even though we found no inhabited planets, why the yi-Induran Bubble took over control of it when the Central Bubble finally wished to abolish it for being impractical. This is the one event all our effort was preparing for. If you do not send me down there now, you make nonsense of it!"

The Archon looked at Nibbana. "In spite of your efforts, Lawchild Nibbana, we have a volunteer." She shrugged.

"Will you tell us, Natheless, how you would go about establishing contact with the people on the planet below?"

Natheless suddenly felt exhausted. She wondered whether she would have spoken so fervently if she had not been upset about Agni. "I believe you would get more detailed information about that from the Computer."

"We have already," said the Archon, "but we were hoping you could personify it for us."

Natheless nodded, and tried to detach herself from all thoughts of Agni. She finally managed to fix her mind on an important Contact text and began to restate it. "The initial problem is determining how to communicate with the inhabitants of a planet whose history has never touched Urith's, who might not even communicate by voice as we do. Therefore, it's been decided the Contact department would train its members to approach communication from different perspectives and in various thought modes. This implied learning many Urithian languages, because our own foreign languages were the only cross-references on varying approaches to reality we had. We also hoped they would protect our theoretical works from becoming too wildly impractical. With this in view our ancestors carried enough texts and documents from Urith to provide complete mastery of twelve languages. Some were chosen because they were closely related to our own language, some because they were not related at all. Since it was assumed different perspectives were more likely than similar ones, it was decided students would first begin studying the languages less closely related to ours. Only at the end of a long program would they be permitted to study the evolution of our own language and the texts compiled before the Great Phonetic Revolution. That is why we start everyone on Zankrid and Zwahli and then take them directly to the theoretical works."

"How will you communicate with the people on this planet?"

"That depends entirely on them. They may not even have the same vocal apparatus we do."

"The communication Agni sent contains background noises the computer has certainly identified as human voices."

"Well, then," said Natheless, "it's certain we could learn their language. It is only difficult to predict how soon. There are all sorts of factors that would make it easy or hard."

"The Council decided before you came to us that, unless you were proven mentally unstable, the rank you hold within the yi-Induran Bubble over the Contact department would be converted to formal governmental rank. You would therefore work with us in our attempt to enforce the Prime Directive. I am still in favor of that procedure. Are there any objections?"

Four voices said, "None," very softly.

"Then you are advanced to the rank of Sixfold, Natheless yi-Induran," said the Archon. Natheless felt a little feverish. "We should begin selecting the other members of the official landing party as soon as possible," said the Archon, "but perhaps you need some time to yourself."

"Could you spare me about an hour?" asked Natheless wearily.

"We can surely spare you that long. Please return when you feel ready, Sixfold."

"I will," said Natheless. She rose a bit hesitantly from the table. The door slid noiselessly open before her at the Archon's gesture and as noiselessly closed behind her, leaving the elders to themselves.

After a pause, Nibbana whispered, "Do you really believe, Sevenfold, that an inexperienced seventeen-year-old with emotional problems can both establish contact with the alien people on that planet and formulate strategies for outwitting two dangerous, armed hatcherbrats? Do you really think she's that capable?"

The Archon's thoughts were already far beyond the meeting. He answered abstractedly, "With the support of a united High Council—possibly."

Nibbana was silent.

5

             Prince Arrigo, second son of King
Manfred, sat on the damp floor of his prison, staring into the dark. He
had been sitting there for two years, and it had become his life. Visions of
the outside world as he had seen it before his imprisonment frequently
came to him, but he had nearly forgotten the difference between
memories and dreams. He often saw his father, King Manfred, riding on
his sleek, rust-colored horse and wearing his hunter's green. (People used
to complain the King was more often seen in his hunting garments than
in his robes of state, but the child had no idea anything was wrong with
this.) Arrigo could remember what it was like to ride behind him. But
only a long argument would have convinced him there was once a time
when it had actually happened, that this was not a picture he had made
up to pass the time of his captivity. And no one spoke to Arrigo these days,
though he sometimes overheard things. There was only one image he
certainly connected with the real past, and he did the best he could to
keep that out of his mind. It was more bitterly painful and frightening
than the cries and gibbering of his brothers, or the threats of the guards
when they were angry.

    It concerned his mother, Queen Helena. Queen Helena was regarded
as a great beauty, and certainly Arrigo considerd her so. To him she was a
glorious vision of dark eyes and black hair, and of garments glittering with

jewels. Arrigo understood vaguely that she was a source of contention between King Manfred and the Pope because her people, the Greeks, would not acknowledge the primacy of the Roman clergy, though to be sure they were schismatics rather than infidels.

Helena would often come to the gardens to watch her four children play. Her eyes then would glow with pride and happiness. But Arrigo no longer liked to recall her. His vision of her happiness in the gardens was blotted out by the other emotion he had witnessed on her face that last night when she had rushed into his room with only a single attendant to drag him from his bed. The nurse, Lucia, had hastily risen and run to her, crying, "Madònna, Madònna!"

"Get the children dressed and bring them to the stables quickly," panted his mother, her face radiating terror. "We must ride at once!" She turned without another word and left the room. The nurse, without even checking to be sure he was awake, began pulling Arrigo's clothes onto him. "What's happening? Where are we going?" he spluttered in protest.

"Be quiet and help me, Arrigo," said Lucia. "Your father has lost a battle and the Frenchman Charles will pursue us." He did not discover until much later that his father was dead.

The little princes were dressed hastily and hurried out to the gate behind the palace, where the Queen and their sister were already waiting. Princess Beatrice, the eldest at seven years, was sitting tall and solemn like a grown woman. Anselino, the youngest at three, was in tears. Manfredino, the oldest boy, called in a shrill, commanding voice, "Let's go! Let's start! Do you want that Frenchman to catch us?" Arrigo had hardly been lifted into the saddle behind one of the knights before they set out. Throughout the long ride he shivered a lot, cried a little, and asked no questions. He assumed they were riding to a port city for a ship that would take them across the sea to his mother's family in Epirus. Probably he was right, but he was never destined to receive confirmation of it.

The rest of the journey was vague and nightmarish. They reached the port safely; he heard someone whisper its name, "Trani." The children and their nurse sat huddled in some dark room while the Queen dispatched one of the knights to procure a ship. He never returned. Instead, a company of Italian soldiers arrived and guarded the door. None of Helena's threats, bribes, pleas and, finally, tears could induce them to leave. At last Charles's Frenchmen arrived and seized them, taking the Queen, her sister-in-law and her daughter in one direction, and the three boys in another. Arrigo had not seen his mother since. He and his brothers were brought to Naples and put into the dungeon under a palace where his father had once gloriously reigned. There they were chained by their wrists and ankles.

They were used to better treatment and complained bitterly at first, but the guards only beat them when they bothered to heed them at all. Gradually the boys learned to speak only among themselves. Then they began to play the picture game. It started when they would take turns telling each other things they remembered, or pretended to remember, about their life in the palace before King Charles had come. Certainly there was nothing to learn in the dungeon, and what there was to see was not worth looking at. Every day was like another. The only event in their lives was the guards' bringing of bread and water—probably daily, but before long Arrigo had no way of being certain about the interval. Anselino was always whimpering, "It's dark," or "I'm hungry," or "I want Lucia," or else pulling on one of his chains and screaming, "It hurts, it hurts, it hurts!" Manfredino used to talk grandly of how their father was not really dead and how he would return and rescue them and put King Charles in chains and behead all the guards. This helped relieve the gloom a little, but one day the guards came in and heard him and hit him on the head so hard he fell down and lay still for hours. Arrigo thought he was dead. When he finally woke up, he complained about a headache for a long time. And the children no longer knew what they dared talk about. They sat for a long time in silence, terrified.

Then, one day, Anselino said, "I see Lucia." At first they thought he was playing the picture game again, and Arrigo encouraged him to go on. All was well for a while, except that Anselino sometimes did not seem to hear his brothers when they spoke, or understand everything they said. But then, he was the youngest and knew less than they. It would not have troubled them if what Anselino saw had continued to be Lucia. However, after a while he began to see things that terrified him—first King Charles, then the Pope, and finally a big black dog with bulging eyes that wanted to eat him up. He would start to scream and cry and beg his brothers for help. Arrigo protested they could not even get over to him, chained to the wall as they both were, let alone save him from things that were not there. But he did not seem to understand this. Arrigo and Manfredino were furious with him, until gradually they realized he could not help it.

After that Manfredino and Arrigo were left to play the picture game by themselves for a while, but they were still restrained by fear of the guards. So they began to spend long hours without talking to each other, only imagining they were all back in the palace with Lucia and sometimes with their mother and father, and the fruit trees were in bloom and they could play with their dogs and birds and ponies. Arrigo could make the pictures in his mind so they were almost real, and imagine sounds as good as audible. He enjoyed making Lucia's sweet voice sing nursery tunes for him. From being too dangerous for Manfredino and him to talk together, it became too much of an effort. And then, one day, Arrigo realized Manfredino could no longer understand him when he did speak. He would just sit there in his chains and mutter things about the pictures he was seeing. He had entirely forgotten they were not real. Only Arrigo could still call up the pictures when he wanted and send them away when he was through, but he realized with vague, calm terror he, too, was losing control.

Arrigo would certainly have become like his brother if he had not discovered what seemed to him a wonderful thing: The guards found the Hohenstaufens' condition amusing, and would bring friends to look and laugh at them. If Arrigo sat in his chains and behaved as they expected, they would stay for long periods of time and sometimes talk about interesting things. It was only through this habit of theirs that he heard the news of the sorcerers in Naples.

One day, which seemed to Arrigo very much like all other days, he was lying on the floor in as much of a supine position as his chains would allow when he heard the door open. The light of a lantern touched his closed eyelids. He did not yet look up, concentrating instead on the sound of the footsteps and guessing all he could. His ears told him there was a third man with the two regular guards, but still he did not open his eyes. Usually the guards brought others of Charles's soldiers, though once they had brought the Italian woman-friend of one of them. She had burst into tears when she had seen the boys, wailing that she had a son of her own, just Anselino's age. For several weeks after that the guards had brought extra gifts of bread, better than what the children usually got. Arrigo believed she had sent them. And he hoped the new visitor might be another woman, or even the same one.

"*Ecco,*" said the guard, Oliver, and Arrigo's heart leaped—because if the visitor had been another soldier, Oliver would have spoken French. "They are still here! The demons have left them just as they were before, filthy, tattered, half-starved and demon-possessed! May he who has escaped be like them soon!"

Anselino was screaming about the black dog and Manfredino was singing a hunting song off-key, jumbling the words. Arrigo kept his eyes closed and waited to hear the visitor.

"Has the King never sent anyone to attend them? No doctors? No priests?" It was a man, after all, with a voice that was low and yet kind. Arrigo opened his eyes and saw that the newcomer was a monk. In the light of the lantern Geoffrey held he seemed a frail man, certainly smaller than Oliver, and his head was bandaged.

Geoffrey snorted in answer to his question. "What would be the good of that, Brother Ambrogio? If anyone knows how incurably evil the Hohenstaufens are, you monks should! Wasn't your abbot beaten and banished during Frederick's reign?"

"We have all had reason to pray for the destruction of the Hohen-staufens and their empire," returned the monk sadly, "but these are only children."

Both guards spluttered incredulously. "Come now! Aren't they just like their parents, the brood of poison-swollen adders? How could you doubt it, after what you have seen today?"

"Frederick was an evil man," sighed the monk. "And yet, what a king he might have been, if he had been a friend to God! Nothing that breathes is beyond God's mercy, Frenchmen, and these children are still alive. It is because of our sins that the misfortunes we have seen today have come upon us—sins of Frenchmen and sins of Italians, too. Be assured, if we had not sinned grievously, God would not have put a man like Frederick of Hohenstaufen over the Empire and allowed him to reign so long. Neither would He have allowed these demons or sorcerers to snatch young Conradin from your King today. And be assured it is a sin to mistreat these helpless children and deny them bodily and spiritual nourishment—perhaps, indeed, it is one of the things we were punished for today."

This speech seemed to anger the guards, who both drew back from the monk in the flickering light and turned away from him.

"If God is angry with our King Charles," protested Oliver, "why was he allowed victory over King Manfred? And why was he able to slay that demon today?"

"O simple men," said the monk quietly, "demons are not easy for flesh and blood to slay. Either nothing was slain today, or else the poor body you saw bleeding belonged to a man, a foolish magician, or an unfortu-nate captive of the demons. Yet, as a result of the encounter, Charles and many others are deprived of the use of their limbs, and Conradin seems to have escaped."

Oliver was silenced, but Geoffrey was angered and he growled, "I don't like the way you talk, monk! You say Charles is cursed by God and the House of Hohenstaufen is in the right! But the Pope himself is on our

King's side, and if you are not careful what you say, you'll soon find yourself bound to a stake with logs piled around your legs."

The monk replied in a tone full of emotion, but without a hint of challenge or anger in it. "May God pardon you for your unjust suspicions, Geoffrey, and grant they lead you into no worse fault! King Charles's misfortune proves him neither right nor wrong, any more than King Manfred's former glory proved him right. If you had studied the precepts of our religion at all, or even if you had lived your thirty years with your eyes wisely open, you would know that Providence does not work that way."

Throughout this conversation, Arrigo was having trouble strangling a cry of exultation. He understood that they were saying his cousin Conradin had escaped. Arrigo knew Conradin was his kinsman and King Charles their common enemy; his idea of their precise relationship was extremely vague.

The monk came back to the children and asked in a puzzled voice, "Why has the pious and devout King Charles not thought to allow these boys spiritual instruction?"

"Why, look at them!" chortled Oliver. "Listen to them gibber! Do you think they would understand?" Arrigo's brothers were indeed making a. great deal of meaningless noise.

"Were they this way when first imprisoned?" murmured Ambrogio. Then his eyes fell on Arrigo. "What about the one in the middle? Is he *alive?*" the monk asked, in a tone of wonder.

Both guards laughed. "Him? He's the most savage of the three! Shall I wake him for you?" cried Geoffrey raucously.

Arrigo had no desire to have Geoffrey's heavy hands on him, and, besides, it was his strategy to keep the guards interested. At these words he jerked his eyes open, leaped to his feet and rushed furiously at his visitors with all the energy in his little body. The chains on his wrists and ankles caught him, tumbling him to the floor, where he lay in a bruised heap, gasping for breath. Then he leaped to his feet again and bared his teeth at them, snarling and barking like a dog.

This was one of his usual tricks. The skin was cut and swollen on his wrists and ankles where the chains galled him, but he kept his act up because of the sensation it invariably created among the Frenchmen. It worked this time, too. All three men stepped back toward the door, Geoffrey laughing nervously and Oliver explaining in a shaky voice, "I told you they were demon-possessed!"

"Strange!" murmured the monk. "I have a younger brother who looks just like that when he plays around the cottage!"

"This one's not playing," said Oliver, and to encourage him, Arrigo flapped his arms as if they were wings and crowed like a rooster.

The Italian monk detached himself from the Frenchmen and started toward the boy. "Take care!" cried Oliver. "The demon will make him leap at you!" He reached out a hand to restrain him, but Brother Ambrogio kept on. "Let it be as God wills," he said.

Arrigo watched the monk come closer. No one had paid so much attention to him since he was first captured. When they were only three feet apart, Ambrogio began to speak. "What's going on in your mind, little Hohenstaufen? Whose thoughts are you thinking? How much of what we say can your marred wits understand?"

Arrigo stood still, disarmed by the monk's gentleness. He was not used to this, and did not know what kind of a show to put on for it. Made suspicious by this silence, Ambrogio said, "I believe you have understood every word we have said."

Within him Arrigo felt the impulse to burst into tears and throw himself at the monk's feet and tell him everything that had ever happened to him. But that was clearly impossible. The guards would beat him. The monk had never come before, and Arrigo did not think he would ever come again. Arrigo looked at the monk and made a gurgling noise in his throat.

That convinced Ambrogio, and he said mournfully, "Your father and your grandfather were afflicted with pride of the intellect. Therefore, your reason has been taken away from you. It is a harsh doom, but a fitting one. God always gives fitting dooms. He visits the sins of the fathers upon their children unto the third and fourth generation."

Arrigo tilted his head back as far as it would go and spat in the monk's face. He did not come near his mark, since Ambrogio was too high above his head, but the monk understood the gesture and leaped back. Geoffrey rushed forward. "Demon-brat! I'll teach you to spit at a holy man!" he cried. Shrieking in terror, Arrigo shrank back against the wall and cowered, raising his hands (smaller than the links of the chains that held them) to protect his face.

But the monk stepped between them, and Geoffrey halted reluctantly. "Pray don't strike the child," he said, his voice fervent. "I have received a blow that caused me pain today, but God knows I would endure much more if I could better this child's lot in any way!"

49

"He's a Hohenstaufen," returned Oliver sullenly. "If he were a peasant, our King would not guard him so severely, but since he has a claim to the throne, he is a trouble to himself and to everyone near him."

Ambrogio sighed. "I know, Oliver. There is little you can do, and yet," he lowered his voice to a whisper, but Arrigo heard it anyway, "for the love you bear God, could you not treat him more gently?"

Arrigo could not hear Oliver's reply. They held a whispered conversation at the door and slowly prepared to leave. As they went, one voice drifted into the cell and was heard by Arrigo: "Your abbot, Sinibaldo, has a great reputation for holiness. If he talked to—" and the door shut. Arrigo sat in the dark pondering with what wits remained to him. Why had the monk never come before? Why had he come now? Would he come again? Had the demons who rescued Conradin changed his status somehow? Would he be rescued, too? Would he see his mother and his sister Beatrice again?

This effort was too much for him, and he soon fell back into his familiar habit of thought, where visions of the beautiful Queen Helena and King Manfred were his own inventions, unrelated to anything past. The monk's appearance only returned to Arrigo's mind in irregular flashes, during which he felt a chaotic excitement indistinguishable from fear.

6

Natheless yi-Induran sat in a room of the Haven Bubble, gazing through the window in front of her desk at the garden of the second level. Gardens aboard the Peleziterea were important areas, since the exiles got most of their exercise and recreation in them. The central core of each Bubble was usually given over to gardens on all levels. It had seemed wiser to add exercise space to each new segment of living space, rather than try to provide exercise grounds for everyone in the Central Bubble, which would become overcrowded as the population increased.

The Founders had expected the population of the Peleziterea to double, triple and quadruple many times. That way the Pelezitereans would never have recourse to inbreeding. For this reason the design of the ship allowed for almost limitless additions. The Central Bubble was spherical in shape. Two other "Bubbles," huge, trapezoidal segments, were attached at their smaller ends to its sides like wings. As the ship traveled and the population grew, other trapezoidal "Bubbles" were added, until the Peleziterea once again had a spherical shape. A few more wings were added beyond those and the process might have gone on indefinitely but for catastrophes that the Founders had not foreseen—the emergence of the hatcherbrats, and three civil wars.

In Natheless's time most of the Pelezitereans lived in four Bubbles.

The Central Bubble still contained the government offices and some of the information systems. But only hatcherbrats lived there now, crowded together in the residential sectors and in the gardens because they did not have the patience or skills to build themselves better facilities and none of the Lawchildren cared to do it for them. The High Families lived in the Eridani, Centauri and yi-Induran Bubbles. The other segments, once the scenes of intense activity, lay empty and deserted, some of them half-dismantled, waiting either to be cannibalized for spare parts or to be revitalized if and when the colony expanded again.

Natheless and Agni yi-Induran had revitalized the old Ceti Bubble. They had the right to do so. Space and building materials were plentiful among the Pelezitereans, so deserted segments belonged by custom to whoever took the trouble to restore them to working order. And the yi-Induran renegades, always at odds with Personality since their parents' death and scorned by the normal Lawchildren because of their neurosis, had spent many hours exploring the disused portions of the colony ship. They thought about the ghosts that had inhabited them, many killed in civil wars fought over half-forgotten causes, or simply killed, no one knew how or why. They found one Bubble they liked more than others. They reactivated the old water synthesizers to set the idle fountains flowing once more, repaired conduits, rebuilt old information systems, reconstructed communicators. Then they named the place Haven. And it had become the favorite haunt for all the respectable and semi-respectable Lawchildren who met to celebrate the God-Myth.

Natheless's office overlooked the tiny artificial brook that trickled languidly among the imitation grasses, and tumbled into a drain at the far wall, where it flowed into the next level and became a larger stream. In the fourth, outermost level (where the water was eventually drawn by the ship's artificial gravity) it became a swimming pool. Outside Natheless's window a group of children—mostly under five years of age—tried their strength against one another and against the climbing frames in the corners. This was not a place for adults to exercise; the running track and treadmills were on the third level.

A purple-haired childcare apprentice, Sumitra Holl, was sitting cross-legged on the cushions beside the brook, watching some of her hatcherbrat charges tussle on the far side of the brook. You could tell they were hatcherbrats because their plain white clothes were standard and machine-made, with none of the distinctive marks that Family-Bubble-made clothing had. Even without their clothes, the vigor of their movements would have given them away, since of the Lawchildren only the yi-Indurans were healthy enough to play so roughly, and they usually had better manners even at this young age.

Natheless and Agni had, like all Bubble-Governors, thrown the main gardens open to all Lawchildren who cared to come, but thus far only some Lawchildren apprentices, whose association with Haven had interested them in working with hatcherbrats, had taken them up on the offer. This was natural, since conditions at the hatcherbrat play areas were deplorable. It was hardly safe even for adult Lawchildren to go there unescorted. As long as the hatcherbrats came, Natheless had often reflected gloomily, no one else would come. Play would be too rough for most of the delicate, inbred, high-family offspring who would stay in their own gardens. The yi-Induran family gardens were similarly isolated. Natheless was not pondering this at present, however. She felt as though her heart had been torn out of her. She wondered whether she would ever be able to think about anything again.

A buzzer sounded, announcing a visitor. Without pausing to ask who it was, Natheless automatically touched the switch that opened the Bubble's main entrance. She was not even aware she had done it, until a door on the opposite side of the gardens slid open, revealing not one but two faces—Alrik Eridani's, with his green eyes and red hair, and Rauhina Telgolarses', with her natural accessories. Several of the hatcherbrats looked up and charged at them with shrieks of delight. Lawchild-baiting was a favorite sport among them, though they had learned to leave Sumitra alone. Sumitra Holl leaped to her feet and shouted an order; two of the children stopped, and reluctantly started back. None of the others even paused. However, the door slid shut again before they reached it, and the two members of the Haven company sought a more roundabout approach to Natheless's office. A moment later the doorbell sounded, and Natheless pressed the switch to admit them into her office. She turned in her chair to face them as they came in.

Alrik hung back at the entrance, Rauhina ran forward with anger in her expression. "Natheless, I was so upset when I heard about Agni, and I was furious when I heard they had called you before the High Council before even telling you!"

Natheless nodded. It felt as though someone were in her stomach, poking around with a steel spike.

"I'm sure it was Nibbana's idea," Alrik contributed. Alrik had been completely unnerved by the High Council's insensitivity, and even more by his knowledge of how deeply Natheless must be hurt. He did not know how to express his sympathy appropriately for such extreme circumstances, and he had to steel himself to appear at Haven at all.

Natheless nodded. "She wanted to make me talk about the God-Myth. She did her best to make me look unbalanced."

"That ghost asteroid!" cried Rauhina. A ghost asteroid was one of the most dangerous and unpredictable hazards scout ships encountered on their expeditions. The word was commonly used among the Pelezitereans to denote a pest or a nuisance. "What makes her certain her own emotions are normal and everyone else's odd?"

Natheless shook her head. "I've always wondered," she murmured.

"Come on," said Rauhina, "let's say a prayer for Agni."

Alrik nervously seconded her request, knowing a prayer would relax Natheless—it always did—but Natheless shook her head in refusal.

"No," she said, and her face was taut. "Agni and I were the only ones who really believed. You and the others put up with it to humor us. It will never be the same anymore. I am tired of being humored. I am a Sixfold now, and I will have to stop acting like a juvenile. I will never say a prayer to the God-Myth again as long as I live."

Alrik cringed, sensing the onset of the storm. Why did Natheless have to feel things so intensely, he wondered unhappily. If he was willing to accept her God-Myth, strange as it was, why couldn't she leave it at that?

Rauhina was outraged. "What do you mean we were humoring you?" she cried. "Why, you almost had us believing it ourselves! And we went along with it because we liked it! Are you going to allow Nibbana Parzes to bully you into admitting she's right, after we've fought her so many years? What would Agni say?"

Natheless was depressed. "Why do I have to be different? And someone has been reporting to Nibbana about us. She knew about the service we held immediately before Agni's expedition—and we only had the six most faithful there."

Alrik felt a pang of guilt. He spoke but found his words with difficulty. Silence would have been worse. "Natheless—I told her. I mean, I didn't really tell her, but she deduced it from something I said."

Natheless stared at Alrik, and then stammered, "Of course, Alrik. I should have guessed it was something like that. I'm sorry. I'm glad it was you. I was afraid that one of . . . the six was an . . . infiltrator."

"No," said Alrik. "She just happened to be visiting my father in our private family room. She turned to me and said, 'I note with pleasure I have heard no word of ceremonies in honor of the God-Myth for at least two years. Is Natheless yi-Induran bored with it, do you think?' All I said was, 'If you really want to know, why don't you ask her?' And she said, 'I see, they've just gone underground.' That was all."

"That ghost asteroid!" cried Rauhina.

"I don't think I could pray to the God-Myth again," said Natheless. "I feel too sick about all of this."

"Well, science and progress, Natheless, if you don't, I don't think I'm going to have the courage to go on this mission with you! Nothing will make sense anymore."

"I couldn't go, either," added Alrik. Not because he couldn't summon the courage, he thought, but because he knew Natheless would be in turmoil the whole time and would probably end up killing herself one way or another. No law of the Founders or their descendants could make him stand by and watch that happen.

Natheless's expression softened ever so slightly. "All right," she said, "I'm sorry to be such a ghost asteroid myself. Let's pray for my brother. " She held out a hand to each of them.

They joined hands and closed their eyes. Everyone understood that the God-Myth consisted of a set of beliefs that had once been taken seriously by the people on Urith. Exactly what these beliefs contained no one now aboard the Peleziterea was in any position to know. At least since the last civil war, a conscious effort had been made to expunge the details. A great many religious texts had either been destroyed or placed on the forbidden file in the information systems. However, Natheless had gathered a hint here and a hint there, partly from the watered-down version customarily taught to children, partly from remarks made in public documents by early Founders whose religious implications had been overlooked by the censors. From these suggestions and their own imaginations, the Haven company had compiled their own version of what they hoped was the Urithian God-Myth. Natheless began to pray softly. "God who created the universe, you who are true, just and loving, who know everything and can do everything, you who are beautiful beyond imagination and description, we would love you beyond all things alive or dead, even if you did not exist. Our brother Agni has died on a faraway planet because he tried to be just. We would pray to you to take good care of him if we were not already sure that because you are the way you are, you have already done so. But we want"—here Natheless's voice faltered—"we want you to tell him for us—that we love him and we miss him terribly. We will try to act rightly in accordance with our beliefs so—when we meet again, we can all be happy to see each other." Natheless's voice cracked and she sobbed. Rauhina spoke encouragingly into the silence. "We all want to join him some day and watch the Universe together."

"Yes, we do," agreed Alrik tensely. There were times when he had really participated in God-Mythmaking. Today he was much too upset about Natheless.

"And," Natheless began again, her voice quavering with emotion, "while we are grieving over his loss, we suffer from the—unkindness of a certain person. Help us—please help us, no matter how difficult—to see things as you see them, to remember she is a human being you created and you have a picture in your mind of something good she could be. Help us not to direct our hatred at anyone you love, and not to destroy anything you are building. Once again, before we depart for this mission, we dedicate all our energy to you, and we ask you to make us your builders, not breakers."

"Yes, help us," whispered Alrik and Rauhina together, realizing the prayer had reached a truly cathartic stage and that Natheless would be more herself again.

There was a moment of silence in which they all recognized that the prayer was finished. They squeezed one another's hands and let go.

Natheless sat down again, and the other two pulled up chairs from the other side of the office. "Wouldn't it have been perfect," said Rauhina softly, "if we could have gone on the mission to this planet with Agni?"

They all nodded. "But he'll be watching us," said Alrik, supplying a familiar argument.

"We will all meet again," said Natheless in a strained voice. There was silence for a considerable while. Finally, Natheless began, "We have about two months to devote to theoretical study before we actually land on the planet. What slows us down is the medical problem. We're used to a germ-free atmosphere. The air on the alpha planet is full of microbes and bacteria. If we go down wearing our helmets and our shield for protection, it will frighten the natives unduly. Consequently, those of us who are actually in the Contact department will have to be specially conditioned, and everyone in the landing party will have to take some precautions. Rauhina, since you're in the technical crew, you will first skim the planet's atmosphere and bring back samples. The Medical department will isolate any dangerous organisms and generate cultures, so we can gradually build up our immunities. In the meantime the rest of us will review the theoretical works on primitive cultures, though I imagine we'll have to halt frequently, because every one of us is going to feel very sick at least once before this is over." She directed a tentative glance at Alrik. "I'm a little worried about you, Alrik. Your constitution is frail. Are you absolutely sure you want to continue in the Contact department?"

"Of course I want to be with you—" began Alrik. At that moment the buzzer sounded again.

"Must be Floress," muttered Natheless, pushing the button. "She's the only other person I've called, so far. Alrik, that's very sweet of you, but you know I'd never forgive myself if anything happened to you."

Alrik objected, "What makes you think you'll survive longer yourself? This is a risky mission."

The door opened, admitting not one but two women. Floress was about twenty years old, with a plump face and figure and lusterless grey-brown hair. She was from what was called an Aspirant family—that is, a family descended from hatcherbrats which was recognized as Lawchild by the yi-Indurans but not by other High Families. Because the yi-Indurans, in their quest for physical vigor, had made greater efforts than other families to find hatcherbrats with potential, train them, and invite them to become Lawchildren, a fairly sizable group of Aspirants and what were called Half-families lived in the yi-Induran Bubble and worked alongside the regular Lawchildren. Many eventually became Lawchildren (usually after displaying extraordinary intelligence or performing some heroic deed), and left the Bubble to join other High Families. But, in the meantime, Haven, for obvious reasons, attracted many children from Aspirant and Half-families. Rauhina was from a Half-family, a term applied to families in which Lawchild qualities such as self-discipline and responsibility were displayed by parents of only one sex (usually the mother), and transferred to children of only one sex (obviously, the daughters).

The uninvited woman was Bodris Hatcherbrat. Her face was considerably younger (she was almost exactly Natheless's age), like Natheless's rather long and thin, and her expressions were mobile and changeable. Natheless wondered why she had come. She had worked in the Contact department before, but no one could guess why, since she seemed to find languages and speculations about theoretical cultures boring, and often said so.

Floress crossed to the desk and said, "I came because you called, Lawchild Natheless."

"Thank you, Lawchild Floress," said Natheless. "Find a chair." As Floress did so, Natheless turned to Bodris.

"Lawchild Natheless," said the hatcherbrat quickly, in a tone that somehow combined excitement and resentment, "Sixfold Lawchild Jimmik Centauri recommends me for the landing party."

"Let's see," mused Natheless, reaching for the card Bodris offered her. It was indeed from Jimmik Centauri, stamped with the official Medical department seal, a double helix. Apart from that, it did not prove very enlightening. The message read, "Sixfold Lawchild Natheless yi-Induran: Being informed you have not yet decided on all the members of your landing party, I have taken it upon myself to suggest Bodris Hatcherbrat. She is young and healthy, tests high for aptitude and has, I hear, experience working in the Contact department. She also has some Medical skills which might prove useful on this hazardous mission." Centauri's signature was scrawled at the end.

Natheless looked up, shaking her head. From anyone else the letter might have made sense. But why was Jimmik Centauri, of all people, becoming so enthusiastic and helpful all of a sudden, about an enterprise which he must consider absurd and wasteful? Centauri was a genius, and his skills and knowledge were indispensable to the sickly Lawchildren. He knew it, and was often inclined to throw his weight around. Even were he to deign to give her advice, Natheless would have expected him to take a more arrogant tone. Why hadn't he, indeed? Not having given Natheless an order since she left his department six months before, was he now uncertain how she might react to a domineering tone and did he want Bodris on the expedition too badly to risk it? It was unlike Centauri to want things so badly. Natheless frowned as she stared at Bodris, wondering whether this woman were Jimmik Centauri's current mistress. He had had a series of hatcherbrat companions since his second divorce ten years before.

Well, it was not for Natheless yi-Induran to dabble in high policy by trying to keep a Sixfold from his mistress. Natheless asked Bodris, "Do you want to go on this expedition?"

Bodris was surprised and offended. "Of course!"

"Why?" Natheless's mind suddenly recalled another scene, which had taken place three years before in Haven's outermost garden. The company of the faithful had been gathered among the padded columns surrounding the pool, looking upward toward the old Ceti viewing screens which showed the passing stars. Natheless and her brother had been in the center of the group. The rest of the company was seated on either side. They were having a ceremonial feast. It usually opened with a rite in which everyone downed a glassful of the synthetic milk fed to Pelezi-terean children. Children after the age of Undeception were given other forms of synthesized food, and the company of Haven would usually not have been able to obtain this nutriment. Of course they were able to synthesize it for themselves. Hence this milk-drinking ceremony was important to them, because their refusal to abandon childish food was symbolic of their refusal to accept adult ways of thought.

On this particular day Bodris Hatcherbrat had found her way to the ceremony (which was not difficult, since Haven had welcomed everyone in those days). She had spent the whole time looking scandalized and asking what the use of all this was. "Why do you drink milk when you're allowed to eat cheese with the adults?" she demanded for the hundredth time.

"We're.all neurotic," Agni had said serenely, as he raised his glass amid the accompanying applause and downed the contents. The rest of the company imitated him.

"I don't think you are," Bodris had said angrily.

"Then why else would we act like this?" Agni had asked. He was already making signals for the company to begin with the rest of the feast.

"I don't know," snapped Bodris. "That's what I want you to tell me."

"We do it because we're crazy," repeated Agni. "If you aren't, why don't you go away and get Seized with the Parzes children?" "Seized," a technical term applying to a ship captured by a star's gravity and unable to escape, was used colloquially to describe intoxication.

"I don't care to," Bodris had replied coldly. "You know only Law-children can do that without being demoted. Besides, I'd rather know why you're doing this." And they had not been able to get rid of her the whole day.

Bodris's face remained perfectly calm as she answered Natheless's question now. "I would like to see the planet," she said.

"Has Lawchild Jimmik told you how risky it is?"

"I don't care."

"Why not, Bodris? Remember how many times you've begun study in the Contact department, and how many times you've left in disgust? I don't believe you have any interest in Contact theory at all. You force yourself to do it. Why?"

Bodris's mouth twisted, as if in pain, but she answered easily, "That was just a bunch of theories. These will be real people."

Well, that much was plausible. Natheless tried to divine why Bodris's presence tended to distress her. It had to do with their extraordinary resemblance to one another. More than one Lawchild had remarked upon it. They had even hinted that her father, Frofor yi-Induran, might not always have behaved as a Lawchild should. Natheless bit her lip. This sort of thing happened; she would have no way of knowing her father had not done so. Her father had died when she was eight, and she had not developed a mature estimate of his character. Yet he had been a loving and devoted father to Agni and her. Could he have ignored his own child as thoroughly as he had ignored Bodris? Bodris had been picked out and brought to the yi-Induran Bubble as a promising child, and Frofor had been kind to her, but no more so than he was to other hatcherbrats-in-training. He had seemed only innocently amazed at Bodris's resemblance to his own daughter. That much did not trouble Natheless. But why had Bodris apparently taken it upon herself to join every group Natheless joined? Why did she hover around the borders of the Haven company instead of joining the frolics of the young Parzes people, which evidently would have suited her personal tastes far better? She was an ambitious hatcherbrat and aspired to Lawchild status. Why had she joined the Contact department? Ordinarily that would not suggest itself as a good way for a hatcherbrat to rise. Wasn't it bad enough she should resemble Natheless, without deliberately striving to shadow her?

Natheless dismissed these thoughts and addressed Bodris again. "I was considering you for the expedition, Bodris. But then again, I thought I might take Izis Centauri instead."

The hatcherbrat's eyes widened. "Lawchild Jimmik's daughter by his first marriage? They can't stand each other! Who's going to pick up the pieces?"

"Well, there's Tau Ceti."

"He's a hemophiliac and vulnerable to strong radiation," objected Bodris.

"Yes, I know," said Natheless, "but then there's also Marduk Eridani."

Bodris was outraged. "He's only thirteen, and has acute anemia!"

"You're still a juvenile yourself, Bodris."

"I'm three days older than you!" retorted the hatcherbrat.

Natheless shrugged and motioned for Bodris to be seated. "Why are we arguing? I've never had any doubt about your aptitude, just your attitude. If you really want to go, and Lawchild Jimmik recommends you, then come. You could do an excellent job if you set your mind to it."

Natheless marveled at the joy that flashed briefly across the hatcherbrat's face. It was quickly erased by the suspicion and resentment that always came to Bodris's rescue when she was in danger of feeling gratitude. She seated herself warily and waited to see what came next. Observing her, Natheless felt irritation, and wondered briefly whether she would regret her easy capitulation to Centauri's request.

7

Within two standard days, the Peleziterea moved from its projected path among the stars to an orbit around the critical planet, a position it was to maintain until the hatcherbrats were returned. Natheless and Rauhina ventured on a preliminary survey, or "skim," of the planet's surface. First they briefly surveyed the whole planet to gain an idea of its population and landmasses. Then they moved in over the peninsula where they were to land to gather samples of the soil, air and water. From these samples Jimmik Centauri and the medical department isolated the potentially dangerous organisms, and grew cultures which were used in various ways to immunize the landing party. This was extremely dangerous therapy for the Pelezitereans, habituated as they were to perfectly germ-free air. Natheless and the other genetically sound members of the party ran slight fevers and had headaches for a few days. Alrik suffered more. The Archon and Jimmik Centauri were virtually prostrated for nearly two and a half weeks. While they were recuperating and conditioning themselves for the descent, Natheless listened over and over again to the computer's tape of the planetary voices. She isolated a few separate words (such as "Charles," "Carlo," "Conradin," "Curradino," "Dieu," "Dio," "Jesu," "Maria" and "misericordia"), which were repeated so often she judged they must either be proper names or extremely important concepts. Beyond that she could make few judgments. The healthy members of the landing party spent their time isolating the sounds that formed the language and learning to imitate them. They also reviewed the theoretical material on pre-atomic peoples with feverish excitement.

Meanwhile the planet serenely continued to rotate on its axis and revolve around its sun. Its days grew shorter and its nights longer in the northern hemisphere. In Naples people still avoided the marketplace, because the demons or sorcerers who had appeared so suddenly before Conradin's execution remained there still, or rather in the nearby church where they had taken refuge. They manifested few signs of life. If one of them had not been glimpsed occasionally, still wearing his armor and glass-fronted helmet, emerging from the bronze doors and looking nervously around, the people might have believed they had vanished into thin air. As it was, no one even dared approach them. One archer, bolder than the others, took up station in a nearby tower and aimed several crossbow bolts at him. But the range was too distant and his missiles fell harmlessly to the ground.

Pious people—Charles and the clerics—sent frantic messages to the Pope at Viterbo, begging him to come himself or at least send some advice to help them in this hour of extraordinary tribulation. Charles also sent his agents far and wide in the attempt to discover where Conradin had gone and what he would do next. An attack from any quarter was possible, particularly from Greece or the Holy Land, where the Emperor Frederick might have gathered his power. There were also definite German possibilities Charles could not overlook. In frustrated indecision, he often had himself carried from the east and the west to the north and the south corners of the city, so he could gaze out in all directions to ponder the dangers from each.

But he did not guess where the real danger lay, because it seemed too removed and insignificant. As a matter of fact, it would have been, except for his faulty assessment of his enemies.

Near the foot of the Alps, the tall mountain range that divides the Italian peninsula from the lands of the French and the Germans lay a region appropriately named the Mountainfoot, Piedmont. There, to complete the work the mountains had begun, stood a series of castles perched atop the hills to guard the passes and defiles. This area had often been the scene of conflict. In the previous generation the Hohenstaufen Emperor Frederick II had tried to gain control of it to ensure safe passage among his wide-stretching domains, which had included Germany and much of Italy. That Empire was now in splinters. Various princelings fought over parts of Germany, the great cities warred for control of Northern Italy, and the Pope sought to consolidate his influence in the South, directly by his own means and through his French ally, Charles.

Most of the Piedmont was now safely in Charles's hands. But some traces remained of Frederick's efforts there. A few castles were still loyal to the Hohenstaufens. One of them, near the Po river, on the western side of Vercelli, had formerly been the seat of the Lancia family. More than fifty years before, it had been the birthplace of a woman called Bianca Lancia, destined to become the favorite mistress and last wife of Emperor Frederick II. Of the two children she bore him, one was the King Manfred whose memory was so dear to the hearts of the common people at Naples. And Arrigo, chained in the dungeon in that city, was her grandchild.

This Bianca was dead. Her descendants were all dead, too, or imprisoned or far away. The castle itself was no longer even controlled by the Lancia family but by Giacomo, Marchese of Caretto, husband of an illegitimate daughter of Frederick II. Another Bianca, a cousin of the Emperor's favorite, was visiting that castle now, along with her husband, Anticoli. Anticoli was only a cognomen. Her husband's real name was Conrad, of which the aspiring king Conradin's name was a diminutive. It seemed something like *lèse majesté* to insist on it however, since Anticoli, with his handsome features and strong limbs, and in the prime of his life, looked more kingly than the slender boy.

Anticoli was also a grandson of the Emperor Frederick, though not through a legitimate son. His grandmother, the Emperor's concubine, was said to have been an Arab slave girl from a city called Antioch or Anticoli; hence, the surname both he and his father had borne. Conrad Anticoli had been unfailingly loyal to his legitimate cousin, fighting by his side and being taken prisoner with him after the battle of Tagliacozzo. He would certainly have been condemned to die along with the young King, had Charles not found it more expedient to release him in exchange for allies of his own who chanced to be in Bianca's hands at their castle of Saracinesco. Anticoli had returned home safe and sound. There therefore had to be a good reason for his return to Piedmont now. If Frederick II were truly planning to reappear, it was to be expected he would keep a dependable kinsman such as Anticoli informed of his movements. Since Anticoli now made a sudden, supposedly secret, journey to the Piedmont, which was uncomfortably far from his own estates in the Abruzzi and dangerously close to the undependable Marchese of Monferrato and the Count of Savoy, people suspected he must know something. Hence, there arose a constant stream of messengers to the castle from all the castle-dwellers in the region and even some from Tuscan and Lombard cities with Imperial sympathies. They all made cautious inquiries, judicious offers of service to the Hohenstaufen dynasty in general, to the Emperor Frederick II in particular, or to his heir, Conradin, or to whoever stood for them. Thus far, although the messengers and their offers were graciously received, only courteous half-answers were given in response. Only the Marchese of Caretto and Anticoli (who both studiously declined to be considered the Emperor's heir) were ever found in residence in the castle.

But Anticoli had traveled specifically to advise a shift in policy. He gathered his wife and their unfortunate young royal cousin into a tower room. From it they could look out over the grape terraces and grain fields on the mountainside. Because no rooms adjoined and the tower stairs below were guarded, they could deliberate freely without fear of being overheard. Still, they spoke in low voices, so as to risk as little as possible.

"Now is the time to act," counseled Anticoli, leaning his chin on his hands. "News of the sorcerers' intervention alone has caused several cities in Tuscany to declare for you. Nobles from all over Apulia and the neighborhood of Rome have journeyed to my castle to express their willingness to serve you. Your escape has put new heart into the Sicilian rebellion. Many are ready to follow you now with men and money, but if you wait long, they will grow tired. They expect Frederick II to appear with an army. If we delay, they will grow suspicious. I advise you to go to Pavia immediately to show yourself, Cousin."

"You must grasp the weapon God has put into your hands," added Bianca.

The boy-King sat on a stiff-backed wooden chair adorned with images of planetary animals carved into its legs. He stared long at the faded oriental carpet beneath his feet. His expression was gloomy—striking in one so young but hardly surprising under the circumstances. Perhaps his black garments also contributed to making him look unnaturally stern, for since arriving in rags at his cousin's castle, he had chosen to wear nothing but mourning. Bianca and Anticoli also wore black, in honor of Bianca's father, Galvano Lancia, whom King Charles had executed less than three months before.

"You say that because you did not see the sorcerers, Cousin Bianca. I did. I tell you, they are not weapons in my hands, and God has given me no weapon against them."

Anticoli and his lady gazed doubtfully on the youth. "Your Majesty is then certain they were really sorcerers, not charlatans frightening the ignorant people?"

"My noble cousins, you know I would not hesitate a moment if it were merely a matter of fighting the Frenchman Charles. But he is nothing compared with these folk. They came from the sky in a flash of light. One of them possessed a rod that shot fire. Whoever the fire touched was deprived of all movement. They have weapons beyond all our science and understanding."

"What are they, then?" demanded Anticoli.

At this point Father Omberto, Bianca's faithful chancellor, could no longer contain himself. "But why are you the last to believe what the people say?" he burst out eagerly. "Everyone says my Lord Anticoli's grandfather, the Emperor Frederick, is not dead, but alive, living with his nobles and scholars and wizards in a great cave under Mongibello. Who but he could have sent such aid to his grandson at such a time?" Omberto was the oldest in the room, five years older than Anticoli. Like the others he was dressed in black, since he was a priest, but unlike them his plump face was full of hope and his eyes gleamed with childlike enthusiasm. Bianca responded sternly to him as if he were a child. "The Emperor Frederick is dead. I walked beside his casket and saw him laid in his tomb."

Omberto was momentarily taken aback, but he quickly recovered. "Yes, *Madònna*, but he had many sorcerers at his court, and they were masters of illusion!"

Still more irritated than Bianca, Anticoli came to his wife's support. "Uncle Manfred was with him when he died and told me all about it," he snapped.

"But, my lord, King Manfred was by all accounts the Emperor's favorite son, and may have been privy to the secret."

This remark reminded Anticoli of Imperial favoritism, and was not calculated to improve his temper. "My father loved the Emperor, too. Why would the Emperor have deceived him?"

"Besides," added the young King, addressing Omberto in slow, condescending tones (for who would deign to be angry with such a fool?),"if the Emperor is alive, as you say, and Manfred was his favorite son, as you say, why would he allow Manfred to be slain at Benevento, yet send sorcerers to help a grandson he had never seen?"

For the first time, doubt seemed to smite Omberto. However, he brightened irrepressibly almost at once. "Perhaps there was no time to send aid—"

"We knew about Charles's invasion months beforehand. A sorcerer or two would have been very welcome indeed." Anticoli's dark eyes grew darker as many bitter recollections flowed back to him.

This gave Omberto time to come up with an even better explanation. "Perhaps Manfred is not dead either! Perhaps that was an illusion, too! You have said the body the Frenchmen buried at Benevento was too mutilated for anyone to be sure—"

"No, Omberto," growled Anticoli. "Only some people said that. But Galvano Lancia was one of the prisoners who recognized Manfred. Galvano was sure."

Bianca buried her face in her hands.

"But he might have been deceived—"

"If my Uncle Manfred were alive," demanded Conradin, "would he allow King Charles to confine poor Queen Helena and his four children so cruelly in his dungeons?"

"Perhaps those are only Charles's boasts—"

"They are there," said the young King shortly. "I have seen them myself." His expression became fierce. "And besides, what of Lady Bianca's kindred? What of Galvano and Federigo and Bartolomeo Lancia?" His eyes filled with angry tears. "The merciless Frenchman had them butchered, too, and my grandfather did nothing? Also, there was my friend, Prince Friedrich von Baden, almost my foster brother. Charles had him beheaded as though he were not a prince. I saw them all die. If my grandfather were still alive, I would have to hate him for having done nothing. Before God, I hope he is dead." Bowing his head, Conradin began to weep. Lady Bianca joined him, and Anticoli, with a few tears gleaming in his own eyes, stared balefully at Father Omberto.

Seeing his optimistic speeches had done nothing to advance the council, but had only awakened painful memories, Omberto sought to repair the damage with brave words. Beseechingly, he addressed Conradin, "Sire, it is noble in a king to weep for the deaths of his subjects, but nobler still to stand strong against adversity."

Conradin did not acknowledge the comment. Anticoli's expression changed to one of mild contempt. "Leave us, Omberto," he said at last.

"Yes, my lord," said Omberto, downcast. He rose slowly, bowed to all, departed, and closed the door softly behind him. When it was firmly shut, Conradin wiped his eyes. "Cousin Anticoli, Fortune has dealt me many harsh blows!" he exclaimed.

"It has dealt them to you and to us," Anticoli replied, "and will deal more unless we take good counsel." Bianca also overcame her tears and was listening intently. "Who did you suggest these sorcerers were?"

Conradin shook his head doubtfully. "What could they be but Infidels from beyond the sea? The Pope used to suspect our grandfather of sorcery because he dealt with Infidels. Perhaps these were messengers from some foreign king he had known. Perhaps they came hoping to speak with Frederick II, not having heard of his death. That would explain why they could not answer Charles's question—they thought the Emperor would know their language or have a scholar in attendance who did."

"What brought them to Naples? The Emperor usually held court at Foggia, when he didn't have to be anywhere else."

Conradin considered the objection. "That is puzzling," he agreed. "Perhaps they did not mean to visit the Emperor after all. We have sent men across the sea to conquer the Infidels. Perhaps the Infidels sent these over the sea in return to conquer us."

"In that case," said Anticoli, getting up abruptly and striding to the window, "why have they done nothing since then? Why do they cower inside a church? What kind of a war of conquest is that?"

"They are ignorant of our language," mused Conradin slowly. "Until they learn it, they cannot possibly exact obedience, no matter how terrifying their weapons may be. Many would be glad to do their bidding, I am sure, if only they could communicate what they wanted."

"Then why," said Anticoli, squinting and staring southward toward the sea, "did their master neglect to send an interpreter with them?"

"Their conduct is really strange," conceded Conradin, following his gaze. He paused a moment and added, "Perhaps they came here by accident." But the idea that sorcerers with powers of the magnitude he had seen demonstrated would ever have done anything by accident was so manifestly ludicrous he pursued it no further.

"Your Majesty," said Anticoli turning deferentially back to the young King, "if you think it is unwise to attack King Charles directly at this time, what shall you do?"

Conradin rested his chin on his hands and spoke with his eyes closed as if to aid his concentration. "I have a plan," he said, "one very easy to describe, but difficult to accomplish. To begin with, we know the sorcerers are more dangerous than Charles; we know they are not on our side; we know they are not demons. We also know their power seems to be entirely contained in their silver rods. And if they come from beyond the sea, there may well be more like them with similar weapons, preparing to come. Therefore, it seems to me we must attempt to get these sorcerers into our power—capture them in an incautious moment, perhaps, and take their silver rod from them. Then we must learn their language if possible, in order to discover where they come from, what they want and whether there are others like them. If there are no others, we can use them and their weapons for our own purposes. If there are others like them"—he stopped, laughing humorlessly—"I don't know quite what we will do, but a least Charles and the Pope will be in no better position than we are."

Anticoli nodded. "You are clearly right. That is the obvious plan. And there is some danger King Charles, being closer to them, may put it into execution first."

"We must count on the fact he will be distracted by his hatred for us," said Conradin. "Since he believes we are wicked enough to bargain with demons, he also believes the sorcerers are our allies against him. He will rely on prayer to fight, since he thinks he has been attacked by supernatural weapons. Since we know we can hope for no extraordinary intervention from either God or the Devil we have only our wits to rely on. We will act. So we have an advantage, though only a small one."

"Then we must get closer to Naples, for more information," said Bianca.

"And for that you will have to show yourself to your allies," added Anticoli, addressing the King. "Return to Savona and take ship for Pisa. Tell everyone you know what the sorcerers are, and that they have come to help you as the people believe. You will gather a following large enough to coerce all the cities between there and Naples. They'll yield to you without a blow. Once all that land is in your power, what will it matter if people are undeceived, especially if you have the sorcerers' rod in your hands by then?"

Conradin straightened. "You are right, Cousin Anticoli. I must set out now to regain my grandfather's Empire. But I must not demean myself by declaring these sorcerers are my friends. After all, we first asserted we knew nothing of them. Why should we change our story? Our denials did nothing to lessen people's belief in our connection with the wizards. Our affirmation will not strengthen it. However, if we openly acknowledge an understanding with the Infidels, we will have to account for anything they might do in the meantime, which might be an unbearable strain on our wits. If we simply welcome the return of our allies promising them forgiveness for past lapses, assure them of our reverence for God and the Church but declare the sorcerers should be dealt with as men, not demons, everyone will follow us assuming we have not taken them fully into our confidence. That will not surprise them greatly, because they themselves know they have not earned our trust." His eyes narrowed.

Anticoli laughed, surprised and delighted at the subtlety of his cousin's exposition. "There speaks a true king!" he exclaimed. Conradin reached toward him and the two men clasped hands.

Conradin, inwardly pleased at his own cleverness, still feared it would prove futile against the mountainous troubles that beset him. Anticoli's words of praise and his support helped to brace his courage. He resolved to face his difficulties one by one, a day at a time, never admitting anything was too difficult for his royal self until it was proved by defeat or death.

8

One night, about forty-eight of the planet's nights after Agni's death, the Peleziterean landing craft settled over the Mountainfoot area. An important Contact theorem stated Pelezitereans ought to land in a time and place when they were least likely to be seen. So Natheless and the technical crew carefully plotted a landing approach that brought them to a sparsely populated area in the darkest hours of the night. The descent was long, and for many hours large portions of the planet were still visible below them. Several of the landing party had never seen a planetary body so close before. They gathered in the lower deck to watch the blue-white surface grow ever larger. The sight filled their hearts with an excitement they had not expected, and which the Contact theorems had not accounted for.

"Father," said Alrik, staring at the screen, "do you think our own planet looked something like this one from high up?"

The Archon, his own eyes riveted to the screen, nodded, and answered with the words of a nursery rhyme:

> *How could we leave our native world,*
> *Where mountains soared and rivers curled,*
> *Where wailed the wind and fell the snow,*
> *On great blue seas of H_2O?*

Bodris tittered at the sound of the Archon's voice reciting nursery rhymes. Alrik and several others returned their attention to the screen after a glance at her.

"To think they don't have to synthesize air for themselves," murmured Rauhina.

"Or even water," added the Archon.

"And day and night come to each part of the planet's surface without having to arrange for it," said Rauhina.

"How could we ever leave our native world?" Alrik queried.

Apparently in a whimsical mood, the Archon repeated the next verse of the nursery rhyme.

> *Karsma Megala of blood was reeking,*
> *So burned with fire and bruised with bars,*
> *He made us exiles from distant stars,*
> *Who always must be seeking.*

Alrik looked back at the screen. The planet had grown massive and powerfully alluring. It had already lost its full, spherical appearance and become humped or gibbous as they drew near the dark side. From that distance all they could see was cloud and ocean, but Alrik's feelings were profoundly stirred by the sight of a material place designed by nature to support human life. He had never personally seen a place like it before, yet he knew his ancestors had come from one such. Now he felt an almost unbearable longing rise in him, as though something ancestral were calling from deep within.

But this beautiful planet would never be a home for the Pelezitereans; they were landing only to preserve it for its rightful inhabitants. Still, once there had been a planet where his ancestors had had a right to live. Alrik spoke hastily and almost without forethought.

"During my apprenticeship they told me our ancestors fled from Urith because Karsma Megala identified himself with the God-Myth. But I never understood why that bothered us so much, if we didn't believe the God-Myth anyway. Couldn't we have humored him and stayed?"

The Archon stared into the screen for another long moment before he even began to answer. Then he turned slowly toward Alrik. He had tried at other times to interest Alrik in detailed discussions of Peleziterean history and its implications, but such a question at such a time struck him as ominous. He searched Alrik's face, unsatisfied by what he saw there. "Alrik, if you would wonder with a little more energy, perhaps the answer would come to you without my saying anything."

Feeling his father's entire attention concentrated on him, Alrik wished he had been silent. He knew he fell short of his father's high standards, and often felt diffident in his presence. Now there was no way out.

"I—I don't really know what you mean, Father," he stammered, "unless the people who did believe in the God-Myth refused to accept Karsma Megala as its manifestation and were persecuted for it?"

"Well, what about *that?* " said the Archon. "Do honest people watch in silence while something like that happens? "

"Well," said Alrik with a shrug, "I don't see any point in their getting themselves killed if there's nothing they can do about it."

"Ah!" said the Archon. "But that's the point. They didn't get themselves killed. They fled in a colony ship."

"Wasn't that a bit drastic?"

The Archon was more deeply troubled than before. "Yes, it was a drastic solution to a drastic problem. Are you suggesting it was unnecessary for our ancestors to leave Urith?"

"I wasn't suggesting anything; I was *asking* you whether it wasn't," said Alrik.

The Archon put a hand on his son's shoulder. "Listen to me, Alrik, and listen well, because I won't always be here to tell you this, but there are things you ought to remember. First of all, men who claim to be gods are bad-humored almost by definition. It takes flattery of a very complex and time-consuming nature to keep them happy. And the talent for producing this form of appeasement profoundly contradicts the scientific analytical ability we have always encouraged among our people. Moreover, people who so set out to deceive others often end up deceiving themselves. If you had to spend half your life addressing Karsma Megala with the grandiloquent names he made up for himself, and if you dared speak the truth, trembling, only in small groups, eventually your ability to pierce the flattery would atrophy. You would forget what you really thought. In a state like Karsma Megala's, when you forget what you really think, you think just like everyone, do just what Karsma Megala commands. That includes informing on dissidents and helping to persecute those believers in the God-Myth who are wise enough to see that Karsma Megala is not the force they really worship.

"On the other hand, under a Karsma Megala, if you do manage to keep your secret thoughts alive, you can be sure that eventually a situation will arise where you will react with more honesty than prudence, more intelligence than tact. Then you will be informed on, branded a believer in the wrong kind of God-Myth, and murdered with the rest.

"So you see, Alrik, drastic as it was, flight was really the only practical course open to our ancestors. And events bore them out—our ship was still within concussion distance when Urith exploded."

"I thought," said Alrik, "it wasn't certain the concussion originated from Urith."

"There was no doubt about that," returned the Archon shortly. "It was only uncertain whether Urith alone had been the source of the explosion. The observed dislocation of familiar stars and the spatial displacement of the Peleziterea itself were much greater than what the dematerialization of a middle-sized planet should have caused. More precisely, the displacement which should have resulted was calculable, and what actually occurred was not. There are, of course, many things we still do not know about the Universe, but there is no doubt whatsoever Urith was destroyed. We can not return no matter how much we want to. Some of our ancestors did want to, you understand."

"I see," said Alrik, wondering uncomfortably whether his father was aware of his intense longing toward the planet. But the Archon had turned once more to look at the screen, where the planet was now a huge crescent, waxing in length but waning in width by the second. Natheless's voice drifted to their ears, reciting the last verse of the nursery rhyme the Archon had been quoting:

> *Therefore, we follow the endless trails,*
> *Through vanishing vapors of comets' tails,*
> *And airless and empty and lifeless space,*
> *Seeking a home for our restless race.*

Startled, Alrik turned to look at his fiancée. She had come to the lower deck apparently for company, but then she had settled in a corner of the room with a small data screen on her lap, and was working busily on some plan. The trouble with this arrangement was that Alrik could never be sure when she was listening and when she was not. Obviously she must have heard most of this last conversation. Alrik reflected back, trying to remember whether he had said anything about the God-Myth that would hurt her.

Natheless was not looking at them now. She was bending over her data screen with a smile on her face, the kind she always wore when she had an especially exciting idea. Natheless always smiled more over her work than she did at people, Alrik reflected. She felt herself at a disadvantage in all but intellectual situations, and was withdrawn and awkward at all social gatherings that were not completely formal and therefore predictable. She was totally different from Alrik in that respect. It amused him.

Natheless could look directly at only a few people without losing some of the intensity of her smile and injecting an element of wariness into her expression. When Alrik Eridani had become one of the favored few about a year before, he had decided to persuade her to marry him. "After all," he had noted ironically in his journal, "if the yi-Induran prodigy finds me almost as exciting as her work, what more could I want out of life?" Lawchild Nibbana had also been very much in favor of the match. Natheless yi-Induran, the Personality sub-Archon had claimed, had talents the Peleziterea could not afford to lose. However, she had a depressive personality. She had never overcome the shock of losing her parents at the age of eight and the subsequent trauma of being isolated from the other children by her brother's refusal to disbelieve the God-Myth. Nibbana feared she did not have enough inner resources to bring her past adolescence. However, if someone good-natured and stable like Alrik would take charge of her, she might still live a healthy and productive life.

Alrik hoped he might be equal to this tremendous responsibility. However, he had to admit that in the months since their engagement, Natheless had really been no trouble at all. In fact, Alrik was convinced she would be as much help to him in their future married life as he to her. There was nothing she was afraid to face. If anything, she was a little too unmovable.

Alrik went over to his fiancée's corner and looked down on the data screen. "What's happening, chief?" he inquired, making a joking reference to the fact that, although he was five years older than she, Natheless, as Sixfold in the Contact department, was now his superior.

Natheless looked up, still smiling. "I think I've figured out how to avoid a certain kind of metaphysical interference."

"What's that?" said Alrik. She had probably explained it to him before, but he couldn't at the moment distinguish it from several other kinds of interference she had talked about. But Natheless never minded when Alrik did not remember. She was too pleased he was willing to listen.

"Metaphysical interference," said Natheless, "is changing the philosophy of the planet's inhabitants. These people have never traveled beyond their planet's atmosphere—in fact, they cannot even fly within its atmosphere. Hence, in all probability, they have no concept of outer space. If we try to explain it to them, we *might* drastically change their way of looking at the world. On the other hand, many primitive peoples on Urith attached great religious significance to the ground and the sky. If we tried to abbreviate our account and tell these people we came from the sky or from under the earth (both equally accurate ways of describing the route we're taking), they might understand it as a claim we are supernatural beings of one sort or another. I don't think we want to get involved with that kind of problem.

"In our preliminary survey we learned the planet below us has seven continents, four of them with highly developed cultures. Now, the culture we are going to seems to have no contact at all with one of these. But it seems to have a thriving trade with the second culture by means of vessels we observed on their internal sea. This second culture, in turn, has contact with the third culture. Hence, our culture knows of the third culture through hearsay, and may have had very distant intermittent contact with it. If we introduce ourselves as human beings, the natives of our culture will probably assume that we come from this third culture. Even if what we do makes them very angry, the civilizations are too far apart for them to make war on each other at the present state of their technology. So I think it would be best, when they ask us where we come from, to point in the direction of that internal sea and say, "Far beyond the sea." That's certainly as true as anything else we could say (we are even approaching the region from that direction), and a great deal less misleading in a metaphysical sense."

Jimmik Centauri, who had been staring at the screen all this time and ignoring the conversation, turned suddenly. "It seems to me you've wasted a lot of effort. We could get quicker results by claiming to be gods."

"Not necessarily," said Natheless. "According to our historical accounts, the God of our own people's God-Myths was an unusually commanding figure. Not all primitive peoples respect their gods so much."

"We'd teach them to respect their gods fast enough!"said Jimmik.

"That," said Natheless, "would be metaphysical interference."

The bluish crescent had disappeared. They were beginning their descent over the dark side of the planet.

"Father," said Alrik, "do we have to leave this planet? It's so big, and Natheless says there are vast unpopulated stretches. Surely we could find an uninhabited island somewhere, and settle there without bothering the great civilizations!"

The Archon shook his head. "No, Alrik. The planet's civilizations will expand and cover the whole world when their science develops, and then they will find us—even assuming we would have the self-restraint to wait until then."

"What if we drop our technology?" pursued his son. "What if we totally destroyed all our records and didn't teach them to our children, and concentrated on learning to subsist on what the planet offered?"

Jimmik let out a whoop of laughter. "Can't you think at all, Alrik Eridani, and you the Archon's son? What do you think you are?"

Flushing, Alrik turned to the Medical sub-Archon. "What do you mean?" The Archon had turned away from both and was staring at the dark screen.

"You are exactly what all the other Peleziterean Lawchildren are, with the exception of your fiancée, Natheless here. She's as healthy as a hatcherbrat and has a lot of hatcherbrat genes in her, too." Alrik winced at the insult to his prospective wife, but she did not seem to notice. "You are," continued Jimmik, "a mass of defective organs held loosely and precariously together by suture, plastic surgery and constant therapy. So dangerous is this journey for your health that I, as chief medical authority aboard the Peleziterea, had to accompany you in order to observe you constantly. And yet you suggest we drop our technology. You wouldn't last a month, and your father wouldn't last a day."

"I guess I just wasn't thinking," muttered Alrik.

"I guess you weren't!" chortled Jimmik, turning his back.

The Archon left the screen. "We can't see anything more from here, and it's nine more hours before we land. I think it best we retire and get some rest. Everyone, be sure to strap yourselves in. We're going to have enough health problems when we land, without having to contend with broken bones." He turned and walked through the door at the back of the room. Rauhina, Bodris and most of the others followed, but Natheless remained working at her data screen. Alrik came to stand over her. Jimmik also remained and stared at them.

"Aren't you going to retire?" he said to Alrik. "Your heart can't take too many consecutive hours of activity."

"I thought you might retire first," said Alrik. "You have to be careful, or your colitis will flare up."

Jimmik grimaced, amused in spite of his best efforts. "Far be it from me to stand in the path of true love," he said, and bowing ironically, he, too, departed. Before he was out of earshot he turned and called back, "Watch it, though, Alrik! She can take a lot more of it than you can." Then he was gone.

Alrik looked at Natheless. Her cheeks were turning very pink. "Don't mind him," he said. "His nose is out of joint because your name was printed above his on the landing party roster."

Natheless looked up with astonishment. "It *was?*"

"Well, of course it was. Didn't you look at it? Think a moment," said Alrik, proud this was an aspect of the situation that seemed to have occurred only to him. "You're now rank six in the Contact department, rank four in the Medical department, and our marriage agreement gives you two extra rank points. Centauri only has five other rank points for administrative duties outside the Medical department, and his marriage rank lapsed. You are carrying more points than any of the Sixfold anyway, so of course the computer had to print your name second after the Archon. I guess that also means, theoretically, you'd have to take charge of the Peleziterea if anything happened to the Archon, until the High Council could elect a new one."

"Theoretically!" said Natheless, standing up. "Alrik, please don't pile any more duties on me." She walked up to him and put her hand on his arm. "Alrik, do you think we can do this successfully?"

"Of course we can!" said Alrik expansively. "You'll do fine. You always do."

Natheless shook her head. "This is an unprecedented situation. I'm scared."

"That's because you're tired. You've been working all day. Put the data screen away and go to bed. You're going to need all your energy when we land on that planet. And don't forget to strap yourself in."

Natheless smiled slightly. "Don't you forget either, Alrik."

"Wish I could come and make sure you were strapped in," said Alrik tenderly.

"No need," said Natheless, blushing again. "I can do it fine." Unmarried Lawchildren were forbidden to be in one another's quarters, as there were plenty of other places for them to meet; however, Sixfold were considered legally irreproachable. Alrik and Natheless had debated whether the rule applied in her case (there had never been a juvenile Sixfold before), but did not dare test it. So, the two kissed affectionately in the doorway and parted, feeling somewhat less alone and somewhat less angry at the Universe.

9

It was the nineteenth day of December, some fifty-one days after the sorcerers' appearance. Since then, the marketplace had stood deserted. Such people as had to engage in commerce now brought their goods to a different square on the other side of the city. But today the square was occupied by a crowd with different concerns. Instead of the usual crowd of gaily-clothed, chattering market-goers, a somber procession of penitents and priests filled the streets, bearing candles and holy objects and chanting prayers. Some tried to arouse God's compassion by more violent methods. They dressed themselves in the dirtiest and most ragged clothing they could find, and went back and forth across the marketplace beating themselves with sticks or leather thongs and shrieking "Mercy, mercy!" in their hoarse voices. Occasionally, when one drew too much blood, a priest would try to stop him, but generally the self-beaters were ignored. Who could be sure they had not really committed some secret crime which was now causing God to turn away from Naples and permit the sorcerers to remain in the house where he should be worshiped?

The procession on this day was much larger and its mood more intense than it had ever been before, because the Pope had arrived the previous night and was walking with them. For weeks they had almost given up hope of his arrival. He had set out from Viterbo almost as soon as he had heard of the attack. But Conradin's escape had thrown the countryside into confusion, and a number of cities along his path had conspired to block his march. The Pope had been forced to take refuge in a castle along the route and lie hidden for days. He had finally slipped out in disguise with a small escort, eluded his besiegers and made his way to Naples. Here the other priests and the allies of King Charles greeted his arrival with joy, for surely his safe arrival was a sign that God was relenting. Perhaps now he would even drive away the wicked sorcerers. Some urged the High Priest to enter the church at once and exorcise the demonic presences, but nothing would induce their leader to put God to the test in that fashion. The Pontiff insisted he had come to comfort the faithful and to confer with his ally, King Charles. He only consented to lead a procession through the marketplace and pray for God's mercy. So he was there now, dressed in his elaborate robes of office, with several other devout and important clergymen—including Cardinal Ughetto and Abbot Sinibaldo—at his side. Nearly a third of the population of Naples followed him, shouting, weeping, chanting and praying, hoping at every moment for a miracle.

The noise from outside could not help but arouse the anxieties of the two Pelezitereans within the church. Jori and Nelsik Hatcherbrat crouched on the floor in what seemed to be the main room of the building, feeling gloomier and more doubtful, if that were possible, than did King Charles as he lay in his royal bed, unable to move hand or foot.

They had chosen to stay in the main room because of all the open space it contained. As long as they stayed there, they reasoned, no one could come close without being seen. In any smaller room, there might be secret entrances. One of the barbarians might sneak in and be upon them before they had time to draw the energet. So the main room it was. Still, Jori and Nelsik did not much care for the architecture. The columns reminded them too much of the Lawchildren's Council room aboard the Peleziterea, though to be sure this room was much bigger, about six times as high as Jori and three times as long as it was high. It was full of decorations the hatcherbrats found unpleasant. Nevertheless, they spent a lot of time looking at them, because it gave them something to do.

Many of the designs painted on the walls and windows or carved into the pillars seemed at least partly based on the human figure, but with incomprehensible additions. Besides the usual eyes, noses, mouths, hands, arms and legs, some of these figures had features which the hatcherbrats had only learned to name a month or so before, and then only from pictures of Urithian animals with wings, horns, claws and tails the computer had printed out. The natives seemed fond of depicting human beings undergoing tortures of various forms. Even in designs with none of these unpleasant themes, Jori was puzzled by the white or yellow disc frequently painted behind a human head which did not seem to represent a part of the body. It might be an article of clothing. But Jori was sure none of the barbarians had been wearing one, and he wondered how it would be fastened on.

The figure whose presence dominated the entire room was painted on the wall at the far end, its feet starting at a level with Jori's chin. It was an enormous human shape about half again as tall as Jori. It had wings as well as one of those yellow discs around its head. In its right hand it held a weapon very much like the one the barbarian chieftain had used to attack Agni—a sort of very large, long-bladed knife. The figure had a poised, ominous, threatening appearance, and its dark eyes seemed to follow the hatcherbrats wherever they went in the room. It gave them the creeps, but they felt they had to keep their eyes on it, almost in self-defense.

"What do you think it means?" Jori asked aloud for about the hundredth time.

Nelsik was sitting uneasily on the floor, trying to keep one eye on the ominous picture and the other on the door through which the chants of the savages came. "It means a crowd of barbarians is outside carrying weapons like that and waiting to cut us up the way they cut Lawchild Agni," he said. As if to emphasize the truth of his assertions, the sound of the chanting outside grew louder.

"What *are* they doing out there?" growled Jori. "I've never heard so many of them together since the first day."

"Maybe they've finally found a way to attack us," said Nelsik nervously. He was more worried about Jori's reaction than the crowd outside. His contempt for the barbarians' power was as great as his companion's. But he was tired to death of the long wait inside the strange building on the strange planet, and made a habit of putting the worst possible interpretation on everything.

"You know they can't attack us," said Jori flatly.

"You're so sure?" Nelsik retorted.

Jori did not deign to answer, and Nelsik, partly encouraged and partly provoked by his silence, went on. "Why don't we call the ship and ask them to come get us?" It was not the first time he had suggested this, but since he had no new arguments, he hoped to wear down his companion's resistance by constant repetition.

Jori's answer was predictable. "We can't," he said matter-of-factly. "We've killed the Lawchild."

"*We* didn't," argued Nelsik. "It was the barbarian with the big knife."

Jori again spoke from his superior knowledge. Unlike Nelsik, he had been brought to the yi-Induran Bubble at an early age, and understood Lawchild mentality better. "Lawchildren don't think that way. They will say the barbarian could never have come close enough to Lawchild Agni to use his big knife if we hadn't crash-landed our ship right over their city. So it's our fault he died."

Seeing himself doomed to permanent exile and perhaps death because of a crime he had never intended to commit, Nelsik complained, "It was all your idea. If you hadn't disobeyed the Lawchild, I could be sitting by the pool on deck right now, watching all the legs go by."

It was the first open accusation Nelsik had made, and he trembled, waiting for a reaction. Jori considered the matter dispassionately for a moment, and then slowly drew the energet.

Nelsik backed away. "You're not going to shoot me with that," he asserted, not quite with conviction.

Jori sneered. "It's only set on paralyze, you numbskull." Jori wished he were able to set it on something else. He had no serious desire to injure his only companion, but the barbarians were outside. He had not yet even figured out how to reverse the paralyze setting. Hatcherbrats were not generally taught to use weapons at all. One of the yi-Indurans had picked Jori out as a promising boy and had educated him in their Bubble, but even so he had been trained only in marksmanship. The energet handed to him at practice sessions had always been set on a designated mode, and it had always been taken from him immediately after his turn. He had no idea how to change settings. If he had obtained the weapon in its locked position, the chances were a million to one against his even being able to get it working at all. For that reason, he had waited until Agni laid it down momentarily in the course of using it. Jori had no idea how to turn it off, and lived in constant fear it would go off some night while he slept.

He continued addressing Nelsik. "There's no reason why I couldn't stun you first and beat your stupid brains out afterward."

"Then who'd keep watch and drive the savages off while you slept?" Nelsik sneered in return.

"I'd sooner see you dead," said Jori calmly, "and die myself, than let you go back up to the ship and sit peacefully by the pool while the barbarians tear me to pieces here."

Nelsik sat down on the floor again. "All right, Jori, if that's what you meant, why didn't you say so? I wouldn't leave you, even if this whole mess is your fault. You can put away that stupid energet. If you want me to stay, I'll stay. You don't have to be such a hatcherbrat."

Jori paused thoughtfully, judging whether or not this was sufficient. Slowly he lowered the energet. "You just gave me a good idea," he said.

"I did?" said Nelsik suspiciously.

"Yes. Don't you see, if we're ever going to get any benefit from being on this planet, we've got to make those barbarians do what we want."

"How can we, when we don't even know their language?"

"That's just the point. There's a whole crowd of them out there, yelling and screaming. All we have to do is emerge and paralyze a few. The rest will run away. Then we just fetch one or two of the paralyzed ones and bring them in here. We should learn their words for food and water in less than a day, and that's mostly what we want." The hatcherbrats were in no danger of starvation, but the food synthesized by their small transformers designed only for travel was bland even by Peleziterean standards.

"We want women, too," said Nelsik, biting his lips.

"And better clothes," said Jori. "And the freedom to move around."

"And peace," said Nelsik. "And safety from the Lawchildren."

"You can't have everything," said Jori. "Let's go." He turned abruptly away from the picture of the winged man and began to walk down the center of the room. Every painting and statue seemed to stare at him as he moved, but he ignored them. Finally, he stood before the massive doors that led out. "Open the doors," he said to Nelsik, as he took out the energet.

Nelsik had learned the trick by now. He drew out the heavy iron bolt, and threw his weight against the doors. They swung open slowly with many squeals and squeaks, revealing the bright light of the afternoon sun in the dusty street beyond. Cries and gasps rose from the crowd outside as Jori stepped through the doors, but they were quickly suppressed and the people continued their strange low chants.

At the front of the crowd stood five men whose stance and apparel attracted Jori's eyes. These were clearly the leaders, for their robes were more brightly colored and more richly decorated than any of the others. Besides, they carried bright objects, some gold, some decorated with gems. As Jori came out, these men did not even pause in their chanting; instead, they fell to their knees, raised the objects they were holding high into the air and turned their eyes skyward. Jori even felt a stab of nervousness, and wondered if somehow or other they were in contact with the Peleziterea.

Overcoming that ridiculous suspicion, Jori studied these five more closely. As leaders they were apt to be among the least tractable members of the crowd, and therefore the least useful from his point of view, yet their clothes were highly interesting and he would have liked to examine them more closely.

But Nelsik's voice distracted him. "Jori, look, *women!*" Jori turned quickly and followed Nelsik's gesture. It wasn't easy for inexperienced eyes to discern sexual differences among the Italians because of their clothing. Everyone wore loose garments. The chief distinction seemed to be that the men wore less covering on their heads and legs. Jori probably could not have figured this out for himself, but once Nelsik cracked the code, there was no denying it. From a group of Italians with thick robes and well-covered heads he picked out one young face that was uncovered, and squeezed the trigger.

He had aimed well. The girl uttered a terrified shriek and crumpled. Cries and exclamations rose from the Italians all around, and about half the group broke and fled. Unfortunately for Jori, the people around her quickly lifted the stricken girl and carried her off with the fleeing crowd. So swiftly was she lost in the swirl of bodies, he was not even able to fire on her bearers.

The other half of the crowd rushed at Jori. In a wash of light from the energet he brought about ten of them to the ground. The rest turned and fled. Some of these tried to carry away their paralyzed companions, but by firing on would-be rescuers, Jori succeeded in discouraging their attempts. In a few moments all was quiet again, except for the fervent chanting of about twenty barbarians who had remained. The five gorgeously dressed leaders had neither fled nor attacked. Neither had a few men standing behind them, dressed all in black, white and grey. Jori focused on them and considered a moment. Then he aimed the energet again and struck five blows. One by one the magnificently dressed barbarians tumbled to the ground. Four of them uttered terrified cries, but the fifth continued his chanting without pause as he crumpled, and he continued it as he lay on the ground.

The confidence of the others broke at once. They leaped to their feet, crying confusedly to one another. Only one came forward in the attempt to help his leader—the man who had continued to chant as he fell—but Jori brought him down with a flash. All the others fled shrieking across the market square, losing themselves quickly in the narrow alleys on the opposite side.

No Italian except the ones who had been rendered helpless by the energet now stood anywhere near the marketplace. Jori ventured a closer look at the five leaders. All were chanting again now, but Jori had watched them as they fell. Ignoring the one who had never stopped chanting, Jori bent carefully over the others. It was easy to choose among them. The one in the middle had far more beautiful robes, and his headgear gleamed with many more precious stones. Jori motioned to Nelsik. "Let's take this one."

Obediently Nelsik tried to raise the paralyzed barbarian. "Give me a hand," he said to Jori.

Jori glanced carefully around to make sure no unstricken barbarians were lurking nearby. Then he returned his energet to his silver vest and took hold of the prisoner's legs.

Feeling the sorcerer's hands upon him, the native screamed and tried to struggle, but of course he could not move his limbs. Instead, he thrashed his neck wildly about. "Spare our ears," growled Jori as the two men heaved him through the door. A few feet beyond it, they laid their captive on the floor and returned to secure the bolt. When they had done this, they approached the Italian.

"Why isn't he moving?" demanded Jori, looking down at him.

"He's paralyzed," said Nelsik, wondering why Jori would ask such a stupid question.

"He can move his head, neck, eyes and mouth. He was doing so a moment ago." Jori bent over the captive. He was obviously not a young man. His hair, now loosened from under his headgear, was sparse and white, and his skin wrinkled. His face was very red. Jori did not think it had been that color when they first took hold of him. He put a hand on the unresisting neck. "I don't feel any pulse. It doesn't look like he's breathing, either." Jori stood up. "I think he's dead."

"But how?" cried Nelsik, surprised and a little frightened. "We didn't do anything to him!"

"Fear," said Jori. "A lot of Lawchildren die of that, too. We'll have to go out and get one of the others." He started toward the door and Nelsik followed.

10

The Roman Emperor was holding court at Grosseto. Or perhaps it would be more accurate to say that the Emperor-elect was holding court there, since the German king did not officially receive the Imperial title until the Pope had crowned him at Rome. It might have been even more accurate to say that the would-be Emperor-elect was holding court, since Conradin's election to the German kingship was disputed, and only a small party recognized his claim. But strict legal accuracy was obviously not really possible when both sides in the conflict had done their utmost to obstruct regular procedures.

So Conradin, as German King, Lombard King, King of Jerusalem and Emperor-elect, held court at Grosseto. All around him in the hall sat the nobles who had flocked to him from the surrounding castles and cities. With a show of force he had passed by Asti and Lavagna, was welcomed at Genoa, took a ship there and went to Frederick II's old camp at Grosseto, where still more allies gathered around him. The terror of the Hohenstaufen name, combined with news that King Charles was crippled by mysterious means, caused several wavering towns in the area to drive out the pro-papal party and install imperial sympathizers in their leadership. Other cities, pro-papal to the marrow, shut their gates against Conradin with renewed imprecations, their courage stiffened rather than broken by the demonic intervention. But Conradin did not think it was time yet to attack them. He was gathering his forces for an attack centered on Naples, or whatever place his arch-foe Charles might see fit to meet him.

It was evening, and the court was feasting. The tables were spread with white cloths and heavily laden with dishes of pewter, for Conradin did not have sufficient plates of silver.

Some of his new allies had brought him the robes of imperial scarlet which had been worn by Frederick II until the camp at Victoria was taken. He wore a rich mantle with a crown of laurel leaves on his head, since the Imperial crown had not likewise been returned. Conradin put on the Imperial robes at their donor's earnest request, but under the mantle he still wore the black tunic and hose that signified mourning in honor of Friedrich von Baden, Galvano Lancia and many others who had died at Charles's hands. Bianca and Anticoli, who sat on his right and left, however, were gaily dressed in scarlet, gold and yellow. For them the joy of the young King's escape and renewed fortune must outweigh all other considerations. The Bishop of Verona and the fickle Marchese of Monferrato filled the other spaces at the high table, and Conradin could be seen turning his smiling and gracious countenance first on one and then on the other. The other dignitaries, seated at the lower tables, were loyally dressed in the colors of the rainbow and many colors that were not in it.

He had changed a great deal since they last saw him. Many whispered he had become more "kingly," more "serene." That was all they dared say about it. Certainly he was no longer the boy-Emperor who had descended from Germany the year before, flushed with boyish enthusiasm for the struggle he was about to undertake and filled with spontaneous delight at the welcome he received. This Conradin had a calmer manner. Though he welcomed them pleasantly and drank their health with lordly expansiveness, there was a much greater air of self-possession about him. The meaningful, intimate smile he sometimes directed at Bianca or Anticoli was quite distinct from the gracious but obviously willed and ceremonial smile he reserved for the public at large. That was all very well, his allies whispered. He had increased in wisdom, and it might even be a sign that this time he would make fewer mistakes. But, on the other hand, when a man would not be open with you about the sorcerers who saved him from death or what they intend to do, how could you be sure you were really accepted as an ally or forgiven your past lapses? What was the young Emperor planning? Would Frederick himself return with a huge army and destroy them all, or confiscate all their property? Frederick was known as a severe and vindictive man who would stop at nothing, not even murdering a priest. Conradin might very well take after him in that respect. What was Conradin thinking now, as his eyes scanned the empty space in front of him?

Conradin was thinking about the past. Only one year before, he had had three times as many allies around him as he did now, including his almost-foster-brother, Friedrich von Baden, many of his cousins and Bianca's brothers and kin. Rome itself had opened its gates to him and decorated its streets with banners. The women of the city had banded together to sing songs in his praise as he rode through, claiming his title as Emperor. But after he had been defeated at Tagliacozzo, Guido of Montefeltro had cast him out of Rome. Those who had been faithful to him in his misfortune were killed at King Charles's hands. And nobles gathered around him in this fortress were mostly the fair-weather sort, who would quickly desert him again if he were defeated. Hence, there was no point in making himself particularly charming to these people. If he could obtain the sorcerers' rod, their loyalty would take care of itself. Meanwhile let them wonder at his new reserve.

Anticoli had been right in predicting ally after ally would come to him. Indeed, they had nearly succeeded in capturing the Pope himself, which would certainly have been a masterstroke. Unfortunately the Pope had evaded them, and now his two chief enemies were doubtless consulting about him in Naples. Only, since they would devote large parts of their conference to the supposed relationship between the young Emperor and the sorcerers, they would be wasting a lot of time. They might not think of a practical method for defeating the wizards themselves. Conradin longed to speak to Omberto, whose duty it was to gather any news he might from Naples. But he could not leave the great hall so early.

The meal was over and a musician struck up a song that Frederick II was supposed to have written himself, "Alas for my lady." The song had been chosen for a purpose, Conradin realized. Ostensibly it expressed the poet's grief over the imprisonment of a lady he loved. But no one believed anyone would dare imprison a woman this dreadful Emperor desired. So many speculated that the song really expressed the Emperor's grief over the captive state of the Empire. Obviously this was no song to walk out on. Conradin decided to wait, applaud the singer loudly when he ended (whether he sang well or ill), and depart. Indeed, he was hard put to tell whether the man sang well or ill because he had not been listening. He forced his mind to attend a moment:

> *Alas for my lady, fair and good, I sing,*
> *Who used to love to carol, play and dance,*

More fair her sight to me than dawn or spring,
My heart was swiftly vanquished at her glance.
But now in prison she sadly languishes,
Watched strictly by a wretch who hates me sore,
And I, pierced deep with many anguishes,
Now aim to show my courage as of yore.

A loud gasp breaking from many in the assembly stopped the musician in mid-note. Conradin forced his eyes to look and saw one of his retainers had rushed inside the doorway, looking pale and thoroughly terrified. The nobles in the assembly looked from him to the king, wondering what they should do.

"What's the matter, Paolo?" demanded Conradin without rising.

The knight could only stammer, 'S-sire, there are m-m-messengers at the gate who s-say they want to sp-speak to you."

The arrival of another offer of alliance would have been announced with the same words, but not in the same voice.

"Who sent them?" inquired Conradin.

"They s-s-say their King is called Benrik and he rules over a people called the Pelezitereans. They are s-s-sorcerers." A murmur swept through the hall. Conradin was not satisfied.

"How do you know they are sorcerers?"

The knight shuddered. "One of them—a lady—has a silver rod which can deprive people of the use of their limbs and then return it."

The nobles in the great hall no longer bothered to whisper. Conradin could only hope their excitement would keep them from noticing how pale his own face had become. But there was no escaping this. There was only one answer he could give his knight. "Bring them in," he said. The hall fell silent. No one dared protest.

A few terrible moments followed. A silence fell. Conradin could not consult with Bianca or Anticoli though they shared the same question. He could not risk allowing the dignitaries at the main table to realize the sorcerers were not sent by Frederick—at least not before it was absolutely necessary. The dignitaries with him did not speak, either, because they had no one near in whom they could confide their doubts. Everyone else was too busy watching the door and the High Table by turns to think of talking.

Then the door opened once more, and in walked the sorcerers in a glitter of silver armor. They looked exactly like the ones Conradin had seen at Naples, except that there were more of them and they had removed their helmets. The leader, a man with reddish hair only a little brighter than Conradin's (but bright enough to look strange and un-natural) was also the tallest. As he drew closer, Conradin could see his eyes were also an unnatural color—green, but just a little *too* green. The woman beside him, dressed in the same kind of silver armor, was proba-bly the one Paolo had referred to. There was nothing strange about her; she was about an inch shorter than the man, had long brown hair (a very ordinary color) and brown eyes. Later, when chronicles reported the arrival of the Pelezitereans in Italy, most writers attributed to Natheless all the qualities young witches need to make their mark in the world, includ-ing astonishing beauty and a seductive manner. Looking at her for the first time, however, Conradin found himself marveling at the complete absence of such qualities. Why did a sorceress with such amazing powers neglect taking the trouble to make herself more seductive? There was nothing wrong with her, of course. Her features were delicate, though she had a long face which gave her a solemn, melancholy look. She certainly did not have the self-confident poise of an accomplished seductress; she moved warily, sometimes awkwardly, like a convent-bred girl entering the world for the first time, not at all sure of what she would encounter there. All this if he was not misreading some foreign mannerism.

The other women in the group did not look remarkably different from the first, except one who had a much rounder face.

Infidels from beyond the sea were, as a rule, very dark. Of course, these might come from a very distant country. Or they might even be the descendants of captured Italians. Legends spoke of such things. But why had King Benrik sent so many women?

The four strangers advanced as far as the High Table. They did not kneel, but they bowed briefly. The leader then spoke, slowly and with a thick accent. "Hail to you, Conradin, King of the Italians. My name is Alrik Eridani and I bear a message from my father Benrik, the Archon of the Pelezitereans. We come in peace. This lady will speak for me, be-cause she knows your language better."

"Welcome, Prince Alrik of the Pelezitereans," returned Conradin, pleased at their tone of respect. "What would the lady say?"

The lady's eyes were fixed on him. Her gaze was more intense and somehow more comprehending than the King's son's. She spoke. "We greet you, King Conradin. We have come to seek your help and to offer you ours. Will you grant us audience?"

Conradin nodded. "I will hear you." He almost added, "after the revel," which he knew would be better suited to his dignity, but his desire to learn who these people were overcame him. After all, they might dissolve into thin air if he did not question them at once. "Now," he concluded, standing up and motioning for Anticoli to follow him. Bianca would remain to act as hostess now, for she would hear all about the interview from Anticoli. He walked to the doorway, where Omberto still stood. He walked through while the whispers in the great hall grew into a hubbub behind him. Conradin considered halting in the antechamber, but that was not private enough. So he proceeded on to his bedchamber beyond. A fire crackled on the hearth. The bed's scarlet silk glowed in the flickering light, and there were benches set around against the walls. Conradin and Anticoli sat down on the bed, and the young King motioned for the infidels to take the benches near the wall.

"You say you come from King Benrik of the Pelezitereans?" He had addressed Prince Alrik, but the lady answered, "Yes, the Archon sent us."

"You say you have come to seek help and to offer it. What then do you seek, and what do you offer?"

The lady turned and spoke in a foreign tongue to Prince Alrik for a moment. Then she turned back and spoke slowly, as if she were on dangerous ground. "Sire, it appears subjects of ours have landed in your kingdom and caused a deal of confusion. We have heard their arrival was of some personal advantage to you. If so, we rejoice. But they did not mean to do you good, Sire, and if they are not stopped, they will do much evil. They are wicked men who have disobeyed our laws, stolen our property and brought about the death of their lord, my noble brother, Agni. If you will help us seize them and bring them to justice, we will bear them and their machines away so you and your people will not be molested again." The lady finished her speech, and all four Infidels stared at the boy-King expectantly.

Conradin stirred uneasily as he tried to figure out which aspect of this complex situation he should deal with first. If these sorcerers had powers equal to the ones he had seen at Naples, why did they come to him seeking help? If they were not as powerful as the Neapolitans, to help them might mean disaster. On the other hand, if the Neapolitan sorcerers were as bad as they said, it would be disastrous not to cooperate with the newcomers. And then, what if they succeeded? Even the prospect of their going away and troubling him no more was not as attractive as it might seem. Their departure would prove to everyone that Frederick II was not going to return with an army, and his allies might desert him.

Conradin stared intensely at Prince Alrik and temporized. "From what land do the Pelezitereans come?" he demanded.

The Infidel Prince met his gaze unflinchingly. In fact, he did not seem to have any idea what had been asked until the lady turned and spoke to him. Then he started. He and the lady held a brief exchange; finally the lady spoke. "We come from far beyond the sea."

"From what land far beyond the sea?" pursued the young King.

"From a land so far away that you have never heard of it," replied the lady. Prince Alrik was watching her anxiously.

"Do you come from India?"

"No. It is farther than that."

"Do you come from Cathay?"

"No, we come from farther than that."

Conradin was frustrated. He had been proud of his geographical knowledge, but it did not seem to be doing him any good. He tried another line of inquiry. "Had you heard of my grandfather, the Emperor Frederick?"

"We had not the fortune to hear his name until we reached your shores," returned the lady. "We are sorry, for from what we hear he was a very great and wise Emperor."

Conradin nodded, slightly mollified. "Do you know of the Saladin?" he inquired, naming a famous Infidel.

"We had not the fortune to hear his name until we reached your shores."

Conradin shifted uncomfortably. Anticoli, beside him, had not said a word or made a move. The lady, too, sat with her hands folded on her lap, her eyes moving watchfully from Conradin to Anticoli and back.

Conradin tried once more. "Have you heard of Genghis Khan?" He gave the name of a great barbarian chieftain whose hordes, supposedly coming from the eastern edge of the world (though some believed the Emperor Frederick had created them), had terrorized Christendom a little more than a quarter-century before.

"We had not the fortune to hear his name until this moment," replied the lady.

Conradin was angry. She could not be telling the truth. "If you come from so far away, how did you get here without passing through these realms and hearing about these men?" he demanded. "How did your subjects get so far away from home, and if they are so far away, how did you learn they were here?" The last question seemed rather silly, since obviously they must know by magic. However, the lady winced as if she had been struck and bowed her head, apparently trying to think. Prince Alrik tapped her shoulder, apparently wanting to be told what had been said. When the lady explained, it seemed to upset him, and he began to speak quickly in an agitated manner. The sorceress calmed him down. Then she began to speak. "Let the King not be angry, but it would weary you to hear a full reply to the question you have asked. Moreover, King Benrik gave us no instructions about what we were to say if you asked it. Is it not enough that, if you help us, we will take our subjects and our machines away and trouble you no more?"

Conradin paused. If they were trying to deceive him, there was no use in provoking them directly; the lady had a silver rod and might use it. But then, if they were so powerful, it might be a question of defying them now and dying, or living and working with them and becoming their slave later. Ultimately it was his overpowering curiosity rather than his sense of policy that made Conradin's decision for him.

"How are we to know whether or not you have gone? How are we to believe that you will trouble us no more, when you have troubled us so much already? If you have the power to move with such ease, how can we be certain you will not come back?"

The sorceress did not wince this time. Her eyes kindled slowly. "Sire, we Pelezitereans live in an unpleasant, barren land. For many years we have been seeking a better one. Our King is a just man, and does not wish to take what is not his. There are, however, others among us who are not so scrupulous. As long as Benrik is King of the Pelezitereans, you may trust you will not be troubled. Otherwise, who knows what may happen? Your land is very pleasant. The longer our company remains here, the more time there will be for the resolution of those among us who are just to weaken, and for the evil ones to practice strategems against our leaders. Sire, it would be well if we were not detained here long."

Conradin looked away from the lady. Perhaps he had been mistaken in his first assessment, he thought—the lady really was seductive, only in a more subtle way, against which he had fewer defenses. It was better not to look at her as he considered what she said.

Apparently she had said her people had both the power and the desire to conquer Italy, and only refrained from doing so because of the kindness of their hearts. Was this plausible? If some vague sense of justice was all that stood between Italy and slavery to the Infidel, then Italy had come to a sorry pass. Her argument was: the quicker they passed through the country, the less likely they were to return. But travel did not seem to be difficult for them, and the Emperor Frederick, who had passed through many lands during his life, including those of the Infidels beyond the sea, was known to have considered Italy the most beautiful. Helping this group of Infidels fight the other would not ensure safety for Italy, let alone himself and his surviving kinsmen. The only thing for it was to learn in detail what they wanted, have them settled in for the night and discuss this interview with Anticoli, Bianca and Omberto.

He turned back to the enchantress, who was still watching him closely. "What is the help you seek from me?" he demanded.

The lady made no pretense of consulting Prince Alrik this time. "We have the same sort of weapons the men you saw in Naples have, only more of them, and we can use them better. The closer we can come to them without their knowing it, however, the better it will be, because we do not want them to take warning and depart. If we could find someone who knows the way into the city and into the building where they're hiding, it would be most helpful to us. Even if we cannot, your written permission for us to travel through your realm would be a great benefit—for we do not wish to molest your subjects if we can avoid it."

Conradin nodded. "It may be we can do these things. I must consult my advisers to determine the best plan. The Lady Bianca will find you lodging for the night."

The lady seemed about to acknowledge the remark, but they were interrupted by a loud knock on the thick wooden door of the royal chamber. Everyone started, and Conradin jumped up in his irritation. He had been interrupted suddenly once already that evening, and wondered what could justify it a second time. Another group of sorcerers could hardly have arrived. "Who is it?" he demanded angrily.

"It is I, Omberto," came an insistent voice from the other side. "I bring you urgent news. Will you admit me?"

Conradin clenched his fist in annoyance. He did not think it would be a good idea to introduce the superstitious priest to the Infidels just now. "Can not this news wait a few more minutes?" he inquired.

"Your life may be in danger," replied the determined priest.

The lady understood. She whispered something to Prince Alrik and both brought their hands close to their breasts, the position from which the Neapolitan sorcerer had snatched his silver rod. Were these the only two that were so armed, Conradin wondered?

"I will come out to you," returned Conradin. He turned to his guests. "My cousin Anticoli will lead you to the hall and show you where you are to lodge." Anticoli had risen at the same time as the boy-King. He looked at Conradin in alarm, but made no protest. The lady, who had already relaxed somewhat, bowed to him. "We will follow you, Lord Anticoli."

"Lady, we do not yet know your name," said Conradin.

The lady bowed slightly again. "I am called Natheless. These others are Bodris and Floress."

"Welcome to Italy," said Conradin, not thinking to wonder whether or not he meant it. "Follow us." He turned and unbolted the door. It opened easily and revealed Omberto on the threshold, stubborn but trembling. Behind him was Tomaso, who guarded the door to the anteroom. "Pardon, Sire, if the intrusion was unwelcome, but Father Omberto made me think your life depended—"

"You did well, Tomaso," growled Conradin. "Omberto will answer for both your fault and his. Go back to your post."

Tomaso went away, and Anticoli addressed the Infidels. "Come this way." They followed him out of the anteroom while Omberto stared after them. "Dare you trust him among them? Might they not do him an injury?"

Conradin shrugged. "They might have done us both injury by now, if they had so desired." He took hold of Omberto's arm and drew him to a narrow window that overlooked the stone courtyard. "Now then, what is this urgent news?"

"Sire, the sorcerers have killed the Pope!"

"*Per Dio!*" cried Conradin. "When did this happen?"

"Three days ago. Many are fleeing the city now. All are in terror. I feared the witch might murder you."

"She is their enemy. They murdered her brother," returned Conradin. "But who brought this news?"

"The witch," Omberto continued, shaking his head, "might be lying to deceive you. The messengers of Satan use many tricks to entrap men."

Controlling an impulse to shout, Conradin managed to adopt a patient tone. "Omberto, I am wary of tricks. But when a man has weapons which can kill from a great distance, what need has he for deceit? Who brought the news, and how many have heard it?"

"It was a cousin of mine fleeing toward his home in Lombardy. I wouldn't know how many have heard. My cousin was exhausted. I had him given dinner and a bed in my chamber instead of the main hall. But I did not forbid him to speak, because many will be passing this way in their flight from the city and the servants will soon learn."

"True," said Conradin. The situation could not be more awkward. Murdering the Pope was about the worst thing the sorcerers could have done. If only they had murdered King Charles instead! Now he would either have to accept responsibility for the crime and gain a reputation for being as ruthless and irreverent as his grandfather, or he must denounce the crime and reveal his weakness and lack of enchanted support. He could not decide which course was wiser. "How was the Pope killed?" he inquired.

"None know. He was leading a procession past the church when the sorcerers came out and struck many with their rods. They carried two inside, the Holy Father and a monk, but when the people sneaked back to carry off the wounded, the Pope was lying among them, dead and stripped of his mantle and mitre."

"Thievery, pure and simple," said Conradin disgustedly.

"Yes, Sire," agreed Omberto, his face lighting up. "Infidels are greedy."

"So are some Christians." Conradin wondered at Omberto's sudden change of opinion about sorcerers. He believed Frederick II had consorted with Infidels and sorcerers and had not held it against him. It was one thing, he supposed, to deal with an Italian Emperor who could control sorcerers, and another to deal with the sorcerers themselves. Furthermore, Omberto might trust the ability of a great Emperor like Frederick to best the sorcerers and keep them subjected and well-behaved, but he would doubt the sixteen-year-old Conradin's ability to do any such thing. Young Conradin apparently would have to change his mind or die.

"I must go somewhere alone to think," said Conradin. He was busy trying to build a complicated pattern in his mind, involving the combinations and permutations of actions, reactions and interactions among King Charles, his French followers and Italian subjects, each important Churchman he knew who might be elected to the Holy See and each of his own chief allies. He also had to consider how his negotiations with the Infidels would affect those interactions. Conradin began to glimpse a few clear paths, but the pattern threatened to unravel every time Omberto interrupted his thoughts. Conradin turned abruptly and walked out of the room. Tomaso made a quick salute as he passed.

11

The planetary natives brought the
Pelezitereans to a smaller stone segment or tower within the massive
rectangular structure of their fortress. At first Anticoli wanted to put Alrik
in a separate room, but he gave up with little protest when the foreigners
expressed a desire to remain together. The natives wanted to know which
Peleziterean would sleep in the huge bed hung with silken curtains and
which would use the trundle bed rolled out from underneath. They were
startled when told the Pelezitereans would decide later.

Having also convinced their hosts, with some difficulty, that they did
not need refreshments, the landing party was finally left alone to rest and
munch on its own synthetic nutriments.

"What a day this has been," said Alrik, sitting down on one of the
benches against the wall and stretching his legs. Natheless was seated
beside him. It was good to feel her near. Between the studying and
relentless drilling they had engaged in since landing on the planet's surface, they had had no time at all to be alone together.

"What a *week!*" returned Natheless. "Never in my life do I want to be
this tired again."

Seven days before, they had met their first contacts, peasants in a small
village near the landing site. The entire first day had been spent con-
vincing the peasants that they wished to communicate. Once this was

accomplished, things moved quickly. They drew out the family's entire vocabulary in conversation, and recorded it in the vocal components of their wrist-units. After each meeting the Peleziterans withdrew, analyzed the language and drilled each other. Then they returned to test their new skills on their contacts. When they were able to hold an intelligible conversation with the peasants, they moved on to their next contact.

This man was a wandering, upper-caste military man (or "knight," as they were called) and a poet and singer, too. He knew several planetary languages and dialects as well as a more educated and poetic Italian. In response to their request, "Take us to your leader," he had led them to Conradin's court. They had learned only along the way of the political chaos the country was now in, and wondered whether Conradin's rank would be of any use to them.

"Do you really think this chieftain will help us?" inquired Alrik.

"Who knows?" answered Natheless. "As long as we're here, we may as well wait to see what he says about it. If he refuses, we can always move directly to that city, Naples. We know now we can speak the language well enough to get by."

Alrik nodded admiringly. "Boundless space, you did a terrific job down there, Natheless!"

Natheless smiled, a glow of pleasure shining through her exhaustion. "It's strange, but for the first time I really had the feeling we understood each other. I wasn't just tapping out a code and hoping it meant something to the people on the other side. This time I almost felt as though it were *my* language." She yawned and rested her head on Alrik's shoulder. "Science and progress, I'll sure be glad when this is over."

Alrik put his arm around her. "Won't we all!"

"Are we going to sleep in shifts?" asked Bodris abruptly.

Natheless looked up, unwilling to give her mind to the problem. "I guess so. The natives may come to investigate us again."

"Two by two," said Alrik. "That way, two can have a bed each, and the other two can keep one another awake."

Alrik and Natheless would have liked the first watch together, but they were the best speakers, so that was judged unwise. After some deliberation, Alrik and Floress took the first watch, while Natheless and Bodris settled down on the beds.

Meanwhile Conradin made his way up the stairs to the chamber over the great hall, to the passage that led along the castle wall and down to the stables. As he passed the entrance, two guards who were seated on benches nearby leaped to their feet and saluted. "Your Majesty!"

"God give you good health, good knights," said Conradin carelessly. "Has anything strange happened since the last thing?"

"No, Sire," returned the knights.

"Good," said Conradin. He nodded and walked past them into the stableyard. Some of the horses watched him as he walked by. One of them, Proteo, snorted. "Thank you for your willingness, Proteo," said Conradin, patting his muzzle, "but I will not ride tonight." He mounted the stairs into the hayloft and sat down among the hay. How undignified he must look, he thought to himself. But no one was watching, and he hoped being away from the trappings of royalty would help him think clearly. He had heard that his grandfather Frederick II had also displayed unseemly manners in his youth. Of course, Frederick had had more excuse. He had lost his father when he was two years old and his mother when he was four. His guardians had allowed him to grow up on the streets of Palermo, learning manners from the lowest sort of people. Conradin had also lost his father when he was two years old, but his mother had raised him carefully.

All the same, a lot more than unseemly manners stood between Conradin and secure possession of the Imperial throne. A letter from his grandfather to his father, which Conradin's mother had carefully read to him many times when he was a boy, came to his mind: "Noble extraction is not sufficient for kings unless it is wedded to noble character. People do not honor kings because they are more highly placed, but because they see farther and act better. Kings have no cause for pride unless they outshine other men in virtue and wisdom." Yes, as Elizabeth of Bavaria used to tell her royal son, there is more to ruling a kingdom than having people kneel and bow and defer to you. You have to be truly great. You must be willing to suffer. In that sense there was nothing unnatural about his having to fight for his throne. But what action resplendent with virtue and wisdom was he to take in this confusing situation?

Conradin pulled off his scarlet mantle and threw it on the hay. "Peacock's feathers," he muttered. Certainly he did not feel like a king at this moment. He looked down quizzically at the black clothes he was wearing underneath. They, too, were for show. They were supposed to make people aware of his grief, but the grief he felt for Friedrich von Baden and Galvano Lancia was not black like a cloudy night, but red like fire or blood. It throbbed like a deep wound; at times it turned green-white like dead flesh on a limb in need of amputation. Sometimes Conradin overflowed with hatred for Charles and the Pope, and sometimes he cried for grief and loneliness at the loss of his friends. Other times a cold disgust settled over him, and he cared for nothing and wondered what there was to fight for in a world where such people were his enemies. The French King was simply greedy for land, yet justified his wars with legal excuses as if his own gain and God's were one. The Pope was the spiritual power behind Charles, whose excuses lacked all plausibility without the Church's endorsement. Most of the other powerful men were weathercocks, shifting to this side and to that according to their notions of who had the upper hand or who would serve their interests best. To win in this conflict, Conradin must force himself to think in their terms, a tedious task. Was such an Empire really worth fighting for, he wondered in these gangrenous moments, but he did not dwell on this question, because it was pointless. As the legitimate heir to the Hohenstaufen fortunes he had only two alternatives—to fight for the Empire or consent to his own annihilation and that of his few remaining supporters. Neither Charles nor the Church would ever forget who he was and what he had a right to claim, no matter how many assurances he offered. They were even less likely to do so now that he had made one expedition into Italy rather than simply staying in Germany.

His scarlet mood would return soon enough. Conradin glanced down at the royal mantle. Perhaps it was not such a bad symbol after all. He picked it up thoughtfully, gently shook off the few wisps of hay adhering to it, folded it and held it on his knees.

What was his mother doing now, Conradin wondered. What would she think when she heard of the Pope's murder? Was she hoping, like so many, that Frederick II had sent the sorcerers across the mountains to help him? Or did she know better? As soon as she had heard her son was captured, she had come across the Alps with all the money she could scrape together, hoping to ransom him. But Italy had been thrown into panic at the news of his escape and the appearance of the sorcerers. Some pro-papal castles had blocked her path and forced her to retire to a more secure castle with her second husband and younger children. Conradin had not dared send her a detailed explanation, lest it fall into the wrong hands. He had sent her letters advising her to stay where she was for the time being. There was nothing she could have done at Grosseto. She was German and understood less about Italian politics than he did by now. Further involvement on her part would only embroil his stepfather and family in problems with the Church, which was especially distressing for them since they were all pious. There would be plenty of time to call them to his side if he triumphed.

But how was he to triumph? None of the alternatives for him were good. If he refused to help the sorcerers, they would leave and perhaps fail in their mission (if they had represented it honestly), leaving the Neapolitan sorcerers to conquer Italy. Or, as the lady had hinted, if they were delayed long, King Benrik himself might be overthrown by his greedy noblemen, who would then conquer Italy. It amounted to the same thing. If they succeeded in their mission, then perhaps the sorcerers would go, but Conradin's party would be doomed. Any gains he might make by playing on the people's belief that he had demonic support would be lost in the reaction that must come, sooner or later, when somebody realized the Pelezitereans were gone. Some deceitful Church-man would arrange a counter-miracle to put heart back into the simple. Then they would advance on Conradin with a crusader's fury, wiping out every man, woman and child who had a drop of Hohenstaufen blood in his veins or had ever aided the family. In that case, if Conradin had been seen accompanying the sorcerers to Naples, it would be so much the worse. Then Conradin's own subjects would know he was cooperating with Infidels, and it would be easy for the Church to seduce them the next time they were feeling pious.

The green-white mood returned to Conradin, and he thought, "If my allies and I must be slaughtered whatever we do, with the Church's curse on us, what does it matter if Charles and the clergymen that fawn on him suffer? They have driven out and destroyed the rightful Emperors; they deserve to be slaves of the Infidels. Why should I save their liberties if they will never thank me for it? If the Infidels remain, at least we will have the chance to die defying them, showing our courage in a way the world cannot deny."

Reasonable as this conclusion was, something in Conradin's heart would not consent to it. Some motive, argument or desire he had not yet considered still urged him toward working with the Pelezitereans in spite of the great risk and small advantage. Where did this impulse come from? Conradin sought its source and found himself remembering the Princess's face and how her eyes had flashed. He began to tremble. He reflected that while no minstrel would ever write a poem praising her beauty, there was an amazing intensity in her expression. Surely a noble spirit burned in that maiden. It made him want to be noble, too. He realized if he refused to help her, he must send a message. What words would he use? Could he reasonably tell her that since he could not get the honor and wealth he deserved as Emperor, the Empire could be destroyed for all he cared? The resounding "no" his heart sent back amused him. How could a total stranger be affecting him this way?

Yet a noble impulse was a noble impulse, whatever inspired it. His mother would also have told him his responsibility to his office did not depend on the loyalty of his subjects to him. What would his mother decide if the choices put before him tonight were before her? Conradin smiled, realizing these choices would never have been put before his mother. She would never have allowed the sorcerers inside the castle if she had any way at all of keeping them out. But if she had understood the matter as he now did, he felt she would decide as he was deciding.

Conradin rose abruptly, his decision made. Then he froze. Had the Peleziterean woman caused all these changes in him? Was it one of her spells perhaps? Why had he received the Infidels with Anticoli alone present, when Bianca might have been a better judge of women? Then a fresh wave of disgust swept over him. Why was he mulling these thoughts as though he were Father Omberto and not the Emperor? The Pelezitereans' strength was in their engines—not their beauty, for they had none; certainly not in their eloquence, for even Natheless, who spoke for them, had not mastered the Italian tongue as well as many ladies he knew. Their power was in their machines. The Emperor Frederick had won great power and wide realms largely because he was able to make the Infidels respect him, and he had done that by dealing with them as human beings, not as demons or demon-possessed creatures. Surely with necromancy or demonic aid, she would have seemed fairer and spoken more fluently. No; although with such great powers the Pelezitereans must be called wizards, their wizardry consisted of natural human wisdom. Hence, their power resided only in their machines. In all other respects they were like ordinary people.

As for casting a spell over Conradin, why would anyone wish to cast such a spell? And if it were a spell, it was not an unpleasant one. It was good to realize he still had heart, and to sense he had something to contribute, after he had been feeling so helpless and impoverished in the weeks since his capture. His mind stirred when he realized how wise the Infidels must be, and how many of the difficulties which had occurred to him as he read his books they might be able to solve. His excitement mounted. An inspiration flooded over him. It was so simple and obvious and so desirable. The Infidels must neither enslave Italy nor leave it; they must unite with the Italian people, live in their land, share their wisdom. That way Conradin would die neither at the hands of the Infidels nor of the Church. His mind truly made up, he climbed back down into the stables. The guards leaped up when they saw him.

"What hour is it?" he asked.

"After midnight, Sire," one answered.

"I will go in now," he replied. He started up the passage.

The corridors were dark, and he had to take a candle from the gate to light his way. He crept back stealthily to the main hall. The tables had been rolled away. The nobles who were not great enough to be assigned rooms of their own or rich enough to hire lodgings elsewhere were sleeping on pallets on the floor. Many snored soundly, but a few stirred and looked up as the King passed. Rather than speak with them, Conradin hurried on. Outside the door, he encountered Ginevra, Bianca's widowed younger sister, accompanied by two maidens carrying candles. When they saw him, they all curtsied, spreading their skirts around them. "Your Majesty!"

"Good evening, ladies and my fair cousin," he said, addressing Ginevra. "Has your sister retired?"

"Yes, Sire. Everyone has retired now, and I, too, am on my way to my chamber with my maids."

Conradin nodded and motioned for Ginevra to walk beside him. She came up to him, and since the corridor here was narrow, the other maidens were left walking behind.

"I see you have shed your widow's white and donned black for your father," he remarked.

Ginevra dropped her eyes. "It was the nearer wound, Sire. And the customary period has ended."

Conradin nodded. "No one will reproach you, my cousin. Adherence to these forms can be tiresome, especially when the heart is not there, but all the same. . . ." He did not finish. Ginevra remembered Bianca's comment made in anger on the day Ginevra's elderly husband was laid in his grave. "We all know he was four times your age, ill-tempered and unkind to you, Ginevra. But if you could contrive to look a little less like a blessed soul having its first glimpse of Paradise at the requiem mass, it would be beneficial to our family's honor." She said nothing.

"Have you spoken with your sister and brother-in-law, *Madònna?*" Conradin began again.

Ginevra made a quick but graceful affirmative nod. Conradin studied her in the flickering candlelight. She was crowned with bright golden hair. By courtly standards she was a beautiful woman, with the blue eyes and delicate features that had graced her famous relative, Bianca Lancia,

---

103

the Emperor's last wife. Her bearing was noble, her eyes lively and her face intelligent. Another inspiration struck him, but he arrested it and held it within him, realizing he did not yet know enough to take it seriously. He knew little enough about Italian women, especially ones his own age, and nothing at all about the Pelezitereans. He considered Ginevra's intelligent face. How much would a young, beautiful woman know about the dangers that threatened the Empire, and how much would she care? Conradin decided to test her quickness. Turning from her abruptly, he pointed to the door of the great hall. "Do they know?" he asked.

Ginevra blushed a little when she realized what he was asking. She nodded again. "Yes, Sire," she said, her heart singing because he had sought information from her on such a solemn matter—though of course the feeling was ridiculous, since the King was such an innocent boy, younger than herself. "The news came hours ago. Anticoli kept away, because he did not know what you wanted him to say. Bianca and I mingled with the guests, listening to their conversations. Bianca insisted you had never consented to the murder of the Pope, so that either it was an accident or the rumor was false."

"Were many of them angry?"

Ginevra shook her head gently. "My sister says we don't have the angry kind here at the castle. They are out in the countryside or else in the Pope's court or with Charles in Naples. She said people here were frightened only because you would certainly have no scruples about killing them when they have served your purpose, if you were cruel enough to order the death of the Pope."

Conradin nodded. "I see. Their bad consciences are tormenting them. It's a shame their consciences weren't strong enough to keep them from doing wrong in the first place, but now they're strong enough to stampede them into more crimes."

Ginevra hesitated. Conradin was the Emperor-elect, after all, and she had no right to question him. But it was difficult to take his dignity seriously when he was younger than she. Anyway he had started the conversation. "Sire, what are you going to *do?*"

Conradin turned his eyes on her and kept them there for a long moment. Ginevra was a little embarrassed. She had spoken almost condescendingly, as if he were a younger brother. Now somehow he looked older than Anticoli and full of worldly wisdom. "How much do you know already, Ginevra? How much have they told you?"

Ginevra dropped her eyes in alarm, feeling like someone who had asked for a duckling and received an eaglet. "Why do you ask, Sire? Will you reprimand my brother-in-law for being garrulous if he has told me too much?"

The boy-King considered his answer carefully, but he had to give it quickly. "On the contrary, I trust Anticoli's discretion absolutely. If he has taken you into his confidence, I have no doubt you are worthy of it."

Ginevra answered cautiously. "My brother told me the substance of what the wizards said. He said the sorcerers in Naples who saved you did so by accident, and the ones who came here tonight were their enemies. If you said anything more to him about this, he did not tell either me or Bianca."

Conradin studied her again. "If I tell you something that borders on a secret of State, can you be discreet about it?"

It was really too late for Ginevra to draw back now. She demurred only as a matter of course. "God knows I would never willingly betray you, Cousin, but why would you confide in me, a woman and young? It is true your years are less than mine, but if you cannot choose your age, you can choose your counselors."

"The secret may concern you," said Conradin.

"How could that be?" quavered Ginevra.

He drew her even farther ahead of the maids and whispered, "Did Anticoli tell you I fear that these sorcerers, whatever they claim, are here to stay from now until the world's end? No? But I think that is true. It is merely a question of whether they work for themselves alone or for one of us, and for which one."

Ginevra's voice rose in alarm. "Can it be so bad? Is everything lost? Would God allow it?"

Conradin warned her to speak more quietly. "How should I know what God will and will not allow? We can, however, avert the danger by finding the most just among them and attaching them to our cause with bonds of love too strong to be easily broken."

"Oh!" cried Ginevra, feeling a jolt of exotic terror. "You're thinking of a marriage alliance!"

Conradin nodded. "You are one-and-twenty, and free to marry again. Your family and mine are bound by ties of blood and traditions of loyalty. Another lady from your family married an Emperor."

The prospect was not without a certain glamour, but Ginevra protested, "Surely, Cousin, you would not marry me to an Infidel!"

"As for *that*," said Conradin, dismissing the subject with a gesture, "we know nothing of these people as yet. We do not even know whether they are worthy of trust. I am going now to speak with them to discover all I can about them. It may turn out that we would not wish to be allied to them, or that they will not honor any sort of pact. I only discuss this with you because it is an idea. Infidels have sometimes changed their religion, you know. And kings are often bound by marriage alliances. But, don't discuss this with anyone."

"Not even Bianca?" queried Ginerva anxiously.

"Not even your sister," he said sternly, wishing it were possible to withdraw his words. He had let his boyish enthusiasm carry him away. Now the very thought of unfolding his plan before Bianca and Anticoli made all his fine ideas shrivel like cut flowers. "Return to your maidens and retire now," he said. "I am going to speak with the strangers."

"Alone?" protested Ginevra, in fresh alarm.

"Yes, alone," returned Conradin. "Does anyone have a weapon that could protect me? What difference does it make whether I am alone?"

"But from their demons and their spells—"

"I have my mother's cross, and her prayers, too, no doubt," said Conradin, smiling grimly.

Ginevra relaxed. "May God be with you, Sire! I will be praying for you, too!" She gathered her skirts and rejoined her maidens. The three of them disappeared in a halo of flickering light.

Conradin walked toward the royal chamber, where he found his personal attendants sitting in the doorway. They looked anxious and were wondering whether they should go seek him. He glanced around the room briefly to be sure all was well, then took a better candle from one of the wall-holders.

"I am going to walk abroad tonight," he announced to his attendants. "You may as well sleep, and do not be anxious if I do not return by dawn." They watched him, quite surprised, but did not dare protest. As a matter of fact, Conradin indeed wished there were someone who could accompany him. But all his closest friends and most trusted servants had perished at Tagliacozzo, and he had not had the time to become acquainted with these new ones.

A long corridor and then a narrow stair in the thickness of the castle wall led to the Northwestern tower. Conradin proceeded softly, trying to keep his leather shoes from squeaking, and stepped carefully, since the light his candle cast on the walls and floor was weak and flickering. He was a bit afraid he might meet Anticoli walking in that direction, but it seemed everyone was asleep at that hour, and no one cared to be near the sorcerers.

106

Conradin slowed his steps further as he neared the tower room. Would the sorcerers be awake or asleep? Were any keeping watch? This question was answered quickly enough as he mounted round a bend in the spiral stair, because he heard a shout in an unknown language above him. Looking up, he saw a human form standing outside the door, holding some strange sort of light. He was forced to turn away and cover his eyes, because the Infidel directed the beam at him, nearly blinding him. When he was able to see again, he perceived there were two Pelezitereans at the top of the stairs, the King's red-haired son and one of the attendant women.

The Prince was shouting something, violently, excitedly, in his own language.

"I come in peace," said Conradin, raising his hands to show he had not drawn a dagger, and he came a step closer.

That was a mistake. Alarmed by both the gesture and the approach, the Peleziterean backed away, whipped out his light-throwing rod and pointed it at the intruder. Conradin threw both hands over his face and turned away, but too late. A strange, dizzy, burning feeling began in his neck and spread through his whole body. All at once his legs became dead weight beneath him. He tried frantically to make them respond but felt himself toppling helplessly onto the stairs. Just before he struck the sharp edges, someone seized his shoulders and set him down softly. It was the woman, the one the lady had called Floress. She had dashed down the stairs to break his fall. His candle had gone out, and had spilled several drops of hot tallow on his neck.

Conradin tried to struggle to a sitting position, but none of his limbs would respond. He was paralyzed, just like King Charles. Desperately he looked to the top of the stairs to see whether Prince Alrik were still standing there, but he could not tell. At last he looked at Floress. "Why have you done this?" he demanded. "I came in peace. I made no threats."

The sorceress, eyes wide and frightened, repeated one phrase. "We come in peace. We come in peace."

It did not seem particularly appropriate to the situation. Conradin wondered whether it was the only phrase she knew.

He heard the door open. At last the Lady Natheless appeared, coming down the stairs with the Prince, who was talking fast in agitated tones. Conradin called loudly, "I came in peace! I meant no harm! Why have you done this?"

The speed of Prince Alrik's words redoubled. But the Lady Natheless turned to him and spoke six or seven quiet words. The Prince fell silent, and the lady continued down the steps to kneel over Conradin. Her eyes were concerned. "Are you hurt, Your Majesty?"

Conradin struggled to face her more directly, but could only move his neck a little. "I cannot move my arms or legs," he answered, trying to keep tears of anger from his voice.

"That can be mended easily," answered the sorceress, "but I must use my silver rod to do it. Will you be angry if I take it out?"

"*Nein*," said Conradin emphatically, lapsing into German vernacular in his agitation. When he saw she did not understand, he repeated the Italian equivalent. Natheless took out her rod. He closed his eyes, trying to hide his tears. His limbs would not follow the commands of his will, but they began to tremble without his command. Suppose she tried to restore him and it did not work?

Almost before he had time to formulate that thought, a dizzy shudder passed through his head and neck, and control returned to his limbs. Incredulously he tried his fingers and toes. As he pulled himself into a sitting position, his perception of the Pelezitereans' overwhelming power, their ability to deprive him of his own limbs and return them at will, overcame him. He bowed his head against his knees and wept for himself and for Christendom.

The lady settled beside him on the stair. "You are not hurt, Sire?" she pursued.

In fact, the only remaining sign of his mishap was the slight burn the tallow had made on his neck. But his dignity had been impaired, and had to be restored. "Why did you do this? I am King here, and I came to you in peace."

"It was a grievous mistake, Sire," returned the Lady Natheless, "and we are heartily sorry. Prince Alrik ought to be able to understand your tongue, but when you came he was so startled he forgot everything he knew. It was ill-mannered of him to draw his silver rod on you. But he saw that you had weapons and was afraid. He is very sorry for what he did."

"I am very sorry for it," agreed Alrik, who was standing behind the lady, looking awkward. Conradin studied his face and had the same impression he had had before—that even if Prince Alrik knew, in some fashion, what Conradin's words meant, he did not really understand what Conradin himself meant.

"Is there anything we can do to compensate for the insult we have done you?" inquired the lady. There was deeper comprehension in her expression, but also a hidden warning which said, "Don't ask too much, or I will have to refuse."

But Conradin was in a fairly foul mood. He shook himself into a more upright position and demanded, "I would like to know the truth. Is he the messenger of King Benrik, or are you?"

The lady looked askance. "That question is of less interest to you than you think, Sire. We are all sent by the Archon to accomplish a task and to gain your help in doing it, if we can. Since I am the one who knows the language best, I suppose I am the messenger."

"But it is also you who give the orders to come and go, isn't it?" said Conradin. "And it is you who will decide whether or not to accept the help I offer, is that not so?"

"It is," agreed the sorceress carelessly.

"Why did you not say so from the first?"

"Was it important, King Conradin?" The lady looked at him steadily. "We have told you no lies. But we do not measure rank as you do; it is possible for some of us to rank above others in one capacity and below them in another. I have indeed been put in control of this expedition, but did you need to know that? There are a great many things about the Pelezitereans which we have not told you, for behold, it would take a thousand years, and you have not the leisure to listen nor I to tell. We believed it would be most acceptable to let you believe Prince Alrik was in control of our expedition, because although women are equal in rank with men among the Pelezitereans, we learned that was not so among your people. The Archon feared we would appear to do you too little honor if we sent a woman to treat with you."

"I do not think you need fear anger, *Madònna*; only surprise. Then I suppose you are a princess?"

Her response was guarded. "As I said, we do not measure rank as you do. But yes, if you call Alrik a prince, you would call me a princess."

"What of the other two?"

Here the Princess hesitated. Finally she said, "They are not of as high a rank, yet they are not inconsiderable. We are all kinsmen."

Conradin decided to let that pass for the moment. He studied the four strangers, who stared back watchfully. "I came to speak further with you about the sorcerers who landed in Naples," he said.

"Good," replied the Princess promptly. "What have you decided?"

"I say," said Conradin, "the power your people wield is too great. I say that if your land is unpleasant and you are looking for a better one, you will come back to ours someday, whether or not you succeed in capturing your brother's murderers. Therefore, after you have captured your brother's murderers, I believe it would be better if you would settle here on some land I will give you and teach your science to our people. That way we can all live together permanently and in peace."

A gasp escaped from Prince Alrik. The female attendants stared at him, saying nothing. The Princess's expression remained unchanged, but she made a slow gesture of denial. "King Conradin, your offer is gracious, but we cannot accept it. It is forbidden."

"How many Pelezitereans are there?" pursued Conradin, nervously preparing for a staggering number.

"It cannot be," repeated the Princess in the same tone. "It is forbidden."

"Who has forbidden it? Your King? I wish then to speak with your King."

The sorceress was becoming increasingly flustered. "No, Sire! He will tell you nothing I have not already told you. He is bound as much as we are. It is our law."

Conradin knew, of course there were laws even kings could not change; this was true also in Italy. But he also knew kings and subjects sometimes had vastly different conceptions about which laws could be altered and which not. "I wish to speak with King Benrik," he replied.

"He will not change what he bade me tell you."

"I wish to speak with him."

"His mind will not change."

Conradin allowed his anger to show. "Why do you speak thus to the Emperor of the Italians, to whom you come for help? Your King sends you to me and I declare I am willing to help—I am even willing to accompany you myself and lead you straight into Naples, to the church where the sorcerers hide—for why should not a king help a king? But I wish to speak with the King about his other plans. If he will not change, he will not change. But if I wish to see him, if only to satisfy my curiosity, who are you to forbid me?"

The Princess closed her eyes. Conradin gathered he had scored a point—just exactly what *kind* of point he could not be certain. When the sorceress opened her eyes again, a small smile, half-annoyed, half-amused, was playing about her mouth. "The Archon would have come to you himself, King Conradin, were he not grievously ill."

Conradin was taken aback. "Ah! May God grant him better health!"

"As we have said," the Princess continued, "haste is important to us. If you delay us, it would be better for us to continue on our own, even if we are more likely to bungle. It took us three days, traveling in the manner of your people, to reach you from the place where our King is encamped. However, we could go back to him by quicker methods. You were in Naples and saw the sorcerers come from the air. If we summoned one of our craft, we could bring you to our King in less than an hour—if you have the courage to travel that way."

Conradin paled involuntarily, although he knew for a king there was only one answer to a question like that. "Do demons carry you through the air?" he demanded sternly.

"No, Sire," replied Natheless calmly. "We make use of natural wisdom in our machines. Your people have already done some of that. None of them could possibly swim across the entire sea, but they cross it constantly in their ships. Your people have learned the wisdom of the fish. Mine have also learned the wisdom of the birds."

Conradin eyed her narrowly. "I have heard of such things," he said. "The Greeks tell the story of a man named Daedalus. He was imprisoned with Icarus, his son, on the island of Crete. In order to escape, he made wings of birds' feathers and wax. He escaped alive, but his son, Icarus, flew too close to the sun, and the wax holding his wings together melted. He fell into the sea and drowned."

Conradin thought the wise Infidel would certainly have heard the story before, but she stared as though he had said something remarkable. "Accidents, of course, do happen," she answered at last, "but our ship is not made of wax, and the distance we must cross is not dangerous."

"I will come with you," said Conradin slowly.

The sorceress inclined her head briefly in his direction. "There indeed you show courage worthy of an Emperor."

That was the least she could say. Conradin felt a wry pleasure that partly compensated for his recent humiliation. Securing her admiration was a necessary first step in his plan. He looked at her more directly and said, "There are also other matters, however. I received some news a few hours ago about your rebellious subjects. I wonder whether you know it."

The Princess's expression became sharper, and the others leaned forward tensely.

"What news is this?" demanded Natheless.

"Did you know that your subjects have killed the Pope?"

Only the Princess seemed as startled as she should be. The others just continued to look tense. "They killed him?" demanded the Princess anxiously. "How? And why?"

Conradin looked searchingly at her. "I thought you might know the answers to those questions. We only know they took him prisoner alive and later brought him out dead, stripped of his jewels and ornaments."

The Princess showed her anger and rose quickly to her feet. "The fools!" she cried.

Conradin also rose. "Furthermore," he said, "in many people's minds I will have the blame for this, because your people's first appearance saved my life. Now that you have come to me, they will believe it more strongly."

The Princess mounted to a higher step in her agitation. "Then of course we will leave at once!"

"Your leaving would make no difference. It is enough you have come, and on the very night the news arrived, too."

The Princess settled down a little. "Well, then, what do you suggest we do?"

"If I could have the sorcerers' heads to set on poles in the marketplace here, the people will believe I was against them."

The other three foreigners drew back in what appeared to be aversion. Conradin could not understand that. His request was very reasonable.

The Princess looked distressed. "I cannot promise that, Sire. It is true we may have to kill them if they resist, or if they seem about to escape. Otherwise our laws require me to take them alive and deliver them to the High Council for judgment according to our own laws."

"But *our* laws also have been broken," returned Conradin coolly.

"And your life was saved, too," answered the Princess steadily. "You might take that into account as well."

Unfortunately she had found the weak point in his argument. Conradin had to back down. "If they are killed in the attack, you will give me their heads?"

For whatever reason, the Princess looked pained, but she said, "I believe the Archon might give permission for that—since . . . we . . . would have to dispose of the bodies. . . in any case."

Conradin decided he would accept that much for the time being.

"What will you do now?" Conradin inquired. "Do you wish to return to your rest?"

The Princess gestured her hair back from her face. "I have rested enough for the present. The Prince will sleep now, while I keep watch."

"Well, then, we can sit and speak longer about our plans."

"Even so," said the Princess. She turned and nodded to Prince Alrik and the handmaid who had kept watch with him. They mounted the stairs, retiring into the chamber. The other handmaid, Lady Bodris, seated herself two steps above her mistress. Conradin saw her sharp eyes fixed on him, and was struck by the almost perfect congruence between her features and Natheless's. Why had he not remarked it before? Perhaps because the difference in her manner was enough to distinguish her identity when he engaged Natheless in conversation; but when they were both perfectly still they looked exactly alike. He sank down once more on the stairs beside Natheless.

12

When Alrik woke, the planet's sun was halfway to its meridian, directing strong yellow beams through the small eastern windows. In this light Alrik could see strange designs on the silken wall-cloths, which were woven in rich shades of red, gold, blue, brown, green and yellow. Through native skill, many kinds of planetary animals (or Alrik assumed they were planetary; without having done a thorough survey of animal forms existing here, it was really impossible to tell) were depicted. Alrik sat up, drawn to a section of the tapestry where one large bird swooped down on another and sank huge talons into its back. Out of the corner of his eye he saw Natheless sitting on a bench near the door, working over her wrist-computer. He pointed to the figure in the hanging. "Isn't that amazing?" he said.

Natheless looked up and smiled. "It's maddening, isn't it? It's just as well we're on this planet trying to fulfill an important mission. If I were here just trying to learn about the culture, I think I might die from the frustration of not being able to decide where to start."

Alrik nodded, grunting. "The people here live rich lives. All of them probably lead richer lives than we exiles do."

Natheless's face clouded a little. "Well, Alrik, we've only made contact with the elite, and they're giving us the treatment of visiting royalty. Most of the population live in those little, one-room, dirt-floored huts, the way our first contacts did, in the company of their livestock. Most of them have never seen anything like this in all their lives, and they have chronic troubles with starvation, parasitism and infectious diseases. Let's bear that in mind before we get too jealous."

Alrik grunted again, momentarily ashamed of his resentment against the Prime Directive. "Mmmm. Well, it was nice to dream for a moment."

Natheless sighed. "Alrik, we'll find our own planet someday."

Alrik silently cursed himself for speaking so childishly and upsetting Natheless. He returned his attention to the wall-hanging. "It's absolutely amazing, isn't it? I hope you've recorded it with the visual component of your wrist-unit?"

Natheless brightened. "I did it while you were sleeping. If I'd known you'd be so interested, I'd have waited for you and let you do it."

Alrik shook his head. "It doesn't matter. As long as I get a chance to study it later. But what happens next, Natheless? Are we going to have more discussions with the native chieftain, or what?"

The Sixfold nodded again, her face tightening. "We have a bit of an ordeal in front of us, Alrik. The chieftain has invited all of us to dine privately with him and his family. Before that we are to pass through the main hall, where his retainers are gathered. One of us is to say a few words to the effect that we are the enemies of the sorcerers at Naples and are going there to see what happened."

"Can you do that, Natheless?"

"I could, of course, but it would be better if you did. You were introduced as the Prince last night, and besides, this culture seems to find female witches more sinister than male ones. I could act as your spokesman, as before, if you prefer."

"Have you worked out the speech? Can I learn it?"

"Yes, I composed it with the chieftain. But another thing, Alrik. We're then going to eat with them. The chieftain gave me what he thought was a complete summary of the customs and ceremonies surrounding meals in this culture, but I'm afraid he omitted something significant. It's impossible to guess how our cultures differ, probably in ways we can't imagine. Besides, the food itself is apt to be quite unsanitary, laced with microbes and bacteria. I can't decide whether I should try to excuse you from dinner altogether on grounds of illness, or advise you to go and eat as little as possible."

"What about you and the Aspirants?" demanded Alrik.

"You know we have stronger constitutions."

"I'll go and eat with you," said Alrik testily. "I'm not an invalid."

Natheless regarded him anxiously, trying to decide which was more fragile, his health or his dignity. Finally, she said, "Well, do what you think best, but take care."

Alrik was embarrassed again. He had not really recovered from the previous night's humiliation, when he had fired needlessly upon the boy-King. Aboard the Peleziterea he knew his way through every situation. Here on the planet he never knew what to expect or what to do next. And he seemed much more nervous about it than his fiancée. "Never mind, no harm done," she had assured him, but he could not forget it so easily. How come Natheless, usually so awkward and nervous around people, was so much more at ease here than he was? Perhaps her nature was so out of tune with Peleziterean culture that it was not much harder for her to interpret the planetary people's actions than her own people's? Alrik dismissed these thoughts, and grimly set about learning his speech.

He had it by heart when the pageboy dressed in scarlet and black finally came to summon them to the banquet hall. All four Pelezitereans rose and followed. They were led down the tower stairs, along a narrow corridor, down more stairs into the royal chambers, through these to the inner door of the great hall. They found themselves standing across from a dais. The King, dressed in a rich but somber mantle of purple over his black tunic, stood on it flanked by the counselor who had been with him the previous evening and by several other people, all richly and gaily dressed. As the strangers entered, everyone turned, and Conradin motioned the Pelezitereans to come forward. Natheless escorted Alrik up to Conradin, who took his arm and turned to the hundreds of nobles. They were festively dressed because they dared not go into mourning for the Pope when the rumors of his death were being denied. Signs of mourning might in fact bring them punishment. Conradin spoke, "Behold, *Signori* and *Dònne*, the Prince who came last night to consult with us. He too has complaints against the sorcerers who linger in the cathedral at Naples. We depart together soon to learn the truth of what has happened there, and to see whether the Pope has indeed been murdered. If this is so, we shall certainly do the work of justice!"

A low murmur of approval swept through the crowd. A few cheered. Conradin gestured for Alrik to speak, but he did not understand until Natheless signaled. Then he recited the words he had memorized: "Noblemen and ladies of Italy, we Pelezitereans are heartily sorry if our rebellious subjects have done harm among your people. Be assured it was done by no consent of our good King Benrik. We will do everything in our power to punish them and bring them to justice." There was another low murmur, this time more of surprise. Then there were a few polite cheers. Conradin smiled encouragingly at Alrik and turned to guide him to the entrance of the hall. Alrik found himself facing the retainers he had passed on the way in—Anticoli, the King's cousin whom they had met the night before, and two richly-dressed women. The native chieftain spoke. "Prince Alrik, you are already acquainted with our noble cousin, Conrad Anticoli. Here also is his gentle lady, the noble Bianca, and her sister, *Madònna* Ginevra the fair." Alrik looked closely at the women for the first time. The elder of the two was pleasing to look upon, a dignified lady with fair hair and blue eyes, though her complexion was somewhat faded. Her younger sister, however, was truly beautiful. Her gown was of green with a pattern of gold-ray embroidered through it. The mantle she wore was deep reddish brown and a bright yellow on the underside, which was visible at the edges and rippled as she walked. All of these colors reflected in the gleam of the white jewels attached to the net restraining her golden hair. Alrik knew no name for these stones, but the Italians called them *margarite* or pearls. The younger woman smiled and curtsied. Alrik found himself marveling that such a beautiful and obviously healthy woman should almost undoubtedly be a Lawchild. He knew for Italians to be born in wedlock was the rule rather than the exception.

When Ginevra rose, Alrik gave what he hoped was an appropriate phrase of greeting. He realized Conradin had already returned to lead Natheless from the room, and the two women had taken charge of him. "Will it please you to follow us, my lord?" said Bianca politely. With a lady on each arm, Alrik passed through the door into the royal antechamber.

Ginevra's feelings on being presented to the Infidel Prince consisted of equal parts of amusement and disgust. The previous night he had seemed more imposing—taller than he looked at close quarters, and clothed in the mystery of his secret powers. In conversation she expected him to prove either obscure and condescending, arrogantly reserved or, at worst, insultingly familiar. Instead, he proved to be awkward, ill at ease, timid and, it seemed, hardly competent in Italian.

He followed the ladies to the table in the antechamber and sank docilely into the place they indicated, glancing anxiously around to see what was happening to the rest of his party. All the Pelezitereans were placed at the same table, since Conradin was confused about the precise rank of the Princess's two attendants and had chosen to risk honoring them too much rather than too little. The Princess was seated at the Emperor's right, with her two maidens beside her. Anticoli sat at Conradin's left, beside Bianca, with Alrik and Ginevra to their left. This made the Peleziterean Prince the only foreigner completely surrounded by Italians, a fact which appeared to alarm him, though Ginevra could not imagine why. Conradin had decided not to question whether it was courteous for the Infidels to come to dinner armed, so doubtless the Princess had her silver rod. Among the Italians no one was armed except the guards at the entrance.

The pages poured the wine and carved the meat. Silver dishes were placed between each pair of guests, for this was the custom at especially elaborate feasts. Bianca and Conradin had arranged things so the Infidel Princess and Conradin would share a plate, as would Prince Alrik and Ginevra. The wisdom of this arrangement was immediately apparent when the food was served. The Princess seemed wary at first both of the food and the drink, but allowed the boy-King to persuade her to try a little of everything. Her ladies quickly followed her example. This process was well under way while Alrik still stared at the food as though it were some kind of dangerous animal. Ginevra realized she was failing in her duty to her King. She turned to Alrik cheerfully. "My lord, will you not try some of the roasted goose? Though the provender here is poor and our cooks' skill humble, you have traveled far and must be weary, and even such fare as this might refresh you."

The stranger started and turned his oddly green eyes toward her. She could not quite judge his emotion. He seemed a little alarmed and almost annoyed she had spoken, as though watching Conradin and the Princess and listening to their conversation was all he had time for. Perhaps he thought it was too much to ask that he should speak to her, too. He answered haltingly, "My lady—uh—jests—this is the finest meal I— uh—have enjoyed in a long time." So saying, he reached carefully down to the part of the plate she indicated. He delicately separated a tiny fragment of the goose with his fingers, and raised it deliberately to his mouth. He chewed it carefully and for a long time, wearing an expression of intense concentration.

Ginevra felt a stab of something like resentment. The cooks had put themselves out to prepare a really splendid meal. Yet this foreigner assumed this attitude. Of course it was not his fault; he was used to better things. Aloud she tried to make light of it. "Pish! So great a man as you could never be pleased here! You come from the ends of the earth and have seen so many strange and wonderful things. Doubtless you have sat at hundreds of feasts a thousand times as splendid as this, and have seen thousands and thousands of things beautiful beyond description."

This perfectly obvious remark seemed to thoroughly discomfit the Peleziterean. It was a while before he could rise above his stammers. "No, *Madònna*—that is not—that is to say, I have not—uh—I mean the food is—uh—excellent—and I have never seen—uh—the things you say—that is—I have never seen anything—beautiful beyond description—" The Peleziterean stopped, dumb for a moment. Then an inspiration seemed to strike him. "Except, of course, yourself, *Madònna*," he concluded. Quite overcome with his own boldness, Alrik directed his eyes on the table. He knew in a general way Italian nobles loved to exchange elaborate compliments, but not having learned all the rules, he had no idea how his would go over.

Ginevra was impressed. Perhaps all the awkward prince needed after all was encouragement. Smiling, her cheeks a little pink, her eyes modestly downcast, she said, "Prince, wheresoever you may have traveled, you have certainly learned the ways of courtesy. Perhaps, then, you will try the mushrooms?"

Grateful, possibly, that it gave him an opportunity to stop talking, the Infidel took another tiny bite and chewed it for a long time. Momentarily weary from the effort of urging him, Ginevra turned her attention to the foreign women. Princess Natheless was taking small bites and sips, but more regularly than the Prince, and talking brightly to the Emperor at the same time. The other women were doing likewise, but talking to each other. Ginevra caught the drift of what they were saying.

"Come," said Conradin, "you have wandered beyond the borders of the lands we know and have beheld many kingdoms and peoples. Have you no tales to tell us to while away the time before nightfall?"

The Princess, a small, straight girl, sat erect in her chair, alert and smiling but tense. "She is cold," thought Ginevra, and from then on Natheless was "the Cold Princess" to her.

"My Emperor," said the Princess quietly, "our land is barren and our wanderings filled with haste. There are few tales among us, and these are doubtless inferior to those you know. It would delight us greatly to hear some stories of your people."

Conradin smiled and shook his head. "No, truly, Princess; it would not be fair for you to hear so much of us and we so little of you. However, since we are both so eager to hear of one another, perhaps you will tell us a tale first, and then we shall tell you one afterward."

The Cold Princess, her expression unchanged, reiterated, "Truly, Emperor, we are no great tellers of tales. We are too intent on our search to learn much else, and tale-telling is one thing we have been forced to give up. I assure you, the few stories we have would amuse you but little."

"Then tell us at least," persisted Conradin, "how you came to be exiles living in a barren land? Surely a tale hangs there."

The Princess considered a moment, her expression becoming very distant. She focused on Conradin again and said, "Very well, Sire, if you wish to know, I will tell you that, though I only hope it will give you pleasure." She raised the goblet she shared with Conradin, took a small sip from it and put it down. Everyone else at the table fell silent, waiting for her to begin. A page or two who ought to have been returning to the kitchens for the cakes and tarts lingered nearby to hear what she said.

"Long, long ago," began the Cold Princess, "more than a thousand years by your count—we lived in a prosperous land. It would be difficult to tell you how prosperous it was. Crops were plentiful; in fact, there was never famine. Everyone had a roof over his head. No one had fewer clothes than he needed; medical treatment was available to everyone. Nearly everyone in our land could read and write." Conradin, Anticoli and Bianca drew in their breath, astonished. The Princess continued, "Diseases of filth and contagion were all but unknown. As for the luxury, the music, the gaiety of the costumes, the festivals and games, the amusements—well, there were many of them, but I have heard little of detail because it was so long ago and their descendants were ashamed to speak of them. If I leave it to your imagination, I am sure you will do it more than justice. Many of the pleasures were wholesome. Yet, alas, too many people who live with peace and plenty become bored with gentle recreation. They make up cruel and wicked games for themselves and others. This was bad, but this is not what drove our people to exile.

"Through the wickedness of many people, and also through their cowardice, their carelessness and their foolishness, a man came to power who was more crafty, more wicked and crueler than most of them. His name was Karsma Megala. After he had destroyed or reduced to submission anyone among our people who might have been a good and wise ruler, he claimed to be the god who created the heavens and the earth. He commanded the people to worship him as such. He also commanded them to do various evil and filthy things in his honor, the exact nature of which I cannot tell you because I do not know—such things are not told to juveniles among my people.

"So many of our people were ready to obey Karsma Megala in these things, he could not be overthrown. Many indeed rebelled against him, but they were informed on and betrayed. Those who were not killed outright were taken prisoner and tortured so cruelly they lost their minds."

The Cold Princess paused and took up the goblet for another sip. Everyone waited for her to begin again. "So how did your people escape?" demanded Conradin.

"They fled," said the Princess simply. "One day a man was walking upon the ocean's shore. He looked into the sky and saw the stars." Natheless lifted the winecup yet again, while she considered her next words. It would not do at all to explain that the Founders had believed many of the stars in the sky had planets around them, some similar to Urith. They also had believed stars of certain colors and rotational speeds were more likely to have them than others. Natheless said, "His eyes were drawn to a certain star, and he said to himself, 'That star is shining down now upon a land which will give shelter to my company.' That very moment he laid aside his old name—no one now remembers what it was—and took the name of that star—Epsilon Eridani. Then he gathered his friends—in the first generation there were more than six hundred, including women and children—and procured vessels, some by stealth, some by petition—to flee to the land upon which Epsilon Eridani shone."

Natheless watched hopefully for Conradin's reactions. She knew his people often steered by the stars. And although all stars except those at the poles moved, shining above one region at one time and another later, she believed it would make sense to them to speak of a land over which a star shone at a given moment. Still, Conradin looked puzzled. "Why did he choose that star? How could he know it was not shining over water?"

Natheless hedged carefully. "He was wise in the science. Of course, not all his companions agreed with him. Several other members of his company took the names of other stars when they set out."

Conradin's face was shining with interest. "But did you ever find that land?"

Natheless shook her head. "No, we never found it. When we were still within sight of our land, there was a—a great disturbance. We were tossed about violently and driven from our course. When we came to ourselves, we were not able to determine our relationship to our former position, and we never saw that star again."

Conradin looked puzzled. "Couldn't you navigate from the other stars?"

"No, indeed; the stars then were so very different from the ones we knew, we thought we might well be in another universe," said Natheless.

This, perhaps, was letting too much of the uncanny into the tale. But after all it was uncanny and had puzzled the Pelezitereans, so why not puzzle the Italians?

Conradin eyed her speculatively. "Did you come from Fairyland?" he asked.

Natheless found herself in unknown territory again. "I have not heard of such a land. What do you mean by it?"

Suddenly recollecting their duties, two pages set down a plate of tarts on the table and departed for the kitchen. Conradin said, "Fairyland is a name that comes into many tales, but none of them give the same account of it. I have heard it is a land where people have strange powers like yours. Some are good and some are evil. The land is governed by laws different from ours, and it may be they have different stars as well, though I cannot recall a tale about that."

"Perhaps that is where we came from," said Natheless uncertainly.

"And yet," said Conradin, "it seems someone who comes from Fairyland ought to know it. What was the cause of the storm that drove you so far? Was it an earthquake?"

Natheless took a small piece from one of the tarts and began to chew it carefully. No doubt the earth had quaked, if it came to that. "That may have been part of it," she said neutrally.

"Did it rain fire and brimstone?" asked Father Omberto from the foot of the table where he sat.

"We could not tell exactly what it was," said Natheless. "It certainly hammered us well, however."

"Do you not see," said Conradin intensely, "your city was destroyed for its wickedness?"

Natheless shrugged. "No one has any doubt about that."

"But because you hated the tyrant, God allowed you to escape and brought you to this land so you might be baptized in the faith and come to live among us."

Natheless shook her head. "No, do not say so, *Signore*. It is forbidden. Now, will you not tell us a tale of your own people, as you promised?"

Since this was obviously not the moment to start a debate on a matter of high policy, Conradin nodded graciously and clapped his hands. A page standing nearby jumped. "One of you find Cino and tell him to bring his lute," he commanded. The boy rushed off, and the Princess's spell was broken. Ginevra turned to Alrik and said in a low voice, "Your Princess has told a wonderful story, you who claim you have no stories. Was it true?"

The Infidel, who during all this time had consumed about three bites of goose, one mushroom, three sips of wine and a small bite of plum tart, turned to her and stammered, "Y-yes, it is true."

"You must have rejoiced greatly when you escaped the fate which overtook the others."

"We—uh—we do," replied the Prince. "Except," he added, "that it all happened so long ago we have almost forgotten."

The minstrel for whom Conradin had sent arrived, preceded by the page. He was a short man, rather thin, but well-dressed in the Emperor's scarlet. He stood before the company, bowing low, and asked, "What is your pleasure, Your Majesty? Shall I sing a song of adventure, or one of love, or perhaps one in praise of God or of the Queen of Heaven?"

Conradin turned to Natheless. "What would you prefer, *Madònna*?" he inquired.

"Any of those would be delightful," replied the Cold Princess.

Conradin tried to think of a song that would serve his purpose, gave it up and motioned to Cino. "You choose the song," he said. However, as the minstrel plucked the first chords, Conradin recognized the song and exclaimed, "But not that one!"

The music ceased as the minstrel waited for further instruction. "Why not that song?" inquired the Princess.

Conradin answered, confused. "May it not displease you, *Madònna*, Cino hoped to display all the kinds of song in one, which is a love song, a song about a great adventure and a song addressed to God. However, it is about the holy wars fought in Palestine against the followers of the prophet Mohammed. I think you are not Mohammedan—for you drank the wine at table—yet I feared it might be discourteous."

Natheless shook her head. "Have no fear; we are not Mohammedans and will not take offense. Perhaps we shall need some explanation from you, however, in order to understand the story, if it is about a foreign war."

"That is no great hardship," said Conradin easily. He waved for Cino to begin his song again.

The chords sounded, and the minstrel's voice, mellow and smooth, began to sing.

> *I never will stop crying,*
> *Kind words will not avail;*
> *The navies at the port are lying,*
> *All eager to set sail.*

And with them goes the noblest knight,
To the lands beyond the sea.
For him I weep all day and night,
What will become of me?

He was seized by other longings,
And he never sent me word;
Now thick my tears are thronging,
And everything is blurred.
I cannot tell the land from sea,
Or know if it be dusk or dawn;
So cruel my lover is to me,
He deceived me and is gone.

"The song was composed by one of Frederick II's knights, Rinaldo d'Aquino," said Conradin softly. The song continued.

O God so great and holy,
Once of a maiden born,
Have pity on the lowly,
And guard your pilgrims night and morn.
Highest and most dreaded power,
Ah, keep my lover whole and free,
I pray to you each waking hour,
Since you've stolen him from me.

Ginevra, irked by her neighbor's blank expression, leaned over and whispered to Alrik, "You hear him say God was born of a maiden? That is one of the things we fought the Mohammedans about." Bianca heard and sent her a quick warning frown. The Infidel answered falteringly, "Uh—I know of no reason why—why your God should not—uh—do whatever he likes." The Cold Princess was now speaking. "It sounds as though the lady in the song is jealous of God."

"So she is," agreed Conradin. "After all, her lover swore once he loved her above all things. Yet now he deserts her for Christ. Anyone would be jealous."

"Then why," inquired Natheless, "does she pray for God to protect him?"

Conradin shrugged. "I suppose she still loves him nonetheless."

Ginevra added, speaking especially to Alrik, "He means more to her than her own happiness."

"She is a generous lady," remarked Alrik. Natheless had already asked another question which he could not hear, nor could he catch Conradin's reply. Ginevra spoke in answer to his remark.

"All true lovers act in that fashion," she said matter-of-factly. "They will never stoop to baseness as some do who only feel base desire. This is also in the story of Tristan and Isolde. Tristan's wife desired him, but he did not desire her. So she deceived him, causing him to believe that his true love refused to come and heal him. He died of grief. It was not nobly done of her."

Alrik thought, "Natheless already has an interpreter herself." She would be pleased if he could gather information from a second source. He turned to Ginevra probing cautiously, choosing his words carefully. "If it was not—uh—noble of her—was it noble of Tristan to love a woman who was not his wife?"

Ginevra's eyes widened and she stared at him. "You ask that, Prince? Many noble knights do it."

"Yet," stumbled Alrik, "it is difficult for a wife if her husband loves another woman."

Ginevra responded, "This is certainly true." She knew a husband's infidelities were a trial to many women, but never before had she heard a man acknowledge the fact. Even among women it was generally allowed that a wife who was properly clothed and fed, and not beaten or scolded in front of guests or servants, had little to complain about. And Ginevra, whose position in her first marriage had given her reason to complain even by these standards, had often told herself if only her husband would treat her kindly, she would not trouble herself about his mistress. Aloud she said, "It is hard for women indeed. Many things are, but no one considers that when marriages are made." Bianca heard the note of personal anger in her voice and sent her another warning frown. Ginevra tried to retrieve the situation. "After all," she concluded, "there are so many more important things to think of."

"What are these concerns more important than happiness?" pursued Alrik nervously, wondering how long he could go on before making a serious mistake.

Ginevra was shaken. Her inner voice had often asked her the same question, but because it was inner, she had never bothered to answer it. Bianca, sensing danger, was trying to think of a way to turn the conversation. But nothing came quickly to her lips, and she remained silent. At last Ginevra said gently, "Perhaps nothing is as important as happiness, but since it is impossible to obtain, the weak and the helpless are sometimes pleased to strike bargains allowing them at least their lives."

Ginevra thought she saw understanding and compassion awaken in the Infidel's eyes. Ginevra's heart overflowed with warmth, and suddenly she seemed to see a huge castle wall, standing between them until then, crumbling into dust. She turned away, afraid if she looked longer into his eyes, her soul would flow out of hers into his.

Bianca interrupted sharply. "Pish, Ginevra! You, a great and wealthy lady, to talk of being weak and helpless!"

At another time Ginevra might have snapped in anger at this attempt to make light of her trials, but the new emotion made her gentle and soft-spoken. "I know, sister, my sufferings are small compared to what has befallen others. Yet, do not belittle them, lest you provoke me into wearying our guest with a longer account."

Duly alarmed, Bianca fell silent. As they had been speaking, three other verses of the song had gone by without comment or explanation, and the minstrel was beginning the last.

> *My patient friend the poet,*
> *I have told you all my woe.*
> *Pray write of it a sonnet,*
> *To bring him when you go.*
> *In Syria tell my pilgrim-friend,*
> *I have no rest by night or day,*
> *For to the land his arms defend,*
> *He has borne my life away.*

The end of the song brought silence, except for the soft strumming of the chords. In order to break it, Alrik asked, "Did Rinaldo really bring this song to Syria for a distressed lady?"

"*Ahi!* How would I know?" exclaimed Ginevra. "Some ladies really sent messages that way, yet sometimes poets have invented such songs when no ladies confide in them. People will never learn the true from the false, because the wise poet keeps it secret from all but the knight most nearly concerned, especially if he does not wish to bring more sorrow upon the poor lady. For as soon as her lover left her, she was seized and imprisoned by her jealous husband, as you would have heard if you had listened to the other verses."

"Poor lady!" cried Alrik spontaneously. "How could a lover leave her in such a state and go pursue a spiritual being he had never even seen?" Then he stopped, wondering if he had said something too daring.

Ginevra felt an amazing warmth in her heart. She spoke gravely, "Men have good cause to love Christ. When he was born among us, he will-

126

ingly died a shameful death for our sins." But inwardly, Alrik's sympathy for the woman with the jealous husband released a flood of feeling. Tears sprang to her unwilling eyes. She recalled a day when she had awakened to find her chamber door locked and her female attendant dismissed, all because she had sent a small embroidered belt to a young cousin of whose father her husband was jealous. Anger rose with the memory. How dare he treat her like a liar and a criminal, when she had given him no reason? And why would no one take her part? Husbands were often like hers. True, some were not; she knew one or two women who had excellent husbands with whom they lived in mutual love. Bianca, for one, was happy with Anticoli. But that was a special gift of providence, not something anyone could expect to have as a matter of course. One had to marry for land and political connections. Character came extra, and was often not predictable unless something outstandingly horrible was concerned. How could it be otherwise? Marriage was a set of obligations, binding both you and your family. Love was something untamed, wild, appearing at unexpected times and unlikely places when no one asked for it. It often disappeared just as suddenly, completely unbound by laws of justice or prudence.

Ginevra said to Alrik, "Among our people it is believed true love ennobles the heart and must be given freely, it cannot be required. Therefore, it cannot exist in marriage."

"Uh—among our people," said Alrik, "the love that exists in marriage is believed greater than any other kind. Dreams and stolen moments are only deceits, and the greatest of all loves is expressed in everyday actions."

Ginevra was entranced. "There are tales among us of husbands and wives who are lovers, too, but surely not everyone who contracts a marriage is worthy of the kind of love that ennobles the heart!"

"If they are worthy, there is no need to marry," said Prince Alrik. "And besides, they must become worthy, for when two parties to a contract are equally powerful, the contract will only last as long as it is pleasing to both. Women have equal honor among us." Alrik started, knowing he had really said too much this time. Bianca was staring at him in genuine alarm.

"But how can your women be as powerful as your men?" inquired Ginevra. "Surely the women are weaker!"

Alrik felt very nervous. He had gone much too far, and the rest of the table had fallen silent. Natheless and Conradin were both watching him. However, it was too late to withdraw. "You think women cannot be equal because you still conduct warfare with your bodies, rushing together with spears on horseback. Our power is in our minds. A woman can wield our weapons as well as a man can."

A wave of exultation swept over Ginevra. "Then why not teach us your wisdom, Prince? Teach us so our women, too, can have equal honor, and no one can lock us up when we have lovers, even though no one reproaches them when they have lovers themselves!"

Alrik, now really distressed, stared down at the table. "It is not—uh—that I do not want it—but—uh—it is forbidden."

Silence fell on the whole table. Conradin broke it. "Sing us another song, Cino."

13

For many hours that evening Ginevra sat before her mirror while her maidens combed her long golden hair. Yet she could not concentrate on her own image. The Infidel Prince's pale yet striking face appeared before her eyes, shining with compassion for the weak and helpless. Her heart burned gently and her lips silently formed the words, "What Conradin says must be true. These people are here to stay. If I ever marry again, it must be Prince Alrik. It must be Prince Alrik. I will have no one, if not him." She was so absorbed in her thoughts she did not hear her sister enter the room, even when her maidens left their brushing and turned to curtsy to the great lady.

"Ginevra," said Bianca.

Ginevra almost dropped her polished silver mirror. Then she stood. "Bianca, *dolcetta*, I did not hear you enter!"

Lady Bianca had come in with a stern face, prepared to chide. But at the innocent affection of the greeting her expression softened. It was hard for most people to be stern with Ginevra. Like all Galvano Lancia's daughters she had been strictly brought up, but as the youngest of six, she had never lacked a sibling's indulgent attention. Naturally affectionate, she had learned to expect others to melt before her winsome ways, and usually they did.

"You were rapt, little sister," said Bianca gravely.

"Indeed, my thoughts were far away," responded Ginevra dreamily.

"Perhaps," said her sister more sharply, "you ought to keep them near at hand, in case you might need them in a hurry."

Ginevra smiled. "Surely I am safe in my chamber with my maidens!"

"What use is it to build dream castles in Fairyland?" retorted Bianca.

Ginevra crossed the room to her sister and took her hand to lead her to a seat. "Come, dear heart. Why should we stand and quarrel? Do you begrudge me a sweet thought or two?"

Again Bianca could not help softening. "Only do not set your heart on the strange Prince, sister, and all the absurdities he spoke of. You may well complain about your husband's treatment of you, child, but such is woman's lot. You'll find if you live long that things get worse more easily than better."

"What of that?" said Ginevra serenely. "Was not the strangers' story marvelous? And was not Prince Alrik wonderfully kind?"

"Fine words," scoffed Bianca. "Fine words, but what do you know of his deeds?"

Ginevra laughed softly. "What deeds would you have him do, lovely sister? Would you have him drive away and imprison all the ill-tempered, jealous old husbands in Italy? That would make him many enemies."

"So I meant when I said fine words were easy," replied Bianca.

Ginevra led Bianca to the luxurious bed and they both sat down. Ginevra glanced away and complained, "I don't know why you tell me this, sister! Do you think I have no sense of honor? Or that my wits are feeble?"

Bianca shook her head gravely. "I think nothing of the kind. I am only afraid for you."

"Poor Bianca," said Ginevra, as she turned back to stroke her sister's cheek playfully. "Was I a scatterbrained child? I must have been, for you trouble about me so much when I am a widow of one-and-twenty years with property of my own."

"You were sometimes reckless, child," said Bianca earnestly. "Be careful." The two sisters turned the conversation to a discussion of the previous night's dinner and plans for the next one, and soon parted affectionately.

After walking her sister to the door, Ginevra called her maidens. "Come, you must finish braiding my hair."

"Do you still mean to do it?" asked the maiden Gualdrada excitedly.

"Of course. The Infidel is on the Emperor's side in this conflict and he is fighting for our sake and for the sake of all Italy. Surely there is nothing shameful in giving such a man a token of my favor. Bring me my scarf."

Gualdrada brought the scarf Ginevra had selected from her wardrobe. It was blue-green silk, profusely embroidered with outlines of fish, serpents and sea creatures in gold, white, red and other colors. It was among her best work, and Ginevra looked it over proudly for a moment before setting it beside her on the bed and calling to her maidens again, "Come, finish my hair."

When Ginevra's hair was freshly braided and bound under her pearl-sewn net, Gualdrada, too, was carefully brushed and adorned (for the whole embassy had to make a good impression). By this time it was sunset.

"We must hurry," said Ginevra, "for they will leave when the moon has set." Finding the opportune moment might have been difficult, but Ginevra had sent her maids out to inquire. They found the Emperor was still with the Cold Princess and one of her maidens, while Prince Alrik and the other had returned to the tower room. The strangers must be nearly ready to depart, and Ginevra hastened accordingly.

Alrik was waiting in the tower room while Floress snatched a few moments of sleep. His emotions were churning. He had apologized over and over to Natheless for the possible metaphysical interference he had generated by talking about the equal honor of women. Natheless seemed to find the whole thing amusing. The first time he apologized, she had said, "Oh, never mind, Alrik, it isn't that important." The second time she had said, "The main point of our mission is to remove technological traces. Avoiding metaphysical interference is an amusing game we play. I thing it's good you were able to hold such a long conversation with the native woman." The third time she said, "Look, Alrik, you probably did more good than harm. Now, the Italian men have a reason for not wanting our science—and most of the women have probably been conditioned to feel that way, too." These reasons comforted him a little, but he still felt tense.

There was a soft knock on the door, the native signal someone wished to enter. Alrik leaped to his feet. A native was coming to see him, and Natheless was not there. What was he to do? Should he make no response at all and risk being considered rude, or was he to make another absurd mistake and paralyze a friendly visitor? For a moment it seemed his native vocabulary had once more been knocked out of his brain, but then he formed a phrase, a little warily, "Who's there?"

A female voice answered through the door. "A lady wishes to speak with you, Prince Alrik. Will you open?"

Alrik felt relief, then tension. He knew nothing of these women, or what they might want. What should he do? He decided it would be wiser to open the door and see. He drew the latch. When the door slid open, the vision of Ginevra's beauty struck him. He stepped backward, a bit dazzled.

She remained in the doorway, unmoved, her face smiling but distant, sweet but imperious. Not she, but the other maiden with her, the one who had knocked, spoke. "*Signore,* the lady Ginevra offers you a token of her favor." Ginevra was holding a magnificent piece of cloth with intricate designs of living forms depicted on it. Alrik warmed to its beauty, but he racked his brains in an attempt to understand what was happening. .

"That cloth is a token of your favor?" he got out, repeating the maiden's message.

"Yes, indeed," said the maiden, and Ginevra lowered the cloth, as though disappointed.

Ginevra spoke for the first time. "It is the custom among our people for a lady to give a favor to a knight she wishes well. He wears it attached to his armor or his helmet, so anyone who sees it knows a lady's prayers are with him. Yet if such things mean nothing to Infidels—" She began to withdraw the scarf, but Alrik stepped forward in alarm. "No, *Madònna!* It means a great deal to me, more than I can say!"

The lady, mollified, stretched out her hand again. "Then it is yours," she said softly. Hesitantly Alrik reached forward and took hold of a corner of the beautiful cloth. As he did so, his fingers brushed Ginevra's. Her eyes rested on him appealingly, as though she expected something more. What did she expect? Words of thanks? Another elaborate compliment? Science and progress, how was he ever to think of one? A kiss? Alrik was paralyzed with indecision.

"*Madònna,* I thank you heartily for your gift and your good will, both so undeserved," he said at last.

This appeared to satisfy her. The native woman smiled and made a slight bow. "*Signore,* no man who spoke as nobly as you did today may be counted unworthy. I must go now. May God keep you safe!" Her attendant also curtsied, and they both turned and left. Alrik closed the door. His relief was almost ecstatic.

What had it meant? Was it mere courtesy? Or a courtship ritual? That was dangerous. With any luck the mission would be completed before anything else could come of it. Lady Ginevra liked him! He could not have made so bad an impression at the meal then. He quickened at the thought and he rebuked himself. No Italian beauty would take a fancy to a sickly foreigner like Alrik.

But these denials did not prevent a subtle euphoria from suffusing him and surrounding him like a cloud as he went to wake Floress so they could leave the tower.

Natheless and the native chieftain were waiting at the postern gate, surrounded by the low steady light from Natheless's wrist-unit. They were restless and seemed anxious to get started.

"Come on, Alrik," said Natheless when she saw him. "The Emperor is going to lead us to a spot outside the city where the Skimmer can land without being seen." Then she caught sight of the cloth he had in his hands.

"Science and progress, what a beautiful thing!" she exclaimed. "How in the Universe did you get *that?*"

Alrik blushed, and for the first time in his life, he found Peleziterean as difficult as Italian. "A gift—" he stammered, "—of a native woman, of the lady, the lady—"

"The lady? The beautiful one you sat with at dinner? Boundless space, I always seem to be in the wrong places at the wrong times! What happened?" Nightmares of taboos violated and of native vengeance rose in her mind.

Alrik was still groping for words, when Conradin interposed cautiously. He could not understand their speech, but had seen Natheless point to the scarf. Moreover, he had recognized the embroidery, and his own heart was beating with alarm. Natheless had told him she and Alrik were betrothed, but he had not bothered to convey that information to Ginevra. And while it was true most political betrothals did not mean much, Ginevra might have been more discreet.

"Prince Alrik," he interrupted, "did Lady Ginevra give you a token of her favor?"

"That's what she said," Alrik replied.

Conradin nodded understandingly. "It shows her favor, indeed, if she gave you that. I have seen her taking pains with it for many weeks. Will you not wear it in her honor, Prince? She is a wise and noble lady."

Natheless stared at the native chieftain. "Is that a custom among your people? Is there no harm in it, remembering the Prince and I are betrothed?"

Conradin nodded gently. "It is a custom among our people. There is no harm in it where there is no evil intent."

That was certainly a vague reply. And Alrik's awkwardness increased with Natheless's uneasiness. However, this was not the time to analyze a complicated native gesture. For the moment they had Conradin outnumbered, and if all went well, Alrik would never see Lady Ginevra again. Natheless smiled deliberately and stretched out her hand for the scarf. Alrik surrendered it without a struggle. "I think you could wear it best like this," she said, running the scarf through a loop in the collar of Alrik's suit which was there chiefly to hold a small pouch of emergency medication. From there the native cloth trailed down across the front of his silver suit, making strongly colored reflections in it. "How does that look?" asked Natheless, turning to Conradin.

"It becomes him well," said the native gravely.

Natheless nodded. "Yes, when we return to our people, he will start a new fashion, I think. Come, let's depart."

Conradin, feeling a cautious triumph, led the way through the postern gate.

14

The Lander was waiting in the Piedmont region. It was by all counts a tense wait. It was natural those aboard should amuse themselves by trying to learn as much as they could about the planet, both by studying the Contact expedition's first reports and examining the terrain and life forms at first hand. But on the third day after Natheless's departure, the Archon ordered Lawchild Jimmik Centauri to send no more crew members out on the planet's surface. The order was given flatly and listed no reasons. Those aboard speculated that the Archon was concerned about the health of the landing party, most of whom were accustomed to germ-free air. Perhaps he also did not fully trust the precautions Centauri had taken. After the fact, it became usual to speculate that the Archon even then had some inkling about Jimmik's motives for sending his subordinates out so far and so often. Were they completely scientific? If this were the case, the Archon did not record it, and no one else seemed to think of it at the time.

When Alrik Eridani contacted the Lander, the Archon and the Medical sub-Archon were sitting together in its lower deck without any apparent discord. Whether Jimmik had been on board all along, Alrik could not know. There had been no reason for the Archon to allude to Jimmik's presence in the coded messages he had been sending them. Visual contact had been avoided up to this point. Natheless had warned that the

Italian potentate they were bringing along would have trouble enough accepting flight through the air, without having to deal with immaterial visions and disembodied voices as well.

Now, when they finally made contact with the Lander, its screen lit up with the image only of Alrik's broad shoulders and red hair. Rauhina Telgolarses was the only other person visible in the Skimmer's control room. A blue-green cloth with strange, colorful patterns on it hung from Alrik's collar and rested across his breast.

"At last, Alrik!" exclaimed his father. "What's that you're wearing around your neck?"

Alrik colored only a little. "A gift from a native," he said.

The Archon frowned. "We should be wary of receiving gifts when we can give little in return—but I suppose Natheless has been over all that with you."

"What's happened to the barbarian?" he added.

"We had a little trouble with him. He was so fascinated by all the controls he didn't want to leave the room. He also didn't want us to drug him so he wouldn't be frightened. Finally Natheless and Bodris just left the room and he followed. He didn't want to be alone with me, I guess. They're in the Sleeping Room now." Alrik chuckled.

"Can you give us a look at him on the viewer?" inquired the Archon.

"Certainly." Alrik adjusted the necessary controls. The interior of the Sleeping Room appeared on the Lander's second screen.

The Skimmer was a small, disk-shaped vessel designed for close planetary explorations by crews of ten or less. It had two main rooms—the control room, where Alrik, Floress and Rauhina Telgolarses now sat, and the Sleeping Room, where Natheless had led the Italian. The Sleeping Room was designed, as the name implied, primarily for resting the crew on extended missions. Since it could not contain separate quarters for every passenger, it had absolutely no personal touches. The walls were a noncommital blue without decorations. The ten identical bunks were set around the walls on two levels. The only other features were cupboards beneath each bunk, where Lawchildren stored their wrist-computers, wigs and eyes (if detachable), and where everyone could stow his clothes. The communication system was designed to work only when the light was on, or in an emergency.

As they appeared in the Lander's screen, Natheless and Bodris were sitting on one of the lower bunks nearest the door, while the young Italian sat on the adjoining one, facing them. Bodris was leaning against the wall, asleep or nearly so. It was understandable. The Pelezitereans had journeyed across a great deal of the planet's surface, and neither Bodris nor Natheless had had her share of sleep the previous night. Natheless was deliberately away from the wall so that the effort of holding her back straight would keep her from sleeping. Her eyes were wide open, but her tiredness was evident.

The Archon's attention naturally focused on the young barbarian. He gasped, and even Jimmik Centauri beside him almost whistled in pure aesthetic delight. "What a fine physical specimen he is!" he exclaimed.

Alrik, visible in the other screen, nodded. "He is, indeed. And he is not as robust or handsome as many of the others. He has a relative, an older man—called Anticoli—who is much more remarkable. And you should see their women!"

"Watch *your* woman, Alrik," guffawed Centauri inappropriately. Alrik's expression did not change. On the other screen, Natheless smiled at something the boy-King had said. She leaned forward, apparently asking a question. The boy-King was telling a tale with great feeling and many gestures.

"He's been talking about his family and its history for the last ten generations or so," said Alrik. "Natheless has had her wrist-recorder going all this while, and she's almost been dying of excitement. She's having the time of her life, let me tell you. Have you seen enough?" Alrik poised over the switches.

"Yes," said the Archon. Alrik disengaged the connection. "Now, Alrik," said the Archon, "Natheless outlined the situation to me in our last communication, but I'm still not sure I understand. Why are you bringing this native ruler to me?"

Alrik rested both hands on the panel in front of him. It was an awkward question. The main reason they were coming, the only real reason, was Conradin's offer of land to the Pelezitereans in exchange for their science. But Natheless had forbidden him to reveal this. "I'll play it straight when we see the Archon," she said, "and translate the offer. Until then, the fewer people who know, the better. You never can tell what might happen if the wrong people hear about it."

The reasons Alrik was allowed to communicate sounded trivial and unconvincing. "He wanted to see you," Alrik said. "He's a stubborn creature, and wants to know for sure we are what we say we are and will indeed leave the planet when we have recaptured our hatcherbrats."

Centauri sneered. "This seems like an awfully complicated maneuver simply to satisfy the whims of a savage."

Alrik was rather annoyed. "Actually it isn't," he said. "Traveling across the ground, native fashion, takes a long time. We've already explained in our preliminary reports how complex the political situation here is. The natives have already assigned us a side and a part in their own political quarrels. The city where our hatcherbrats are—it's called Naples—is in the hands of the opposed priestly party, which distrusts us most of all. It believes we derive our powers from evil beings who live in the air. To win them to our side would require the overthrow of many preconceived notions and would be very difficult, leaving aside the question of metaphysical interference. It's better for us to deal with the less prejudiced party, represented by this young chieftain, if we can. Besides, Natheless believes this chieftain is an especially lucky find for us. He knows several of the native languages, and is able to understand us on our own terms better than any other we have encountered.

"In addition, he was even willing to ride to you in the Skimmer. That opens a variety of possibilities in our strategies against the hatcherbrats, if he can be persuaded to help us. If we can win him over, we might be able to finish this whole business within twenty-four hours." Then Alrik reconsidered. "But don't tell Natheless I told you that. She told me not to raise your hopes too high."

The Archon was amused. "Your secret is safe with me, Alrik. I'll do my best to look honorable and treaty-abiding. Is there anything else Natheless warned to be careful about?"

"No, Natheless thinks you should be very straightforward, wear your star insignia and say what you mean. But"—Alrik hesitated—"she also suggested it's fortunate you have your hair and eyes done in natural colors. Cosmic accessories would certainly terrify the natives if they saw them."

"Does that imply we should keep Jimmik out of sight?" inquired the Archon.

"It might make things easier," admitted Alrik.

"We'll see to it then. Is there anything else?"

"No; that's pretty much it."

"Very well, close communication. Contact us again when you land. The computers will monitor you meanwhile." The screen went black.

The Archon turned to Sixfold Jimmik Centauri. "You're not disappointed, are you?"

Centauri was noncommital. "You're going to need another vifin injection, Sevenfold."

Benrik Eridani was surprised. "Do you really believe so? I had one just three days ago."

138

"These aren't normal times for you, Lawchild Benrik. You've been under tremendous stress, and you haven't been sleeping properly. The last injection has already worn off. I can tell your blood isn't as red as it should be. You will need to be in prime condition for your interview with the barbarian."

"You're right, of course," replied the Archon. "Shall we go immediately to the medical sector?"

"At once," replied the Sixfold. They climbed to the next level. Benrik moved aside so Centauri could come abreast of him as they walked. "No need to be concerned about not seeing the chieftain when he comes aboard, Jimmik. You can watch everything from the data screen in your quarters."

Centauri continued without saying a word. Assuming he was absorbed in some other concern, the Archon fell silent.

Centauri was indeed so preoccupied he had not even heard the Sevenfold speak. He was pondering dosages—dosages and the Archon's medical records. How much soporin was required to put him out—kill the Archon and leave nothing to point the finger of suspicion at himself? Who would dare suspect him in any event? Who among the landing party could detect him? Natheless was the only one with the necessary expertise. She was ordinarily too naïve to suspect anything. Even if she weren't, he could prevent her from obtaining whatever evidence she needed. He was her superior, whatever the computer's stupid formality dictated.

The suddenness of it made him uncomfortable. And removal of the Archon, whose dictates had been almost a datum of nature, as important as the laws of the Universe, made Centauri uneasy.

Nonetheless, he would have to act at once, before the barbarian arrived and agreed to work with them. He required at least weeks to mature his project—weeks to ensure the whole landing party would fall desperately in love with the planet. If Natheless had not worked so accursedly fast, the matter might have been settled without harming anyone. Now his hand was being forced.

Still, acting suddenly would arouse suspicion. Perhaps it would suffice to render the Archon unconscious and declare him ill—for now. The fatal dose could be administered later, when he and everyone else had gotten used to the idea of the Archon's illness.

The two men entered the medical section, and the Archon sat down as usual on the medical table. "Imagine how it would be to be like that barbarian and live without weekly injections," he remarked.

139

"This will only take a moment," said Jimmik abstractedly as he went into the adjoining room, where the synthesized medicines were kept. He shook a little as he prepared the dosage. What he was doing was necessary and best for everyone concerned, but a vision of the fury and hatred that would shine from Alrik's and Natheless's faces if they knew what he was doing disturbed him. They were fools. They did not understand the real cost of survival, juveniles that they were. And they would never find out.

When Centauri returned holding the injector, the Archon was wondering aloud. "What will we do with Jori if we take him alive?"

"No need to think too far ahead," said Centauri, handing him the injector. Though his coordination was too poor to perform surgery unaided, Sixfold Centauri could still make injections when necessary. Most of his patients however preferred he not do so. The Archon completed the injection himself and started to rise. But Centauri interrupted, "Sit there a moment longer. Let your system absorb it."

"But I feel fine."

"You don't look fine." Centauri was watching Benrik narrowly, with an expression that made the Archon uneasy. "Is something wrong? Is there more to this than you're telling me?"

"You know very well you're not to worry," retorted the doctor, "and when I know anything definite, I'll tell you about it."

Benrik suddenly raised his hands to his temples. "I feel dizzy!" he exclaimed.

"Lie down for a moment," suggested Centauri in a leisurely manner. He was pressing keys on the computer data board, changing items in the Archon's record. Later he could alter the main computer aboard the Peleziterea to agree with it. By the time he completed his immediate alterations, the Archon was unconscious.

15

The sun was well below the horizon when the Skimmer settled over the Lander. Guided by the homing signal, it slid precisely into its lodging cavity, and the Lander's covering hatch closed over it. Alrik opened visual communication with the mother ship. "Archon, shall we come aboard?"

To Alrik's surprise, the discordant, cosmic colors of Jimmik Centauri's accessories filled the screen instead of his father's brown eyes and gray hair. "This is the Interim Archon," he declared. "Fourfold Alrik Eridani, you are to come aboard at once, but leave Sixfold Natheless and the chieftain until further notice."

Alrik had not absorbed the first piece of information yet. "Lawchild Jimmik! Where's my father?"

"In the infirmary. He's very ill. Come aboard."

"What's the matter with him?" demanded Alrik anxiously.

"You'll learn as soon as necessary, Alrik Eridani. Now do as I have said."

Alrik was alarmed at his father's sudden illness and furious with Jimmik Centauri for his refusal to supply particulars. He could see there was no use in further bickering at this point. "I'll come, Lawchild Centauri, but first I'll have to inform Lawchild Natheless about what is happening."

"Do so by video screen."

"She's instructed me not to. It will frighten the native."

Centauri grimaced. "Of course we mustn't risk that. Talk to her in person then." Abruptly Jimmik's image vanished from the screen.

Alrik found Floress staring at him. "Lawchild—I'm so sorry about the Archon," she offered.

"Thank you," said Alrik, as he moved from the control room. The hatch leading to the Sleeping Room opened, and he descended the ladder. There on the bunk lay the King, feet on the ground, otherwise outstretched on the bed, carefully strapped down to avoid jarring. Bodris was asleep on the neighboring bunk. Only Natheless was awake. She sat on the edge of her bunk in front of Bodris, eyes fixed on Conradin. She looked up when Alrik entered.

"All set?" she inquired.

"No," said Alrik.

"No?" Natheless straightened. "Is something wrong?"

"My father is in the infirmary. Jimmik has proclaimed him incompetent, and has assumed the office of Interim Archon. He won't tell me exactly what is wrong with my father, but commands me to go to him first and send for you and the chieftain later."

Natheless considered the possibilities. "How serious is your father's illness?"

"I told you he wouldn't say," replied Alrik impatiently. He was trying, with considerable effort, to distinguish his personal concerns from the implications this had for their mission. "I suppose the chieftain will just have to be frightened by Centauri's cosmic accessories."

Natheless's voice sank to a whisper. "Alrik, it's worse than that. *Lawchild Centauri will agree to Conradin's proposition.*"

"What?" Alrik was lost in his own train of thought and had not followed hers.

"Conradin's proposal," whispered Natheless, "to give us land."

"Supernova!" exclaimed Alrik.

"I guess you'll have to go now and hear what he has in mind, Alrik. He *is* the Interim Archon," continued Natheless.

"But if he agrees?"

"If he agrees, it will be a clearcut violation of the Prime Directive, and we can appeal to the High Council."

"But everyone on the Council is now so dubious about the Prime Directive, and they're all afraid of Jimmik Centauri. What if they don't dare oppose him?"

"Then," shrugged Natheless, "the fault for violation of the Prime Directive will clearly be theirs. If they cannot enforce it, how can we be expected to?"

"True," said Alrik. The idea it might happen without his fault comforted him a little. It would be delightful to live on this planet, as long as he were not responsible for the decision. "Shall I simply do as he orders?"

Natheless nodded. "Then send someone for us when he suggests."

"Fine." Alrik and Natheless walked together to the doorway, took leave of one another and parted. Alrik reentered the control room and signaled Floress to follow him.

Jimmik Centauri was pacing up and down the Lander's lower deck when Alrik and Floress entered. In spite of his resolve to maintain appearances, Alrik shot off his first question. "How ill is my father? I want to see him."

"It will do no good. He's in coma," said Centauri, without checking his pace. He continued to the end of the room, halted and waited for Alrik to reapproach him. "When did it happen?" Alrik demanded.

"Shortly after your communication."

"How did it happen?"

"Your father received unpleasant news."

"Unpleasant news?" Alrik was filled with foreboding.

"Yes. Very unpleasant." Centauri turned and walked to the other end of the room. This time Alrik did not follow, but stood where he was, suddenly aware of the contrast between Centauri's green hair and the pale orange wall. The Interim Archon returned to Alrik.

"It's going to be difficult for me to explain this to you," he said, with what might pass for sympathy on his face.

"You may as well start trying," suggested Alrik.

Centauri fixed his gaze on the ceiling. "The chieftain you have with you," he began slowly, "was mentioned in your early reports. He was accidentally saved from death by the intervention of our hatcherbrats. Isn't that so?"

Alrik nodded. "True."

"The hatcherbrats did not only save his life, however. Their very appearance received a political interpretation that vastly strengthened your chieftain's party, which by all other indications was about to be extirpated. So, since the hatcherbrats' arrival, the entire political configuration of this portion of the planet's surface has been altered drastically."

"Exactly," conceded Alrik.

Centauri now faced him squarely. "Don't you see that in allowing this chieftain to continue living, and even collaborating with him, you are interfering grossly, overtly and unjustifiably with the planet's history? Don't you see that this chieftain must die if we are to preserve the Prime Directive?"

A chill went up Alrik's spine. "But no one thought of that before!"

Centauri began to pace again. "No. It was my misfortune I was the first to think of it. Perhaps I should have spared your father. The idea proved too much for him, though I couldn't have foreseen that. He's been under stress lately. And he cares intensely about the Prime Directive." Centauri looked at Alrik. "In all events, the chieftain must die."

Alrik was stunned. He had indeed conceived a mild dislike for Conradin, but certainly had no desire to see him die. Such an act was, to begin with, foreign to his conceptions of right and wrong. Capital punishment had not been inflicted among the Pelezitereans for many generations. But it was conceivable one might kill legally as a punishment for serious crime, or as an immediate necessity for self-defense. But to kill a man who had done no harm, in the name of an abstract principle he did not fully understand and with which in any event he did not totally agree, was completely abhorrent. Like most Pelezitereans of his generation, however, he had never been taught to speak directly of ethics or morals *per se*, so he fumbled and had to approach the question from another angle.

"We need Conradin. He is not afraid to fly with us, and we can simultaneously exploit his knowledge and our machines if we work with him."

Centauri shook his head emphatically. "No. He must die now. Do you imagine Natheless would let you kill him after he's worked closely with you? Nonsense."

"Natheless *is* soft-hearted, but not insubordinate, and if you *order* her—"

"Nonsense. It's clear you don't understand your fiancée as well as I do. Send for her now and fire on the barbarian as soon as he enters. Take my advice—simply aim and squeeze the trigger—it works better that way. Don't think."

Of course, Alrik would have to handle the energet. For one thing, it was beneath Centauri's dignity as Interim Archon to do the job himself. For another, his coordination was too poor for it.

Alrik felt as though conflicting forces were tearing him to pieces. Killing the Italian went wholly against his nature, and would also certainly delay or even permanently obstruct the fulfillment of their mission. Yet he was bound to obey the Interim Archon. Even Natheless had told him that. In despair he drew his energet and turned it to a fatal setting.

144

Centauri motioned Floress to fetch Natheless. "Don't tell her what we've been talking about," he commanded.

Natheless walked into the room a few minutes later. Her eyes still showed her exhaustion. But she was quite alert, for her adrenaline had been flowing in anticipation of the confrontation she was expecting—so different in fact from what she was actually facing. After her came Conradin, trying not to seem apprehensive. The Interim Archon had no idea he was receiving the name by which he would soon be known in scores of Italian chronicles, "the sorcerer of hideous aspect," or "the wizard of terrifying visage."

Centauri was intent on other matters. He realized Alrik was standing with the energet half-raised, doing nothing. Would he or would he not obey his order? Natheless glanced at her fiancé as she passed him; Conradin followed, easily within Alrik's range. Still the Fourfold did nothing. About three feet from Centauri, Natheless paused and declared, "Interim Archon, I present King Conradin of the Italians to you."

Jimmik leapt backward and cried, "Strike *now*, Alrik!" Floress backed against the wall and covered her eyes. Alrik slowly raised his energet. But with a surprised shout, Natheless stepped between him and Conradin. "What's going on? What *is* this all about?"

"Get out of the way, Natheless," directed Jimmik. "The barbarian must die."

Conradin was clearly bewildered. He did not understand a word being said, but sensed danger. Alrik was attempting to step around Natheless, but she moved with him, and Conradin, feeling she was the one to trust, contrived to stay behind her. "What is this, Alrik? What are you doing?" pleaded Natheless.

"She refuses obedience at a time of emergency," cried Jimmik. "Kill her, Alrik."

Alrik was by no means the stuff of which mutiny is made. On the other hand, blind obedience was equally certainly not a habit ingrained in Peleziterean Lawchildren. Alrik might have understood why the Prime Directive required Conradin's death, but never Natheless's. He lowered his energet. The moment had passed.

Meanwhile Natheless's thoughts were racing. "You are all acting in violation of the Constitution! If the Archon is really incapacitated, the law states the highest ranking Sixfold is to become Interim Archon. I am the highest ranking Sixfold. Alrik, turn that energet to stun!" Since Alrik was already doing that, nothing happened immediately. He stood expectantly, watching Natheless. Natheless turned determinedly on Jimmik

Centauri. "Lead me to the Archon, Lawchild Jimmik," she declared, "or I'll order Alrik to fire on *you*."

Alrik felt clearer about facing Centauri with his energet. Jimmik Centauri felt the allegiance in the room shift from himself to Natheless.

"You know very well you are still legally a juvenile, Natheless. Your recent increase in rank was an emergency measure, not comporting the least claim to the Archonate."

"If you dispute my authority, the Constitution rules we must both step down until the High Council decides on the permanent Archon. In that case, the Lawchild third in rank becomes Interim Archon. That would be Alrik."

Centauri clearly wanted to say more, but found no words. If this matter were appealed to the High Council, everything would come out. And whatever decision might be made concerning the powers of a juvenile Sixfold in general, Natheless was certain to be praised for raising the question when she did. Whoever became the next Archon (assuming they did not succeed in reviving Benrik Eridani and adding his testimony to everything else), it would certainly not be Jimmik Centauri. His only hope therefore lay in forestalling the intervention of the High Council as long as possible.

Jimmik countered. "Would a mere Medical sub-Archon challenge the yi-Induran prodigy? By no means! If you are convinced you can bring this expedition to a successful conclusion, I'll gladly be rid of responsibility. Don't hold me accountable, however, for the clear violation of the Prime Directive."

"What has this possibly to do with violation of the Prime Directive?" retorted Natheless.

"How can you possibly justify saving this chieftain's life, when you yourself can see his survival has already profoundly altered his planet's configuration?"

"We didn't save him. We found him alive."

"But the hatcherbrats were responsible for that."

"Are you suggesting we should erase every trace of what they did? That is not what the Prime Directive specifies. The Prime Directive requires only that we remove all technological aspects of our intervention. We can accomplish that and be certain of it. Of course, we should keep all other forms of interference to a minimum—if we can. Nonetheless, we knew, under the best of circumstances we would generate some interference. And we certainly never flattered ourselves into believing we could return every speck of cosmic dust to where it was before the hatcherbrats intervened. So the history of this planet has doubtless been changed, though we will never know by how much. And murdering a living man without cause is as certainly murder under these circumstances as under any other. Perhaps the change will be fortunate; perhaps it won't be. All we can do is remove our technology and let the normal cultural laws start operating naturally again." Her explanation flowed smoothly because she had frequently pondered this very question while preparing for this expedition. She had never previously discussed it with anyone. It was no one else's concern. But she was in charge of Contact theory and had to think of its implications. The question was, why had Jimmik Centauri thought of it when he was not in the least concerned with Contact theory?

Jimmik Centauri was almost stymied for the moment. His motive had been to prevent enforcement of the Prime Directive. And he had derived ironic pleasure from believing he was foiling an absurd, impractical law by exploiting its own logical implications. He was astonished by Natheless's ready answer for him. And she was firing more words at him: "If you assent to my Interim Archonate, Sixfold, I want you to lead me to the Archon."

Centauri advanced toward the door. "If you plan to take over my medical duties as well as my administrative ones, you'll be busy."

Natheless spoke to Alrik. "Remain here with Conradin. Try to make him understand what has happened without getting him too upset." The Italian King wanted strongly to follow Natheless. But Alrik successfully persuaded Conradin to stay, explaining he had only acted under direct orders from Jimmik, who no longer had authority. Conradin was in any case not as upset as he might have been, since he had never seen an energet used as a deadly weapon and did not fully understand the danger he'd been in.

In the infirmary, Natheless closely examined the Archon, keeping one eye on Jimmik and one hand near her energet. She was puzzled by the unconscious man's strong breathing, and the absence of emergency equipment. The Archon's face was a shade paler than usual, but that was the only sign of difficulty.

"It looks as though he missed his weekly vifin injection," she observed. "Did he?"

Jimmik demurred. "You ask a doctor with more than thirty years of experience a question like that?"

"Exactly what is wrong with him?"

"I'm a doctor, not an oracle. Since you're so much smarter than I, perhaps you can deduce an answer yourself."

Natheless responded very calmly, "I was asking for your medical opinion, Lawchild Jimmik."

"I have not yet formed one. The tests are not complete."

"I would like to see the records."

"Go right ahead." Jimmik pointed to the data screen.

Still watchful of the sub-Archon, Natheless operated the computer. She was cross-checking facts in her head. She had worked under Centauri for a time in the medical sector. It so happened she had once routinely employed Benrik Eridani's medical history for a special project. And the basic data were still stored in her wrist-computer. Among Jimmik's entries into the computer, Natheless thought she saw an important strand which had been falsified. Consultation with her wrist-computer removed all doubt. Natheless shut down both units and turned her full attention on Jimmik Centauri.

"The Contact expedition must leave for Naples after Jori and Nelsik. We will take the Archon with us and treat him aboard the Skimmer."

Her impudence astonished Centauri. "Are you trying to murder him?"

"Merely overseeing his treatment." Natheless felt quite tense and frightened. She was assuming full command of the landing party on an unproved legal technicality. Now she was also snatching a most important sick man from the care of the Peleziterea's most skilled and honored doctor. Her impulse was to drop everything and flee from the room. But she was certain of what she had seen and of what she knew. She had to act on that knowledge.

Steadying herself, Natheless addressed the Sixfold. "While we are away, neither you nor anyone else is to set foot outside this Lander. I shall prepare for our departure and will personally gather all the medicines the Archon requires. I therefore don't need you for anything. Please return to your quarters."

Jimmik reacted in cold fury. But he was too clever to reveal himself. He shrugged elaborately, and proceeded to leave.

16

Benrik Eridani opened his eyes, unable to understand immediately where he was. These bare blue walls certainly did not belong to his quarters. Yet he had certainly been asleep and where would he be sleeping, if not in his quarters? He tried to recall his last moments of wakefulness, but only normal images connected with arising and the duties of the day came to mind. The last thing he distinctly remembered was sitting on the table in the medical sector after his vifin injection, waiting for the dizziness to go away and looking forward with apprehension to his meeting with the barbarian chieftain. Sleep had not been part of the plan at all. Had he had an attack of some sort? But then, he was surely not in the medical sector, either.

Benrik tried to raise himself, only to find he was strapped around his ankles, thighs, and wrists. He rested back to ponder this. There could be no need to secure anyone so thoroughly except on a moving ship. But the Lander was not supposed to take off, without his order.

Benrik reopened his eyes and found a face looking down at him. Whose? It was a young face, sixteen or seventeen years old, perhaps. Its blue eyes and red hair looked natural, but it was more alert and inquisitive than any hatcherbrat's he had ever seen. Seeing a totally unfamiliar face was an experience adult Pelezitereans rarely had, Lawchildren still more rarely, and Archons never at all. Perhaps he was losing his mind.

The possibility had to be faced. Apprehensive lest the face prove its nonexistence by failure to respond, Benrik whispered, "Who are you?"

He waited a few seconds in utter silence before he heard a series of sounds which might have been organized by an intention but did not resolve themselves into a pattern of words with meaning. Benrik saw the young face staring down at him with concern. Finally, despite a new wave of dizziness, he understood. From his memory sprang the words he had heard from Natheless: "Conradin. King. Italian."

The face lit up. "King Benrik. Peleziterean," said the strange youth, bringing one of his hands to rest on Benrik's arm.

This was the native with whom the Archon was supposed to meet. But, strapped down and helpless as he was, he ought not to have been left alone with him. Who had arranged this? And in any case, a translator was necessary. For the moment the barbarian was Benrik's only resource, and as he looked both friendly and sympathetic, Benrik inquired, "Natheless?"

The youth pointed toward the door. "Natheless," he agreed. "Alrik," he continued. "Floress. Rauhina." Then he pointed to the bunk behind Benrik, out of his field of vision. "Bodris," he said.

"Natheless," repeated the Archon.

The barbarian disappeared momentarily and said something in his own language. A woman groaned and exclaimed, "What? *Cosa?*" Bodris leaped to her feet and stood before the Archon. "You're awake, Sevenfold? I was supposed to be watching you, but I must have fallen asleep. We've had a very bad time." The Italian had already disappeared through the door.

"Where am I?" demanded the Archon.

Bodris responded, "On the Skimmer. We're on our way to Naples. I'm supposed to summon Lawchild Natheless so she can tell you about it."

The Archon continued impatiently, "Unstrap me now, and summon Lawchild Natheless at once."

Bodris released the straps. Before she had quite finished, Alrik rushed into the room with Natheless at his heels. "Father! Are you all right?" demanded Alrik.

"How do you feel, Sevenfold?" inquired Natheless in a more subdued manner.

"I feel fine," said Benrik. "Is there any reason why I shouldn't?"

Alrik fell silent and Natheless answered, "There's no reason why you shouldn't; as far as I know, it was only soporin."

"Soporin? But I don't take soporin. I was supposed to be getting vifin."

Natheless shook her head. "You were certainly given soporin."

The Archon adjusted his wig and pushed some of its stray hairs out of his face. "Did Lawchild Centauri make a mistake?" he asked thoughtfully.

Natheless shook her head. "It wasn't a mistake."

The Archon quickly realized something was deeply wrong. He knew Centauri would never have consented to his boarding the Skimmer. "What happened?" he demanded.

Alrik opened his mouth to speak, but halted. Natheless slowly recounted the series of events, pausing frequently to make sure she wasn't overlooking some essential point. When she finished, the Archon sat pondering for a long time.

"What I don't understand," he said finally, "is how Centauri planned to justify all this to me when I revived. It's perfectly clear his only real motive for murdering the chieftain was to hinder the fulfillment of the Prime Directive. A double violation."

Natheless seemed unwilling to continue speaking, but she took this last remark as a prod. "Lawchild Benrik, he never meant for you to revive. He changed your medical record to make it look as though you needed treatment with soporin. If he had continued with the therapy your altered records indicate you need, it would have killed you in a very short time."

The Archon clutched his heart, and Natheless was alarmed.

"I'm all right," said the Archon dismally. "I'm fine. Tell me precisely what measures you've taken concerning Jimmik Centauri."

Apprehensively Natheless said, "He has been removed from all authority and forbidden to enter the Control Room of both the Lander and the Skimmer.

"Why," demanded the Archon, "didn't you arrest him and inform the High Council? In fact, you should have had him transported back to the Peleziterea before proceeding with this mission."

Natheless was nonplussed. "I—I—I've never put anyone under arrest before, I'm not even sure how it's done. And I wasn't sure the High Council would back me."

Never had she seemed so young, thought the Archon, and never was there a greater need for her to be mature. He tried to imagine her confrontation with Centauri. Of course, she had been on her own in most unusual circumstances. Benrik continued, "Centauri could be stealing the Lander right now, and raising a much greater problem for us than ever Jori or Nelsik have."

"Kappa and Petrik are under orders not to allow him near the controls.

I see no reason why they would disobey—they don't *like* him."

"Of course not, but they're used to obeying his orders and being punished severely when they don't."

"Perhaps we should return and arrest him?" asked Natheless.

The Archon shook his head. "It may already be too late for that. And if we turn back, it will only delay our accomplishment of our other objective. That might even provide an opportunity for the two forces to join. At this point, the only thing we can do is proceed with whatever plan you had in mind, and as quickly as possible."

"That means proceed to Naples?" asked Natheless.

"Yes. But let me call the Peleziterea."

The two stepped back respectfully as Benrik rose. He briefly considered whether he should put on his ceremonial dress, which had been removed during his supposed illness and replaced with a bedgown. He decided against it, and assumed only the seven-star insignia Alrik offered him. Then he went up to the Control room. Rauhina had been at the instruments. She rose respectfully as he appeared. The barbarian, who had been completely absorbed in a viewing screen trained on the surface of the planet below, also turned to face him. "Lawchild Rauhina, can you contact the Peleziterea for me?" said the Archon.

"Yes, Lawchild." Rauhina worked the controls and established contact almost immediately. "I wish to speak with Lawchild Nibbana Parzes," he stated. In a moment, Nibbana appeared in the screen.

"What is it, Sevenfold?" Her eyes expressed wonder at the ruffled appearance of his own image, which she saw in the screen at the other end.

"I am calling to lodge a complaint against Sixfold Jimmik Centauri. It is a matter of attempted murder and treason against the Prime Directive. I or my successor will lay the full details before the High Council and the Full Council when the present emergency has been resolved. In the meantime, Lawchild Centauri is relieved of all duties and confined within the Lander. Under no circumstances is any order of his to be obeyed. In case of my death or incapacitation before the completion of this mission, I formally appoint Sixfold Natheless yi-Induran to act as Interim Archon until the emergency is over and the Full Council can meet to elect a regular Archon."

Nibbana hardly reacted. "Your orders are recorded and will be acted on. Do you wish to supply further details?"

"Not at this time. The Skimmer's computer will feed the account of the events directly to the main computer. We must attend to pressing business. Lawchild Nibbana, have you got an Orbiter in working order?"

Nibbana showed no sign of surprise. "Yes, Sevenfold, we have one ready to go."

"I want Sixfold Rho Smide to take it out right away, with all the operational combat equipment that might be useful. I want him to take a position above the Lander at our base near the mountains. Have him report any changes or movements."

"As you say, Sevenfold." The communication closed, and Benrik turned away. "Maybe that'll make him cautious," he said.

Natheless was watching with a horrified expression. "Me the Interim Archon? I—I thought—"

"You volunteered, didn't you?"

"But I did *that* because—"

"That's no argument. There will always be plenty of becauses."

"But I don't know if I can do—and even you said I made a bad mistake by not arresting Jimmik Centauri and appealing at once to the High Council!"

He reassured her sympathetically. "My child, your mistake is beside the point. You did far better than could reasonably be expected from one of your age and experience in such a situation. You'll find there are times when even your very best is not enough, not nearly enough. But as you yourself say, we can only try, can't we?"

Natheless was touched and upset at the same time. The Archon led her toward the screen where Conradin still watched. "Life's hard, Natheless. It's always been that way. Cheer up. After all, life is also short, fortunately."

Noticing their approach, Conradin regarded them expectantly.

"Am I still supposed to convince this King Conradin I abide by treaties?" inquired Benrik.

"It would certainly help," said Natheless.

"Well, then, let's get to it."

17

It was deep night as the Skimmer flew along the Italian coast toward the Bay of Naples. Conradin was staring intently into a Peleziterean crystal viewer empowered by Pelezite-rean science to show the ground despite the darkness. At least Natheless had explained the crystal box was operated by science rather than witch-craft. He had believed her because he had little choice. The mountains rolling under him looked like intricate carvings, and the lakes were deep-set jewels. The rivers from above looked like grey snakes. As a boy Con-radin had sometimes wondered what the world looked like to birds. Now he was learning.

He concentrated on details, both of the countryside below and of the actions of the people around him, to keep his sense of helplessness from overwhelming him. He understood he had no power to defend himself against these people. Had Natheless wanted him killed, crippled or im-prisoned, she could have arranged it with little trouble. Because his wits would become unhinged if he dwelt on what he could not do, he turned his mind to what he could do and where his hopes lay. Neither Christen-dom nor the Empire, he mused, would ever be safe with such people free to roam the world. The only hope for either lay in his ability to persuade them to share their wisdom with the Italians. He could do this only if he succeeded in learning enough about them to discover the reasons that

would persuade them to abandon the strange law that forbade their set-
tling in Italy. So, with considerable effort, Conradin kept his fear under
control and watched every move the foreigners made.

He watched Natheless the most carefully. He watched her partly because he trusted her to warn him of danger, as she had when they arrived
in the strangers' great Silver Tower. Conradin was almost irritated at how
much he had to depend on her. Yet he resisted yielding to this feeling,
too. Considering the staggering superiority of their power and knowledge,
Princess Natheless was behaving with considerable tact. Conradin was
grateful for that and resolved to reward her appropriately should the
opportunity present itself.

Conradin also watched Natheless because marriage with a Peleziterean
princess was the most obvious means of cementing an alliance between
the two peoples. And Natheless was the highest ranking Peleziterean
woman available for his observation. The more he deliberated, the more
inclined Conradin became to regarding Natheless as a possible match for
himself. Better her than some unknown, possibly higher-ranking, princess who might still be somewhere aboard their ships. From what he
understood of the Infidels' government, the kingship was not hereditary.
In that case a woman from any of the several powerful families was a good
match. Natheless was also obviously high in King Benrik's favor, and
events proved her extremely influential. When he banished the resentment created by his dependence on her, he could observe objectively that
the Princess was good-natured, courteous, wise and quick-witted. True,
Prince Alrik's talk, and hers, about equal honor for women was a little
alarming. But that was an unavoidable hurdle if the Italians intended to
gain Peleziterean science. Anyway, Conradin's close observation had not
detected arrogance in the Princess's manner toward men in her party. She
was evidently devoted to King Benrik, and he seemed to rely on her. She
even contrived to be courteous to her fiancé for the present, Prince
Alrik—quite an accomplishment, since he seemed a complete dolt.

As far as Conradin could judge, an alliance between the Hohenstaufens and the Pelezitereans, sealed by his marriage to Princess Natheless (perhaps reinforced by a union of Prince Alrik to Ginevra, and
doubtless by others as time went on) would produce many advantages.
First of all, it would ensure the victory of the Hohenstaufens over King
Charles, put the Church in its place, and bring new learning and science
to Italy. At the same time it would provide the Empire with an intelligent,
capable Empress, worthy to be recounted in song. Finally, it would
provide Conradin with a wife he could trust and rely on and who might

even (under circumstances more propitious than these), learn to admire and love him. With this last idea, Conradin became truly enthusiastic, for Emperors were rarely able to obtain such a combination of advantages from a marriage. However, he brushed his personal emotions aside and sought to focus on political matters. With both his life and his Empire at stake, this was no time to be dreaming about domestic happiness.

All this while the Pelezitereans stood gathered around another of their crystal viewers, conversing with a red-haired, red-eyed image that appeared within it. Conradin had seen too many strange things in the last few hours to be seriously disturbed by this one. And since he could not understand their speech, he could only watch them. The image spent most of its time listening to King Benrik, and responded only in brief sentences. At length the image vanished and the Pelezitereans turned their attention to him.

"Your pardon, Emperor," said Natheless, as she led the other two toward him. "We regret having left you alone so long, but we have been confronted with great treachery and have had to make many quick decisions."

Conradin assented and gestured toward the crystal viewer, now empty of images. "What were you doing there?"

The Princess answered in the tone she always assumed whenever he asked about her science—something between distress and reluctance. "The King was issuing orders to his lieutenant back with the fleet. He made certain that, in event of his death, I, and not Jimmik Centauri, would act as regent until a new king can be elected."

"Indeed! Then you choose your rulers as the German princes do!" exclaimed Conradin. "The kings of most nations used so to be elected by their nobles and princes, but now most kingdoms have become hereditary."

The Princess nodded. "Customs change, and often change back again. But the basic fashion among us would probably seem strange to you—we assign rank only with duties. Anyone who attains a rank of more than four in any department becomes a prince or a princess and can help to choose, or even be chosen, Archon."

Conradin was really surprised. "The basest, most uneducated peasant can become king?"

Natheless did not agree. "Not really. Positions bearing ranks of four or more are difficult and are not given lightly. Moreover, attainment of the rank of four or more tends to run in families, though legally it is not so-limited."

Conradin was actually amused. "Why would that appear strange to me? High positions in the Church are granted in just such a fashion."

Alrik was translating for the Archon, who studied Conradin with fascination. Conradin waited for the translation to end; then silence fell. It was obvious an important moment had arrived.

"What do you wish to say to the Archon?" asked Natheless, at last. As she spoke, Benrik and his son seated themselves in nearby chairs.

Conradin studied Benrik Eridani's brown eyes, grey hair and pale, tired face. Here, indeed, was a man weighed down by many cares. How could he make him see how much easier it would be for him to consent to Conradin's proposal? Uncertainly, Conradin began, "The Princess has told me you are reluctant to use your science to oppress my people. For that I render you both thanks and honor, and I pray God may reward you. Yet, she also has spoken of your determination to return to a barren land you hate. I see no reason for you to do this. There is land enough and plenty in Italy for your people—great lands, rich lands. You could have them if you will teach us your science and grant us other guarantees to prove your intentions are peaceful." He stopped short of mentioning a marriage alliance; that would come later, after King Benrik had reacted to his first proposal.

The Princess translated. King Benrik listened attentively and sat silent for a moment. Then he spoke to Natheless with a tone which suggested his words were for her approval. She nodded and translated.

"King Benrik thanks you much for your generous offer. He says you cannot know how much it appeals to him. But his conscience forbids him to agree to it. Our science would bring you evils which at present you cannot even imagine."

The earnestness in all three faces regarding him impressed Conradin. Sorcery was dangerous in unexplainable ways; he had heard that. Sorcery was managed by demon-conjuring, and demons were treacherous and deceitful. Yet, surely there was nothing evil about learning natural laws? "Did you not tell me you never dealt with the powers of darkness?" Conradin asked hesitantly.

Natheless translated. As the Archon heard, he said nothing and shrugged. Natheless said, "The Archon does not understand what you mean by powers of darkness, and bids me explain our reasons. I repeat, we do not deal with demons. But I also assure you the more power men gain, the more they control their own fate, and men may not be wise enough to control their own fates."

Conradin gestured. "God made man a creature who mars himself.

157

That is no less true among us as you. How does your science change that?"

The Princess seemed interested, yet sad. Conradin wondered and ached to know what she knew. "You pose a difficult question, Emperor. Must I tell you of all the ways our knowledge has harmed us? We need only be here a short time. Must I teach you to despise us before we go?"

Conradin answered courteously, yet firmly, "I doubt you can, Princess. But if you do not instruct us, I will think bitterly of your people for leaving Italy when you could have done us so much good."

The Princess remained silent. Prince Alrik had again taken to translating both speakers for his father. Natheless continued, "I will tell you a long and weary story." She glanced at the crystal box for a moment. "When our people originally set out on their flight from the land of Urith, they were few in number and had no property. They were all friends. Rank and duties were defined clearly only for the most important positions. When men and women married, their children were housed in one central place, for which duties were assigned, and our many machines, such as this viewer, made the burdens of those who cared for the children light. It was not necessary for parents to see their children frequently to be sure their needs were taken care of. Nothing hindered parents from visiting their children, so many did visit them frequently and took them places. But many others did not bother to take the trouble.

"At first no one noticed any harm. But after several generations, it was noticed only adults whose parents visited them frequently during childhood tended to attain ranks of four or more. Furthermore, people who had been neglected as children neglected their children in turn and often did not even bother to marry. These people, whose fathers were usually unknown and whose mothers paid little heed to them, came in time to be called hatcherbrats. Like everyone, they had the power to vote for the Archon—since that was our law originally—but they were irresponsible, and could not be trusted to perform their duties without the closest supervision. Often they caused riots or even committed impulsive murders. Finally, after one of them in a rage had murdered an Archon during a quarrel over a matter of protocol, the High Council convened and restricted the voting right to Pelezitereans with a rank of four or higher. It also decreed that all persons under the rank of four whose fathers were unknown and who were not married should thenceforward be forbidden to employ dangerous tools or weapons. The hatcherbrats were infuriated. A group of them gathered their silver rods and hunted down whatever

Lawchildren they could find (that is to say, the people who were born into families) and killed them. Lawchildren who could took to their ships and set off away from the fleet. They waited at a distance until the hatcherbrats ran low on food and needed the Lawchildren to return to provide it for them. The Lawchildren agreed, on condition the hatcherbrats would surrender their weapons. It was agreed. The Lawchildren returned, and have enforced these laws against hatcherbrats ever since. Furthermore, because hatcherbrats cruelly taunted young Lawchildren, the families from then on constructed private nurseries to rear their children separately. Some Lawchildren subsequently experimented with various ways to turn hatcherbrats into Lawchildren once more, sending family members in to train them and even bringing young hatcherbrats into Lawchild nurseries. But there were too few Lawchildren and too many hatcherbrats for more than a handful to be influenced in any generation. Come, is that enough of a curse for you?"

Conradin could hardly believe what he had heard. "These hatcherbrats, as you call them, live among you like animals, without law or decency?"

The Princess did not react. "Judge as you will about them; I have told you the truth."

"And the sorcerers in Naples?" Conradin asked shrewdly.

"Precisely! They are hatcherbrats we tried to convert into Lawchildren. That explains why one of them can use the silver rod a little, though not in as many ways as we can."

"Why did you not destroy them all like vermin?" demanded Conradin.

The Princess shrugged. "What would have been the point? They could not understand what they had done. They have no more discernment than babies. That is the deceit our machines worked on us—they enabled us to rear people with healthy adult bodies and full minds but essentially infantile emotions and judgment.

"We could, indeed, have rendered them infertile and so allowed their kind to die out in a generation. But the few remaining Lawchildren at the time deemed that unwise. We needed the vigor of their blood. That was the second part of the curse. Must you hear that also?"

Conradin nodded. The Princess went on. "There were only a few Lawchildren left alive. They could affect only a few hatcherbrats and raise them as Lawchildren. Hence, in the following generations, more and more frequently cousins had to marry cousins. Your people have laws discouraging that. So did ours, before. One reason for it was our belief

159

this kind of intermarriage results in the births of more sickly and deformed children than there should normally be. And so it does.

"Now, when a child is born among us blind or crippled, or with an organ incomplete or missing, the child can be repaired or have the damaged parts replaced with synthetic ones by our wise doctors. So the child lives and grows like other children, and marries and produces children with the same faults. Within a few generations of the first civil war, almost all the Lawchildren were born with not one but many deformities. These can be repaired, but there are too many repairs in each child. The Lawchildren are never strong and must always take medicines. At last, some time in their lives, too many things go wrong simultaneously and they die. So you see, our machines essentially drew all our powers into themselves and grew ever more mighty as we became more feeble."

Conradin was disturbed and doubtful. "I have never known you to lie, Princess—yet your words are strange."

"You doubt me?" the Princess asked. Prince Alrik had continued translating and suddenly the Archon spoke.

"What did he say?" demanded Conradin.

"He says," answered the Princess, "there are ways to prove what I say, only perhaps they would horrify you too much."

Something like terror passed through Conradin, but he answered, "I don't understand."

"The eyes of King Benrik and of Prince Alrik here are artificial, made by our craft because the ones they were born with were defective," said Natheless. "They can prove it by taking them out of their heads. Have you the courage to look upon it?"

Conradin shuddered, but he would be the biggest fool ever born in Christendom if he believed such a thing without seeing it. "Yes," he said.

The Princess signaled his agreement. The Archon and his son reached to their eyes, manipulating their eyelids with their fingers. Suddenly their eyes were rolling in the palms of their hands. Before Conradin could get a full view of the empty sockets, he choked and threw his hands over his own eyes. The Princess's voice broke in. "I'm sorry, Conradin. That was too much to show you. Be patient a moment. They can quickly put them back." A brief moment later Natheless said, "You may look again, Conradin."

Conradin reopened his eyes. He was still upset. But as she had said, the Archon and Prince Alrik looked as before. He turned directly to Princess Natheless, whose lovely eyes had attracted his admiration.

"Are yours counterfeit too?" he demanded.

Natheless was taken aback. She responded, "No, Emperor, our people's curse does not express itself in my body. My family, the yi-Indurans, have given me a double gift. If anything, our problem consists of the hatred we have borne as a consequence. You see, Epsilon Eridani and his companions set up rules when we began our voyage which were meant to keep our race healthy. The yi-Indurans alone among all the Lawchildren have kept them. According to those rules, any child who could not survive with the organs he was born with was not to be allowed to die, but was to be rendered infertile. That way its deformities would not descend to a subsequent generation. But many of us came to consider this practice unwise because there is so much more to a person than his body. Who could say for sure a deformed child did not possess virtues or intelligence which would outweigh physical weakness? So a clause was added to the law allowing special exceptions for children of superior parents. Then exceptions became more common. And after the first civil war—the one with the hatcherbrats—the Council as a rule granted an exception for any Lawchild if it was requested by the family. As a result, only sickly hatcherbrats continued to be sterilized, since only on their behalf did no one bother to make petitions.

"Soon, however, it became clear that by being indulgent with themselves and stern with the others, the Lawchildren were in fact weakening themselves, strengthening the hatcherbrats. So the yi-Induran coalition was formed. The yi-Indurans believe virtue and intelligence are more matters of training and development than of blood, and therefore do not provide reasons for breeding the sickly. They alone, of all the Lawchildren, continued to have their sickly infants sterilized, and simultaneously encouraged such adults to adopt healthy hatcherbrats and rear them as their own. When such children—that is, adopted hatcherbrats—become adults, most Lawchildren disdain them on the grounds of their blood. But for many generations healthy yi-Indurans have been willing to marry them to avoid marrying close cousins. Eventually the other Lawchildren discern their families are not as healthy or strong and marry yi-Indurans. That is why our race has not died out completely.

"Nonetheless my family is often disdained as foolish and body-minded, and we are often jibed at for being related to hatcherbrats."

Natheless paused and waited rather uncertainly. She wondered how Conradin, with his prejudice in favor of kingly bloodlines and sharing the Italians' general horror of anything that interfered with fertility, would react to all this. Although he was pale, he seemed to be trying to weigh the evidence coolly. "None of this poses a problem," he finally said, shrewdly. "If the Pelezitereans settled in Italy, there would in effect be no need to marry so many close cousins. And when we have your example before us, we will see for ourselves how much wiser the yi-Indurans' course was. And we can avoid the mistake your technology led the other families into."

Natheless nodded. "Perhaps you might for a while. Eventually, your people will make the same mistake and not notice it before it is too late. It is always so among men." Natheless could not clarify. If Conradin's culture was to make the same mistakes, it would have to happen on their own, not from the Pelezitereans.

Conradin parried. "Why must you insist on predicting the future? Men can avoid mistakes for themselves, never for their children. Let each generation be wary of its own dangers."

Natheless disagreed. "Your words are wise, yet unwise, Conradin. In many ways you simply cannot protect your children from their own foolishness. But you must understand you now have the opportunity of protecting them from weapons they could easily use to destroy themselves."

"Have I?" retorted Conradin. "You have these weapons, and you say you are attracted by this land. If you leave now, how do I know your descendants with fewer scruples will not return and annihilate all of mine, precisely because you depart today without sharing your science?"

Alrik translated for the Archon. Everyone seemed to sympathize with Conradin's fear. The Princess looked disturbed. "We will erase our navigation records so we can never find this place again."

"Impossible! Among so wise a people there will always be someone who remembers or can guess," said Conradin.

The Princess looked truly distressed. "There are risks, yes. But you can trust us to take the necessary precautions."

"Why, finally, are you so averse to living among us?" demanded Conradin, cutting past all the discussion. Natheless glanced anxiously at the viewing screen, where she could see the white sands of the seashore already rushing to meet them. They were about five minutes from landing, and Conradin was not yet convinced. Did she know the language well enough to manage without him? Would she be able to find her way around inside the city?

Following her gaze, Conradin guessed her thoughts. "Do not be-troubled, fair Princess," he said. "I told you I would help you recapture your subjects, and so I will."

Natheless brightened. "You sounded as though you had begun to disagree with our plans."

"For your sake, we shall first capture the vile hatcherbrats. We can discuss the other things later."

Alrik translated for the Archon. Everyone seemed to relax.

18

"O, God, deliver me from my affliction," Brother Ambrogio prayed, "and release me from my captivity." The words had almost become a habit, a formula he repeated without conscious hope. Most of the time his mind was working on other matters. He certainly understood he and many other people in Naples were being justly punished for someone's sins, probably his own among them. But he could make no clear connection between anything he had actually done and what he was undergoing. His own sins, however serious in nature, had seldom been translated into action; he had never had either power or opportunity, and he had always spent his time, as perfectly as he could remember, avoiding getting them. Obviously his sufferings were therefore part of God's deeper plan. So he could be sure there were opportunities here as well as trial. Consequently, while he kept his prayers for himself and the others who had been struck by the sorcerer's fire-throwing rod rising heavenward, he also kept his attention trained on his captors, trying to divine their thoughts and watching for any opportunity they might offer to speak to them about God.

Considering they were barbaric Infidels probably in league with Satan, they were not particularly cruel. Cardinal Ughetto was known to treat his prisoners more harshly. If anything, the sorcerers' attitude tended to be neglectful rather than malevolent. Since Ambrogio was paralyzed from the neck down and completely dependent on them for food, water and help with his natural functions, this was uncomfortable enough. But the smaller man had taken it upon himself to help Ambrogio a number of times. Since the monk had been careful to smile and express his gratitude in all ways possible, the sorcerer had been touched and in time became devoted to him. He often helped change his position, and even moved him to different parts of the room so he could face different pictures. Ambrogio himself had grown rather fond of this smaller man, whose name was Nelsik. He even found himself wondering doubtfully whether he was really a sorcerer at all or only a victim of the other man, Jori, who wielded the fire-throwing rod.

Jori was perfectly willing to leave difficult or unpleasant tasks to Nelsik, but he often spoke with Ambrogio, clearly trying to learn his language. Thanks to the many pictures, they had done quite well and could already converse in short sentences. Seizing this opportunity, Ambrogio had spoken to them at length of Christ and Mary the Queen of Heaven, of life after death and punishment for the wicked. Often he indicated pictures to illustrate his points, but though both Jori and Nelsik would listen for long stretches, apparently fascinated, Ambrogio somehow felt they were not really absorbing much of it. The ribald laughter and obscene gestures even Nelsik sometimes made when pointing to pictures of the blessed women confirmed his suspicions.

So Ambrogio had passed the last few days, sleeping and waking and praying and conversing with his captors, waiting helplessly for his needs to be attended to. Since he could not work and had no ability to control his body, Ambrogio had lost track of time, waking at irrational hours, without reference to light or darkness. Right now he thought it must be night, because the stained-glass windows were opaque and Nelsik was keeping watch with the light that shone from a sort of band on his wrist. Ambrogio wondered why he had wakened. In his supine position on the church floor, had he felt a slight tremor in the building's structure? Was his suspicion that something was about to happen based on sensation or imagination? Ambrogio strained his head toward the main door, but could not turn far enough to see anything. "Lord God," he prayed fervently, "deliver us, deliver us from bondage and from the servants of the powers of darkness." So even Ambrogio was startled when his prayer was answered by a flash of bright light which lit up the entire room and the appearance of three angels, but not as surprised as he would have been under other circumstances.

The newcomers did not look as Ambrogio imagined angels would, but human imagination was notoriously undependable when it came to divine things. Certainly their stature was erect and commanding as angels' ought to be, and the light shining around them could hardly be interpreted as coming from anything else. But their clothing, at least from what he could see, was dull, somber and rough-looking, just like the homespun worn by Italian peasants. Although that was strange attire for angels, Ambrogio also knew he was unworthy of seeing their true celestial array; perhaps indeed he could not have looked upon it and lived.

Nelsik had seen the apparition and leaped to his feet, staring in mute terror. The foremost angel, who was dressed as a woman, stood facing him and held one finger to her mouth in a gesture clearly commanding silence. Then slowly she made one brisk, emphatic gesture, "Come." Nelsik stared, hesitated, looking anxiously behind him at Jori and back at the commanding angel. Reluctantly, as if unable to resist, Nelsik started toward her. Halfway across the floor, however, he seemed overcome by the desire to defend or excuse himself. He suddenly blurted out a loud babble of incomprehensible words. The lady gestured again for silence, but it was too late. Jori had awakened and leaped up. There was another flash of light, originating from somewhere near the second angel, and Jori immediately crashed back down to the ground. Nelsik cried out, apparently in supplication. The second angel started toward him. Nelsik resignedly held out his hands and the angel bound them with a short chain. The second angel then proceeded on to Jori. But Ambrogio's attention was drawn away because the lady was now standing over him.

He looked up at her, eager and amazed, puzzled by the nondescript color of her hair and her uncertain hazel eyes. Still, there was an unspeakable sweetness in her expression that served suddenly to remind Ambrogio of the error of his assumptions and of the true nature of spiritual beauty. He shut his eyes and praised God.

The angel spoke in a gentle voice, like a woman's. "How goes it with you, Brother Ambrogio?"

"Surely you know, lady," replied Ambrogio, almost without thinking. Then, he hastily opened his eyes, remembering angels have no sex. "If it is proper to call you 'lady.'"

She looked down on him calmly, with the hint of a smile. "You may call me so if you wish. I have come to help you. You are not afraid?"

"Is it right for me to fear anything God has sent?" answered Ambrogio.

The lady paused a moment. It appeared she removed something from her sleeve—something that looked just like the silver rod Jori carried.

166

"Impossible," Ambrogio thought anxiously. "That could not be." Some demon was playing tricks on his eyes. Firmly he closed them again and prayed to God for deliverance. The next moment a vibration passed through his body. With overwhelming joy Ambrogio realized he could once more command his limbs. In an ecstasy he leaped up and threw himself on his knees before her. "Lady, I beg you, tell me your name."

But the lady, quite correctly, backed away. "Why do you wish to know my name?" This was quite in keeping with what Ambrogio had heard of the behavior of angels and the blessed dead who came to the help of unfortunates. Yet she did not give the entire usual disclaimer, so Ambrogio did it for her. "I will thank God for sending you to me."

"Then you will do well," replied the lady. She was apparently preparing to go. Alarmed, Ambrogio pursued her on his knees and grasped at her brown robe. He closed his hand on it, puzzled by its realness, its coarse brown fibers. But there was no use in wondering about that; when God chose to make the invisible visible, you could never tell exactly where he would stop. "Lady, lady, there are many scores in this city afflicted by the sorcerers' rod. Surely you were sent to deliver them also!"

The lady hesitated. "Where may these many afflicted be found?" It was a strange question from one who presumably had instruction from Omnipotence, but now the monk realized he was being tested. "Many are at the bishop's house; some are at the hospital; King Charles is in his palace; and some of the others were carried to their own homes to be tended by their families."

"I will go to the bishop's house," replied the lady, "and to the hospital and to the palace, but as for the others, if they can be brought here within three hours, I will heal them also."

Strictly speaking, there was no reason why one of the saints would need to have people brought to her instead of going to them herself. But when the messengers of God condescended to communicate in human terms, it was better not to argue with them. Therefore, Ambrogio rose with a great show of eagerness. "Shall I run to summon them?"

"Raise your brothers and let others go," returned the lady. "Your limbs are weakened from long inactivity. You will not be able to bear much running tonight."

How wonderfully thoughtful of God's messenger to consider a little thing like that. Ambrogio bowed low before her. "I will obey you, lady. Praise be to God!" He was about to leave, when a sudden thought struck him. The third angel was still standing by the far wall of the room and had not moved the whole time. The second angel had finished binding Jori and Nelsik and was leading them to the lady at the center of the room. Ambrogio pointed to them. "Lady, are these men or demons?"

The lady looked questioningly at him. "They are men. Why do you ask?"

"What will you do with them?"

The lady gestured in a very human manner. "I will do nothing to them. That is for others to decide."

"Lady, I think the smaller man, Nelsik, is not as wicked as the other. He was good to me when I was helpless, and I think it was his terror of the other's weapon that drove him into crime. I hope there is a chance for him?"

To his amazement, the lady bowed to him. "It is good of you to say so, Brother Ambrogio. I will see that it is taken into consideration."

"Praise be to God!" exclaimed Ambrogio. "You are indeed gracious."

"Do not say so," replied the lady, looking almost embarrassed. Ambrogio decided it was high time he left, since the angels seemed weary of his presence. He walked swiftly but carefully to the door and found himself standing in the marketplace before the house of worship. The· night was advancing and there was no moon. Bright stars were shining in the heavens.

Ambrogio dashed through the marketplace, rejoicing in his new strength. He let memory alone guide his feet beyond the square, up the narrow streets. The pungent smell of spices, livestock and dung confronted him in all these narrow ways, but nothing could have seemed more delightful. Presently, after proceeding through many twists and turns, he found himself standing before the great wooden doors of the bishop's house. Despite the hour he banged on them eagerly. "Brothers! Open! It is Brother Ambrogio! I have been freed!"

Voices inside at first rose in disgruntled protest, then cried out in wonder. "Ambrogio! Is it really you?" There came noises from the inside of someone working the bolt, but another voice interrupted, "No! It is a demon's cheat! Bolt the door fast and pray, or he will burst in and destroy us all!"

"Open, fools!" cried Ambrogio, "pray if you like, but open! Angels are visiting the city tonight, and if you do not welcome them, you cause the many who are afflicted by the sorcerers never to be healed! For the angels have told me they would come to our hospital. If you shut them out, they will not come."

The door was hastily flung open. Nearly ten men poured out and surrounded Ambrogio. "Ambrogio! What happened? What angels? Will they also heal the abbot? What did they look like? What did they say? When will they come?"

"Someone must go," panted Ambrogio—his exhaustion was catching up with him—"to the houses where the sick are to tell them they must be carried to the church if they are to be freed from the sorcerer's curse."

"But what did they look like?"

"Like people. A woman and two men in homespun," he panted.

"Those weren't angels, you goose! They must have been saints."

"So I think," replied Ambrogio, "only I will be able to talk better later. I asked the lady her name, but she wouldn't tell me."

"She would not tell you?" repeated another monk suspiciously. The others began to whisper. This was important. If the lady had been some hitherto unknown newcomer into the ranks of the Blessed Dead, she would surely have told him her name. That would increase the glory of God and the joy of those on earth to learn of new blessedness. Hence, her decision not to identify herself indicated she was someone about whom they already knew a great deal, who in modesty would not reveal her name.

"Do you suppose it was *the* Lady?" whispered one.

"The Queen of Heaven?" returned the other.

"In peasant's homespun?" argued a third.

"Why not?" the first rebuked him. "She is humble and loves the poor."

"Brothers," panted Ambrogio, "there will be time enough for disputes later. She has asked for those struck down by the sorcerers to be brought to the square. If this is not done, she will be very angry with you, no matter *who* she is."

Still talking excitedly, they prepared to rush off to complete the mission she had indicated to him.

19

After the Italian monk departed, Natheless found herself in the midst of a verbal crossfire. Nelsik was exclaiming as loudly as he could, "I did not kill the Lawchild Agni. I didn't kill the Lawchild Agni!" Alrik was demanding, "Shouldn't I call the Skimmer now?" Conradin was musing, "He took you for an angel. No doubt he will raise the whole city." Jori had recovered from his temporary stun and was adding to the din. "Isn't this really stupid? If any of you had any sense, you'd join us instead of attacking us."

Natheless turned to Alrik. "Yes, summon the Skimmer." Then she faced the hatcherbrats. "Quiet! Your time to speak will come at the inquest, not before. Right now I want to know what you did with Agni's body."

Nelsik looked away. Jori answered defiantly, "You know we couldn't disintegrate the body properly with the energet only set on stun. We had to leave the body outside, and the barbarians took it. They cut off his head and stuck it on a pole on the other side of the square. I have no idea what they did with the rest of the body. I was going to make them bury it as soon as I learned their language." He didn't appear to think that made much difference.

Natheless felt sick with anger and grief. "What about his equipment?"

"There." Jori nodded toward the middle of the room, where a heap of blankets and the portable food-transformer were also stacked. Natheless knelt over the pile and sorted for the particular items she had been looking for—Agni's helmet and suit and his personal wrist-unit where his apprenticeship experiments and his records of a number of mutually shared adventures were stored. Conradin watched curiously as she strapped it to her wrist behind her own.

Alrik had already taken the energet. With the portable survival kit, it completed the list of Peleziterean implements which had to be removed from the planet's surface. Seeing she had every item, Natheless was enormously relieved. "Once these things are inside the ship, our mission is virtually complete—assuming Jimmik has done nothing to the contrary in our absence," she said to Conradin. At that moment she felt the signal from her wrist-unit. "The Skimmer is outside," she added. "Let's go," she called to the hatcherbrats.

Their hands were cuffed and they knew she had her energet, so she had no need to draw it. They followed her sullenly. Jori continued to protest, "I did not kill your brother." Nelsik had already given up and was silent.

"I am glad about that," said Natheless quietly. "Agni selected the two of you from among the hatcherbrats because he believed you had the greatest promise. He hoped someday you might be admitted to the ranks of the Lawchildren. He wished the best for you. It would have grieved him immeasurably to know you had turned on him. But according to the Constitution, members of the victim's immediate family may not sit in judgment at a murder trial. It is a wise law, for which we may all be grateful."

The Skimmer had settled noiselessly to the ground before the church. Alrik entered. The hatcherbrats were quickly hustled aboard. Natheless spoke to Conradin, "Rauhina, Alrik and the Archon can remain aboard to guard the prisoners and the Skimmer. I alone can heal the other paralyzed people, if you will lead me to the bishop's house, the hospital and King Charles's palace. Do you know these places?"

"I will lead you there," said Conradin, though his distaste for the final part of the task was obvious.

"First I must remove Agni's head from the pole." They crossed the square; Natheless tried to detect an odor and simultaneously to block her awareness that it would be her brother's head exuding it. She swept the square with her wrist-light. "There it is," said Conradin. Natheless saw a long wooden pole firmly stuck into the dusty ground. Atop it a blackened, insect-ravaged piece of flesh was hardly recognizable as a human head. She turned the light away and nearly groaned. She was dimly aware

Conradin had approached. She heard him speak, but the meaning did not register. "What?" she murmured distractedly.

"Did you know him well?" repeated Conradin.

"He was my brother!" Natheless choked. She clutched involuntarily at her throat, wondering how this critical piece of information had somehow not been conveyed in all their past conversations.

"May God have mercy! You did not tell me!" exclaimed Conradin.

"I thought I had, from the first!"

"You said your subjects had killed your brother. This is the man King Charles killed."

"My meaning was our subjects are responsible," said Natheless. "King Charles cannot be held responsible for striking a frightening interloper who suddenly appeared before him in a way which probably marked him as evil according to his own understanding. It was Jori's and Nelsik's fault my brother came there in that fashion."

Conradin protested, "The sorcerer made no threats, though there was a bright and terrifying light when he appeared. Yet he drew no weapon. It was Charles who struck first. *I* would not have attacked him, if I had been in command. But then King Charles had a guilty conscience." Conradin pursued, "Do you really mean to heal this man who murdered your brother?"

"In truth, Emperor," replied Natheless as she also signaled the Skimmer, "I cannot feel anger against King Charles. He struck against a terrifying creature of his own imagination and knew nothing whatsoever about my brother. I am angry with the hatcherbrats. They knew perfectly well Agni would sacrifice his life for the Prime Directive, yet they betrayed it and therefore him—though I must say I do not think they really intended his death."

"You amaze me, Princess," said Conradin slowly. "Your words are just, but without feeling."

"We Pelezitereans are a cold people, Emperor. A sad, cold people. Be thankful that you do not bear our burdens."

One benefit of their conversation was that it distracted her from the memories of the living Agni which his head had raised. The head on the pole was only a mass of decaying flesh to be disposed of. The Archon's reply came from her wrist-computer.

"Incinerate the head at once. What do you hope to gain by staring at it?"

Natheless raised her energet, turned it to a middle setting and aimed it at the head. A brief, blinding flash, and both head and pole had disappeared. Natheless turned quickly, suddenly aware she had not prepared Conradin adequately for what would happen. He had already seen the energet noiselessly burn a hole through the stone wall of the church large enough to admit them all, so he was not too startled. The young Italian was staring at her, but the question he asked caught her completely off guard. "Do you believe in the afterlife?"

Natheless replied distantly, "Why do you ask that?"

Recollecting their purpose, Conradin started down a narrow alley beneath an unsightly collection of wooden balconies. "Come. The hospital you wish to visit is this way." Natheless followed him, and Conradin continued, "I asked because I wanted to say the comforting things Christians say to their friends when members of their family die. We say, 'He is in God's hands; may he rest in peace.' But I do not know what you believe, so I had no idea whether those words would have any meaning for you."

Natheless responded. "I thank you, Conradin. We do not believe as you do, but it comforts me that you wished to say something comforting."

That caused Conradin to check his stride long enough for her to come abreast of him. "Poor Natheless, have you no other comfort? Do you believe you will see your brother again? It must be a grievous loss for you if you do not."

She had, for the first time, addressed him with the familiar *tu* form, and he had immediately responded in kind. Natheless pondered before deciding what to respond. It was a touchy subject, not that she was opposed to discussing it. But how far could she go without risking metaphysical interference? She knew by now Conradin was quite unusual for his society and culture. Perhaps no idea she could put into his head would have any effect at all on the metaphysics of the planet. Besides, he was really being very generous, helping the Pelezitereans in a manner that might rebound to his disadvantage. If she could not give him the material rewards he desired, the least she might do was offer frankness and honesty since he seemed to want that. Natheless gave up debating the possible consequences of her words and answered honestly, "My brother's death really is grievous to me, as were the deaths of my mother and father. I do not know whether I will ever see them again. My people believe not as you do. The topic is seldom even discussed among us. I do not especially agree with what my people tell me is the truth, but I do not know of any other. I am glad your beliefs give you so much comfort."

"They do not always give me comfort," retorted Conradin. "The priestly party claims to control who goes to the happy places in the next world and who to the wretched ones. And my family has been at war with the priests for years. So I believe I will meet my friends again in the land where God reigns over the blessed, but Charles would tell you I will meet them where Satan is eternally tormented with the wicked. Since your people have gained great power over nature and have flown near Heaven where God dwells, I thought you might also know the truth of these matters."

"You are not, then, satisfied with the truths your priests have told you?"

"At times I am not. I think they have often said things in hatred rather than justice, and sometimes I think they are not very wise."

"Yet you seem to think the truth is something worth knowing?" inquired Natheless.

"How not?" returned Conradin, apparently quite surprised.

Natheless considered. It was imprudent to speak, but in a way it was exhilarating to think he could not immediately dash off to inform Personality, as some of her Peleziterean confidants had done. "Suppose, Conradin," she said slowly, "suppose you learned beyond a shadow of a doubt that the Universe was wide, cold and empty. Suppose the things that give warmth and joy to human beings have no meaning there but are only accidents, and unlikely ones at that. If you learned this, would you go forth to tell others, or would you keep it to yourself?"

"I believe I would keep it to myself," replied Conradin, after some thought.

"So would I, Conradin," said Natheless. "Let's proceed."

Conradin led her out of the narrow alley and into a broader avenue flanked by massive buildings. "But, Princess Natheless," he said, "you did not keep it to yourself. You just told me."

"Did I?" Natheless asked. "I'm sorry. I deserve your censure. But now you know the full nature of the burden on us which must not be spread."

"Yes, I know now. I wanted you to stay in Italy believing your people could help mine. Now I see you are in worse trouble than I am."

"Do you think so? You're probably right. But one's own troubles usually seem worse to oneself."

"You ought to stay in Italy, to find a cure for yourselves."

"How does one cure the truth, Conradin?"

"There is no cure for the truth, but for lies that masquerade as the truth, there is a cure."

"What's this?" Natheless glanced at a patch of stars which suddenly became visible to them through a gap in the houses. "A moment ago we were discussing the truth. Now you talk as though you have it."

"As danger makes a warrior bolder, so your despair has increased my hope."

"I am glad of that, Conradin. So may it ever be for you. I wish it were so for me. When the yi-Induran family was founded so many years ago, its founders took their name from a scholarly language. In that language yi-Induran means 'I hope.' Ever since then members of my family have borne names which express 'I hope.' The first founder was Garik yi-Induran, 'I hope in the years.' My father was Frofor yi-Induran, 'I hope for consolation,' and my mother was Urmis yi-Induran, 'I hope in compassion.' But I was born just after a series of deaths among the Lawchildren, and the head of our family was on trial for treason because he assigned too many yi-Indurans of great ability to duties outside the central government. At any rate, my parents named my brother Agni yi-Induran, 'I am fiery with hope.' But when I was born they were running out of things to hope for, so they gave me the name derived from the old form of a word in our language, 'in spite of everything,' or 'Nevertheless.' So my name means, 'Nevertheless I hope.' But it is not easy to hope 'nevertheless,' or for no reason at all."

They had gone a considerable way along the avenue and had arrived at the large building Conradin said was the bishop's palace. A number of robed men bearing oil lamps hurried their way past them along the opposite side of the avenue. Natheless extinguished her wrist-light and drew closer to Conradin. "Who are they?"

"Monks, canons—perhaps bearing your message, perhaps looking for you. They took you for a messenger from God, come to heal them in response to their prayers, and they are greatly excited."

"What does all that imply?" inquired Natheless a bit edgily.

"If you sustain the pretense, they will do anything you say, so long as it doesn't discord with their conception of you too drastically. But if they discover what you really are, they will certainly try to kill you. If they did take you alive, they would chain you to a stake, pile wood around the base of it and set it ablaze, to burn you to death for being in league with Satan or other demons. They would treat me the same way for being your accomplice."

"I have my energet to protect us. Are you worried at all?"

"Not I; but it will take you forever to get anything accomplished unless you keep up your role."

175

"How can I to do that best?"

"That's fairly simple. Act precisely as you did with Brother Ambrogio. Refuse to tell anyone your name. Whenever anyone tries to thank you, instruct him to give thanks to God. The main danger is from your silver rod. The monk Ambrogio shut his eyes when he saw it, but you cannot count on everyone to do that. If too many people see it at once, they may become suspicious. Can you keep it hidden?"

"I suppose I could keep all but the very point inside my sleeve," said Natheless. Her brown native garment had long, flowing sleeves. "But if anyone were close enough, he might see it anyway. If everyone attacked at once, they would seize me before I had a chance to knock them all out."

"Then command them not to approach within twenty paces of you," said Conradin. "They'll ask no questions. That would also be wise for another reason—there might be cause for me to say something to you while we're in there. If they heard us speaking in the vulgar tongue, they would certainly be suspicious."

"Why, what language do angels generally speak?"

"I do not know; either Latin or a heavenly one, I imagine," said Conradin. "But it is perfectly acceptable to address them in the vulgar, because you are condescending to communicate with them. Many of them do not know Latin very well beyond the words of the mass."

The details seemed clear. Natheless tuned her wrist-unit to its highest intensity. Six of the monks cried out in astonishment. "Hail!" she called to them solemnly.

The monks fell instantly to their knees. Some bowed their heads, while others raised their hands heavenward and returned her greeting. "Hail, messenger, if you be from God. What is your will with us?"

"I have come to release those who are under the sorcerer's spell," replied Natheless. "Am I welcome in your house?"

"Who are we to deny you entrance?" replied the canon who had made himself their spokesman.

"That is well. Pray open the door and go before me, but do not approach within twenty paces, for fear of the Power.

"It shall be, lady, as you command."

When it was over, this part of the episode would stand out in Natheless's mind as effortless. They opened the great door, and ushered her and Conradin in just as she instructed. The six priests preceded them at a respectful distance. They followed a long corridor to a room containing a bed where lay a man whom Conradin called the Abbot Sinibaldo. There followed other corridors and more stairs and rows of beds, first in the canons' infirmary, then in the hospital. She kept the energet concealed within her sleeve the whole while, and if anyone noticed it, no one said or did anything about it. When they were done, Conradin led the way to the palace. As they were proceeding, an urgent signal came in on her wrist-unit from the Skimmer in Naples.

"Sixfold Natheless yi-Induran, the Orbiter reports that the Lander has taken off from our base in the Mountainfoot. Sixfold Jimmik must have won over our hatcherbrats. How much more business do you have?"

"Just one more appointment, Sevenfold."

"Finish as quickly as you can. At the moment he's not coming fast, but try to be back soon. I'll let you know if there's a change."

Natheless quickened her pace. "How fast can we go, Conradin?" she inquired.

20

Young Prince Charles of Salerno could not sleep that night. Though the walls of his gaily decorated chamber were thick and strong, and loyal guards stood vigilant at the doorway, for him his room was filled with a shapeless dread. He had tossed and turned for several hours, trying to sleep. He knew his father despised him for his lameness and the sensitivity he called weakness. He was sincerely ashamed of his failings and wished he could ameliorate them. But his uneasiness grew ever stronger, until he could hardly endure it. Finally, throwing back his covers, the Prince sat up and called out, "Étienne!"

His tutor rose from his pallet in the neighboring room and entered. "What troubles you, Your Highness? Can't you sleep?"

"No," replied the youth, shaking his head. "I keep imagining King Manfred's sons. They haunt me. And Conradin. How could a king be sentenced to death for trying to recover his kingdom! What would he do to us if he had us in his power?" Prince Charles threw on his shirt to ward off the night air.

"Are these thoughts fit for a prince?" demanded Étienne in his sternest tone. "Wicked men always persecute the just when they get them in their power. Let them meditate what crimes they will in their black hearts but do not let them disturb your slumber."

Prince Charles was not moved by the argument. He took hold of his crutch and stood. "I'm not really afraid of what they might actually *do*—it's more the idea of their doing it, and everyone's believing we might *deserve* it—including me."

"Your Highness's conscience is overscrupulous," grumbled Étienne. "Conradin is a criminal, excommunicated by the Pope."

"I know," said the youth, making his way restlessly to the window, "but is that so strange? Churchmen are often troublesome. My father doesn't always agree with them either. Suppose the Pope excommunicated my father? Would that give someone the right to chop off *his* head?"

"The Pope would never *dare* condemn King Charles," returned his tutor, following him to the window. "He has no one else to rely on."

"Does that mean my father would deserve it if the Pope had other resources? Or that Conradin wouldn't if he had served the Pope's interests?" pursued Prince Charles.

"Your Highness has an oversubtle mind," his tutor got out. "Remember, you are King Charles's heir, and not destined for the Church. Lay aside such quibbles. Perhaps a walk along the walls would calm you."

"Perhaps," remarked the youth. "I will go. You need not accompany me if you wish to rest."

"I'll come," rasped his tutor.

In his heart, Étienne cursed the young Queen who had caused all this misery. He personally would have been delighted to live on, happily oblivious of the captives' sufferings. But Queen Marguerite had taken it into her head to inquire into the dungeon where Conradin's cousins, King Manfred's three sons, had been kept in chains since their capture two years before. Abbot Sinibaldo had originally made her conscience uncomfortable with something he had mentioned to her about it. Besides that, the Queen believed it might also be expedient to placate the Hohenstaufens by treating their children better. Moreover, releasing them might actually stir confusion and dissension in the Hohenstaufen camp because Manfred's children were more closely related to Anticoli and Bianca then Conradin was.

Marguerite therefore believed her approach to be superior on several levels. But as soon as the children were produced, it became apparent her stratagem could not be put into play immediately. The young Princes were in no condition to win over or confuse anyone among the Hohenstaufens' allies. They were filthy, sick, and half-starved, matters which could be rectified with comparative ease. But more distressingly, two of the three appeared totally mad, uninterested in their surroundings in spite of everything the Queen and her ladies attempted. They would not respond to blandishments or offers of playthings or sweets. They simply sat in the middle of the Queen's private chamber, rocking back and forth and muttering to themselves. The second child had eventually been persuaded to tell them his name—Arrigo—but then he had proceeded to work himself into a passion, running from one brother to the other, calling out their names and weeping when they would not respond.

At that very moment, Prince Charles and Étienne had unfortunately stumbled upon the proceedings. The Prince was shocked when he learned what the Queen had dared do behind her husband's back, and threatened to reveal it. But the young Queen had burst into a rage, letting loose the fury of bad temper that had been accumulating since her marriage ceremony less than a month before. "You miserable, spiteful cripple, if you tell your ailing father about this, I'll take my dowry and return to France! Two years ago all these boys were stronger and more promising than you, and though you're older, had you been treated as they were, you'd have become an idiot much faster than they, legal-minded, frail and faint-hearted as you are! Consider that! Unless your father recovers quickly enough to start leading his knights, that's precisely what will happen to you, unless you give the Hohenstaufens some reason to show you mercy! I was a fool to throw in my lot with yours after Conradin's escape! If I'd also known your father had done this, I'd have made my decision another way." She gestured angrily toward the wretched children and exclaimed, "Look at them! Perhaps you'd like to be treated in this fashion!"

Struck by her anger, her fear and the force of her arguments, as well as by the awkward secret thus put into his possession, Prince Charles had retired from the scene in confusion. And it had troubled him ever since.

"Étienne," mused the Prince, "I am going to see King Manfred's children." He returned to his bed and finished dressing.

"Those idiots?" His tutor shuddered. "Haven't you had enough of them?"

"No," returned the Prince firmly. "I'm going to them, no need for discussion."

"But, Your Highness, they will disturb your thoughts even more!"

"It is sometimes strangely soothing to know the worst," said Prince Charles as he proceeded slowly along, relying on his crutch.

"The worst what? What are you talking about?" demanded his tutor, anxiously keeping pace with him.

"The worst I may deserve. And perhaps I can do something for them."

For a soft-hearted prince he could be obstinate. His tutor uttered a low groan of resignation and could only follow him. Prince Charles made his way doggedly until he reached the door of the private chamber where the young prisoners had been lodged. Two stout French guards were on duty there. They saluted the Prince but blocked his path.

"The Prince wishes to converse with the Hohenstaufen Princes," said Étienne. "Let him enter."

One of the Queen's ladies, Marie, heard their conversation and came out from the chamber. "What does His Highness wish here? Only one of the captives will speak at all, and even he is fairly sullen."

"I wish to see him, Lady Marie," said the youth patiently. "Allow me to enter."

At a sign from Marie, the guards parted to allow them past.

If King Charles had had another son, this might have served as a chamber for him. It was like Charles's room, richly furnished, with bright pictures of hunters, hounds and game painted on the walls. Because of the condition of the room's present occupants, the lights had not been extinguished that evening. Three candles burned low in the holders along the wall behind the straight-backed chair in which Marie had been sitting. Her gigantic shadow leaped and flickered confusedly against the opposite wall, projected by the movements of the three flames. The curtains on the single large bed had not been drawn, either, and all three boys could be seen clearly. One of them was lying on the far side of the bed, a hand in his mouth, sound asleep. The second was sitting bolt upright, rocking back and forth rhythmically. The third sat on the edge of the bed toward them, following their approach steadily but uncuriously. Charles approached slowly until he stood within five paces of him. The two Princes stared at one another in silence.

"I wish you good health," began Charles at last, politely.

Arrigo stared back and said nothing. Charles continued, his tongue almost lame, "I am Prince Charles of Salerno, the heir to the throne. I would like to be your friend."

The boy's face seemed to flicker, but he continued his silence. Charles thought he understood why. He said, a little defensively, "Yes, I know you believed you were the heir to the throne, but your father was a usurper."

"*Your* father is a French swine." For a small and rather haggard boy, he hurled his insult with the tremendous force of conviction. Prince Charles was shocked. He tried to conjure a reply at once conciliatory, true and consistent with his loyalty to his father. But nothing came to him, and tears welled in his eyes instead.

Étienne intervened. "Prince Arrigo, His Highness has come in friendship, hoping to comfort you. Is there anything he can do for you?"

Arrigo looked away from the lame Prince and regarded the tutor for a moment, trying to gauge his argument. At length he spoke indifferently. "Why did you wait so long? It was dark down there and they beat us whenever we talked about escape. All we could do was make pictures in our head. And now my brothers have forgotten how to see anything else." He pointed to the others on the bed and stared gravely at Prince Charles.

The youth felt himself guilty. A few tears rolled uncontrollably down his cheeks. "I didn't know," he protested. "No one told me. If I had known, I would have begged my father—" But of course, his father would not have paid him any attention. King Charles never paid any attention to his lame, tender-hearted son. He turned his head to wipe his eyes.

This display of emotion stimulated a sympathetic reaction from Arrigo, but Arrigo did not know precisely how to interpret Prince Charles. Following a vague impulse to move closer to Charles, he slid to the floor. After a few steps he pointed to the crutch. "Why do you need this?" he demanded.

Prince Charles was startled out of his tears. "I'm lame," he said. "When I was a small boy, I fell from a horse. I broke my leg and it healed crooked. So I have to walk with a crutch." Arrigo stared, and Charles added by way of pleasantry, "I will never be able to dance, but I can ride well enough."

Arrigo looked at him thoughtfully. "I have not ridden for a long time, except when I dreamed in the dark. But it wasn't really good, because I was always alone in the dreams. Even when I brought Manfredino and Anselino into them, it wasn't really they, it was only my picture of them. That's why I tried to dismiss the pictures and really talk to them, but the guards wouldn't allow me. Now my brothers won't even answer when I call their names!"

Arrigo spoke so fervently, Prince Charles could not doubt he told the truth. Still the older boy could make little sense of what Arrigo was saying. Therefore, he tried to turn the conversation to a more comprehensible topic. "Perhaps they will let us ride together."

Arrigo's face brightened. "I would like that!"

Just then the silence of the night was rent by cries from the area of the postern gate. "Who goes there? Halt! *Mon Dieu!*" There were shouts, roars and sounds of scuffling, and then suddenly all was silent. Marie and Étienne were alarmed. Étienne exclaimed, "What was that?"

"Shall we inquire, my lady?" asked one of the guards outside the doorway.

Marie nodded. "Run immediately, find out and report to us quickly."

The two retainers ran off down the hall. The noise of their footsteps faded into the distance. They all waited tensely for the sound of their return.

It never came. All was silent. And in the silence only the tense sound of their breathing grew louder and louder. "They've been gone a long time," whispered Marie. "Why haven't they—"

At that moment, they heard the sound of other footsteps in the hall— not bold and hasty like those of the knights who had just left, but slow, steady, rather stealthy. Marie drew in her breath slowly, and Étienne strode nervously toward the door. As he did so, two figures passed through it. Both were dressed in coarse brown peasant homespun. The first remained hooded and stood in the background; the other's hood fell back to reveal Germanic red hair. There were some red-haired peasants near Naples, but Charles knew this man was not one of them. He had only seen him once before, but he recognized him immediately as he might recognize a nightmare. "Conradin! You're Conradin!" he cried, frozen still in the center of the room.

21

Conradin was momentarily unnerved. If the Pelezitereans were not going to join him, there was no use in his gaining a reputation for accompanying Infidels and sorcerers on their journeys through the air. His falling hood had not helped matters, but even so, he had not expected to be recognized quite so quickly. He studied the youth in the center of the room, and suddenly understood. "Ah! You are the lame Prince Charles!" he cried, in a tone mingling contempt with impatience.

"So you've come to kill us all with sorcery, Hohenstaufen?" challenged Prince Charles with the best defiance he could muster. "You have quite despaired of finding *men* to follow you?"

Conradin let his emotions flow. "Son of a vagabond French plunderer, I would be only too happy to drive my sword through your heart. But I have come here not on my own business. It is your good fortune I serve a gentle lady who has begged your life in advance."

Charles was struck speechless, especially since the lady in question now came forward and laid a nervous restraining hand on Conradin's arm, thereby apparently confirming his words.

Arrigo was already running across the room. "King Conradin! My cousin Conradin! Take us away from here!" With desperate haste the child threw himself at Conradin's feet. "Take us away, Cousin!"

Conradin stared down in bewilderment at the haggard face and ulcerated wrists. He shuddered in recognition. "You are one of my Uncle Manfred's sons! But how came you to be here?"

"They brought us up here out of our prison! I am Arrigo, and my brothers no longer answer when people speak to them."

Natheless was bewildered. "Who are all these people, Conradin?" she asked. "Charles isn't here, and we must make haste."

At the mention of Charles's name, Étienne, Marie and Prince Charles cried out. Arrigo only kept exclaiming, "Take us away from here, King Conradin! I beg you, I beg you!"

Conradin addressed the lady. "These are my own cousins, grandsons of an Emperor, who have been bound in chains as if they were animals, and treated with as much charity as if they were snakes. Surely as good and kind as you are, you would not insist I leave them here!"

Natheless studied the boy at Conradin's feet and the other two on the bed. "These are King Manfred's children, about whom you told me? It's clear they have been ill-treated! But it looks as though they are being better dealt with now."

"Because I have escaped and Charles fears me! After you leave and my cause is weakened, they will be thrown back into chains again. You cannot desire that, Princess. It ought not anger your King if you succor them; their release will not aid my cause by very much. But the children will live and die among their own kindred instead of among enemies."

Natheless recalled an unhappy Peleziterean Lawchild who had tried to starve herself to death when she was sequestered from her family in the Personality Bubble. "Believe me, Conradin," she said, "I would like to help these three children, but how are we to bring them away? Two seem to be of unsound mind, and we must travel with all possible haste!"

"We could borrow horses from Charles's stable and ride back."

"Ride!" The lady seemed appalled. "I have never ridden one of those animals you call horses. I'm sure I don't know how."

It was Conradin's turn to be startled. "Never ridden!"

"We do not have them in our country. I told you how barren it was," Natheless explained.

"It is obviously more barren than I ever dreamed a land could be!" returned Conradin. "Can you not summon your flying ship to come for us here?"

Natheless shook her head vehemently. "There is no time. They must be poised and watchful for Jimmik Centauri."

"You have already told me we hardly have the time to return before the one of hideous aspect arrives, even if we start back right now. I am certainly loath to spend time healing my enemy Charles, who is merciless, and spend no time saving my blood relatives who need mercy." Conradin seemed determined.

"You are right," replied Natheless. "Let us go." She rushed from the room. Conradin and Arrigo rushed after her.

Conradin inquired, "Are we going to accomplish both tasks then? A fair balance—let us indeed heal King Charles as you planned, and then bring all three of my cousins away."

"Good," declared Natheless. "Now where is he?"

Conradin turned to Prince Charles. "Order these people to lead us to your father," he said, indicating Marie and Étienne. "They know where he is, and we can't leave them here anyway, or they'll remove my cousins."

Marie and Étienne refused. "We'll tell you nothing, slave of Satan!"

Natheless pleaded with them. "Do not be frightened, and do not delay us. We have come to heal Charles, not to harm him. I have the power to cure King Charles's affliction, and I shall, if you lead me to him. But we are in a great hurry and if you resist telling us where he is, you will force us to leave him uncured."

"A likely story, witch!" sneered Étienne. "Doubtless that is why you came to Charles's palace in the company of his mortal enemy."

Natheless continued. "His mortal enemy, as you call him, has been a courteous friend to me. He has helped me accomplish a task which is my responsibility and concerns him little. However, since I can't persuade you, I'll have to put you to sleep as I already have the guards. It won't permanently deprive you of your limbs as the other sorcerer's blows did, but it will put you into a deep sleep for at most half an hour. When you wake you will not even remember having seen me. If you will take my advice, you should lie down to avoid being bruised when you fall."

Étienne paid no attention and took his fall to the ground. Prince Charles was terrified.

But when Natheless turned her energet on Marie, she cried out, "No, don't strike me! I will take you to the King—only—spare the Queen. She is innocent, and took no part in any of the attacks on the Hohenstaufen house."

"Treason!" cried Prince Charles. Marie stood her ground, frightened as she was. Charles rushed not toward her but at Conradin. "Son of a viper!" he cried, cursing himself for not having a weapon with him. He wished the Hohenstaufen would draw his sword as he had threatened and run him through, ending his humiliation. But Conradin met his hand-to-hand attack in kind.

"Lame Foot, you're not a very sharp arrow in your murderous father's quiver!" Conradin grappled with him briefly and threw him to the ground.

"You'll—burn in Hell!" gasped the French Prince helplessly. Conradin held him pinned with one hand.

Conradin spoke mockingly. "What did you say? I don't think I heard you."

"I said you'll burn in Hell!" panted Charles, struggling frantically to escape from his hold. Conradin snapped his fingers before the frantic Prince's face. "So you're stubborn, Frenchman! You could still be wrong."

Charles heard the lady speak. "Conradin, get out of the way if I am to stun him without stunning you."

But Marie pleaded, "In God's name, don't harm the boy! You see he's crippled and can do no harm. I will lead you to his father."

"Then do so and let us be done with talking," said Conradin.

"No!" cried Prince Charles, struggling desperately to rise. Conradin pinned his arms behind his back and pulled him to his feet. "Be quiet, Prince Charles. It so happens we mean no harm to your father this night."

Since he had been fairly overpowered and had said everything appropriate to his honor, Prince Charles allowed himself to be led from the room in silence.

King Charles was not asleep when they arrived in his chamber. His helplessness generally made him restless at night and suspicious of those who guarded him. This night he had already been awake for about an hour, believing he heard strange noises. But weary from many nights of little sleep and wary of doubts that led to nothing, he was unwilling to summon his sentries to demand yet another fruitless search. As the suspicious noises approached closer to his chamber, however, he grew increasingly tense. The sounds followed no pattern he could understand. Surely if it were a matter of a surprise attack on the castle, at least one of his many servants would have had the chance to sound the alarm. Finally, when he heard a slight disturbance in his anteroom and then the wooden door to his chamber slid slowly open, he was alarmed beyond measure. Instinctively he tried to rise, forgetting he could move little more than his head. He fell back, in anguish, and called out, "Guards! Where are you?"

There was no answer except the low sound of voices outside his room. The King was further mystified when he recognized one of them as the voice of his eldest son.

"—and let God be the judge in a fair fight!"

A youthful voice with Germanic intonations answered scornfully, "You'll have to find a champion, because I won't fight a cripple." King Charles had not heard much from Conradin, but he believed he recognized the voice. The subsequent exchanges confirmed his suspicions.

"I could make you eat your words, coward, if only you would let me have a sword!"

"I don't recall your making me that offer when I was the prisoner here," returned the German voice.

King Charles once more struggled to rise. "Are you there, Conradin?" he bellowed. "Why do you tarry? Come quickly! Do you think I am afraid to die?"

The voices fell silent at once. The footsteps, however, entered his chamber. Most of them halted, but a single figure continued across the floor. Finally a woman's face swam into his field of vision in the dim light. Charles stared at her. She was dressed in peasant garments, but her face was too pale for a woman used to labor in the sun. She addressed him courteously in Italian, but with an accent he could not place. "What cheer, Sire?"

"Most ill, slut!" he replied shortly. "Where is Conradin?"

Quite unperturbed, she answered, "I have come to heal you of the affliction the sorcerers have laid upon you."

"You lie, witch! I will do nothing at your bidding. God may deliver my body into Conradin's hands, but my soul at least is proof against your wiles! Go and tell your youthful dupe he will have to use his weapons after all, though I suppose killing a bedridden man will not cause him much inconvenience!"

Despite his bravado, the King could not suppress his fear when the witch suddenly drew a gleaming rod of silver, like the one the others had used, from her sleeve. He cried in alarm and tried to raise his hands. A kind of sting passed through his body, and suddenly he found himself able to move his arm. He sat up. But the woman continued to point her rod at him and said, "Lie back down, Charles, and don't move. If you do, I will be forced to put you to sleep."

The King hesitated. The cure's undoubted effectiveness made him doubt his visitor was a witch, but he remembered the voice that had aroused his suspicions. "Who are you?" he demanded.

"One who means you no harm," she returned quietly. "Please lie down."

Though it had been obvious to Ambrogio that Natheless was either an angel or a saint, neither of these possibilities occurred to Charles. Ambrogio, after all, was Italian, and was delighted to be addressed in Italian. But Charles expected an angel to speak to him in French or Latin. As for her being a saint, many Italians had allied themselves to him for reasons of political expediency but he doubted the blessed spirits had any like motive for doing so. "Did I not hear Conradin's voice in the corridor?" he demanded.

"Go back to sleep," returned the woman. "How should I know what you think you've heard?"

Her quiet confidence and unaggressive manner almost laid his fears to rest, but not quite. "Is Conradin with you?" he persisted.

"My Lord King, I am here on my own business. I do have companions. Who they are does not concern you. I assure you they have not done, and will not do, harm to you or any of yours tonight. More I cannot say. Go back to sleep."

Charles started to sit up, not to attack her, but to finally get a good view of who else was in the room. Something hit him and everything went black.

When he next opened his eyes, the curtains of his huge bed were drawn fully open, and the flickering light of several candles was shining on his face. His lame son, Prince Charles, sat crouched on the edge of the bed, and his new Queen Marguerite stood nearby. Many of the Queen's ladies and one or two of his own knights stood around the room. Following a month-old habit, he started to get up, then checked the impulse, remembering his paralysis. But before he could stop himself, he had actually moved. He sat up surprisedly and directed a questioning glance to the Queen. "What's happened? What are you all doing here?"

The Queen showed her amazement. "You are healed, My Lord. That is all we know."

Charles swung his feet off the side of his bed and stood up. "God's life, I can walk again! What did you do?"

The Queen was noncommital. "I know only what your son and one of my ladies have told me. It's a strange tale."

Prince Charles shook his head. He could hardly utter a sound. When he did speak, his voice was choked. "It was an Infidel sorceress, Father, in the company of Conradin. They came and put all your guards into an enchanted sleep. The sorceress freed you from your affliction; but they also mean to carry King Manfred's children off with them."

King Charles started. "What? What are you talking about?"

Just then a clatter of hooves erupted from the pavement below. Charles strode to the window. Two horses, their dark coats dull in the lantern light, galloped beneath him toward the bridge connecting the island castle with the mainland. A man rode one bareback with a boy holding on behind him. The second was saddled, and the man on the first horse led its reins. A woman rode it, holding both herself and a child before her tight to the saddle. It also looked as though some sort of large bundle was lashed to the saddle behind her, but Charles could not see that clearly. As they approached the entry to the bridge a shutter opened suddenly, and a large stone tabletop was hurled into their path. Someone in his palace was loyal after all. The woman leaned forward in the saddle, disengaged one of her hands and pointed at the obstacle. For one moment the tabletop dazzled in silver light, the next moment it had vanished. Before Charles could comprehend the empty space, another event caught his eye. As she lowered her hand, the witch lost her balance and tumbled to the ground. He saw her twist, in order to break the child's fall. Then her shouts rose to his window. That startled him. She sounded exactly like any Italian girl would on taking such a spill. The horseman drew up both horses, leaped to the ground, lifted the girl back into the saddle, handed the child back up to her and remounted his own horse. In the process, his hood fell back, and Charles recognized Conradin, the boy-King. Then they both galloped off. Charles turned from the window, too thoroughly bewildered to be angry, at least for a while.

22

Alrik and Benrik Eridani stood in the marketplace in Naples, dealing with their share of the paralyzed Italians waiting to be cured by the angelic touch. Nearly a hundred people had already been brought, and still they came, in ones and twos, as the news of the heavenly visitors reached them. The energet made undoing the paralysis a simple matter for Alrik. But when word spread that a messenger of God was in the city, people did not confine themselves to bringing Jori's victims alone to him. They carried anyone crippled, sick or blind from whatever cause from everywhere in the city to the market square. An occasional tumor or boil could be healed by the energet, but most medical problems were far too complicated for it and Alrik had to dismiss these sufferers with a barely satisfying word of advice. Yet the people continued to listen attentively and went away with little further argument. The hardest to deal with were the ones he couldn't help at all. One woman brought a child, still warm, who had just died of a serious disease.

"I cannot help you," Alrik said, scrutinizing the small body. "This child is dead. You must take her away and dispose of her body in accordance with your customs."

The child's mother, a woman dressed in homespun as coarse as Alrik's but far more brightly embroidered, knelt tearfully on the ground before him. "But you are from God! You can raise the dead. Have mercy on me!" she protested.

She grabbed for the hem of Alrik's robe, but he managed to draw it away before she touched it. "Lord, if you will restore my child to me, I will give half my sheep and chickens to the Church!"

"You must take the child away," reiterated Alrik, badly flustered.

"I'll give them *all* to the Church!" cried the woman, bursting into more tears and throwing herself prostrate.

"It makes no difference. I cannot help you!" insisted Alrik desperately.

"Ah, my God, you have seen through my false words and into my sinful black heart," moaned the woman. "My husband is dead that I never loved, but you have seen this is a child of adultery. Ah, *Dio*, I beg you, if you will only bring her back to life, I will devote the rest of my life to prayer and penitence! *Ahimè*, have mercy! My husband used to beat me, and my lover was so kind!"

Alrik was speechless. He was mercifully distracted by footsteps behind him. It was the Archon, coming from the Skimmer. "No sign of them?" he inquired, speaking in Peleziterean.

The distressed adulteress heard them speaking the angelic tongue, and decided they might be reviewing her case. She began to wonder at the ways God chose to convert sinners.

"Natheless has signaled she's returning. I thought it might be too late and signaled her to take refuge away from the ship. But she just kept repeating she was definitely coming back, and met my inquiries with the 'can't explain now' code."

"How much longer can we wait before we have to take off?" asked Alrik anxiously.

The Archon showed his ambivalence. "If we took off and drew Centauri's attention, they would in fact have a better chance of surviving than we do. The problem is we need Natheless because she's a sharpshooter."

"This is calling it too close. We shouldn't have allowed Natheless to go so far in order to cure that barbarian king. They could have brought him here to us if he wanted to be healed."

The Archon assented absently. The distressed mother continued watching them. The more they conversed in the angelic tongue, the more she began to hope the outcome of their consultation might prove favorable to her.

Suddenly a distant clattering sound could be heard.

"What's that?" demanded the Archon.

"It's the sound of those animals the Italians use for locomotion," said

Alrik attentively. "Could someone have declared an alarm?" He drew his energet and held it ready. In a moment, however, what could only have been Natheless's wrist-light shone in the narrow alley approaching the square. He backed away a bit as the two horses galloped into view. The Italian woman took her dead child back up into her arms and stood.

Conradin dismounted first, lifting Arrigo to the ground. Then he helped Natheless and Manfredino off their horse. Alrik approached. "Natheless, you're none too soon. But who are these children?"

"Conradin's cousins," Natheless explained. "They won't make a great deal of difference in this planet's history, and we could not bear leaving them there, the way they had been abused. Besides, Conradin might have mutinied if I hadn't agreed to bring them away with us."

Manfredino seemed shocked out of his months-long stupor by his fall from the horse. For the first time in a long while he appeared fully aware of his surroundings. He was holding tenaciously onto Natheless's sleeve and staring at Alrik with a mixture of curiosity and wariness. Alrik thought he seemed a very sullen and unattractive child. More importantly, he wondered how they were going to look after children during the battle which certainly lay ahead of them.

Natheless had administered a small dose of soporin to Anselino when Conradin bound him to the saddle. In his haste at this moment, Conradin did not take the time to release him from his bundle. He unstrapped the entire saddle from the horse and carried it, child and all, toward the Skimmer. Natheless and the others turned to follow him. But with a piercing cry, the Italian woman threw herself once more at their feet. "My lady, whether you are a deathless spirit made by God before the world or a spirit of the blessed dead, if you ever had a child of your own, you know how I feel! Have mercy on me, restore my Alicia to me!"

Natheless was startled and Manfredino drew closer to her. "What's this all about?" demanded Natheless, throwing a glance at Alrik.

"She wants you to raise her child from the dead," groaned Alrik.

Conradin made a sign to Natheless, and her face brightened. She looked down at the imploring woman. "God has not given us the power to raise the dead, lady. Behold, today I saw my own and only brother lying dead, and I could do nothing. You must entreat God by other means. Depart in peace." The woman rose confusedly, child in arms, and finally turned to leave.

The entire party entered the Skimmer. The Archon signaled to Rauhina for immediate takeoff. The others busied themselves with preparing the children for the flight. Anselino, unconscious, was easy.

Manfredino was visibly upset at the process, and stared uncertainly at Natheless, demanding, "What are we inside of here? Where are you going?"

"I'll be in the very next room," Natheless assured him. "We are preparing to fight a terrible wizard. But I will return when we have succeeded."

Arrigo was less upset, but was full of questions. "What are we doing here?" he inquired.

"We will travel up in the air with the birds," explained Conradin, who was holding him.

"Will Father be there?" cried Arrigo excitedly.

"*Nein*—we aren't going as high as that," returned Conradin. It took Natheless a moment to follow the drift of the conversation.

"How high *are* we going?" pursued Arrigo.

"You will have to ask the Princess," replied Conradin. Natheless said, "That depends how far and in what ways the wizard chases us." Natheless departed, leaving to Conradin the task of explaining who the wizard, Jimmik, was.

The Skimmer rose as Natheless entered the control room and she braced herself temporarily in the doorway. The Archon was standing before the main screen and Alrik was at one of the four energet ports. Natheless, knowing what her duties would be, went to one of the others and checked the sights on the carriage into which the energet would be set.

"I've checked all four," said Alrik. "They're fine." The Archon spoke.

"The object is to get above the Lander as it tries to reach us. It has a high-powered energet-beam strong enough to dematerialize this Skimmer and simultaneously level this city. But it is set in a fixed position on the rear section. Our ships are not designed for combat. After each civil war, our technologists try to redesign them so they're even less apt for that kind of conflict. So if we can stay in front of him, we stand a chance. If I've guessed right, we should be meeting Jimmik just about—ah!"

"*Gran Dio eccolo!*" exclaimed Conradin excitedly. The Lander's form appeared in the main screen, hurtling toward them. Obviously aware of their presence, it was in the process of turning slowly.

"Dive left, Rauhina!" cried the Archon. "We've got to stay ahead of him!" The Skimmer veered and dived in the direction of the Lander's nose until it sped before it. A powerful bolt of energy from the Lander proved Jimmik Centauri meant business. But it cleanly missed them. The Archon adjusted the Skimmer's position before the Lander. Maneuverability was their only advantage. From below they heard wailing—one of the children was crying.

"Fire when ready," cried the Archon to Natheless and Alrik. "The Lander is powerfully built, but if we can score some kind of lucky hit we're bound to damage him—perhaps persuade him to leave off."

Their energets turned to maximum, Alrik and Natheless shot repeatedly back at the Lander, but with little visible effect. The sturdy metal hull absorbed their shots.

During these maneuvers, the ground slipped out from beneath the ships. They had traversed the entire Italian peninsula and passed over the Adriatic and over Albania, where Arrigo's mother had been born. Alrik and Natheless continued to bombard the Lander. But the Skimmer had to veer and dive to stay ahead of the Lander.

They were over a wide, dry, plateau. "He wants to trap us between him and the ground," said the Archon. "He knows the Orbiter is not built to intervene this far down safely. Rauhina, do your best to stay above the Lander."

The Lander again began to turn, but the Skimmer kept nimbly ahead of it. Suddenly, Centauri pulled the Lander into an unexpected climb. High into the climb, he as suddenly spun his ship through ninety degrees, giving him an awkward but clear shot at the Skimmer. He fired.

The Skimmer trembled violently. The children were no longer screaming. Natheless hurled herself away from her shooting port across the ship to the second one, beside Alrik. Swinging her energet viciously into the difficult angle, she fired repeatedly. Alrik did likewise. The Skimmer made a dive while Jimmik tried another shot. But Natheless and Alrik's combined fire finally succeeded in blasting a huge gash in the Lander's bow.

"Good work!" cried the Archon. "The damage is serious!"

"But Skimmer II," cried Rauhina. From its place near the tail of the Lander the second Skimmer cleanly separated itself from its berth in the mother ship.

"Fire!" cried the Archon. Alrik and Natheless directed their fire at the fleeing ship, but it was fast moving out of their range, since Rauhina was having difficulty maintaining control of their own Skimmer.

Suddenly, from high above them came a powerful bright flash. "The Orbiter!" cried Natheless. They watched breathless as the huge sphere descended high over Skimmer II. Centauri dodged, descended to the lowest possible altitude, nearly treetop level and sped safely out of range.

23

As Skimmer I settled back into smooth flight, the Archon turned to Rauhina Telgolarses. "Can we pursue him?" he demanded.

Rauhina, crouched over the controls, looked shaken. "Not by my advice, Sevenfold! That last bolt damaged our shield. If we catch up with him, he'll just shoot us down."

"Look at that!" exclaimed Natheless, pointing to the tracking screen. Skimmer II's path was now represented by a red streak. "He's flying off at more than safe speed!"

"Let's hope the acceleration gives him a stroke!" exclaimed the Archon.

But no mishap showed on the screen and the streak soon disappeared.

"Why didn't he come back and finish us?" wondered Alrik.

"He must fear the Orbiter can still hit him from the ground," said Rauhina.

"We'd better get close to the Orbiter, then, if we're going to have to land to make repairs," said the Archon.

They retraced their flight path, following the large vessel's distress signal. The Archon made contact. "Orbiter, are you there? Any casualties? Sixfold Rho, come in."

The response came swiftly. "I hear you, Sevenfold. Have you spotted us now?"

"We see you." The massive form of the Orbiter appeared on the dry plain below. It was all there, but not in one piece. The Orbiter was not built for dives close to the surfaces of large planets, but it had effective accident-protection systems.

Rho Smide continued. "No serious injuries. Since you see us, we may as well turn off the distress signal, Sevenfold. We don't want to attract unwelcome attention, do we?"

Benrik Eridani was alarmed. Rho Smide was evidently nervous about Centauri's coming back, which might mean the main energet was knocked out. He considered calling the Peleziterea for another vessel, but decided to postpone it. To ask for reinforcements would advertise his vulnerability and besides, from the last he had heard they had no other ship ready. Also, the High Council might balk at sending out more personnel. "Turn off the signal," he said. "We'll come down and join you."

The distress signal stopped, and the Skimmer began its descent to the crippled ship. Seeing their plans concluded, Natheless finally found time to descend into the Sleeping Room to find Conradin and the children. Arrigo and both his brothers were strapped to their bunks, the elder two together, Anselino by himself. They were all sound asleep, their chests rising and falling in a steady rhythm. Bodris sat opposite them, absorbed in a game of solitaire with her wrist-computer. Floress and Conradin were sitting on another bunk, watching the children.

"I can't believe the children could sleep through a battle," said Natheless. "What happened?"

Bodris looked up innocently. "I couldn't quiet them down. I gave them all soporin."

"That's hardly what I intended you to do, Bodris," said Natheless, trying to control her exasperation, "unless they were really distraught."

Bodris did her best to look surprised. "What did you mean for me to do?"

"I thought you might try to reassure or distract them—for a good example, by playing a game with them instead of with yourself."

"The baby kept screaming, no matter what I did. The older ones listened to Conradin for a while, but every time the ship swerved they would yell. And Conradin kept going to the control room to see what was happening."

"Well, Conradin isn't under my orders. It sounds to me as if you might have put Anselino to sleep and talked to the other ones."

"I couldn't think of anything appropriate," retorted Bodris rather lamely, having exhausted her list of legitimate excuses.

Bodris returned to her game of solitaire. Natheless saw there was little more to be accomplished with her. She turned to Conradin, who had been listening attentively, though all he could understand was that the conversation in some way concerned his cousins. "I hear you watched a considerable portion of the battle, Conradin. How much of it could you understand?"

"I saw a shadow like your Silver Tower flying toward us in that crystal box. I assume it was the one of hideous aspect?" said Conradin.

"It was," said Natheless. She explained the action as best she could. "Our people have sent us another flying ship, but one that could not easily come close to the ground. You see, the larger the ship, the faster it must fly in order not to fall. Had this second ship not arrived, Jimmik Centauri could have chased us into the high heavens and the outer darkness."

"Where is the hideous wizard now?" said the boy-King. "And how will you fight him?"

"Ah," sighed Natheless, "that isn't an easy question to answer. At the rate he was flying, he could be halfway around the world shortly."

Conradin looked impressed. "Will you be able to pursue him?" he asked.

"We'll have to see about that," said Natheless.

There was no use in discussing it for the next twenty-four hours, while the Orbiter was repaired and readied for flight.

Conradin fretted and fumed about what was going on in his court. His disappearance the very night after the sorcerers' arrival was bound to be mischievously construed by many of his subjects, not to mention the priests. His appearance in Naples would create even more confusion. Conradin wondered what kind of reaction there would be throughout Italy when the news spread. It was hardly likely to help him. Charles and the Church would certainly not attribute to him any good motives, and his allies would be angry with him for injuring his cause and theirs. He could not blame them.

Natheless was occupied, so Conradin passed his time with his young cousins. He worried a little about the complications they would cause, but found their companionship meant much more to him than he had expected. Arrigo, who had shared the horse with him on his hasty flight from Charles's castle, set no bounds to his gratitude and his admiration for his older cousin. He followed Conradin around the Skimmer and the recreation room of the Orbiter, and outdoors on the arid plateau whenever Conradin walked. Manfredino was more devoted to his own rescuer, Natheless, and shadowed her as much as he could. Considering his mental state, she couldn't bring herself to prevent it, but she could seldom give him her full attention. Manfredino was also drawn to the young King by an attraction which apparently worked against his will. He followed Conradin at a distance with a wary and uncertain look. Conradin could easily understand why he was reluctant to show his feelings after so much pain. He felt much the same way himself, and respected the child's silence. It was Manfredino who finally broke it.

"Did you love my father?"

Manfredino had come up quietly behind while Conradin was squinting into the grey distance, trying to figure out exactly where this dry plateau stood in relation to Italy. He was wondering whether he could associate it with some place mentioned in a history or chronicle he had read. Was it perhaps the eastern land from which Genghis Khan had descended with his barbarian horde upon a shocked and horrified Germany a quarter of a century or so before? He turned and faced his cousin. "I never met your father, Manfredino."

"Charles's men said you hated us, and would never help us because our father usurped your kingdom." It sounded like an accusation.

Conradin had to pause. "It was Charles who stole my father's kingdom. Conrad, my father, died when I was an infant of two years, and the Pope's allies overran Italy while I was safe with my mother in Bavaria. It was your father who drove out the priests. He might have acted as a regent for me, but he preferred to have himself proclaimed King, by right of conquest, he said. The Hohenstaufen allies were glad to have a grown man who was a skilled ruler and accomplished warrior as their king instead of a baby, and they raised no questions. Your father wrote me explaining all this and sent me some pleasant trinkets. Of course, the Pope was furious to find so strong a ruler succeeding Frederick, so he sent to me, urging me to claim my kingdom. But my wise mother knew they only meant to divide the Hohenstaufens and weaken them, so she paid no attention. That's what led the Pope to turn to the Frenchman Charles, who overthrew your father at Benevento and me at Tagliacozzo. So you see, I never came to blows with your father."

Manfredino continued to appear unsatisfied. Conradin said, "I might have, however, if he had still been King in Naples by the time I came of age."

Manfredino said, "What will you do with us?"

"Your father is dead," replied Conradin, "and I am too angry with Charles and the Church to hate you. If you are good and loyal cousins to me, perhaps when I regain my kingdom, I will return your father's princedom to you—perhaps." He poked Manfredino lightly on his shoulder, and the boy grinned.

Since Conradin was in such a communicative mood, Arrigo also spoke up. "You never told us how you yourself came to be rescued, *Signore*. Who are these people with the flying ships? Did our grandfather send them?"

"No, they are merely wise Infidels from far beyond the sea. They just happened to pass this way," answered Conradin.

"What land do they come from?" pursued Arrigo.

"You would not like it. It is barren and there are no horses. They are searching for a better one."

"Why don't they stay in Italy?" demanded Arrigo, skipping around Conradin in his eagerness. "Why don't you marry the Princess and ask them to stay?"

Conradin smiled and patted Arrigo's cheek. "You think I should marry the Princess?"

Arrigo nodded eagerly, and Manfredino assented more shyly. "I think she would be a good Empress!"

"Be sure to tell her so some time," advised Conradin.

In the dark hours of the morning after the crash, the Orbiter, with Skimmer I aboard, lifted off again. They soon found the Lander on the plain some distance from the Orbiter's crash-site and brought it aboard for repairs. It was then they discovered the only fatality of the battle; Petrik Hatcherbrat had been left in charge of the control room while Jimmik made ready for flight in Skimmer II. He had died in the crash. It was little enough for the Archon's party to triumph over, since they realized that Jimmik Centauri did not care about this as deeply as they would.

Then they began the work of pursuing Jimmik Centauri. Their first hope was in following the ion trail he had left in his flight at near-maximum speed. Despite atmospheric dispersion, they were able to trace him on a straight path over a southern continent and an ocean. But at the South Pole the trail rose into the ionosphere and disappeared amid a magnetic storm. Try as they might, they could find no trail leading away from the region.

"He might have left this planet and landed on another body in the star system," said Sixfold Rho Smide. "He knew the Peleziterea's position, and if he left in the region of the South Pole, the planet would block the ship's view of him."

"He couldn't have gotten to any of the larger planets without being charted on their screen, though," said Alrik. "The Peleziterea is above the plane of their orbits and would see him cross from one to another if that's what he did."

"True," said Sixfold Rho Smide a bit irritably, "but he might be sitting on an asteroid somewhere."

"He wouldn't do that, though," said the Archon grimly. "It's this planet he has designs on. If he left the planet, it would be ludicrously easy for us to watch the planet's atmosphere and catch him when he comes back."

"True. In any case, the extraplanetary search can be conducted by scout ships," said Sixfold Rho. "What he probably did was shift to a sonic or subsonic speed and find a hiding place on the ground or under the ocean."

Then began the much slower business of scanning the planet's surface for Skimmer II. Yet, after forty exhausting hours, they had found nothing. They met in the conference room to discuss it.

"If he's still on the planet, he's doing one of two things," said Sixfold Rho. "He's found a way to block our detectors, or else he's lined himself up with some underground metallic deposits from which we can't distinguish him."

The Archon protested, "The Skimmer's metal isn't quite like anything that occurs naturally here. Surely, we can distinguish the natural from the artifical?"

"Of course," said Sixfold Rho wearily, "if we employ several times the level we're using. Unfortunately, our technology tends to be designed for dead planets. It would destroy the ecosystem here wherever we used it. There are so *many* places he could be!"

There was a long despondent pause. "Well," said Alrik, "we could easily spend the rest of our lives looking for him. With transformers and synthesizers to make everything he needs, he could hide himself for years without communicating with the people at all."

"No!" said the Archon, coming out of a reverie. "We cannot resign ourselves to that. We must lure him into betraying himself somehow. But he's an impatient man. If we let him get the idea we've left, he'll attack the natives."

"And since he doesn't know any planetary language and has no Contact training," said Natheless, "he will have to use gross technological aggression to make any impression on the people. We could keep the Skimmer searching low on the planetary surface, near populations, and investigating closely in places where there seems to be great unrest."

An idea struck the Archon. "This is what we must do. We must give the planet a thorough search with all our beams—at the advisable levels, of course—and allow Jimmik Centauri a few hints that we are doing it. Then we must pretend to believe he has left the planet—escaped out of the solar system under the shelter of the South Pole. We can instruct Nibbana to find some suggestive trails in the Peleziterea's record of that area and report them to us. Then we will withdraw all our vessels, supposedly to search space. We will return in two of the planet's years and try to find out what Centauri has done. If we are careful to make a detailed environmental and technical chart of the planet before we leave, we will probably be able to detect his doings when we come back. Of course, this solution may allow more destruction of the planet's people and culture than we were hoping, but what else can we really do? Sixfold Natheless, what do you think?"

Natheless looked sadly over the tired faces of the two older leaders and then at the empty space of the conference room, which had been built with five times as many people in mind. "As you say, Archon, this solution is more destructive than we hoped for. In two years, Jimmik Centauri might kill countless people to gain his ends, might drastically alter political configurations, might beget children, might even pass on our knowledge. All the same, it seems the best plan. I would only add one refinement. Since we know the Italian language, why not leave a party in Italy, and check back with them periodically without making communications Jimmik Centauri could overhear? The Italian peninsula has a good central location, and rumors from a wide stretch of territory would eventually reach it if something extraordinary happened. We might trace Jimmik Centauri faster that way, if he decides to operate in one of those places."

Ultimately, that was the plan they adopted. This concluded, most of the exhausted Lawchildren went to rest, while the technical search continued the rest of the night and throughtout the day with a skeleton crew.

24

In Naples, Abbot Sinibaldo spent days trying to untangle the conflicting accounts of the miraculous events. First, his faithful secretary, Brother Ambrogio, for whom he had grieved since that terrible day the sorcerers emerged from the church and seized him, had mysteriously returned in the middle of the night, healed of his paralysis and claiming he had seen an angel. As though to confirm his words, the same angel appeared that very night and lifted the affliction of the abbot himself and many other sufferers in the city. To Sinibaldo the visitors seemed like strange-looking angels, but he did not dare set too much store by that, since God was known to take an almost perverse pleasure in overthrowing the expectations of the learned. One was supposed to judge above all by the fruits, and thus far the fruits of the visit were undeniably effective cures.

Sinibaldo would have posed no futher questions, had not a frantic messenger come to him that same morning, crying that the dreaded Conradin had been seen in the city, in the company of a witch. The abbot at first believed some terrible disaster had befallen King Charles. But it turned out the necromancer had healed the French invader, too. As more news followed, the story from Charles's palace proved to be even stranger than what occured in the rest of the city.

"And then," said Sinibaldo, speaking to Archbishop Ruggeri, who had come to visit him in his chamber and congratulate him on his recovery, "there's the story of the woman with the dead child. She saw a lady with bright light shining all around her come to the market square, where another was healing the sick who were brought to him. When she asked the lady to raise her dead child to life, she said she had seen her only brother dead that very day and could not raise him. Have you ever heard anything stranger?"

"Than a witch not being able to raise the dead?" asked the Archbishop, squirming a little on the cushioned bench where he sat.

"No, that she had seen her brother dead that very day. I've sent inquiries all over the city trying to discover the name of any young Neapolitan girl, recently dead, who had a reputation for performing miracles. But I can find no one answering her description. And if I did, how could I explain her being in Conradin's company?"

Ruggeri laughed cynically. "I myself find the story of the flight on horseback most incongruous with angelic identity. I can image why God might want one of his messengers to appear riding a horse, but to fall off? Impossible."

Sinibaldo frowned and nodded. "That does seem strange. Yet I dislike branding Ambrogio's tale nonsense."

"He's a blessed innocent," said the Archbishop. "He will be in paradise long before you and I, Sinibaldo, but in this world he sees things unclearly. There are so many angelic spirits inside his head he becomes confused and believes he sees them around other people. No, don't let the sheep lead the shepherd, Sinibaldo."

Sinibaldo grunted. "We have yet to discover who this woman really was, what she wants, why Conradin was with her, and what they mean to do next."

Ruggeri chuckled. "Those are the questions, Sinibaldo. How are we going to answer them?"

Sinibaldo stared through the broad window. The shutters were opened wide, and the narrow street below could be seen, empty. "I have sent out inquiries, mostly to find people who saw and heard them when they came. We have been looking especially hard to find the woman with the dead child. Others have gone to the palace to speak with the King and the Lady Marie. It is possible we shall learn more."

The Archbishop stared hard at the abbot. "I find it most difficult to believe any of this really happened. However, yesterday you could move nothing below your neck, and today you move as ever. What did she look like?"

Sinibaldo was meditative as he spoke. "Not very striking, apart from her healing abilities. She was a young woman, a girl really, not beautiful, not ugly. She was dressed in peasant's homespun and spoke the Italian vernacular, but ornamented with words and figures of speech which she must have learned at a king's court or a nobleman's house. She had an unusual accent, but I couldn't place her by region. She was gentle, though, and had a soft voice. I remember thinking if she was one of the Blessed Dead, she was probably a nun of Saint Clare who had spent a large part of her life tending the sick."

Ruggeri shook his head with disbelief. "Was she alone?"

"No, she had a companion, a hooded man who watched and said nothing."

"That would be Conradin! And he only stood there and looked at you, when he might have cut your throat!"

"I shudder to think of it," said the abbot, "but imagine how much worse it must be for the King. Except, of course, that he cannot remember it."

There was a soft knock on the door. Sinibaldo realized he had been so intent on the conversation he had not seen his messenger enter from the street below."Brother Ambrogio? Come in."

The door opened and the young monk entered hesitantly, stopping when he saw Ruggeri. The Archbishop was friendly but distant. "Good day, Brother Ambrogio. Are you out pursuing angels or sorcerers today?"

The monk looked to his abbot, who said, "Sit down, Ambrogio. The Archbishop would like to hear your story, too. What have you discovered?"

Ambrogio sank down on the stool Sinibaldo had indicated, and answered, "I learned a lot, but little of immediate use."

Ruggeri chuckled. "It's good you know it!"

"Tell us that," said Sinibaldo, without change of expression.

"It seems last night's visitors were quite mortal. The witnesses to Conradin's appearance are unimpeachable; they include the King himself, the Prince of Salerno and several others who had seen the boy-pretender when he was in prison. Furthermore, I myself witnessed the young woman's use of the silver rod, though I did not acknowledge it. I pushed it out of my mind because I thought some evil demon was trying to deceive me, but it seems my senses were telling the truth all along. I have been at fault."

"My son," said Sinibaldo, "we have yet to see whether any harm has been done. Did you speak to the Lady Marie also?"

"I spoke with her." Ambrogio raised his hand as if to adjust the position of his head-covering. As he did so he brought one finger before his mouth for a fraction of a second, signaling the abbot he had heard something he did not wish to tell the Archbishop. Then he went on. "When I pressed her, Lady Marie admitted the young woman had never claimed in so many words to be a messenger from God. She only said she had power over Charles's illness and was under orders from some authority, which she did not identify, to use it."

Ruggeri scowled. "Why did you ask questions like that, Ambrogio? In truth, you're still trying to cover your fault! Since it turns out the messenger of God you saw was neither an angel nor a saint, you want to prove that she's at least an honest witch. Why can't you simply admit you were disastrously mistaken?"

Ambrogio bowed his head and looked down at the tiled floor. Sinibaldo turned rapidly on Ruggeri. "What do you wish, Ruggeri? Do you wish to hear Ambrogio's explanation, or shall I dismiss him until we've finished discussing other matters?"

"The boy can speak," growled the Archbishop, squirming again on his bench and trying to find a comfortable position for his fat legs.

"Ambrogio, is it true?" inquired Sinibaldo. "Have you been working to save your own fame?"

The monk's face was open and frank, without a trace of rancor. "I never saw an angel before, Father Abbot, so I could easily be misled about the appearance of one. I have never seen a saint, either, except in the pictures and sculptures in the monastery and the church, so I might easily be deceived about that, too. But I know that in my own life I have seen the light of God's love shining from a human face. And about that I think it would be very difficult to deceive me." Then, almost embarrassed at having spoken so feelingly, he stared down at the floor again.

Ruggeri snorted. "I've no doubt you saw light in her eyes, Ambrogio, but you might be mistaken about its inspiration. You're a handsome lad, however little you may care to think about it."

Ambrogio remained staring at the floor. His cheeks were turning red.

Sinibaldo addressed Ruggeri with gentle sarcasm. "Personal failings make all of us unsuited for understanding the world. Just as Brother Ambrogio may underestimate the power of lust, I believe you stress it far too much. Even if the witch thought Ambrogio was a handsome lad, and she would have unless there was something wrong with her eyes, it still does not explain why she wandered through the rest of the city healing scores of other people, including myself, who certainly am not handsome. It also does not explain why the young Hohenstaufen accompanied her to the bedside of a man he considers a usurper, and yet refrained from killing him."

"It *is* a mystery, especially since you say the girl wasn't pretty." Ruggeri smirked. "If she were beautiful, it would be easy to explain."

Sinibaldo turned back to his monk. "Did you speak with the King?" he asked.

"The King received me," said Ambrogio, "and treated me graciously even though he wished me to carry some of his complaints to you."

The Archbishop started. "Complaints! What's this?"

"King Manfred's sons, I imagine," said Sinibaldo placidly. "I was expecting it as soon as I heard they had been carried off. It was I who spoke to Queen Marguerite and suggested it was barbarous to keep the children chained to the wall, and without priests or doctors, too. I did not, however, say anything to her I hadn't already said to the King, nor did I urge her to do anything about it behind her husband's back. My conscience is quite clear about that."

Ruggeri leaned forward, furious. "You did that? When you know one of Charles's dearest desires is to find an excuse for dismissing the Italian priests and replacing them with Frenchmen? You'll be the ruin of us all!"

Sinibaldo looked serenely through him at the flower design painted on the wooden wall behind him. When he saw that Sinibaldo would not reply, Ruggeri continued, "I know you think I'm a despicable coward and a disgrace to the Church, but perhaps you'll understand my attitude better when you find yourself at the bottom of the sea with a stone hanging around your neck."

"At the orders of a King who was called in by the Pope? To protect the interests of the Church?" returned Sinibaldo. "That would show the world a few things."

"If all priests were like you, the Church would have no defenses at all," protested Ruggeri with real feeling.

"She would have God as her protector," replied Sinibaldo firmly. "Men who protect priests because they compromise with wickedness and cruelty to keep themselves in power are not the friends of the Church; they are her worst enemies."

"Sophistry!" said Ruggeri, standing up. "And I wouldn't be surprised if it bordered on heresy, too!"

"Heresy is half-truth," shrugged Sinibaldo. "If a man wished to avoid bordering on it, he would have to tell many lies. And then, of course, he would be on the other border."

Ruggeri leaned back again as if exhausted. "I can see the doom hanging over me and my kind. You will become Pope, and the kings of the world will drive the whole Church into hiding."

Sinibaldo was ironic. "I become Pope? How can you suggest it, Ruggeri? I have neither the wealth nor the connections for that, and as you just said, King Charles wants a Frenchman."

"How innocent you are," said Ruggeri archly. "You forget that in times of great turmoil, even cardinals will become pious. You have a reputation for sanctity and you were here in the midst of all these miracles, however they be interpreted."

"It shall be as God wills," said Sinibaldo serenely.

The Archbishop rose slowly to his feet, his face expressing his weariness. "I don't hate you, Sinibaldo, in spite of your inflexibility. But men like you are fated to bring misery on yourself and others. The world will not change for all your efforts, and at the end of your life you will find yourself worn to the bone and broken on the rocks of human hardheartedness. It is better to enjoy a few pleasant things along the way, as I have, or else you will never know anything but bitterness."

Sinibaldo rose to walk with him to the door. "This world was never meant to be pleasant, Ruggeri. In the next world the sorrow of the righteous shall be turned to glory. I grieve to see you waste your time and your gifts as you do, because you ought to be more steadfast."

The Archbishop took his leave without another word. Sinibaldo returned to find Ambrogio still standing. "Father Abbot?" he said.

"Speak," said Sinibaldo, sitting down on his bed again and motioning for the monk to do likewise.

"I hope you do not believe I am in love, in a carnal way, with the sorceress who healed me. If I were, it would be my duty to confess it, but it is not so. I am not as young as Archbishop Ruggeri thinks, and I know the kind of look he meant. This is different."

"Leave that aside for the moment," said Sinibaldo with an impatient gesture. "What is the secret matter you signed me about?"

Ambrogio's face darkened a little further. He seemed reluctant to speak. "It is a matter of little import, I suppose. When I spoke to the Lady Marie, I thought her story contradicted itself in several ways, but I was unable to guess which part was truer than the other. Then the lame prince, Charles of Salerno, sent for me. He told me a number of things on condition they go no farther than you. As it happens, telling them does little good, but the Prince seemed to want to talk. I comforted him as best I could." Ambrogio described Queen Marguerite's threat to return to

France, and Lady Marie's attempt to protect the Queen at the King's expense. Lady Marie's account had suppressed this last detail, and Queen Marguerite, though aware of the truth, had endorsed her friend's version of the story. "The Prince believes King Charles would have pardoned Lady Marie, out of respect for the Queen, even if he had known the truth. But now the Prince is afraid to make his knowledge public, lest it provoke a quarrel between the royal pair."

Sinibaldo shook his head. "This does not bode well for King Charles's domestic life. But did the Prince know anything more about the young woman who did the healing?"

Ambrogio nodded slightly. "His more detailed description of their conversation revealed a few things. Neither Conradin nor the Princess (Conradin called her that) appeared to be in a superior position. It was certainly the Princess's influence that restrained Conradin from harming the Frenchman, but he did not seem to be especially afraid of her. Prince Charles said she appeared more like some influential person Conradin was trying to impress, and he seemed to be succeeding."

"That's *something*," said Sinibaldo. "But then, who *is* she?"

"You heard she fell from her horse?" said Ambrogio. "King Charles added that as she fell, she turned to catch Prince Manfredino above her to shelter him from the fall. The King does not believe that sort of devotion can be bought for money or comes as part of a mere alliance. He believes the Princess must be a cousin of Conradin's, probably related to King Manfred—possibly another daughter of the Emperor Frederick and his last wife, Bianca Lancia."

"Of course!" Sinibaldo's face lit up. Then it immediately darkened. "But we keep coming back to the same question. Why would a daughter of the Emperor Frederick and his last wife, no doubt sent by him from his subterranean court under Mongibello to aid his descendants, heal King Charles of a spell put on him by the same group of sorcerers?"

"The King believes the cure was only a subterfuge intended to conceal some more subtle damage they may have done at the same time. He wishes his whole palace, and the portions of the city where Conradin and his companions are known to have walked, to be exorcised and blessed."

Sinibaldo grunted. "That's plausible, but—what do you think, my son?"

"You saw the Princess yourself, Father Abbot. Do you believe her healing was done with evil intent?"

"It did not seem so to me," said Sinibaldo, "but I do not claim to judge the motives of strangers. You cannot trust your eyes when you are dealing with the powers of darkness, or so it is said. And can you think of any reason why Conradin would aid a true healing?"

"Perhaps," said the monk cautiously, "perhaps Conradin is not as evil as we fear."

Sinibaldo shifted impatiently. "We knew nothing evil of Conradin before this. He was only a boy of fourteen when he first came to claim his throne. Before that the Church offered to support his rights against his uncle Manfred, but he refused her help. Only after the Church had chosen another protector did he see fit to assert his claims by force, and even then the boy might have been influenced by the Hohenstaufens' supporters who flocked to him after Manfred's death, without being wicked himself. I do not deny there might be a streak of real generosity in Conradin—his grandfather and even his uncle did not lack something of the sort in their best moments. But if Conradin were merely a generous king, he would in fact refrain from using sorcery against his rival. He would hardly return, after King Charles had condemned him to death as a common thief, and heal his enemy. That kind of compassion comes only from God's blessed, and nothing we know of Conradin's character would lead us to suspect that of him."

"But he did not order the cure," said Ambrogio. "The Princess spoke of a higher authority. Perhaps Frederick II himself commanded it. He first sent Jori and Nelsik to prevent Conradin's execution, but they disobeyed him and injured more people than they should have in order to seize power for themselves. So the Emperor sent a nearer relation to undo the damage they caused, and Conradin also obeys him."

"Why not overthrow Charles in the same blow?"

"Who knows what Frederick II would plan? Perhaps he knows God would not permit it. Perhaps he is waiting for the Church to weary of Charles, or for the people to weary of the Church and Charles, to be sure of a warmer welcome."

The Abbot gasped. "What a thought!"

25

While the court at Grosseto awaited
Conradin's return, his cousins Bianca and Anticoli were driven nearly to
distraction with anxiety. For three days they presided, tight-lipped and
reserved, over the great hall, hardly daring to leave the palace for fear of
treachery. But the fickle supporters of the Hohenstaufen dynasty only
huddled about and whispered among themselves. Fear that the boy-
Emperor might have unseen magical spies in their midst kept them from
whispering more loudly or pressing Anticoli with awkward questions.

On the third day confused reports of the events in Naples began to
reach them. This raised their spirits, since it proved the young King had
reached the city alive and accomplished his mission. Why he had not
returned they could not imagine. The Bishop of Verona had a *Te Deum*
sung in the chapel, and later Anticoli went out hunting with some of
the other nobles. It was unsafe to leave the palace unguarded, however,
which is why Ginevra was there to receive the first definite tidings.

Ginevra was sitting in one of Bianca's chambers, working on a mantle she intended for a niece, when one of the pages announced the
Emperor had returned and was addressing the assembly in the great hall.
All aflutter, she set aside her embroidery and, summoning her attendants,
made her way through the corridors. She heard the cheering as she
approached. An amazing sight awaited her. Conradin, dressed in rough

peasant clothes, was standing on the dais at the end of the hall, holding aloft a helmet of strange metal and foreign design. It looked remarkably impractical judged by good Italian standards.

"The sorcerers who killed the Pope have been banished from this world!" he cried. Great cheers responded, and some of the nobles and ladies threw their caps, scarves or mantles into the air. Conradin turned the helmet upside down to show the charred underside, and Ginevra, like most of the Italians, assumed the sorcerers had met their deaths by burning. Of course, they had been returned to the Peleziterea to await trial. But Conradin informed Natheless he would need a trophy. So she had blasted all the technologically significant parts from the helmet and given it to him. In doing so, she warned him he would have to return it later, because she could not risk the natives' discovering and duplicating the alloy of metal it was made of which was different from anything they presently used.

Conradin continued, "Yet this battle fills me with awe. For behold, Italy and all Christendom are threatened by a grave danger, even greater than when Genghis Khan advanced with his barbarian hordes!"

"Ahi! Alas! May God have mercy!" exclaimed some, while others whispered among themselves.

"I know," Conradin called out clearly, lowering the helmet, "some of you did not believe your King when he informed you he knew nothing of these sorcerers, nor where they came from, nor what they wanted. But I have never lied on that score. I would never seek the help of Satan or any other demon to obtain what is mine, nor did my grandfather Frederick or my father Conrad. These sorcerers are descendants of a great people who have been driven to a barren land, and now some of them are trying to escape from it. Two of them entered Naples intent entirely on their own gain. King Benrik sent his son, Prince Alrik, not to find me but to pursue them. They came to me instead of to the Pope because they feared an incourteous reception from one who would harbor such bitter suspicions about them. And now, although we have captured the first two, a worse trial yet remains. There is an evil wizard greater than either of these, with eyes as red as blood and locks greener than a grass serpent. His purpose, it seems, may be nothing less than becoming ruler of the whole world. Even King Benrik fears him, for he is learned and crafty and will stop at no sort of treachery."

Gasps of consternation could be heard from the assembly. Ginevra wondered how much of what he said was true, and how much policy. The King certainly looked calm and strong, not at all like someone who had confronted a terrible red-eyed, green-haired wizard. But perhaps a person who has stood at the point of his own execution fears nothing else ever again.

Conradin lifted the helmet again. "Courage, my people!" he cried. "There is reason for hope! I have told you the sorcerers did not come here to rescue me from Charles or to establish me as your ruler. Therefore, since my escape was the work of no human agency, it could only have been the will of God!"

There was a cheer or two, but the fear was so desperate and the hope so distant, most only murmured. Ginevra felt tears coming to her eyes. She regarded the proud, erect, lonely youth in ragged garments, on whom all their hopes rested. Would God really work through him? Was he innocent enough? Pious enough? At the moment he certainly looked humble enough, at least in apparel. He was the meanest-dressed in the hall, Ginevra thought, nervously comparing him to the Bishop of Verona, who was gorgeously robed in crimson, with a ruby-studded mitre. Was it wise of Conradin to make such a spectacle of himself? People did notice. It wasn't as if he didn't possess the proper clothing; he *could* have changed before going to the hall.

She brushed these thoughts aside and tried to concentrate on what really mattered: Would God work through Conradin? Fervently she prayed, "May it be so! May it be so!"

"For the moment," the Emperor continued, "the terrible wizard, Jimmik, has been driven beyond our borders. But he may return. Therefore, we must keep watch for him! Our allies, King Benrik and his son, Prince Alrik, and the Princess Natheless, will be here to help us as much as they can. They are honest and trustworthy, though they be Infidels, and I have hopes they may soon be won for our Faith. We need the aid and the prayers of all believers, if this peril is to be overcome. It will be deeply grievous if Charles and the new Pope whom the Cardinals elect do not cease their relentless war against my family. The peril is so great, even important quarrels, such as ours, must be set aside for a time."

The nobles in the hall clustered together and debated in low tones. If Conradin was sincere, they thought, the danger from the sorcerer Jimmik must be serious indeed. If he was not sincere, his speech was a most clever device for separating the Church from its French allies. Of course, it would work only if he could succeed in fooling them all.

Conradin stepped down from the dais and started to leave the hall with a swift and purposeful stride. He signaled to Ginevra as he passed. She followed quickly, her maidens trailing behind them.

Conradin allowed her to draw closer at the main entrance to the great hall. "Where are your sister and Anticoli?" he asked.

"Out hunting, Sire," Ginevra replied. "They thought it would divert our allies' suspicions if they seemed less worried than they are."

Conradin nodded. "I'm sure they were right. I will ride out to meet them. How have things gone here since my departure?"

"Everything has been quiet—before this morning hardly anyone dared stir outside the palace, for fear of the sorcerers. Then news came of the events in Naples."

"How was this news received?"

"As you might expect, *Signore*, everyone is mystified. What really happened?"

"I haven't time to say," said Conradin, continuing swiftly, "but I will tell you we have rescued King Manfred's three sons from the Castel dell' Ovo."

"Then it is true!" cried Ginevra.

"Yes, it is true. They were in the Infidels' Silver Tower, which has come to earth outside our city. I am going to put them into Bianca's charge. If you would go out to meet the Infidels—Prince Alrik is with them—and take charge of the children, you will be able to ask them what happened in Naples."

Ginevra's heart leaped at the thought of seeing the green-eyed Prince again and having so rich a topic for discussion. "Sire, I will go at once. Where shall I find this tower?"

"It stands on the west side beyond the palace walls, but Prince Alrik and Princess Natheless have already started out with the children. You will meet them. But beware. The children are in a sorry state. The youngest has lost his reason and the other two nearly have."

"*Ahimè!*" Ginevra cried in horror. "Is Charles so cruel?"

"He is certainly not tender-hearted," said Conradin. "I will ride after Anticoli."

"Wait!" Ginevra called after him. "Cousin—" He looked back, and she asked softly, "How do you fare with the Cold Princess?"

He flushed slightly, but Ginevra could not tell whether it was in annoyance or embarrassment. His answer was a reproof. "Why do you call her that, *Madònna*? She is a great and wise lady."

Ginevra felt defensive. "All the while she sat at the feast, I hardly ever saw her expression change! Her heart seemed frozen into a single attitude."

Conradin continued firmly, "She is not so frivolous as you, fair cousin." He walked swiftly toward the passage leading to the stable.

Ginevra remained alone in the corridor. Her maidens rushed up around her. "*Madònna*, what did he say? What did you talk about, *Madònna*?"

Ginevra shook off her embarrassment. "We are to fetch my cousins, King Manfred's children," she said. The suddenness of this news pushed all other ideas out of their minds.

"Where are they?" demanded Gualdrada.

"Outside the castle gates," said Ginevra. "We must have a guard with us—and at least one woman who's been a nurse—a doctor and perhaps a priest."

As it happened, no doctor was available, but Father Omberto was quickly summoned, along with two women who had been nurses to Bianca's children. By the time the group assembled, word was brought to Ginevra that the Infidels were at the castle gate, requesting admittance.

"Bring them to the gardens on the south side," returned Ginevra.

It was late in the year. The peaches had been harvested and the branches were bare. Prince Alrik was standing in the orchard, staring intensely at the tree limbs. Beside him stood the Cold Princess, lost in concentration. On seeing her, Ginevra checked her pace and approached more slowly. Some instinct told her the Cold Princess was hostile to her, and an obstacle to her designs on Prince Alrik.

When they saw her, both Infidels stepped forward and made their typically shallow bows. "Good day, *Madònna*," said the Princess in her clear, precise way. Alrik echoed her more softly. Ginevra felt a wave of resentment. Obviously she was not going to have much of a conversation with Alrik while this other woman was present.

Ginevra bowed. "Well met, my lord and lady," she said. "The Emperor has ordered me to take charge of the children."

Alrik held the smallest of the Princes, a tiny boy who lay quite still. His eyes were wide open and staring, but seemed to find nothing that interested them. Ginevra forgot about the Princess in her distress. "Sweet Queen of Heaven," she whispered, "this is the youngest who has lost his reason! Merciful God, it is altogether dreadful!"

"We cannot—get him to talk," Alrik explained as he surrendered the child into her arms. She noticed the gleam of gold as he did so, and felt a quick joy. He was wearing her gift. But when she looked at the child, her elation vanished. There was no trace of the filth and stench of the prison; the Infidels had bathed him. His clothes were also quite clean. Ginevra had heard the Infidels had an unholy obsession with washing, clearly misinterpreting Christ's stress on cleansing as demand for physical washing. The child's blond hair also hung evenly to his shoulders. It was more likely the Infidels than the French who had cut it. But he was distressingly thin and his face was even wrinkled, and his eyes stared at her from terrible depths. She called to him, "Anselino? Anselino? That is your name, isn't it?" The blue eyes stared through her rather than at her. The child said nothing.

"Yes, he is Anselino," said a helpful voice at her feet. She glanced down at the second brother standing beside her. Then she looked for the third child. He was hanging back, tenaciously clinging to the Princess Natheless's sleeve. She observed he was larger than the one who stood in front of her. "You are Prince Arrigo?" she asked uncertainly.

The child smiled delightedly on hearing his name. "How did you know?" he demanded.

Tears crowded into Ginevra's eyes. She handed Anselino to Gualdrada and opened her arms for Arrigo. "Didn't they tell you, Prince Arrigo? I am your cousin Ginevra. My grandfather was your grandmother's brother. Your old tutor came to us after you were captured and told us all about you. We have some of your old clothes, and even some of your old playthings, waiting for you in the palace."

Arrigo burst into tears and rushed into Ginevra's arms. She clung to him, unable to restrain her own tears. "Don't cry, Arrigo—that French monster will never see you again—from now on you will be well-treated—and you will learn to ride and fight and read books until you are just as good a man as your father was!"

Manfredino's interest was finally piqued by all this. He edged away from Natheless and drew closer to Ginevra. However, he continued clinging to the Infidel Princess's sleeve and drew her after him. Seeing him approach, Ginevra opened her arms to him. But suddenly she caught sight of the marks on Arrigo's wrists. "What are these?" she demanded, seizing his hands. She understood. "The marks of the fetters on his tiny hands! How could Charles be so cruel? He is a coward and a bully who fears little children!" She saw Alrik's sympathy. But before she could regain her composure, another voice interrupted. The Princess had nudged the other boy forward. Ginevra barely heard a whisper, "Why don't you show your noble cousin that you have marks on your wrists, too?"

Manfredino's voice rose, filled with outrage. "I have marks on my wrists, too, *Madònna*! Charles is a wicked usurper who ought to be hanged!"

Ginevra turned to him and swept him into her arms. "Spoken like a prince! Spoken like a true prince!" she cried.

"How can you who have the power to stop such things—how can you simply let them happen?" She spoke directly to Alrik, but Alrik seemed unable to reply. She turned to the Princess, whose expression as usual did not change. Something burned inside Ginevra at that moment. Some instinct told her it was the Princess, not Alrik, who objected to the Pelezitereans' intervention in their affairs. Her suspicion was confirmed when Alrik looked to Natheless for an answer. The Princess looked very grave. "Alrik, I think she was asking you," she said.

Ginevra understood the subtlety of the Infidel Princess. She sensed Ginevra liked Alrik better than her. Therefore she made Alrik accept the responsibility for her hateful opinions.

Alrik seemed confused. "*Madònna*, your words pain me more than I can say. Understand that what you are asking is forbidden."

"Why is it forbidden?" demanded Ginevra. "Why are your people forbidden to do good?"

The Prince seemed bewildered. "The point is we cannot trust our understanding of what is good. We know little of your people. We cannot be sure your own party might not act similarly under like circumstances." He looked to the Princess, who nodded her approval. Ginevra realized the argument originally came from her. That stung. There were stories about allies of the Hohenstaufens treating captured children with terrible cruelty. The force of these stories struck her now with a violence they never had before. It was too much, too much, too much for an Infidel to raise this question.

"I would never do such a thing, and neither would Bianca or Anticoli—or Conradin," she added as an afterthought.

Alrik was silent. The Princess spoke. "Please understand, *Madònna*, we do not mean to insult you. It is simply not for us to decide what is right or wrong in Christendom. I believe you are telling the truth. Despite everything, we must keep our law."

Ginevra realized nothing could be gained from further discussion. "I am sorry I spoke so, *Madònna*, and I am sorry I caused pain to the Prince. It was my full heart, not my doubt of your goodness, that drove me. We must proceed to the palace now to measure the children for their new clothes. Pray accompany us and recount what happened at Naples."

Natheless and Alrik fell into step beside Ginevra, and they entered the palace.

26

Conradin's court moved to Tuscanella, because Natheless thought it unwise to remain near a location known to Jimmik Centauri. After that, however, the boy-King made no further attempt to advance. Little could be accomplished by quick action when he was uncertain against whom it should be taken. Soon after his recovery from paralysis King Charles had mustered his best knights to the neighborhood of Rome in an effort to influence the Cardinals into selecting an acceptable Pope. He himself was continuously in and out of the city in his newly established capacity as Senator, attempting to hasten the process. Meanwhile, he kept a wary eye on the not-very-distant Tuscanella.

Conradin could have attacked with his superior forces. But in that case he would almost certainly lose whatever chance he had of conciliating the new Pope the Cardinals elected. Without assurance of the Pelezitereans' continuing support, Conradin thought it unwise to run that risk. There was an even greater danger: alienating Natheless by taking what she would consider unfair advantage of her people's reputation. Futhermore, if he became engrossed in a military campaign, he might overlook Jimmik Centauri's whereabouts. Hence, Conradin deemed it best to wait with the Pelezitereans for all these considerations to clarify.

Natheless was in the process of collecting what information she could about sorcerers in the history of Christendom—in poems, tales, chronicles and proclamations. "Your people will describe Jimmik Centauri in terms they understand," she said. "We must learn what these terms are." Whenever Conradin turned the subject to politics, her reaction was indifferent, detached. "If our presence compromises you with the Church too badly, we will do something to restore the balance before we go. Or," she reassured him privately, "you can take refuge among us."

In private, Bianca and Anticoli fluctuated between hope and terror. In public, before the volatile allies, they always appeared supremely confidant. King Manfred's three sons were unaffected by the fears of their elders. The youngest, Anselino, still did not respond as most children did, but he was learning to recognize his new nurse, and he sometimes conversed with his brothers. Moreover, he saw the black dog less frequently. Manfredino and Arrigo ranged all over the castle, playing with the dogs and cats, chatting excitedly about horses, hawks and armor, and observing the behavior of the noblemen and ladies and their servants. Conradin was extremely gracious to them when they gathered at dinner, and sometimes he would direct a word or two to them. The Peleziterean Princess who had been their salvation always greeted them in a friendly fashion, made a point of asking them about their activities and concerns and sometimes bestowed a restrained, nervous caress on them. Lady Bianca made much of them, but with all her duties she had as little time to spare as Conradin. It was Lady Ginevra, among the nobility, who spent the most time with them. And spending time with Lady Ginevra during those days meant spending time with the Peleziterean Prince Alrik.

Alrik was the least busy and most unhappy of the Lawchildren during this period; or at any rate, he thought so. The landing mission's success now probably rested with the efforts of the technical searchers—Rauhina Telgolarses and Sixfold Rho. On the other hand, the Contact department's efforts were probably in vain, though there was a faint possibility something might turn up. Natheless seldom had time to be alone with him, and any contact with the suffering people of Italy troubled him. Alrik was ill-equipped to bear the continuous pressures of helplessness. He pleaded for duties with the searchers, but his father did not respond to the idea. "Alrik, there are dozens of technicians on the Peleziterea who could take the place of anyone under Rauhina Telgolarses or Sixfold Rho. It would take months to train somebody to take your place in the Contact department. We need you to work where you are most effective."

Natheless had given Alrik a general order to increase his knowledge of Italian and to gather as much folklore, especially regarding magicians, as he could. But though he was not shy among his own people, he found it difficult to approach Italians. The only one easy to talk to was becoming another kind of agony. Alrik found her perfect features burned into his memory and would return to him in his dreams. Sometimes, when her eyes flashed, he even believed the tales she told him that little arrows did fly from her eyes to his when she looked at him that way, piercing his heart. "That's one of their descriptions for falling in love," he told Natheless on one occasion when they met to exchange data. As he spoke the words, something inside him jolted. No, that could not possibly be it! She was a stranger, and therefore she fascinated him. He was not in love with her. He had made her a symbol for everything about the planet he desired. To him she stood for everything that had potential here, everything that was beautiful, sensitive and vulnerable and likely to be destroyed if the Pelezitereans left the planet to its own devices. He was not in love with her. He knew how difficult it would be if he fell in love with an Italian.

But even as he reached this noble conclusion, he suspected otherwise. Natheless had gently taken his hand, murmuring some joke which he did not catch. The recoil he felt at her touch shocked him. How could he feel this way toward Natheless? He forced a smile and playfully squeezed her hand. "Our way is better, of course," he tried to continue.

Natheless was not content to let it go at that. She spoke with a note of apprehension, of wariness. "Alrik—it seems to me that your Italian has improved phenomenally in these last weeks."

"I've been working hard!" he said, with an edge in his voice that should not have been there. Observing his reaction, Natheless's face became a mask.

"I would almost think you had found new inspiration, Alrik."

Alrik felt himself reddening. "What are you suggesting?"

Natheless said nothing, but Alrik saw tears running down each cheek. How difficult this was. He struggled with his feelings. "Alrik," she begged, her voice more genuinely pleading than he had ever heard it, "if there is something wrong, please tell me! You can trust me."

He supposed if they could just talk about it, the problem might simply dissolve, or perhaps she could say a word to get him transferred to the technical search, or even speak to the Italians and prevent further meetings between him and Ginevra. Part of him longed for such a separation and part of him dreaded it. Perhaps it would be best to speak and get it over with. He tried to find the words, but could not even find the courage. "There's nothing wrong," he insisted swiftly.

220

"Are you sure, Alrik? Are you sure?" said Natheless. And she would not look him in the face. "It seems I keep losing people and never getting anyone back." She buried her face in her hands, and actually sobbed before struggling to gain control of herself.

For the love of science and progress, there's no need for a lonely-orphan act. Aloud Alrik said sharply, "Natheless, I think you're overtired."

She blinked back her tears. "I probably am. Perhaps we all are?"

"You work harder than the rest of us put together. Besides, it's getting late, and you're the one who insists we keep regular hours."

"As you say, Alrik. I guess I should retire."

She got up and walked across the room. At the door she turned and said, "You usually kiss me good night, Alrik."

Guiltily he leaped to his feet and started toward her, but she had already crossed the threshold. "Never mind. It's late now." In a moment she was up the stairs and out of sight.

Alrik knew he ought to run after her, talk to her playfully. He knew he could soften her hurt, but somehow he could not find the strength. Besides, he had never been much of a liar. He had believed he loved Natheless. He still did love her, he thought wearily. He cared about her deeply, and it would be terrible for him if anything happened to her. But for Ginevra his feelings were overpoweringly different. It had always been pleasant to turn his thoughts to Natheless; now his whole mind focused on Ginevra without his command and sometimes against his will. The attraction was often as painful as it was pleasurable, but there was no escaping it. It felt like being burned and frozen by turns, or being held by a star's gravity. Why had no one warned him real love was like this? At least he would have known enough not to say he loved Natheless.

As the following weeks dragged by, Alrik found it impossible to conceal his attraction for Ginevra. When they were together, a powerful magnetism seemed to draw them to one another. He often had to look away from her. There was a special deepening in her eyes and a special tone in her voice when they spoke. No matter, he kept telling himself. Soon necessity would snatch him away from her. Then his feelings could beat themselves to death against the cold metal walls of the Peleziterea or die of starvation across the widening vacuum of space.

But these rationalizations became progressively less credible. And what if he were selected to remain on the planet when the technical crew withdrew? He could never endure this tension for two years.

One day when he saw Ginevra walking across the grassy courtyard toward the Lander he resolved to act. Bodris asked him rather insolently,

"That's Lady Ginevra coming across, isn't it, Lawchild?"

"Yes," replied Alrik. "I'll see what she wants."

Alrik left the lower deck of the Lander and entered the courtyard just a few paces from the Italian lady. He trembled at her nearness. She wore a dark sea-green cloak lined at the neck with animal fur of some kind. Her head was covered with a fur-lined hood of the same color. She stopped when she saw him, and looked to the side as if missing her attendants.

"My lady Ginevra," said Alrik, in a carefully controlled voice, "my delight at seeing you here passes all bounds. Yet it grieves me you are obliged to weary yourself by coming here on some errand."

Ginevra flushed. "My lord, my brother Anticoli bid see whether the King was with you, and to inform him that a letter has come from a friend in Rome."

"King Conradin is in the eastern tower there," said Alrik, pointing, "with Princess Natheless and King Benrik, studying an old chronicle, I believe. Shall I lead you there?"

"It is not necessary—I know the way." Ginevra turned quickly and Alrik followed.

"Am I, then, forbidden to accompany you?"

"Forbidden?" Ginevra smiled mischievously. "Who could forbid a powerful wizard like you from doing anything he wished?"

Alrik kept telling himself there was nothing but playfulness in what she said. But he couldn't prevent his emotions from reacting to her flattery. He smiled uncertainly. "You might forbid me, my lady; one word from you would stop me in my tracks."

Ginevra's eyes filled with surprise and pleasure. He had not spoken so openly before. But she challenged, "You say I could stop you from following me. But what if I requested the opposite? Supposing I asked you not to return to your barren land, not to leave Italy? Suppose I bid you stay here? Would you heed me then?"

"You know I could not do that," said Alrik.

Ginevra sniffed. "Great power I have over you. But I tarry and must seek my cousin. Farewell!"

She started to walk. Alrik knew he should be glad his position had been made so clear. He should leave the matter where it stood, but he dashed impulsively after her. "*Madònna, Madònna*, I beg you not to leave me so!"

She turned with a mixture of pique and amusement. "So, already you break your word. You follow me despite my command, my Lord Prince?"

"Pray do not be so harsh with me, my lady. Your every word is an arrow in my heart. Therefore—therefore, I must tell you that it is for your sake I am leaving Italy with my people."

Ginevra was skeptical. "For our sake? When you could drive Charles from Naples, force sickness and uncleanliness from our borders and banish famine?"

Alrik bowed his head. "I have disobeyed my King's command. I have boasted too much."

Ginevra seemed surprised. "Boasted! Can you not do all the things you said?"

Alrik answered without restraint, "I have told you no lies, *Madònna*. All the same, I have not told you the entire truth. My people have indeed gained great powers. Only, to obtain them, we have paid a terrible price. Things you cannot even imagine living without we have had to surrender permanently to become what we are. If you could grasp what has happened to us, you would not really want to share our fate."

Ginevra became really doubtful, since this was more like the stories she had heard of people who dealt with demons and fairies. But she was unwilling to abandon ideas she had become fixed upon. "What kind of price?" she said at last.

"Alas, *Madònna*, would you have me describe our great shame?"

"What a trifler you are! Do you mean nothing more than the illness the King told me of, that which comes of marrying first cousins? I am not your first cousin."

Alrik was astounded. "You know?"

She responded serenely. "That the eyes you see with were made by your wise men because you were born blind? The King told me. He was interested in an alliance between our peoples and thought I should know the disadvantages. Did you think I would love you the less for it?" True enough, Conradin had believed she would love him less for it, and had told her precisely in order to end her interest in the Infidel. But Ginevra ignored that side of the matter. Until she thought about it later, Ginevra did not realize she had let the word "love" slip for the first time in her exchange with Alrik. Her words were so sincere Alrik was overwhelmed. He could only stare at the grey rocks of the castle wall across the way. "I thought you could never bear to look upon me again," he admitted.

"*Ahimè*, Infidel, it's little you understand the love of a Christian lady!"

He looked at her then, filled with an enormous respect for more than her beauty. She stood, firm and straight, radiating a power that had to come from an extraordinary inner vitality, a perfect psychic harmony

223

which came so naturally to these Italians, but which his Pelezitereans had lost forever. He felt irresistible desire to take her into his arms. "Lady Ginevra—" he began, stepping forward.

But she backed away. "Have a care, Prince! Many people may be watching from the walls or towers!"

Alrik flinched, wondering whether anyone had already seen something which he could not explain. But Ginevra was walking toward the tower again. "I must find my cousin the King," she said. "I did not invent that errand. But you may walk with me if you like."

Alrik fell into step with her. They crossed the yard in silence until she urged him, "Have you no more to say, Prince Alrik?"

"I might say a great deal," murmured Alrik, "if I thought words would help."

Ginevra did not really understand what he meant. But his expression bore a slight resemblance to one of the conventions of Italian love-talk, so she responded accordingly, "You accuse me of being too cruel to listen? You know it is not so. Many knights and noblemen—yes, even a prince,— have sighed for some of the words I have given you today. They never got them, though I gave them to you with little asking. I would give you greater gifts—perhaps I would give you the most precious thing I have— but I will not give it unsought."

Ginevra trembled at her own audacity. She was behaving with little of the modesty becoming a woman of her rank. What would Bianca or Anticoli or Conradin think if they could hear her? Her face became scarlet at the thought. She had never acted like this before. She had never given herself to any man except her husband, and since his death she had received the attentions of other men graciously but modestly. She had the right to take a second husband. And even if she took a lover, she was less likely to be punished than an unmarried girl of her rank. Even so, it was filled with danger, and forbidden by the priests. Why was she acting this way? It had to be a combination of her fascination with this foreigner and his peculiar sensitivity to the suffering to which she had become hard-ened. His gentleness was also a factor. He did not frighten her as some of her more forward admirers had.

He was speaking, his voice aflame with passion just as she desired it to be. "O, Ginevra, I could not bear it. They would separate us—they would tear us apart as soon as they discovered we had let our hearts become linked!"

"Do you mean my people?" Ginevra whispered back. They had just entered the tower's arched doorway, and it protected them from others' view. "My people would be glad to receive you as an ally. They would be happy to give me to you in marriage."

"My people—they intend to leave—"

"They will never leave. They will require years and years to find the wizard of hideous aspect. By that time who knows what sorts of other things will have happened."

"No." Alrik shook his head. "They will catch Jimmik. And if I tried to do what you suggest, they would search me out and capture me, too, just as they will him now."

Ginevra looked shrewdly. "They have not caught him. Could they catch you so easily? Will they not grow weary of hunting after a while?"

Alrik denied it. "No, Lady Ginevra." He searched frantically for a metaphor. "I am one of the chief pillars supporting my people. I cannot give way beneath them."

"So many fools speak," answered Ginevra scornfully. "They refuse to abandon a hopeless cause because their leaders hold to it, and their leaders will not learn how bad a cause it is until everything is lost. Among us, some people leave their leaders when they are fixed upon a bad cause. Then their leaders abandon the cause, and all are reconciled and all survive. How do you think you would show more loyalty, by helping your people have life or helping them die?"

It happened. Her words altered Alrik's perspective. He suddenly realized if he acted quickly, he could rescue his father and Natheless (for whom he felt a pang of guilt) and all the others from their aimless wanderings in the vacuum of space under the inflexible dictates of the Prime Directive. He could do all that and have the beautiful Italian woman for his wife, too. He reached for her.

"Ginevra, how wise you are—"

Her face showed her delight, but again she drew back. "Not here! Not now! Tonight. There is a walled orchard off the east side of the castle. The gate is just below the tower, and I have the key to it. Can you find your way?"

Alrik nodded, his mouth going dry.

"At midnight. But now I must find the King. Farewell!" She hurried up the stairs away from him.

27

Cardinal Ughetto's lodgings in Rome were luxurious. The walls were hung with velvet curtains, the chairs and tables inlaid with marble and gold. Ughetto approved of luxury on principle. People respected it, and when they saw jewels glistening from his fingers and head, they knew he was a man with power and significance. However, not everything that came with luxury was good. Many clergymen who exhibited it developed a reputation for softness and effeminacy. Therefore, Ughetto made it clear that while he had a right to luxury, he was not dependent on it. He kept the fast during Lent with the utmost strictness. And on Good Friday, barefoot and wearing sackcloth, he always led a procession through the streets of whatever city he happened to be in. Hence, although rumors occasionally did fly to the effect that he had several illegitimate children and had ordered more than one murder, the people at large thought of Cardinal Ughetto as a holy man. Left to their own devices, they might even have chosen him Pope. For some reason, however, which they never thought of probing deeply, another holy man had been imported from Naples. People passed among them telling stories of his integrity and virtue and of how the Conclave of Cardinals had chosen him to be Pope. It seemed he was so modest he declined, and was only prevented from leaving the city altogether by the orders of the Cardinals. It had not been hard to arouse their enthusiasm.

Large crowds were now surrounding Abbot Sinibaldo's lodgings, shouting and pleading for him to accept his election. Ughetto was preparing to give their pleas added support.

After considerable deliberation he had decided to involve his mistress, too. He would not have to do this to fool the people. But it was required if he intended to fool other Cardinals. Too many of them knew about Selvaggia to believe in his repentance if it did not include a renunciation of her. About the murders he had been discreet enough—they did not have to come up.

Most people would have said Selvaggia was no longer a beauty. Her delicate features were as perfect as before, and her neck as graceful, but age was making its marks. Her figure was still slender because she was careful of it, though no longer girlish. She used makeup carefully, but her complexion was no longer fresh. She stood before him now, her hair carefully dressed within a hairnet studded with diamonds at the interstices. Ughetto remembered overhearing some members of his household marvel that so ruthless a man as the Cardinal would allow his fading mistress to remain by his side. He smiled at their naïveté. An innocent, untried young girl in his household would have represented a gap in his armor, an ever-present source of weakness and vulnerability. Selvaggia, instinctively attuned to all his wishes, spoken and unspoken, was one of his greatest strengths.

When he was a younger man, before Pope Innocent IV had made him a Cardinal, he had had a succession of pretty mistresses. Then he had met Selvaggia. Although her beauty, her learning and her penetrating wit had immediately impressed him, he had not thought of making her his sole concubine. However, several other beautiful girls who had interested the Cardinal suddenly began to have unpleasant, and in one case disfiguring, accidents. Flattered by having aroused such a ferocious passion in so remarkable a woman, Ughetto had allowed Selvaggia to establish herself permanently in his household and drive others away. Indeed, she had been such a help to him during his career he had not even been mentioned in connection with half the murders for which he was responsible.

Ughetto spoke ironically. "You look splendid as usual, *Madònna*, but you will have to change your costume. We have some penitential pageantry to perform."

She registered no surprise, even though they had not previously discussed this. "Has Your Eminence decided when?"

"As soon as we've talked to the boy. Where is he?"

"He's waiting in the anteroom. I'll call him." Selvaggia returned to the door, and called softly, "Geoffredo!" A youth of about eighteen appeared on the threshold. He was dressed brightly like one of the lower nobility who hoped to rise in the courts of greater men—in cloth of green and yellow. Closing the door carefully behind him, he turned to the Cardinal, bowed very low and whispered, "Father!"

Ughetto smiled slightly and studied the boy. He had not seen him in five years, and was pleased at his growth. But when he spoke, all he said was, "Now, more than ever, Geoffredo, you must remember that we are only distant cousins on my mother's side. Do you understand why?"

The youth nodded. His face, like his father's, seemed strong and ready for adventure. His eyes were intelligent, but his posture, like his mother's, was pliant. Ughetto's heart swelled with pride. He was a promising boy, a worthy tool in the enterprise. "You are a page in the household of Count Guido. Has he any suspicion about who you really are?"

"No, Father. I keep my secret well. I believe it will be a better joke if I surprise him with it someday."

"Good. Now he must never know. Count Guido has come to Rome for the ostensible purpose of adding his pleas to the others who are trying to persuade the pious and simpleminded Abbot Sinibaldo to accept his elevation to the Holy See. I have reason to believe he is really traveling through Rome to gain intelligence of what is happening. As soon as he is satisfied, he will immediately proceed to Tuscanella. He will offer his service to Conradin, conveying whatever information he has gained as a sort of peace offering."

Geoffredo reacted. "Shall I do away with him then, Father?" he cried.

Ughetto held up a restraining hand. "Not so hasty! You must learn policy, my boy. Let your master be. I have already made certain most of his information will be misleading. You are to go with him to the Emperor's court—"

"The Emperor's!" cried the boy, surprised because the Church party did not concede the young Hohenstaufen that title.

"You will refer to him so from now on," returned Ughetto smoothly. "Go to the Emperor's court, and as soon as a reasonable opportunity offers itself, leave Count Guido and attach yourself to the Emperor's personal service. You are an intelligent and courageous boy. You will find ways to make him notice you, especially if you are diligent and faithful. Make yourself invaluable to him and serve him better than you would yourself. The more you make yourself trusted, the more your betrayal will be worth when I order it."

The youth's expression showed wonder. He understood his father's loyalty to the Church party was a matter of expediency. And he himself felt no special loyalty to the Papacy. He only wondered at how something so expedient until now had suddenly become not so. But his only response was, "Yes, Father."

"Conradin will win this struggle," continued Ughetto, "unless the Church changes its policy. This does not trouble me greatly, for the Empire will always need the Church. I would go over to Conradin now myself, if he were as wise as his grandfather Frederick II. But he is a hot-headed youth like you, and he would dwell on the injuries I have done his family in the past rather than the services I could render him in the future. So I must pursue other policies. I have a plan which will induce Abbot Sinibaldo to accept his election and fill your master's ears with a strange story. Just be sure you don't pay any heed to it."

"Yes, my lord," replied the youth, knowing it was not his part to ask for more information than his father was willing to give.

"The Emperor has spread rumors," continued the Cardinal, "about a red-eyed, green haired wizard. Everyone else dismisses them, but I have reason to believe the story has some foundation. What else but fear of such a man can have kept the Emperor from attacking us with the extraordinary weapons he seems to have at his disposal? Since I cannot ally myself to Conradin, I hope to offer my services to this wizard, and persuade him to make me Pope. Now do you understand why I am sending you to Conradin's court?"

The youth nodded. Ughetto was pleased. "Good. Then go and do as I say."

Geoffredo bowed and slipped out. A moment later a servant popped through the door and announced, "His Eminence Cardinal Tebaldo to see you, Your Eminence."

"Good. I'm expecting him. Send him in."

Cardinal Tebaldo, a thin, well-groomed, self-important man, strode forward impressively dressed in purple velvet. But as soon as he was safely inside the room, he dramatically threw off his mantle to show the sackcloth he was wearing underneath. Pulling off his smoothly-cut black leather boots, he stood in bare feet. "There!" he cried. "I saved the ashes for last. I thought you would have no difficulty providing enough for both."

Ughetto laughed despite himself. "Indeed, I can find that much charity in my heart, my brother."

Tebaldo turned to Selvaggia. "Are you really accompanying us, *Madònna*? I admire your courage! I tried to convince Francesca to come with me, but she dissolved into tears, poor child. I had to send her home to her mother. Now this is real devotion!"

Selvaggia bowed her head politely. "Whatever my lord desires, I desire."

"It's all for the best," Tebaldo reassured her, a little condescendingly. "Besides, it need not last long. The people think Cardinal Ughetto is a holy man, but the Hohenstaufens know him as a bitter enemy. If he were elected Pope, they'd attack at once, and none of us could expect the least mercy. That's the only reason I didn't support my brother's election in the Conclave," he said, with a deferential nod toward Ughetto. "If we can succeed in persuading Abbot Sinibaldo to accept his election, Conradin will pause and negotiate. We don't aim to obey him, really, only we need time to get out of harm's way."

Selvaggia nodded demurely. "I understand your reasons, Your Eminence."

"You're wise," agreed Cardinal Ughetto smoothly, "because, of course, Tebaldo's arguments are always indisputable."

In his own mind Tebaldo was nonetheless puzzled. The strategy he had outlined was valid for both him and Ughetto. Ughetto had committed far more heinous crimes than Tebaldo and might expect far more serious retribution than his fellow Cardinals. He had not, however, believed such a willful man would submit to so much indignity for all that. Yet it seemed he had elected to do so, and Tebaldo was not going to question his good fortune in finding so powerful an ally.

Two hours later these repentant Cardinals were seen parading down the street toward the Lateran Palace, barefoot, their bare heads bowed and covered with ashes, wearing only sackcloth where once they had glittered in silks and jewels. Many had seen Cardinal Ughetto so vested before, but never had he walked with such deep humility. Beside him walked a woman few had ever seen, but under the circumstances no one could doubt who she was. She was Ughetto's partner in contrition, and must have been his partner in sin. In the angry mood that had swept through Italy since the arrival of the demons, the people might have attacked Selvaggia had they recognized her for a clergyman's mistress under any other circumstances. But wearing her penitential garments, proving by her presence that the Cardinal was confessing a sin few had known of, she excited curiosity and sympathy. Her ragged dark clothes could not conceal the grace of her figure. Her veil and short-cropped hair even lent her a certain dignity, in addition to the dignity conferred on such women by Mary Magdalene and other sinners of the flesh who had become saints.

Her delicate feet had already been cut on the royal pavement, and she left a faint red trail on the street behind her. Some saw it all as evidence of God's returning favor and cried, "*Gloria deo!*" The penitents made no response to such jubilation, but kept on, while chanting their penitential hymns. All the same, they were taking no chances. Behind them marched some of Tebaldo's retainers, dressed appropriately in black, but in fact carrying clubs and swords beneath their robes, in case the people were not to be restrained by their feelings of piety alone.

But there was no violence. The crowd followed at a respectful distance, praying or cheering, as they participated in the repentance of these princes of the Church.

At the door of Archbishop Ruggeri's lodgings, the warden bowed low before the Cardinals and ushered them in without further ado. Ruggeri had just finished his dinner. He had eaten amply but alone that day, and his expression was somber. He rose up in surprise as the penitents entered and knelt down before him.

In an instant, Ruggeri was in tears and had thrown himself on his knees, too. "Ughetto—Selvaggia—Tebaldo—in the name of heaven. What is it you want!"

Ughetto glanced austerely at Ruggeri. "Rise, brother, go, remove your rich and frivolous vestures and don sackcloth. Cover your head with ashes as we have. The Abbot Sinibaldo has twice refused to accept his election to the Holy See, largely because of men such as we. Today we must humble ourselves for the good of all Christendom."

Ruggeri wiped his puffy cheeks with his silk handkerchief. "Yes, Your Eminence, of course. I'll prepare myself at once. Wait here." He rose, but Ughetto called out, "You alone are not enough. Lucia must come with you!"

Tears flowed freely from Ruggeri's eyes. "I sent Lucia away this morning. She was terrified. A mob came banging at our gates, threatening to burn us both. She slipped away in servant's dress. God grant she escapes the city safely! Yesterday word came that our son Giovanni was stoned at Rimini. The crowd set upon him and tore him to pieces for being a priest's bastard. Who were they indeed to judge him? He was such a handsome boy, and played the lute so well! What had he ever done to them? They were all so certain they knew what was right and what wrong! But on Judgment Day—"

"Enough!" cried Ughetto sternly. "You have been a bad Archbishop, Ruggeri; you cannot expect the sheep to know the path better than the shepherd! You foolishly see the speck in your brother's eyes and not the boulder in your own. If your paramour is gone, it is too late to send for her now, but go and at least prepare yourself." Ughetto was disappointed. Ruggeri had been the least careful of the three in concealing his irregular life, and although he was guilty of fewer crimes than the other two, the people hated him and his concubine more. He wondered for a moment why Ruggeri had kept Lucia so long. She was not of the nobility as Selvaggia was, and without aristocratic manners, education or intelligence to offset her fading complexion and thickening figure (for she had borne Ruggeri five children), Ughetto judged she had become a liability in the Archbishop's household. But Ruggeri did not seem to think so. Perhaps it was because she kept a good kitchen.

Ruggeri returned presently, dressed in coarse clothes, head and face covered with ashes. The costume seemed to stimulate the appropriate emotions, for tears were coursing down his cheeks. "I'm ready," he said.

When they reached the Lateran Palace, where Sinibaldo had been assigned his residence, the guards admitted them without question.

28

Jimmik Centauri listened absent-mindedly to the rain dripping through the dense leaves onto the dome of Skimmer II. He was finally beginning to feel like himself again. The gravitational pull during that overspeed flight to the South Pole had weakened him alarmingly. He really should not have risked it. But how was he to know that the Orbiter would be disabled so long?

There were huge deposits of iron ore beneath the ground surface where he sat. These had effectively disrupted Peleziterean detection efforts, but there were disadvantages to the environment as well. The atmospheric control inside kept him and Kappa comfortable, but the air outside was stifling, and abounding with microbes and insects. The vegetable matter also teemed with mammalian and reptilian life. Sometime, Centauri hoped, he could study and classify these species more precisely, but preferably not until he could work with dead specimens. He would employ some of the native populations in gathering them, so as not to risk his own life and limb too severely.

Centauri had already observed some natives walking by the ship in groups of ten or less with their game and hunting equipment. They had fled in terror on seeing the Skimmer, but later they had gathered others and come back in larger groups to look from a distance at the strange vessel. When two or three began to approach in a purposeful manner, spears aloft, Centauri had frightened them away with a weak energy bolt.

The natives here were useless because Centauri could not speak their language and had no way of learning it. He had spent all his life studying real science, and was too old to change his orientation.

Rauhina Telgolarses' voice sang from the communication screen. "I'm flying over a wide area, densely grown with large vegetable matter—anthophytic, I think. This sort of place was called a rain forest on Urith. There are great reserves of metallic ore here and all around. This part of the continent is extremely rich in minerals."

"Chart the borders of the deposit carefully. See if there are any exceptionally hot spots."

Centauri chuckled in amusement. "So! They've decided I'm hiding among mineral deposits! Good!" He said this apparently to Kappa, who usually stood near, watching his superior warily. The hatcherbrat seldom answered, because the Sixfold's plans were beyond his understanding. Jimmik laughed again. He was tickled because he had already developed a masking device that made Skimmer II indistinguishable from the ore to the searching Skimmer, and he was about to put finishing touches on one that would block the detectors even without minerals nearby. All the while he lay recovering, the invention had been turning over in his mind, and now he was ready to complete it. He would need it soon because there were few mineral deposits in Italy.

The Archon's party had underestimated not only Centauri's ambition and daring but also the extent of his previous planning. He had heard the Orbiter discussing with the Peleziterea the possibility that Centauri might have left the planet, and he viewed with alarm the idea of the Archon's party leaving. That would ruin all his plans.

When he had first come to the planet, Centauri had been contemptuous of the Italian natives, with their animal locomotion and their primitive methods of agriculture. But now, when he compared them to the inhabitants of the rain forest, he was seized with a burning desire to return to them. They at least had a well-started civilization with roads and bridges and complicated buildings and organized methods for producing food. Here the people had hardly any clothes and only a few tools of wood, stone, bone and clay. Centauri or his heirs would eventually find the time to civilize them, but he would establish his primary base among a more advanced people.

True, from what he had heard, several other civilizations on this planet, including an especially opulent one on the very continent where he was hiding, were equally deserving, or more so, of his first attentions, but there was still the language problem. Italian was the only language known to any Pelezitereans, and the only ones who knew it were Natheless yi-Induran, Alrik Eridani and Bodris Hatcherbrat. The only possible course for Centauri was to go back to Italy and gain control of one or more members of the Contact department.

Centauri smiled, knowing he had already planted the seeds of a betrayal in the Contact department. Although he had decided on his rebellion too suddenly for all the details to have been worked out, if he could get Skimmer II back to the Italian peninsula, he was confident that the situation would play into his hands. He closed his eyes and made plans.

"The Archon must die," he said aloud. He looked expectantly at Kappa, but there was no reaction. With a pang, Centauri realized that he missed even Alrik's naïve moral sensitivity. It was depressing to be far away from all society, cooped up with a dull-witted hatcherbrat who could not even manage a passable gasp of shock. A pain throbbed in his heart, but he suppressed it before he could recognize it as the ache of loneliness. Instead, a picture of Natheless's face rose in his mind, as it had looked at their last meeting. There was something triply insulting about her attitude, the way she had not shouted or screamed or cried, but had only stared at him from wide hazel eyes, alive with emotionless horror. It was as if what he had done was beyond mere human anger. She would pay for that, Centauri thought savagely; she would suffer for making him so miserable. If he took her alive, he would not kill her quickly. She did not belong in the same category as the Archon. He, at least, was a mature man, a seasoned administrator, and the legal head of State. When you are plotting to take over a government, you expect to have trouble from that kind of person. But for a mere seventeen-year-old girl, hitherto considered hopelessly naïve and self-absorbed, to have the temerity to see through his plot, expose him as a traitor and tell him to his face that he was dismissed—that was intolerable. Let him take her alive and he would show her just how insightful, intelligent and important she was. But first he would make her watch the Archon die, and also that pest of a native chieftain she seemed to like so much. Then she could watch the other Pelezitereans land on the planet and submit to his leadership. Certainly none of them would hold out if the Archon were dead.

Centauri wondered briefly whether the death of his father and the torture of his fiancée would thoroughly cow Alrik Eridani or drive him into open rebellion. Here was a point. Would Alrik be of any use, or would it be just as well to kill him, too? Having Bodris as the only translator might give her too much of a sense of self-importance. Perhaps he would have to kill Natheless quickly after all. With these and other half-painful, half-delicious thoughts, Centauri pondered far into the night.

Alrik sat tensely in the gathering darkness. When night came, it was utterly black because of a heavy cloud cover. As midnight approached over Tuscanella, however, the clouds cleared, and millions of stars were ushered into the sky. The familiarity of it all reassured Alrik. He tried to orient himself toward the Peleziterea, where, he knew, they would also be scanning the same starry sky. But the ship was too far off, and on the planet's dark side. As midnight neared, he needed reassurance, for that hour, when the sun was at its lowest point beneath them, was the time set for his meeting with Ginevra. First, he had to get away from the ship without being noticed. But two people were always assigned to each watch to guard the Lander. Bodris, his companion, had not left her place in the Lander all evening. Alrik rose from his chair and paced around the room as he had been doing all evening. Bodris looked up momentarily from her game of solitaire, took a quick glance at the outside screen and returned to her game. Alrik stepped toward the door. "I'm going to check the area outside," he said. "You'll be all right in here, won't you?"

"Afraid I'll start to play with the controls?" she asked sourly.

"I just asked for form's sake," muttered Alrik.

Bodris went back to her game without another word.

He stepped outside. The air was cool and strangely fresh. Alrik shuddered with delight, and for the last time his conscience challenged him. "What are you doing? What about Natheless and your father? What about the Prime Directive? How do you know this isn't some elaborate plot to trap you and steal your energet?"

But the vision of Ginevra's beautiful face rose in his mind, and he had his answer. "No. She loves me." Delight drove away all his doubts.

The grass of the courtyard rustled softly beneath his feet. He dared not use his wrist-light for fear of being seen from the walls. He had memorized his path through the courtyard and kept to the smooth places, guiding himself as much as possible by the lantern that shone from the tower near the orchard. Finally, he reached the wall Ginevra had indicated. He advanced along it cautiously, running his hand along the rough stone until he came to the wooden door. As he pressed against it, it creaked slowly inward, and he stepped through into the garden. The fragrance of peach blossoms immediately filled his nostrils. A voice, Gualdrada's, whispered in the dark, "Who goes there?"

Alrik answered, as he had been instructed, "One who comes to do my lady's will!"

A smooth hand took his and drew him forward. "Welcome, my lord!" said Ginevra's voice, tremulously.

He reached out nervously and took her other hand. "You are really here!" he said.

"My love, I feared you would not come!" she whispered back.

Behind him he heard the wooden door being pulled shut. A key turned, and Gualdrada's footsteps receded. "She will keep watch from a high window in the tower. If there is danger, she will warn us," said Ginevra. Then she called him by name for the first time, hesitantly, but with delight, "Allrrik!"

Alrik was overcome with joy at the feeling in her voice. He reached for her in the dark and touched the soft fabric of hér dress. He closed his arms around her and drew her to him. "That you should love me!" he whispered. When her kiss responded to his, he knew he accepted the fact.

29

Abbot Sinibaldo knelt on the floor beside his bed, frustration and duty warring in his heart. Four deputations of clergymen, laymen, noblemen and merchants had visited him. Through his windows he could hear the mob shouting, pleading, "Sinibaldo for Pope! Be our Holy Father." He knew the Cardinals had summoned him to Rome for that express purpose. And he expected other deputations to call on him to try stronger techniques of persuasion, though he could not imagine what these might be, since every plea and threat imaginable had already been used.

When Ambrogio entered, he knew it had come. Wearily he rose to his feet and said, "Another deputation?"

"Yes, Father Abbot."

"Who is it this time?"

"Cardinal Tebaldo, Archbishop Ruggeri and Cardinal Ughetto."

The abbot's eyes widened in surprise. "The World, the Flesh and the Devil! What have they to say to me?"

"They want to beg you to accept your election."

"Why? And how, even?"

"They are in sackcloth and ashes."

The abbot was surprised. "Truly? Could God touch such hard hearts?"

"So it would seem," replied Ambrogio, though there was conflict in his voice.

"Or else the others threatened them," added the abbot in a tone to cast aside doubt.

Ambrogio made no reply, and the abbot said, "Must I go see them?"

"The Cardinals all implore you to do so," replied Ambrogio.

"Where are they?"

"I'll lead you to them."

They were in the cloistered inner courtyard, standing among the spice flowers, Selvaggia among them. He had only a moment to reflect ironically on the opulent setting chosen for their humility. Upon seeing him, they rushed toward him in a body and threw themselves onto their knees before him. "Have pity on us, Abbot Sinibaldo!" they cried in unison, Ughetto's voice the loudest.

Sinibaldo drew himself together. "What does all this mean? In God's name, stand up! It is I who should kneel before you!"

Ughetto's face was lowered at just the right angle toward the earth, but his reply was dry as usual. "You would not agree to become our Pope, so this is how we must implore."

"But I have told you," said Sinibaldo, pacing a few steps, "I am not worthy of this high office."

Ughetto, still on his knees, looked up at last at the abbot. "So says every man who has been elected to the office. After a decent interval, most of them accept it anyway. Why do you continue to refuse?"

Sinibaldo flushed. He stood where he was and made no effort to raise the penitents, at this point tacitly acknowledging his position of moral superiority. "Do you insist, good Cardinal? Do you insist on making me rebuke you? Do you insist, although I am your inferior?"

Ughetto bowed his head again, but said loudly enough, "Not only do I insist—I implore you! Alas, too few people have rebuked me in these last years!" He beat his breast, and the others imitated him.

In hope of keeping his self-control, Sinibaldo gripped the edge of his own black robes. "Though you try to steal my point by saying it yourself, that is quite true, Your Eminence—much truer than you intend. The Church has grown powerful and fat, and her shepherds have become thieves, robbers and murderers. If I were Pope, I would drive the wolves in sheep's clothing from the fold and return the vast sums that have been mulcted from the poor. If you hope to turn the wrath of God and of the people away from you by electing me and then thwarting me at every turn as I try to do right, you hope in vain. I will not become Pope because, foolish sinner that I am, I am neither wise enough to see how to defeat you nor foolish enough to fall into your trap."

The penitents all beat their breasts and moaned. Ughetto spoke again, plaintively. "Man of God, you are right in everything you say. I am a wicked man. Twice wicked because I am a priest, thrice wicked because I am a prince of the Church. Alas! I think even knowing the depth of my guilt would mean my death; to speak of it would darken the sky—and yet, God's mercy is great! We have seen the wickedness of our ways. We grieve because our sins have brought demons to attack Christendom. Save us at least from this one last sin; do not let us prevent Christendom from having a truly holy man as its leader. We have come before you in sackcloth and ashes. We kneel before you to show you we are utterly at your disposal. We resign all our offices and powers to your care and have agreed we will accept any penance or punishment you wish to prescribe. This we do without even asking you to accept your election—only we beg you to hear our plea, which is made with contrite heart."

A speech like that could not lightly be disregarded. Sinibaldo began to walk slowly toward his visitors. "If you are telling the truth, it is a greater miracle than any I saw at Naples," he said. His gaze fell on Ruggeri's bleeding feet. "Archbishop, why have you done this? Do you think you can substitute self-hate for repentance?"

Ruggeri, overcome by the emotion of the scene, burst into tears. "How can I help hating myself? I have resolved to do right so many times, and have failed to keep my word. I just can't trust myself any more!"

"Do not fall into despair. Trust God's mercy."

Ruggeri and Selvaggia were the only ones bleeding; Ughetto's soles were calloused through previous exercise, and Tebaldo had prudently put on sandals before beginning his trek.

Abbot Sinibaldo turned to Cardinal Ughetto. "Do you really mean, Your Eminence, you would do my bidding?"

"With all my heart," returned the Cardinal.

"First of all, I command you to wash and bandage these others' feet. Brother Ambrogio will bring you what you need." He turned to leave the courtyard.

"Will you accept your election?" demanded Ughetto.

The abbot glanced back with a sigh. "I will consider it. I must pray and meditate upon it."

Back in his chamber he could still hear the crowd shouting, "Sinibaldo must be Pope! A holy man for our Holy Father!"

He sank to his knees. A feeling of uneasiness was growing in him, stronger with every heartbeat. "Blessed Savior, I am unworthy," he whispered.

He felt no reassuring presence within the room. He never had. Some monks in his cloister had had visions and some had dreamed dreams, but never the abbot. He had only good intentions, self-discipline and book-learning to rely on. With only his monastery to supervise, somehow he had never needed more. But it seemed to him Christendom now had problems such resources could not cope with. "I am not the man to lead the Faithful," he whispered. "Not in these times."

There was no answer. There was only emptiness and silence, not the silence of a God who did not exist, but the silence of a God for whose voice Sinibaldo did not know how to listen. Christendom was in confusion. Conradin was advancing on Rome supported by demons. King Charles hovered around the city, for his own purposes, demanding a Pope—at once. The Church was full of wicked men, and four illustrious penitents were calling upon Sinibaldo, a man with just enough faith for himself, to become Pope. Why? With what motives?

Faith, after all, was something you could pray for. "Give me faith, give me faith," whispered the abbot.

The hoarse cries of the mob floated up to him again. "Have mercy on us, man of God! Have mercy on us." Sinibaldo warred with his revulsion. Throughout his life one of his greatest cares had been to keep things orderly. Nothing could come closer to unhinging him than this uncontrollable throng. Since becoming a priest he had been brought closer to the people. But the attitudes he had developed as the petted son of a rich merchant kept reasserting themselves.

However, these were God's creatures. Their faith must mean something to them or they would not be here. On an impulse from duty, he went to the window and threw it open.

Seeing his face, the mob cheered, and redoubled its pleading. Perhaps some of their energy flowed up to him and conveyed their thoughts. "Good people!" he cried, but his voice was lost among theirs.

"Fellow sinners!" he cried. This time they saw he was trying to speak, and gradually they subsided into silence.

"My brothers, you ask too much of a sinner like me! You cannot choose me to be holy for all of you. If you wish God to draw back the doom he has prepared for this world, you must all be holy yourselves!"

They cheered loudly and redoubled their entreaties. "Lead us, Abbot Sinibaldo! Teach us how to be holy! Banish the liars who have lulled us with false teaching!" Almost desperate, Sinibaldo was wrestling with his answer when he heard a knock on the door.

"Brother Ambrogio? Come in," he said. He turned from the window.

The door opened and the monk entered quietly.

"Did Cardinal Ughetto do as I asked?"

"With good grace," said Ambrogio solemnly.

"What do you think of it?"

The monk stared at him, unprepared for having his opinion asked on so delicate a matter. "I could detect no insincerity—but somehow I find his repentance hard to believe. I thought I had forgiven him for that blow he gave me, and yet—so I cannot tell whether it is my own sinfulness or something in his manner that makes me doubt this miracle."

Sinibaldo nodded. "It is the same with me."

He was delaying too long, the crowd began to shout again. "Have mercy on us, man of God!"

"What am I to do?" cried the abbot, almost in desperation. The monk did not answer. Sinibaldo saw him standing in the middle of the floor, his head bowed under his cowl, his eyes cast downward. "What do you think, my son?" he demanded.

Ambrogio straightened. The abbot had subtly elicited his opinion on matters of important policy before, but never had he directly asked for his advice. "You care to know what I think?" he asked.

"Yes. What do you think? I am a man of little faith."

"You, Father Abbot?" said Ambrogio, incredulous.

"I have never had a vision," said Sinibaldo.

"No one knows why God sends visions to some people and not to others," said Ambrogio. "At least—" he faltered, "that is what you told me."

Sinibaldo eyed him narrowly. "Ambrogio, I think you are the godliest man I know. Have you ever had a dream that seemed to come from God?"

Ambrogio watched him in concern. "No, Father Abbot. At least—nothing I could honestly speak of."

"I have heard many people describe their visions—and I have thought more than half of them were nonsense," added Sinibaldo.

"Perhaps they were. How are we to know?"

"If only I were sure," mused the abbot.

"Why do you need to be sure?" inquired the monk in a puzzled tone. "You know God will send you a vision if you need one."

Sinibaldo nodded. "Ambrogio, it's you who should be Pope."

The monk drew back in bewilderment. "Do not even say so, Father Abbot! You have to have good manners and be able to converse with kings and queens! I can only understand the common people! I do not understand political intrigue. Everyone would make a fool of me. You are wise; you understand rulers. It must be you!"

Sinibaldo faced the window. "You believe it should be me?"

The monk was silent.

"So you think I should accept the election?"

Ambrogio spoke in a very low voice. "What would I think except what you have told me? It is the duty of Christ's servants to perform whatever tasks are set them, be they great or small, humbly and without protest. I must have heard you say it at least a thousand times."

The abbot nodded slowly. Then he returned to the window. The cries rose louder. "Be our Holy Father!"

"My people!" cried Sinibaldo, and once again his voice was lost. However, sensing this was his final answer, the crowd quickly fell into a dead silence.

"My people!" cried Sinibaldo. "Do you truly wish it?"

Their response was thunderous. "Sì! Sì! Be our Holy Father!"

Sinibaldo held out his hands for silence, which came immediately. "My answer, too, will be 'sì,'" he said, "although I am unworthy."

The response was thunderous.

30

Ten days after Sinibaldo accepted his election, he was consecrated in Saint Peter's Basilica, taking the name of Innocent V. He was then carried with great pomp across the Tiber and through the rejoicing city to the Lateran Palace. Before him rode a glittering procession of Roman noblemen, dominated by the figure of King Charles, whose robes and accouterments outshone all others except those of the Pope. Beside Charles rode his son, The Prince of Salerno, also spendidly attired. The populace followed in the crisp March air, singing *hosannas*.

King Charles visited the new Pope in his palace almost immediately to urge him to re-excommunicate Conradin without delay. (Conradin had been absolved of his sentence prior to his planned execution, as was the custom.) Innocent was not inclined to act so hastily. He believed the matter deserved careful consideration. Conradin had made no aggressive moves since his escape, and the charges of sorcery had not been proved. Perhaps he was behaving carefully now in order to forestall hostile action from the new Pope. Yet though he remained uncomfortably close to the eternal city, he sent away most of his new allies after merely extracting pledges of loyalty from them.

This alarmed King Charles more than anything his young antagonist could have done. It convinced him Conradin's next move would rely on sorcery rather than the force of arms. Sinibaldo shared his fears, but desired firm proof before proclaiming a sentence. And thus the situation stood for several months. Charles was unwilling to attack a rival whose mysterious rescue had lent him a superhuman aura, unless he was first excommunicated by a Pope whose undoubted holiness would render the condemnation undeniably effective. Sinibaldo plied Conradin with messages demanding to know his intentions. But he received only politely worded, evasive replies. Charles made no attempt to negotiate with Conradin himself.

So the situation appeared to the people at Rome. But Peleziterean strategy was developing somewhat faster. The day was approaching when the ships were scheduled to depart, leaving only the landing party to continue quietly at Conradin's court, waiting for news of Jimmik Centauri. But as it happened this departure never occurred in quite the way Natheless had planned. Bodris Hatcherbrat had plans of her own.

Bodris sometimes wondered why Alrik unquestioningly assumed she would not report the many times he slipped away to visit Ginevra when he was supposed to be on watch with her in the Lander. Did he believe his absences went unnoticed? Ridiculous! Did he perhaps suppose a hatcherbrat aspiring to Lawchild status would not dare report a Lawchild's misdemeanor? She could not believe he would think that of her. Timidity was not one of her failings. Of course, her reporting that the Archon's son was having an affair with a native woman would have caused quite a stir among the Lawchildren. Allowing it to continue would cause even more—that is, unless Bodris herself were planning to bring her own brand of consternation upon them sooner, and in a more direct way.

Under the present administration Bodris's chances of becoming a Lawchild were infinitesimal, she brooded, since Natheless's hostility toward her was increasingly evident—Natheless, who of all people had the least right. For the thousandth time, Bodris wondered what had guided Jimmik Centauri's decision the day he had created her destiny. For his own strange reasons, he had caused the generation of two identical zygotes from one zygote. One of these became Natheless, the other Bodris. Had he chosen the right test tube instead of the left for the hatcherbrat, Natheless would now be Bodris and Bodris Natheless. What would Bodris not have done to be a Lawchild! Certainly she would not have raised all the fuss Natheless was making about the God-Myth.

But it was too late, Bodris thought unhappily. Her hatcherbrat upbringing had formed her irreparably. Everyone who compared her with Natheless commented on the purely physical quality of their resemblance. Bodris was hatcherbrat through and through. Somebody was going to pay for that, she thought with rage. If they knew who she was, the yi-Indurans might be mortified, but it would not make them accept her. They might constrain her to act as a Lawchild, but however they succeeded, she would always be compared unfavorably to Natheless. So her way was quicker and more certain, and she would not be humiliated in the process. Centauri knew her secret.

Bodris was therefore delighted Alrik had so conveniently found something to occupy him while she made her preparations. She was only afraid his affair would end too soon. Judging by her own sexual adventures, it had lasted quite long already. It had endured six months and was still quite intense now, just a few days before the date set for the Pelezitereans' departure. Lawchildren seemed to be like that, Bodris thought angrily; they could relate to each other longer than hatcherbrats did. How they had obtained this privilege and preserved it for themselves was more than she could guess. She knew it was unfair. In any event, she must act quickly, because she had not been selected to remain on the planet.

She had invested her time alone fruitfully, duplicating in her wrist-computer all the information about the planet's language and culture Natheless had compiled so carefully. Bodris had laboriously practiced in secret and could now speak as well as Alrik. Her mind rebelled against taking all the silly tales these people told about their nature and the Universe seriously. But, such information might prove useful. And she would take it with her as a bargaining chip if nothing else.

During the past weeks she had quietly sequestered a good supply of the more easily stored foods and a hand-transformer. She had stashed these within a bundle of Italian clothes, which could conceal them a good deal better than her close-fitting Peleziterean clothing. Then she considered her next step. Obviously the big problem was getting away. But where would the Sixfold be? Certainly he was hiding. Would he be trying to surprise the Archon? Very likely. But how could he discover their precise location? He was probably having difficulty and would not be close. With any luck at all, her only hope was that he would be within reach of her wrist-communicator. In all events, she was as ready as she would ever be, at last.

The problem with her plan was that any wrist-computer could pick up her broadcast. All communication had been forbidden and the hatcher-brats' communicators had even been removed, though Bodris had made use of her nights alone to regain hers. The risk was consequently great. But what would they do if they caught her? They would hold her, send her back to the Peieziterea, place all sorts of labels on her, strip her of any hope of Lawchild status and bring her to the Central Bubble to work off her offense at menial tasks with the other hatcherbrats. In short, she would hardly be worse off than she had been before. Regarding demotion to hatcherbrat status as the worst possible fate, the Lawchildren had failed to devise any worse punishment for people already holding that status. The only other form of confinement, the terrible motionless prison, where paralyzed hatcherbrats lay on bunks and were fed by mechanical means, was reserved for the incurably violent. And Bodris would not fit that category.

In sum, the risk was worth it. The only problem really was how to get away. And far sooner than she had dared hope, Alrik solved that problem for her. More precisely, in this case, Ginevra did. It was early afternoon. The sky was blue, with only a few wispy clouds. The Archon was in his quarters and Natheless was at the castle practicing her skill at riding one of those hideous quadrupeds the Italians used for locomotion. Floress, who had never learned more than a few Italian phrases, was in her own quarters practicing. She was making herself worthy of the place she was to occupy in the crew that remained.

Alrik and Bodris were on duty together in the lower deck. By mutual agreement they had called a map of Italy to the main computer screen, and each was studying it for reasons of his own. A disturbance suddenly appeared on the side viewing screen. It was an Italian. Conradin, Ginevra and one or two other favored natives had been taught to approach and identify themselves at the door. But they usually spoke more loudly than necessary. This time, Ginevra's face appeared on the screen. Bodris could tell at once she was upset. Her face was extremely agitated.

"May I enter, my lord?" she demanded into the screen. Alrik immediately admitted her. In a moment Ginevra was in the room. She regarded Bodris with obvious distress. Finally, seeing no way to avoid her hearing it, she said to Alrik, "I must speak to you privately, my lord."

Alrik was concerned and puzzled. "Tonight?" he whispered.

"Not tonight!" Tears were spilling from her eyes. "Bianca will catch us if we try to meet tonight. If I return to the castle now, she will have me locked up. She suggested I retire to my rooms, and I pretended to do so, but hurried here instead. She'll never trust my word again after this!" She felt a bit weak, and started to lean against one of the screens. But she backed off quickly and rested on something she knew to be a chair, since Alrik had once invited her to sit on one.

Alrik looked anxious. "We'll talk, but not here." Any of the Contact department members might walk into the lower deck at any time. Alrik would take Ginevra to his quarters. "Bodris, can you manage here?"

Bodris could not have been more helpful. "Go ahead. I will manage very well." Alrik noted her strange enthusiasm. That made no difference, thought Bodris jubilantly. The emergency was too great. He would have to take Ginevra off no matter what he feared from Bodris, and as soon as they were alone, he would forget everything else.

Alrik guided Ginevra from the lower deck to his quarters. Bodris stared at the closed door for a moment, wondering exactly what had happened. No doubt Ginevra had been found out. She might well be upset. Bodris understood that violation of the code of sexual taboos among the Italians was punished more severely than breaking any rule among the Lawchildren. Women found guilty of having sexual relations with men not their husbands were punished with gruesome deaths—was it burning alive, or being battered with stones, or had she heard that the virtuous women would join together and beat the offender to death? She could not quite remember. It varied irrationally according to the woman's circumstances and who was related to her. Natheless, who seemed to glory in these complications, had theorized that it differed from region to region and that the customs had varied over time as well. It would be a waste of effort· to study such absurd customs too closely, anyway, since she and Jimmik Centauri were planning to alter them irretrievably as soon as possible.

She spared a final thought for Ginevra. What a stupid girl! Bodris enjoyed sex as much as any hatcherbrat, but she would have managed to refrain from it if someone were going to kill her for it!

This was her chance! She must exploit it at once because a Lawchild might enter at any moment. She swiftly strapped on her wrist-unit and threw her Italian peasant dress over her Peleziterean suit. She checked the main screen for anyone in the courtyard. No one. Few Italians dared approach without invitation. The Pelezitereans were absorbed in other concerns. Bodris exited and started across the yard. Dozens of eyes might be watching her from the walls and towers, but they would not know who she was and why she should not be leaving.

She found her way through the courtyard and into another without being noticed. Most people were at the large noontime meal in the great hall. At the front gate the guards allowed her to pass without question. Bodris assumed they took her for an Italian; in fact, they recognized her as a witch and did not dare interfere.

She hurried through the streets of the city, dodging people, wheeled contraptions and quadrupeds of all shapes and sizes. How easy it would be to die here, crushed beneath a wheel or trampled by the hooved quadrupeds or mangled by the sharp-toothed ones! After what seemed an interminable time, she made her way out of the city in one piece.

She began to ascend the terraces on the hills beyond the city. They were covered by culture of a vine of some sort. Natheless had said the vines produced clusters of small purple fruit which were crushed and fermented to make an intoxicating beverage. The important thing was they were low enough to pose no real threat to the Skimmer's landing, yet high enough to shield her from being spotted easily by the Archon's party.

Bodris walked and walked and walked. Her muscles grew sore and tired. The planet's sun sank lower and lower in the sky. She kept walking. Just once was she followed. Three huge, sunburnt Italian men appeared near the edge of a village and started slowly after her. She tried to ignore them at first. But they looked sinister. Their strides grew longer and stronger than hers. She whirled to face them, and they spread out to encircle her. Bodris flicked her wrist-communicator so it emitted a loud buzz, raised her arm high and shouted a simple phrase: "Beware! I am a witch! I will put a curse on you!" She was on the point of collapsing from terror. She had no energet and could not have used one if she did. And she recalled vaguely that witches who were identified and captured were also put to gruesome deaths—was it strangulation or burning alive? This time she wished she had paid more attention to those absurd Italian customs.

But these three men were not going to challenge witches that day. They hastily fled back down the hillside, shrieking some charm against evil. Bodris was shaken but elated. It had been a useful ruse. It would not be without side effects, however, because those men would spread the tale to everyone. And unless Jimmik came for her tonight, Natheless would easily find her tomorrow. Natheless could ride the hooved quadrupeds and use the toothy ones to sniff her out, and she could get other Italians to help her search by assuring them Bodris had no real powers.

When evening's last light was sinking behind the hills, Bodris finally halted. She must have gotten about six miles beyond the city. Her shift of duty in the Lander was supposed to last four hours longer, but she could not count on that to cover her. She had better act now. Now or never. Her heart beating wildly, she activated her wrist-communicator and spoke into it. "Jimmik Centauri, this is Bodris Hatcherbrat. I have slipped away from the Archon's party. Can you compute from this signal where I am—come and get me." She ended communication and kept her channel open, hoping for a return acknowledgment. Perhaps he would not risk a response until he was much closer and needed to fix her position more exactly.

Her transmission was loud and clear on the main screen of the Lander, but the control room stood empty with no one to hear it. High above the planet's surface the crew of the Orbiter heard nothing, since the signal was too weak to reach so far. On the other side of the world Rauhina Telgolarses of course heard nothing. In the east tower of the palace, Natheless sat with King Conradin, her communicator deactivated because of the ban on signals which might reveal their position to Jimmik Centauri. She heard nothing.

Conradin was discoursing amiably on the peoples of a neighboring Christian kingdom, unaware that his most trusted ally, Bianca, slouched wretched and ashamed in her chamber within a close tower, continuously looking toward the sorcerers' Silver Tower and wondering whether she should confide her sister's disgrace to her husband. What would the King say if he knew?

The only one who heard Bodris's call was the person she had intended to hear it. He had been waiting for it, night and day, for nearly six months.

31

In the darkness after twilight Natheless and Conradin crossed the courtyard wrapped in the light from Natheless' wrist-unit. As usual Natheless pronounced her name into the speaker at the entrance. There was no response. She repeated it. Again no response.

"This is strange," she said to Conradin. "If something has gone wrong with the viewing device, I don't know why they didn't send for me. What could be the matter?" Conradin said nothing. Natheless's wrist computer was programmed to contact the main computer directly when the lower deck was unmanned. She activated the proper code and the door slid open. Hovering between outrage and mystification, she led Conradin into the control room, noting in a glance that both guard seats were unoccupied. Then her entire attention was nailed to the main screen. A strained, hoarse voice was calling over it, "Lander control room, is anyone there? Lander Control, is anyone there?" Rauhina Telgolarses was on the screen with the main room of Skimmer I in the background. The other two crew members were visible and seemed agitated, throwing a series of switches and examining various screens. Rauhina continued to repeat her request for communication almost automatically, as though it were a recorded message from which she now expected no results. Natheless rushed to the screen and established contact.

"Rauhina, this is Natheless. I have just arrived and found the watch deck empty. What's going on?"

Rauhina blurted out a pent-up rush of words. "Natheless yi-Induran, I have been calling for over an hour. The Orbiter has detected Skimmer II heading this way. It'd easily have attacked you before I could contact you. But it halted several miles north of the city. It is clear your position has somehow been betrayed. I was requesting instructions from the Archon, but it's too late for that. I'm going to have to fight—to give you time to take off. Get the Lander off. Great space, he's almost on top of you!"

Rauhina turned abruptly away from the screen and toward another. On it appeared Skimmer II, moving at great speed. Natheless frantically activated a program in her wrist-computer. An emergency communication system aboard the Lander could tune in to quarters usually granted the strictest privacy. Only the first and second in command were allowed access to this system. It was for use only in the extremest of emergencies. Natheless judged this was one indeed.

The Archon's quarters came into view. He was resting, his hands folded neatly behind his head, his eyes closed. At the sound of the buzzer the Archon raised himself quickly. He stared, surprised to see Natheless's face on the seldom-used screen. "What's happened?" he demanded.

"Archon, we have been betrayed. Jimmik is in the process of launching an attack."

The frail man extracted his undependable limbs from his covers with all the haste that was medically prudent. "I'm coming," he said.

Natheless next contacted Floress's quarters.

She was also lying on her bunk when the screen lit up. She bolted upright in surprise. "Lawchild Natheless! Am I late for my shift?"

If the situation had not been so desperate, Natheless might have laughed. "No. This is an emergency. Come to the control room at once."

Bodris's quarters were empty. Natheless knew she would have to search for her later.

Alrik, who was also supposed to be on watch, still had to be accounted for. With inexplicable apprehension, Natheless pressed for his quarters. For a moment, she thought she saw what she had dreaded: murder.

The body on the bed was in no natural position. It was twisted, grotesquely distorted, limbs out of place. Who could have done such a thing? Bodris did not have weapons, and Jimmik had not yet arrived. How could even he have made the body seem to have two heads? And how could it be moving?

All at once the mystery began to clarify, and in some senses became worse. There were two bodies on the bed. Alrik was still asleep. But the golden-haired Italian woman was staring in uncomprehending fear at the sudden light in the crystal box and at the face which obviously was watching her in a place she had believed safe and private. Natheless forced herself to say the first words which came into her head, "Lady Ginevra, wake Prince Alrik and tell him the wizard of hideous aspect is attacking us."

The Italian lady grew yet more terrified. She froze as though paralyzed. Natheless was about to ask whether she understood, but Conradin's voice, vibrating with anger, erupted from behind her. "Do what she says, flower of chastity!"

The Italian woman burst into violent sobs, but started to shake Alrik. Natheless switched off the screen. Only then did she notice the Archon had already entered and was standing behind her. He had also seen everything. His surprise registered clearly in the paleness of his face. But he spoke quietly to Natheless. "Will you be all right, Natheless?"

"I guess I have to be," she answered. She remembered the Archon's weakness. And her concern for him allowed her for the moment to avoid confronting her feelings about Alrik.

The Archon agreed. "I'll complete the call for personnel; you prepare the ship for takeoff. So far all accounted for but Bodris?"

"Yes. She must be linked with Centauri in this."

The Archon proceeded with the search, while Natheless and Floress activated the engines for takeoff. When they were airborne, Natheless felt she had to address Conradin, who had followed on her heels through the various preparations. His face was expressionless and he had made no comment. Conradin had at times exhibited considerable breadth of understanding. But Italian sexual taboos and their reactions to violations of them bordered on the irrational. If Conradin were seriously angry, it might be wise to put him under restraint before proceeding.

"Are you angry with us, King? Do you feel injured?"

Conradin answered calmly, "It is the custom among our people to take vengeance when our women are dishonored."

"Please understand we will do everything possible and lawful to satisfy you, if we survive this ambush."

"I understand," Conradin nodded, his expression enigmatic.

On the main screen by which they were in contact with Skimmer I, Rauhina cried out, "There he is! Fire!" They heard metal boiling, some yells and a piercing scream. Their view screen went black.

"They've been hit!" exclaimed the Archon softly. He worked the controls to bring another image to the screen from outside the Skimmers. The two Skimmers were plunging apart. Skimmer I was crippled, wavering slowly downward toward the planet's surface. Skimmer II was hurtling away.

The door to the control room opened. Alrik entered. "Take the tail gun," the Archon ordered, without looking at him. Alrik rushed to his post while the Archon attempted to maneuver the Lander to bring Skimmer II within range of its weapons. A bolt was fired. But the Skimmer was clearly beyond range and sped on.

"Great space," muttered the Archon, "he'll outrun us if we try to keep him in bolt range, but if we follow straight on, we can't do anything to him."

They chased Jimmik Centauri on a zigzag path for many miles, gradually edging up past the limits of safe-speed. Then suddenly, when they were in the neighborhood of Naples, Skimmer II slowed down. The Archon entered into a swift climb and slowly rolled, readying for a shot. They fired a bolt, but the Skimmer neatly dodged it, turned sharply and dove under the Lander. A sudden burst of flame erupted toward them from the Skimmer.

"Alrik! He's trying to fire at the spot where this ship was hit when we attacked him in it!" The walls of the Lander vibrated wildly and the ship veered at a sudden angle. But the Lander was massively constructed, whatever the previous damage, and withstood the hit. Within a brief time, the Archon had it under control again.

But Skimmer II was nowhere to be seen.

"He can't mount a sustained attack on us," said the Archon. "That attack was only a diversion to cover his escape. He's scuttling back to whatever hiding place he's found. Natheless, contact the Orbiter."

Natheless obeyed. Rho appeared on the screen.

"Rho, can you determine where he's gone?"

"I'm sorry, Sevenfold. He threw something off. Some kind of blocking device. It's hiding a considerable portion of the sky from our detectors."

They might have known. "What about Skimmer I?"

"The ship succeeded in making a soft landing. But they're too badly damaged to fly. And Rauhina Telgolarses is dead. The bolt caught her in its path. She rushed to attack too early. She knew if your Lander and her Skimmer coordinated their attack, together you could have knocked Centauri out of the sky. But as it was, she knew she had to buy you time to take off. Otherwise, Centauri would have caught you on the ground."

"I see," muttered the Archon. "Keep a close watch. Contact me at once if there's any sign of Centauri. We'll join Skimmer I. Where did it come down?"

Rho gave the requested information.

"Understood." The communication was closed. A tired silence settled over the room. The Archon broke it by a remark to Alrik. "Is your guest properly strapped in?"

"Yes," he answered.

"Good. She'd have serious injuries by now if she weren't."

Then Sixfold Rho contacted them again. "Sevenfold, the blocking effect in the planet's atmosphere has ended. But I can't detect Centauri on the ground. He must have devised a very effective shield. But he cannot have left the Italian peninsula. His cover never extended far over the ocean."

"Thank you, Sixfold Rho. Keep the suspected area under surveillance."

"Understood, Sevenfold." The communication closed again, this time for good.

Alrik left the weapon controls and crossed to Natheless, who was still sitting in front of the screen. "Natheless, I'd like to speak with you now."

Natheless had managed to divide the contents of her consciousness. One area contained her thoughts about the larger situation, one contained her feelings about Alrik. She could concentrate on one or the other. She could think clearly or suffer violent emotions. But she was nowhere near a point where the two forms of consciousness could have any meaningful communication with each other. Numbly she asked him, "Why?"

"You know why."

Natheless cast an inquiring glance at the Archon, who said, "It's a question of whom he talks to first, Natheless. We both have claims, but I am willing to grant yours priority, if you wish."

Natheless shrugged. "All right, Alrik, let's talk."

"Floress, you're on watch," said the Archon as they left. They walked up to Natheless's quarters.

"Natheless, I'm in love with Ginevra."

Natheless shook her head slowly. "Is that an excuse, Alrik?" she whispered. "You know you have no right to be, even if you weren't engaged to me. It's against everything we're trying to accomplish."

"You don't understand. I couldn't help it."

"Alrik, Lawchildren don't talk that way."

Alrik paced to the other side of the hall. "There may be some things Lawchildren don't know!"

"Are you a Lawchild or not, Alrik?" Natheless asked in wonderment. "If you aren't, what do you think you are? A hatcherbrat?"

Though she had said it very softly, he grew angry. "Natheless, I never thought you would speak to me like that!"

"Have you become Italian then? You don't seem bound by their sexual taboos. Do you think you are superior to either culture, bound by the obligations of neither?"

Alrik lost his temper. "Perhaps that's always been the trouble with you, Natheless!" he snapped. "Here I was, worried because you'd be terribly hurt. But all you can do is lecture on Contact theorems, culture identification or whatever you'd like to call it!"

A great reservoir of misery stirred inside Natheless. Tears came to her eyes, at last. "You think I'm not hurt, Alrik?" she whispered.

He could not look at her. "Oh, how am I going to discuss this with you? You're not even normal! Your reactions are always so odd. You treasure these neurotic ceremonies in honor of the God-Myth, and always think of death when everyone else is enjoying life. I guess you can't help it. I guess that's just the way you are."

Natheless's voice took on some energy. "What do you mean, Alrik? Haven't I the right to be what I am, just as you have to be what you are?"

"Of course you do. That's what I'm trying to say."

"I see!" exclaimed Natheless. "You're telling me that just as it is my nature to be forever in low spirits, to try always to satisfy other people, to keep my personal feelings under control and do what the Peleziterean laws require—in the same way it is your nature to celebrate your high spirits and enjoy life by disobeying rules, ignoring other people's feelings and getting into legal and cultural difficulties other people will finally have to straighten out. In other words, it is perfectly natural for you to make me wretched and then claim you haven't done so because I am naturally a wretched person."

"That just won't work, Natheless! I don't know anyone else who is as depressed a person as you are. No one else your age still believes in the God-Myth, either." He moderated his tone a little. "You'll just have to face it, Natheless. You aren't like other people. Before, I thought we would work it out, but now I know we can't. We wouldn't make good partners."

The anger faded slowly from Natheless's face. She answered coldly.

"That's true. We aren't good partners. I'm sure you thought it out just like that—calmly, logically, taking all the factors into account—"

Alrik flared again. "There! Calmly! Logically! As if all there were to life was calmness and logic! Nibbana Parzes thought I could help you. I've tried for two years and I know now it simply wouldn't work. You really don't seem to have any emotions at all."

Natheless's voice sank so low it was barely audible. "You asked me to marry you because Nibbana Parzes wanted it?" She looked thinner and more melancholy than ever.

Alrik tried to undo what he had let slip. "No, no! I shouldn't have said that! Never mind! Forget it! Natheless—believe me, I'd have done it anyway!"

"All this while," she whispered, "you were administering therapy to a neurotic?"

"You've got it all wrong!"

Natheless could hardly continue speaking. "I think, Alrik, we have said all that needs to be said. We both agree our engagement is at an end. You need to speak with the Archon now. I believe he can spare me until we reach the downed Skimmer. If he can't, he can call me on the emergency circuit." She brushed past Alrik to the door of her own quarters. Alrik tried to grab her arm.

"Natheless—I never meant to hurt you."

She eluded him. "I believe you, Alrik. You couldn't have meant to hurt me. You weren't thinking about me at all."

32

If Alrik said anything more, Nathe-
less did not hear him. She was too distracted by her pain. She found the
door to her quarters, opened it and locked it behind her. The familiar
brown walls brought a momentary sense of security, but also a feeling of
loss. The only decorations on the walls were two pictures. One was of
Agni in full ceremonial costume, just stepping aboard the vessel for the
voyage which would end in his death, the other of Alrik and herself, also
in full ceremonial dress, just after they had announced their engagement.
She removed it and thrust it into one of the storage compartments, while
the tears she had been restraining began to flow. She felt a scream
struggling to rise out of her but restrained herself—as usual, she thought.
She knelt on the floor beside the bunk and buried her face in the covers.
Then she reached out to the God-Myth.

The vague Peleziterean stories told to children did not specify a precise
appearance for their god, or even a sex, but Natheless had conceived of
him as a cloudlike human form, encompassing the whole universe but
clearly visible in none of it. The features of the cloud figure were noble,
wise and kindly, old, yet young. He gazed eternally and unwaveringly on
things humans could not see and could not bear to see. After only a
glimpse of those eyes, Natheless always looked down into his heart. There

his arms were tenderly folded over the souls of the dead. There were a great many souls there, but only a few were known to Natheless yi-Induran. Some were lying inert, like Rauhina Telgolarses, her cheeks still stained with the suffering she had experienced during the last moments of her life. Others lay in varying degrees of wakefulness. Some opened their eyes occasionally, and quickly closed them again. Others rested against the All-Father's chest and looked around them with increasing intensity.

Still others, awake far longer, had begun to move about. They seemed to be gathered on a planetary slope of some kind, pleasant enough, but not precisely like anything Natheless had ever seen. There was really no reason why it could not have been, except that Natheless preferred it so. For one thing the God-Myth implied that all images or words concerning the deity and the afterlife were strictly figurative and should be abandoned as soon as they proved unhelpful. Natheless concentrated on feeling his presence all around her.

The awakened souls were moving around the hill, sometimes in groups of two, three or more, sometimes alone, but all responsive to the god's unseen influence. Sometimes crowds would join and proceed together for a time. Sometimes large clusters would break into smaller groups, but there was never any sign of disharmony.

At long last Natheless found a small group containing Frofor yi-Induran, Urmis yi-Induran and Agni. They in turn could see Natheless, and sent a greeting full of love and serenity across the distance.

"Mother, Father, Agni!" cried Natheless. "How much longer must I put up with this heartlessness? No one here has any use for me. I want to come home to you!"

Agni spoke for them, because he knew her best. His face was full of fun, as it had always been. "Why give up now, Little Sister? You're doing fine. We're all proud of you."

Natheless continued to protest, "No one thinks the way I think. No one cares about the things I care about. No one wants the things I want, not since you've been gone."

Agni appeared saddened. "You can stand it a little longer, Natheless. There may be a great deal left for you to do. And we will always be here, whenever you come. We have nowhere else to go. What are fifty or seventy years, one way or another, when you have all eternity to wait?"

Natheless felt enormously better. "But I'm not even sure the Prime Directive matters, not now, after all this. Were you sure?"

Agni laughed. "Of course I was sure. I hadn't even met the people though. So I can understand why you're wondering. Are you certain the Prime Directive doesn't matter?"

"No."

"Well then, perhaps you'd better remain, in case it does. That way, we'll certainly have more to talk about when you finally come here."

Natheless rested against the bed. "But it hurts so much," she said.

"You've enjoyed some things, haven't you? Remember those exploring trips we used to take, dodging the larger asteroids in our Scouts?"

"Yes," said Natheless, her tears beginning to flow again. "You and I, Alrik and Rauhina."

"Consider how much you've enjoyed learning this planet's language and its legends, and all the revisions you were hoping to add to Contact Theory after returning to the Peleziterea," said Agni.

"Yes," said Natheless. "Maybe my problem is only Alrik, who really hurt me. He finds me mistrustful and withdrawn. That's precisely because people hurt me when I try to depend on them. He tried to persuade me he was like you, that he cared about me, that he understood and would not turn against me. When I finally let him see where I was vulnerable, he hurt me more than anyone has ever hurt me before, and deliberately."

"You shouldn't take it so seriously, Natheless. It was a defensive reaction because he knew he was in the wrong and was trying to divert the blame from his own behavior. He's got no one to defend his conduct. Even Nibbana Parzes will disapprove."

"He said the worst things he could think of, because he knew they would hurt."

"You've got to be careful whom you let into your heart, Little Sister."

"I will never take the risk again," said Natheless, her emotions rising again. "I will act so no one will ever want to know anything about me again. I'll mark my face." She drew the energet from her suit. "A long ugly scar, from my forehead to my chin, so men will look at me and turn away. They will keep their distance and I'll keep mine. I'll concentrate entirely on my work and be at peace." She held the energet at arm's length before her and studied it. Agni swiftly dashed several paces down the hill. "Don't do that, Natheless, don't dare do that!"

Her father, Frofor yi-Induran, looked intensely at her and spoke calmly. "What is the use of disfiguring your face, Natheless? If you really mean what you have said, you won't need it to keep other people away. Are you really considering it to hurt Alrik and Benrik Eridani? Alrik is probably not sensitive enough to be badly hurt, and the Archon never meant you any harm."

Her mother, Urmis, spoke. "If you must make a mark anywhere, daughter of mine, make it on your soul, so you yourself will not forget what has happened."

Natheless was clutching the energet to her breast, whispering, "A mark on my soul, a mark on my soul," when she became aware of someone else addressing her from her own side of death. Someone was calling her from the corridor outside the door.

"Lawchild Natheless! Natheless yi-Induran! Lawchild Natheless!" The voice sounded familiar, but she could not yet place it.

"Who's there?"

"Benrik Eridani."

Natheless rose dazedly and staggered the step or two to the door. The Archon, pale and distressed, stood in the doorway. She motioned him in, self-consciously wiping away the signs of her tears. In her personal agony she had lost sight of the larger issues. She tried to refocus on them.

"What is it, Sevenfold? Do you need me for something?"

"No," said the Archon, stepping into the room and glancing around as though he were expecting something to jump out and attack him. "May I sit down?"

"Please!" She would ordinarily not have forgotten to invite him.

The Archon sank wearily down onto the bed. "Why don't you sit down, too, Lawchild Natheless? I'd like to talk to you."

Natheless sat beside him and eyed him with concern. "These times are very hard for you. Are you feeling well?"

The Archon flinched as though his thoughts had been interrupted. "I'm bearing up all right, I think, thank you. Actually, I came here because I am worried about you."

"About me?" Natheless spoke without passion.

"I see you have put away your energet."

Natheless gasped. "You were watching me on the emergency viewer! Because Nibbana Parzes says I am unstable, you were watching me!"

"Please believe me, Natheless, I would be derelict in my duty if I had not. You are under tremendous stress, you are only seventeen, and there are reservations on your Personality dossier. Alrik returned with some barely coherent tale about trying to mention something unmentionable to you and your being out of control. He was out of control himself at the time. I sent him to the infirmary to compose himself. Under the circumstances I could do no less than use the emergency screen, to see how you were doing. You were clasping your energet and murmuring to yourself. Floress and I were afraid if I spoke to you on the emergency speaker, it might startle you and precipitate whatever it was you were planning. So I turned the screen off and came to speak to you in person. Floress and the native chieftain are probably still on the lower deck, anxiously waiting."

Natheless shook her head, somewhere between amazement and mortification. "I was talking to myself, Benrik Eridani. I had no idea I was putting on a show for you."

"What were you planning to do with that energet, Natheless yi-Induran?"

"I wasn't planning anything, Lawchild Benrik. Thoughts were flashing through my head. I clutched the energet to symbolize them, I guess. It was close at hand and convenient. If it hadn't been, I'm sure I wouldn't have gone to look for it, because I didn't need it for anything specific. It was locked the whole time. I never even considered turning it on."

"What were you thinking then, Sixfold Natheless?"

"Do you really need to know, Archon? It was a fairly stupid idea. Most people are allowed to have stupid ideas in private. No need to reveal them in public."

The Archon seemed relieved by what she was saying. "That's true enough, Natheless." After a pause, he added, "You know I want to believe you, but would it be right for me to take your word?"

Natheless was in confusion. She was unable, as usual, to escape from the strange circumstances in which she found herself, and unable to see herself as others saw her. "I've told you the truth as far as I understand it myself, Sevenfold. I really don't know what more you're asking."

The Archon was reassuring. "What I want to know is whether I've been asking too much. Most of the other Sixfold believed this mission was too hazardous from the first, and it has become more complex as we go along. You are a juvenile, to begin with, and many among us—not Nibbana Parzes alone—felt this might be too high-pressure an assignment for you. I took several precautions to help you. One was coming myself. If the Contact sub-Archon had been more experienced, I'd probably have left the whole expedition in his charge. Also, Alrik was supposed to exert a stabilizing influence on you. The latest development—Centauri's flight, the obvious fact he has designs on Italy—places the pressure entirely on the Contact department once more, and nearly everything has gone wrong. One member has already deserted to him.

Another has proved to be a *de*stabilizing influence. Is it reasonable of me to continue this mission, or should we abandon or at least postpone it for a while?"

Until this moment the one fixed point Natheless had relied on was the priority of the mission. It seemed to her the Archon's suggestion had dissolved the floors and walls around her. "And leave Jimmik Centauri to make himself a god?" she cried.

"It's a terrible choice," agreed the Archon. Natheless studied him closely. He seemed small, frail and tired. How could she help him? An unexpected reserve of energy was released somewhere inside her. Strength flowed through her. "Lawchild Benrik," she said.

He looked at her. She knew then the strength of the God-Myth and of the dead had come over her. They were all with her, spreading their unseen influence through her.

"Lawchild Benrik, I am ready to go on fighting."

He seemed puzzled by the change in her. "You seem to be, Natheless. But how can it be?"

She responded steadily. "I have called upon the God-Myth for help. He has never failed me yet."

Benrik Eridani looked doubtful. "If only I could find something in myself to help me understand precisely what you mean! Perhaps a mind working alone, a soul talking to itself, is very inefficient? I know I make much better decisions when I pretend to review my ideas with someone else. People often lose many of their natural insights by trying to hide things from themselves. But other people bring such things out in conversation. I suppose when you believe you are reviewing matters before an omniscient being, there's no point trying to hide things."

Natheless was a tiny bit distressed. "What you have said is very true, Lawchild Benrik. What always troubles me is how easy it is to lie to yourself. Theoretically, people could avoid a lot of that by pretending to hold conversations with omniscient beings. But who would really bother, if, at one level or another, they did not truly believe?"

Benrik nodded slowly. "I still don't understand exactly what you're feeling now, Lawchild Natheless. But one thing is clear anyway: you're certainly sound of mind. I'll take you at your word."

Natheless smiled again. "What happens next?"

The Archon looked troubled. "Technical matters are well in hand. I'm afraid, however, the important issues depend on you again. The Italian woman is pregnant. I understand from Floress this might cause severe trouble with our contacts. She wasn't sure what kind. On this point, I gather from the native chieftain's statement that Alrik is no longer capable of speaking comprehensibly, in any language. It remains to be seen whether we still want him working with the Contact department, or whether we should get a replacement."

"I see," said Natheless. Her hurt gathered in her throat to remind her of its existence. She resolved not to consider it. Let her emotions rage as they would; she had to keep working. "I'll start now," she said.

33

Ginevra had no way of knowing how long she had lain within the sorcerers' Silver Tower. Alrik had left hastily, saying he had no idea when he would return and that they were in great danger. Then the room had begun to pitch violently and spin about. Was it an earthquake? Or was the sorcerers' tower possibly flying through the air, propelled by demons? Every pulse in her body beat with terror, but she kept her mouth clenched shut, for fear a scream would summon one of the witches. Between the room's jolts and her own terror, she racked her confused brain for anything to help her understand her position. They were being attacked by the wizard of hideous aspect. Ginevra tried to remember how Conradin had described him. A small, withered man with hatred pouring from his red eyes beneath a mass of ghastly green hair. He sounded like the sort of man who would deal with evil spirits. And in such cases, the worse a man was, the less human he became, the more influence he would have over the demons. Comparatively decent people like Alrik would have no chance against him. What would happen if the hideous wizard found her there, a pregnant woman, alone and helpless, strapped in place? Ginevra pulled frantically against the straps. Though they were gentle, they held fast. Alrik had explained the straps were necessary because—Ginevra could not remember why. She had been too distraught seeing those faces in the crystal box and hearing Conradin call to her so contemptuously.

The Silver Tower pitched again, and she knew clearly she was staring downward at the ceiling. If she had not been strapped in, she would have fallen to the ceiling in a heap! Perhaps that was the reason Alrik had given her.

The turns and twists lasted only a short while longer. Then her situation became even harder to bear. All was still, quiet, quieter than a convent on the remotest mountain. She could have heard mice rustling through straw. But there were neither mice nor straw here. Only those bare walls and the floor made of a material she did not recognize. Where was Alrik, and what was happening to him? Would the King punish him? And what would they do to her? "My people will not hurt you," was one of the things Alrik had said in haste as he was preparing to leave. But in her heart she suspected Alrik did not have complete control over what his people did. The Cold Princess's face returned to haunt her.

Who was this Princess, and what did she have to do with Alrik? No one had ever described their relationship. They were "Prince" and "Princess," while Benrik was King. Were they brother and sister? Or did the Pelezitereans have a custom like the one in Germany, where many princely families elected the king on the death of each ruler? Either way, jealousy was likely in the witch's heart. Alrik, being a man, would not suspect. What could he do if the Princess tried to take vengeance on Ginevra and he were locked in prison? Some Italian ladies were horribly cruel to their brothers' or cousins' sweethearts. Infidels were probably even worse. She had heard a story about an Infidel woman who had captured her husband's pregnant mistress, stripped her naked, cut open her belly, sliced off her breasts and left the rest for the dogs to tear to pieces. Ginevra cried out, "Ahimè! Gran Dio!"

"Lady Ginevra?" A voice suddenly sounded from outside the room. It was the Cold Princess. Neither the voice nor the accent could be mistaken. Ginevra tried to raise her hands to protect herself, but the straps held her.

"Lady Ginevra? Are you hurt? May I enter?" the voice came again.

Ginevra sobbed. The door slid open, and the sorceress, mighty and tall at the angle from which Ginevra saw her, stepped into the room. She bent a moment over the bed.

"How goes it with you, Lady Ginevra?"

Ginevra saw nothing in the pale face above her to which she could appeal. The expression was faraway and impersonal, as it usually was, though her eyes were redder than usual. Could it be from weeping? Weeping for Alrik? Perhaps she was his sister after all. However it might be, Ginevra could do nothing to prevent the sorceress from having her will, whatever she intended.

"I am well," she said, trying to sound confident, but unable to control her fear.

"Good," replied the sorceress. "The battle is over now. The wizard Jimmik Centauri has disappeared. It is safe to release you. Will that please you?"

"Sì," said Ginevra in relief.

The Princess knelt beside the bed and worked the clasps. In a moment Ginevra sat up, stretching her arms and legs. She looked warily up at the Princess. "Where is Prince Alrik?" she quavered. "My betrothed," she added, gaining courage and flushing at the same time.

"Your betrothed?" The Princess seemed startled, but not for long. "Was there, then, talk of marriage between you?"

"He swore he would marry me," insisted Ginevra, "on the image of Mary, Queen of Heaven."

"Is that so?" replied the Princess slowly. She hesitated, as if uncertain whether to reply. "And how were you to live, and where?"

"The King would give him lands. He has powers enough to hold them."

"Did you not know this is strictly forbidden by our people?"

It seemed plain the Princess intended no violence, but her cold, even tone irritated Ginevra. She answered somewhat heatedly, "I knew you had said so."

The Princess's eyes acknowledged the intended insult, but she replied without rancor, "Did Alrik tell you something different?"

Ginevra was about to affirm it. But she caught herself. She remembered these Infidels were strange people. They took this rule of theirs, incomprehensible as it was, very seriously. It was possible they might regard Alrik's rejection of it as something near treason. What had she been doing, giving evidence against him? "He will tell you everything!" she exclaimed, and said nothing more about it.

The Princess smiled grimly. "I see. He was planning either to stay in Italy with you after we had gone, or to persuade us not to go."

Ginevra wanted to deny it. But she couldn't think of a plausible way of doing so, since she had already claimed marriage was part of the plan and she could not deny the child in her womb. Tears flowed from her helplessly.

"Lady Ginevra," said the Princess, her gaze still quite distant, "I am sorry for your distress, but I cannot relieve it. You have desired and trusted in something my people cannot grant you, and we have said so from the beginning. You might have spared yourself this pain if you had heeded us."

Ginevra sobbed, "What will you do with Alrik?"

"Alrik? You have no cause to fear for Alrik. At worst he will be returned to his people. And you to yours."

Ginevra was as distressed at this as at the worst possible news. The Princess continued, "Or perhaps I should have said, 'At worst you will be received among the Pelezitereans as Alrik's wife and granted all the rights and privileges pertaining to Lawchild status.' How do I know what is worst?"

"You would let me marry Prince Alrik?" cried Ginevra, in sudden hope.

"If you would be willing," said the Princess, warning her, "to join the Pelezitereans and depart with us after we have defeated Jimmik Centauri. You may do so. No law forbids it. But we will never return to Italy again."

Nothing in Italy was worth enduring the shame of bearing an illegitimate child and the scorn of her family. "I wish to go where Alrik goes!" she said promptly.

Natheless was gentle. "You ought not decide so hastily, Lady Ginevra. How much do you know about the Pelezitereans? Did Alrik tell you how barren our land is? That we have no animals at all?"

"Sì," said Ginevra, but her heart sank as she considered what it would be like to live in such a country—no horses, no dogs, no hawks, no deer—

"We have no plants, either, except a few kinds of seaweed, grown for food," said Natheless. "And we have no mountains, no oceans, no rivers, no waterfalls. We make all our water ourselves, and all our air, too. And the sky does not look as it does here, blue by day, with great white clouds in wisps and masses blown by the wind into changing patterns. For us it is always the night sky, black with glittering stars. And for us they are not even the same stars as they are for you. Your people have looked up at the sky and seen the same stars year after year. You have noted their patterns and given them names, so you can even measure time and tell your directions by them. But we, we only see our stars once and pass them by forever."

Ginevra was staring at her in uncomprehending wonder.

Natheless paused. "I have already told you more than I should have.

But how else can I be fair, as you consider the choice of becoming one of us? Let me also tell you our great secret, the one I have told no one but the King."

Ginevra's eyes were wide. Natheless tried to think of a way of explaining the matter without misleading her. "Think of the sun," she said. "Now think of a star. We have found it is possible to go close enough to those stars so that, from our vessels, each star looks like a sun. We have also been so far away from your sun that it looked just like one of those little stars."

"*Oeh!*" exclaimed Ginevra.

"In fact, the sun is like many other stars. It only looks different here because it is close to us. Every star you can see in the night sky is a sun, and most of them have worlds close by to light up and keep warm, though few of those worlds have people on them like this one. We came from the only other world we know of, driven away eighty generations ago, because it was dominated by a cruel tyrant. Ever since we have searched through the skies, looking for another world, but we cannot find one. Yours is the first we have found, and because you are here we must leave it."

"Alas!" cried Ginevra. "Is not God's throne in the sky?"

Natheless had to think a moment before replying. "It may be, but we have not found him yet."

"*Ahimè!*" cried Ginevra. "If you long so for our world, why do you not stay here with us, when we are so eager to welcome you?"

Real emotion and conviction came into the Princess's face, and Ginevra was frightened. "It would destroy you, Lady Ginevra, whatever you think. Your King sees our powers as a shortcut out of his present troubles. But I tell you, it is not a way. Our powers are great, but we have paid terribly for them. We know what some of that cost has been, but there are many aspects of it we still do not understand. It is distinctly possible we do not even know the worst of it. The rule we call the Prime Directive was established by wise people, who based their decision on everything they had witnessed during their lives. It would be foolish to disregard their advice. If we remain, you will lose something unspeakably precious, something so important to you that you are not even aware of it now. You would curse the day the Pelezitereans came to your world, and it would be too late."

"God have mercy!" cried Ginevra. The force of the Princess's opinion left no room for doubt. She was telling the truth. All her dreams of glory, with Alrik at her side as an Italian prince, evaporated. Yet somehow she could not quite regret Alrik had not made this clear to her in the first place. The child in her womb could not be unbegotten in any case. "I wish to be a Peleziterean and come with you. If it is something Alrik has borne, I can bear it, too."

"I would urge you again," said the Princess, "do not make your decision in haste. Your wishes will be considered, but others must also be taken into account—those of Alrik, of King Benrik and of your own family and your King. It may be possible to conceal what has happened. You could possibly remain with us only until the child is born, and then Alrik could see it was adopted by one of the families among our Lawchildren. It would be well taken care of, never fear; healthy children are scarce among us."

"I will go where my husband goes," repeated Ginevra. "Where is he now?"

"I believe he is in the infirmary now, talking to his father. Come, I will bring you to your new quarters. You cannot stay here."

Ginevra began to follow Natheless but halted, "Does Alrik know where you're taking me?"

"It won't be concealed from him."

"May I not see him?"

"Not now."

"May I see him soon?"

"That remains to be decided. Have you any messages for him? You may tell me, and I will tell his father, and his father will tell him."

Ginevra looked shrewdly at the Princess. If they were going to be among the same people, it might be worthwhile to try making a friend of her. Ginevra sought a conciliating tone. "Do you have any sympathy for the ways of love?" she asked.

Natheless looked at her a little suspiciously. "Too much. Especially for my own ways."

Something in the Princess's manner alarmed her, but the answer on the whole seemed encouraging. "You have been in love?" she asked interestedly. Who would have thought it of the Cold Princess?

Natheless motioned vigorously for Ginevra to follow her into the hall. "What matters it to you, Lady Ginevra?"

Ginevra followed, a bit chagrined. "I only meant to ask you if you would give Alrik my message yourself. You are a woman."

Natheless proceeded a few steps before answering. "Lady Ginevra, I find it difficult to believe you do not know this, but I suppose you might not if neither your King nor Alrik told you. You will have no trouble understanding why I cannot give your message to Alrik, if you are a woman who has any sympathy with the ways of love. Prince Alrik was betrothed to me before he met you."

Ginevra was stunned. "Betrothed—to you?"

"He was." They had come to another door. Natheless opened it with some device on her wrist-unit. Ginevra hung back and would not enter. Everything Alrik had told her about Peleziterean marriages' being arranged by mutual consent came back to her. "Then you love him!"

"What does that matter to you, Lady Ginevra?" replied Natheless, gesturing for her to go in.

"He betrayed you!" Copious tears began to fall from her eyes. "You will hate me forever! But why did the King not tell me?"

"The King?" Natheless's voice was sharp with surprise.

Wailing loudly, Ginevra threw herself to her knees before Natheless. "Forgive me! If I had known, I would never have looked upon him! I never meant to injure you! Say you forgive me. I will return to Italy and become a nun and donate my property to the Church. My child will be a monk, too!"

"Stand up! Stand up!" cried the Princess nervously. "What is the use of this?"

"Forgive me! Forgive me!" insisted Ginevra.

Seeing her distressed commands had no effect, Natheless tried another approach. Leaning toward the crying girl, she spoke in a softer tone. "I do not understand you, my lady. The gestures you use mean nothing in my culture. I do not know precisely what you mean by forgive. What exactly should I do to grant it? Please stand up, so that we may talk about it."

Ginevra's tears subsided. She looked hopeful. But she did not rise. "You do not understand forgiveness?"

"I have heard the word, but I do not know what you mean by it. Are you asking me not to take vengeance? Surely you do not think I intend you any harm?"

"But you will hate me forever!"

"Would you be harmed by that, my lady?"

"Sì! It would kill my heart within me!"

"Very well, then, since I said I would not harm you, it seems I cannot hate you, either."

Lady Ginevra rose hesitantly to her feet. "But you have been injured because of me!"

Natheless guided Ginevra to her new quarters. They had previously been unoccupied. The walls were the basic Peleziterean blue she had seen on the walls of the Skimmer's Sleeping Room. "What is the use of such talk, Lady Ginevra? There is no question of my marrying Prince Alrik now. It is not so much on your account. When we discussed it afterward, he said something disrespectful about matters that mean a lot to me. I realized then we would not make good partners. Whether Alrik will make a good partner for you is something you must decide yourself. Do what you think best for yourself and your child, or for Alrik, if you care to think of him, but do not trouble about me. I am well enough. The past cannot be undone, so let us take care to manage the future better."

Ginevra watched, still sorrowful, and Natheless held out a hand. "Take my hand, Ginevra. That is a gesture common to our peoples." They clasped hands, and Natheless said, "Shall we be friends?"

"*Sì*," said Ginevra, in a swirl of feelings.

Natheless departed. Ginevra's mind was a chaos as she contemplated being her beloved Alrik's wife and bringing up their children—in a land with no hawks or horses, no priests, no churches, no fixed stars, maybe even no God, and where she would never see her family again.

34

"I want to know what will happen next," said Jimmik Centauri.

Bodris didn't answer immediately. She stretched luxuriously on her bunk opposite Jimmik, savoring her new importance. "I thought you said they couldn't find us," she remarked. "That device of yours is supposed to block the detectors, isn't it?"

"Unquestionably!" declared Jimmik smugly. "But I still don't relish being cooped up here for the rest of my life."

Skimmer II was resting in a cave Jimmik Centauri had hollowed out on a peninsula between the Mediterranean and a small inland sea. As it was at some distance from human settlements, Bodris had ventured outside dressed in Italian clothes. A port city was only a few miles along the coast, and there were scattered villages, none very close.

"Why so impatient?" she said languidly. "It's a nice location."

He didn't take the bait. "Lawchild Bodris," he said, calculating on her pleased response to that title, "I didn't risk my life to rescue you from the Archon's camp so you could lie here and make entertaining quips. Let's talk about the landing party. You told me the Archon's plan, how he intended to lure me from hiding with a pretended departure. But they will hardly try that now, knowing I'm on the Italian peninsula. Obviously they will keep the Orbiter watching this area so I can't ambush them again. But what else will they try? Will they call for reinforcements or more ships?"

"They might," replied Bodris indifferently.

Jimmik was thoughtful. "Their mistake if they do. They can't find me unless I fly the Skimmer. Which, of course, I needn't do. And the more personnel they summon, the greater the chance of desertions." He laughed. "Their record so far has been pitiful. Me, you, and Alrik. By the way, do you think Alrik will get away and join us?"

Bodris looked fastidious. "When he knows you tried to kill his father? Not Alrik. Besides, it was still his guard shift when we attacked. They're sure to have found him out."

"What a shame," sighed Jimmik. "I'd hoped that unpleasant surprise was still in their future." Bodris's indolent and insolent manner was beginning to irritate him slightly, so he fixed his eyes on another part of the room. "As I was saying, it won't do them any good to request reinforcements. They can't find us, and time is on our side."

"They could use ships against us if the Contact department locates us," warned Bodris.

She was trying after all. Jimmik followed her lead. "Yes, the Contact department, now. Who's left in it? Only Natheless?"

"And Floress," said Bodris. "But she has no real flair. Natheless is the dangerous one. She'll trace us by rumor among the natives. That's why we can't risk meeting the natives."

"No!" Jimmik turned quickly back to her. "I said I won't be cooped up here forever. If they're going to trace us through native rumor, two can play that game. You've got contact skills yourself. It's a question of who locates whom first."

Bodris was surprised. "What? You'd attack again? But the Orbiter will detect you, and if they've sent for reinforcements, we're finished!"

Jimmik mused. "Natheless and the Archon are at the root of the problem. If Natheless dies, the Archon can't work among the natives. If the Archon dies, Natheless will have no Peleziterean support. If I knew for certain where they were, I'd risk attacking. But I suppose they'll change their base, as they did before."

"If they don't, they'll certainly have gained reinforcements," said Bodris.

"I see. Then, Lawchild Bodris, it's up to you."

This did not strike Bodris as brilliant strategy, not that she would humor Jimmik by showing fear. "Is that the best you can do? Get us killed?" she demanded.

"I've done more than my share, Lawchild," said Jimmik pointedly. "You should suggest something now. In reality, it's wasteful to use a sophisticated ship like Skimmer II just to kill one ailing man and his raw accomplice. A native knife in the heart would do as well. In fact, for Benrik Eridani, a pat of planetary mud in the face would almost be enough. He's not a healthy man. But for this we need native help. That's up to you. You're my Contact department."

Though immensely pleased at his confidence in her, Bodris tried to needle him by assuming a mask of indifference. "Well, really," she said, "you're the one who wants to conquer the world." Her placidity infuriated him as she added, "I'll see what I can do for you." Then she rolled over on her stomach to ponder her new responsibilities.

Near the middle of the Italian peninsula the Archon's party gathered up the remains of Skimmer I and its forlorn survivors. The Orbiter kept watch against further ambush. Then began the complicated task of smoothing relations with Conradin's family. So intricate were these negotiations that the High Council was transported to the Orbiter to take part. Extraordinary concessions had to be made to Conradin. But oddly enough, from Natheless's point of view, they were not what the High Council balked at. Without a murmur of protest, the High Council agreed to accept Ginevra as a Lawchild, to permit a priest to accompany her, to receive up to three hundred of Conradin's allies as refugees among them should the need arise and to allow all these natives to practice their religion unhindered. Questions about equipment and personnel on the planet engaged them longer. Predictably, Nibbana Parzes had had enough of the mission and did not want to commit anything more to it.

"I don't understand why you need to replace the Skimmer," she remarked. "Now you have Centauri tracked to a small region which the Orbiter can watch all the time. You'll have ample warning in case of attack."

"Yes," the Archon answered patiently, "ample warning for flight. But with the Skimmer we'd have a chance of defeating him, which is our main purpose. The Skimmer would not come with us to the planet but remain with the Orbiter unless and until Jimmik is spotted."

"The presence of a Skimmer didn't help you last time," persisted Nibbana. "And a valuable life was lost." Nibbana often felt impelled to mention the obvious.

Benrik Eridani's anguish was evident and painful to all beholders. "That's true, Sixfold. But it shouldn't have happened that way. It just shouldn't have happened that way. We simply must trust the remaining crew members. That's all that can be said."

No one answered. The culprit they all wanted to upbraid was confined to his quarters, all his rank temporarily suspended. Nibbana directed the discussion elsewhere.

"This catastrophe really shouldn't have startled us. Our instinctive desires for a homeland are powerful. The longer we remain in this planet's neighborhood, the more Pelezitereans will be lured away from the colony. In fact, only three days ago we arrested a group of juveniles trying to commandeer a scout ship. Whether they meant to strike out on their own or join Centauri is unclear. Luckily we caught them before they boarded. Otherwise, it might have been difficult to intercept them before they reached the planet."

This was dismal news, but the Archon was not swayed. "The Peleziterea is too close to the planet now. We will withdraw it to a maximal orbit of the planet's sun. The crew remaining with the Orbiter, and the landing party will be as small as possible and the most trustworthy."

There was a pause while the others absorbed this. "That decreases the likelihood, Sevenfold, but does not eliminate it," said Nibbana. "Besides, each of these desertions was after all unexpected. Doesn't it seem all our efforts to mend the damage of cultural contact have in fact increased it? Isn't Jimmik Centauri more dangerous than the two hatcherbrats you originally went to arrest?"

"Yes," replied the Archon, without hesitation. "There can be no doubt, if every hatcherbrat aboard the Peleziterea descended to the planet now, they couldn't worsen the situation. They might improve it. If we can't make Jimmik leave, the whole colony may as well settle on the planet for all the difference it would make."

The High Council was aghast. "You're saying total negation of the Prime Directive is better than a partial violation, Sevenfold?" queried Nibbana.

The Archon's patience was visibly strained, as though he felt this too obvious to need explanation. "Jimmik's presence on the planet is a total, not a partial, violation. Nothing beyond that is needed to doom the native culture. Other presences might soften his effect by joining with natives and treating their concepts with more respect. They might help the natives advance and refine their own culture, instead of simply destroying it, as Jimmik would make them do. We were not supposed to do this, because we should not entirely trust our own notions of refinement and

276

advancement. Nevertheless, Peleziterean attempts at help might be less destructive than unashamed Peleziterean domination. The joint culture would not be a total wasteland. There would still be birth and death, authority and rebellion, work and rest, love and hate, tears and laughter, selfishness and altruism. And after all, the Prime Directive was designed mainly to protect inhabited planets. Making Pelezitereans miserable was not its major objective.

"If we settled on the planet, life would go on. But not my life. There is no doubt in my mind, the planet would be better off left alone. And the only thing that prevents it from being so is us—our irresponsibility. Our halfheartedness. Our greed. Therefore I do not intend to be halfhearted. I decided long ago I would not outlive the Prime Directive."

This speech shamed the High Council. The Archon was given what he had requested, and the meeting adjourned. Natheless caught Nibbana Parzes as she was stepping out the door. "Lawchild Nibbana, I'd like to talk to you," she said.

"Oh?" The Personality sub-Archon was surprised. Never in her memory had Natheless deliberately sought an interview.

"Preferably alone," added Natheless.

"Certainly," said Nibbana. "Come to my quarters."

Though Nibbana's quarters aboard the Orbiter were only temporary, she had already taken the trouble to decorate them with her discordant oranges and reds. Natheless stared at the walls, wishing they would give her some clues to the intricacies of Nibbana's mind. They didn't. "Something's bothering me," said Natheless, when she had seated herself at the sub-Archon's request.

"I'm glad you have the courage to ask for help," said Nibbana. "It shows maturity."

Nibbana was far from getting the point. "I'm glad you take it that way, Lawchild. It's about Ginevra—I mean the native woman Alrik will marry."

The Personality sub-Archon nodded understandingly. "Yes, of course. I thought it would be that. By the way, it was very mature of you to suggest the idea of adopting her among us. It's hard for you, I know, but you are right in thinking it will be the best thing for the Peleziterea."

Natheless took a deep breath and plunged in. "Yes, I think so, but frankly I'm surprised you do. You've been very dubious about the God-Myth and yet you voted with the others to allow the Italians among us to practice their religion. And even to try to spread it. I did make it clear they'd do that, didn't I?"

"Well, of course, Natheless! You made it very clear! But the natives will be good for us. Their excellent genes and strong family bonds will far outweigh the disadvantages of their primitive outlook. Of course, I'm sure they'll be some trouble. They'll have a lot of learning to do. But ultimately it will be worth it. As for spreading their religion, what chance do they have in a culture like ours?"

"You might be surprised," answered Natheless.

Nibbana found this hilarious. "You're an interesting case, Natheless! You have so thoroughly repressed your jealousy, you think you're trying to protect the Peleziterea, when you're really trying to rob the native woman of her husband."

At this, Natheless had had enough. She stood up, flushing. "Very well, Lawchild! If you want to think I'm so simpleminded I don't know my own motives, go ahead. I'll conclude you're deliberately evading the issue!"

Nibbana also stood up, raising her voice. "Not so fast, Natheless! Most of your troubles stem from your inability to accept your own perfectly normal egotistical strivings. For some reason you feel the need to pretend you're selfless. If you could get over that, you might adapt to normal life."

Natheless answered icily, "I am not one bit ashamed of my own perfectly normal egotistical strivings; I just don't happen to want to discuss them with you right now. And if you're determined not to answer my question seriously, I guess there's no point in my staying here longer."

Nibbana was in a cold fury. "I won't answer your question, you say? In answer to your question: Yes, I have no doubt the presence of the planetary natives will temporarily give an impetus to the society that used to revolve around you and Agni and your worship of the God-Myth. But for Lawchildren who are normal in every other respect, these ceremonies will only be what they always were for everyone except the two of you: an interesting diversion. It is simply not normal for people with as much scientific knowledge as you have to believe in gods."

Natheless felt darkness, the threat of annihilation, pressing on her from all sides. Her vision blurred. When it cleared again, Nibbana was watching her closely. "Don't you think we should talk about your problem now?" she said.

Natheless shook her head. "No. No, Lawchild Nibbana. I don't have any problems. Thank you for answering my question. Good-bye." She turned toward the door, but Nibbana called after her.

"Natheless, I'm sorry if I upset you. But I don't think running away will help."

Natheless answered quietly, "I am sorry if you are sorry, Lawchild Nibbana. After all, you are just trying to do your job. But whether it pleases you or not, it is basically upsetting to be told your mind is not a mind and your heart is not a heart. So if you insist on perceiving me that way, you will have to accept the fact that it upsets me." She went out before Nibbana, who liked to get the last word, could say any more. Swiftly she walked through the corridors, shuddering uncontrollably with the fear Nibbana's words still succeeded in arousing. But gradually that reaction subsided and she felt herself growing angrier and angrier. Suddenly she knew she had the strength to carry out a plan that had occurred to her a while before.

Alrik was in his quarters in the Lander. Natheless made her way there and knocked on his door.

"Who's there?" Alrik's voice was tense and defensive. He was waiting to be summoned before the Council and was in fear of reprimand.

"It's Natheless, Alrik. The meeting's over and they've agreed to everything, if no one's told you already. I wanted to talk about specifics."

The door opened, revealing a haggard Alrik with circles under his eyes and slightly hunched shoulders. "What is it?" he asked dully.

Natheless's energy deserted her, as she had half-known it would. As Alrik stepped aside, she leaned against the doorframe. "Alrik—where are you going to live?"

He stared. "It hasn't been discussed—but I assume nuclear family quarters in the Eridani Bubble, for Ginevra and me. The priest, I guess, would have adjoining quarters, and Anselino will probably be sent to the Personality Bubble."

"Alrik—I think you would all be much better off at Haven."

His mouth dropped open. "But—but you have all the programs, all the combinations to unlock the doors and get the synthesizers working—"

"Yes, but I can give them to you." Natheless unstrapped her wrist unit and held it out to him. He shrank away. "It's all right," she said. "I transferred everything personal from its memory to Agni's. I am keeping Agni's unit for myself—you know why."

Alrik slowly reached toward the wrist unit. "But why, Natheless? Won't you want Haven yourself?"

Natheless shrugged. "I can't live there now, Alrik, and when I come back it would be fairly easy for me to open up another deserted Bubble—if I ever want one."

Alrik nodded. "That's true, I guess." It was all he could think of to say.

Silence fell. At least he added, "Natheless, you've been extremely generous to me—I can never be thankful enough, or tell you how sorry I am. I . . ."

Natheless turned toward the wall of the outside corridor. "Alrik, I don't want you to be sorry. I want—I want you to beat Nibbana Parzes," she concluded somewhat awkwardly.

"You want me to do what?" demanded Alrik, turning to her in his surprise.

She turned back then, and to her relief, a slight smile came easily. "I was just talking to Nibbana Parzes. I was surprised she gave in so easily to allowing Ginevra and the priest to practice their religion without interference. I found out the reason is she has an entirely false picture of the situation. She expects them to abandon their religion spontaneously when they learn what she considers to be the truth. When she realizes that isn't going to happen, she'll make plenty of trouble. The kind of trouble she makes is hard enough on me when I know the God-Myth is a fantasy that I consciously elaborate, but these people take their belief literally. For them to accept there is no God is for them to disbelieve in the validity of all their experiences. If you lived in the Eridani Bubble, Ginevra would be completely under the control of your female cousins and the Parzes children, and would have to live in the environment they arranged. The pressure would be very strong from them to adopt their way of thinking about everything, from the very beginning. If, however, you lived in Haven, you could do several things to arrange the environment as you want it. You could invite people to visit you when you want, and keep them out when you don't. You could take her visiting other Bubbles and researching Peleziterean technology when the time was right, or staying in the Bubble talking about Italian culture when you prefer. Ginevra and the priest and you will have much more control of your immediate surroundings and will be better able to form a synthesis."

Alrik nodded slowly. "I don't understand all of what you're saying, but things will be easier on Ginevra if we live in Haven."

"As long as you see it," said Natheless. "Good-bye, Alrik. I wish you good luck." She backed off slowly, but Alrik called after her.

"Natheless!"

"What?"

He shifted uncomfortably in the doorway. "You're—you're too good to be true."

Natheless bowed her head. "No, Alrik. I just try to do the right thing." Looking up, she added hesitantly, "We've known each other since we were children. I used to think of you as sort of a brother. I guess it was unfair of me to expect you to be—something else."

"Natheless—if we could be friends like that again—if you could forget—is that too much?" Alrik looked down.

Natheless smiled sadly. "Perhaps, Alrik, perhaps it's not too much. It's only—too much right now." He looked up, and she whispered, "Keep the faith, Alrik." She turned quickly and walked away.

35

Many people at Rome had seen two spheres wrapped in their own fire rush together over Tuscanella after sunset that day late in June. The vision caused consternation. Charles was furious about the Pope's inaction. "Conradin remains within your realms, in the patrimony of Saint Peter. He gathers armies to attack me. He consults sorcerers. Yet you do not cut him off from the Church!" he accused.

The Pope was troubled himself, but still undecided. "I did not command him to depart from Tuscanella," he said. "If his account of the Infidels is true, he has reason to linger." And, as Ambrogio diffidently pointed out, the two spheres seemed to be in conflict, suggesting there might be two factions among the Infidels after all.

Instead of acting hastily, Sinibaldo waited for Conradin to send him an account of the action. It arrived in due course, a letter full of courtly hyperbole about a treacherous ambush, a servant's wicked and unnatural disloyalty to her King, the piteous death of a brave warrior and the infuriating escape of the hideous Infidel who would not, however, escape Satan's pursuit. Predictably, the letter glossed over the strangeness of the weapons involved. It touched only briefly on the sex of the warrior killed, deflecting criticism by a subtle allusion to the famous Amazons of ancient times, Camilla and Penthesilea.

Sinibaldo was not prepared, however, for the glowing postscript, in which Conradin suddenly announced the conversion of an Infidel Prince. Gushing with enthusiasm, the letter invited Pope Innocent V to officiate at the ceremony of baptism and the wedding which was to take place several days later. Prince Alrik was to marry Conradin's beloved kinswoman, the Lady Ginevra. There was also the matter of selecting the priest who would accompany the noble bride to her new home among foreigners.

The Pope was mystified at this turn of events. King Charles, however, understood the situation at once. "He prostitutes his own cousin to the Infidel to gain an ally! And he has the impudence to suggest the Pope should countenance it! How can Your Holiness endure his shamelessness?"

Certainly, Sinibaldo could see, the short span between the baptism and the marriage was suspect. "Yet they say the Infidels will receive a priest among them," he mused. "There's a chance there. . . ."

"A chance they won't kill him!" rejoined the King. Then he almost pleaded, "These Infidels want to enslave Christendom. Why will you not denounce and condemn Conradin for harboring them?"

The Pope answered rather abstractedly. "No Infidel can enslave us. Only we can do that by abjuring God and submitting."

This platitude greatly irritated the King. "Then it would not annoy Your Holiness if they merely slaughtered us?"

The Pope recollected himself and dealt with the worldly man on his own level. "Your Majesty doubts my love for Christendom? Why? True, I have no illusions this can be a proper conversion, and I fear they have not allowed time for proper instruction. But if this Infidel will accept baptism in order to marry a fair lady, and his people consent, they cannot be extremely bitter against God. More of them may become Christian."

King Charles was silent, convinced the shepherd of souls was completely uninterested in the bodies of men. Guessing his thoughts, Sinibaldo continued, "Why so dejected, Sire? If I accept these foreign converts, do you imagine I would allow them to remain bound to Conradin alone? Of course you will be included in any permanent peace we arrange."

Conradin knew that the Pope, not recognizing his royal title, could not perform the baptism or marriage at his court. He only hoped the bishop who did perform the ceremonies would not be suspended or excommunicated. In order to minimize the possible offense, he had stressed the shortness of time, asserting that Alrik was urgently needed in his own kingdom and must be both married and Christian before his departure. The Bishop of Verona had already agreed to officiate and recommended an eager protégé of his to act as a missionary to the Pelezitereans.

Both ceremonies were celebrated magnificently. Alrik, dressed in white to represent his cleansing from sin, knelt in the baptistery. The Bishop, dressed in his splendid jeweled vestments and wearing his mitre, sprinkled water on him and said the necessary Latin words.

Since the marriage resulted from a family disgrace, Conradin and Anticoli would have liked to celebrate it quietly. But Ginevra was a well-known member of his family and her disappearance from Italy would be remarked. If the marriage was not public, sinister rumors would abound. Hence, he and Anticoli made a bold show of it. Alrik was bravely decked in robes of purple and gold, altered to fit him for the occasion, and Ginevra was resplendent in a yellow gown and her family jewels. After the ceremony the couple was carried in an open horse-litter through the streets of the city while they scattered gold and silver coins among the cheering crowd. Later they reveled all evening in the great hall. Wine flowed freely and Conradin's supporters were wild with enthusiasm. Alrik's conversion reaffirmed their badly shaken faith in their own culture and Conradin as its effective protector.

Moving among the guests, Conradin was elated. A near disaster had been converted into a modest triumph. He would have preferred, of course, a military alliance against King Charles and Jimmik Centauri. But this at least was an alliance of sorts, sealed with a marriage. He and his family would have a place of refuge if driven from Italy. Conradin thought soberly a moment about life in the ship which wandered among the stars. Thus far the barrenness of the Pelezitereans' environment had daunted him less than their powers and store of knowledge lured him. But no doubt he would soon come to miss his world sorely if he left it. But there might be no choice. If they remained in Italy after the departure of the mighty Infidels, his family would simply be wiped out. Besides, a departure did not end all hope. The Pelezitereans might change their minds and return. He might help make them change their minds.

At midnight the bridal pair was put to bed. Ginevra left the great hall first, accompanied by her sister, Bianca, and their maidens. Alrik remained at the High Table, ill at ease. Anticoli then moved closer to him and tried to entertain him with jests. That was a change for the better, Conradin thought. The day of their return after the battle, Alrik had had to kneel before Anticoli and beg his pardon for seducing his sister-in-law.

At one point this confrontation had grown so tense that Natheless's hand had moved toward her silver rod. Not, thought Conradin, that Anticoli had ever intended violence. But Conradin had feared this scandal might open a permanent breach between himself and his hitherto loyal cousin.

Then it was time to lead Alrik to his bride. As Alrik had no young male companions of his own nation, Conradin took his arm and led him from the room. The knights followed, and so did the tired Princess Natheless, the only Peleziterean besides Alrik still at the castle. King Benrik had stayed only a few minutes before Lady Floress escorted him back to his Silver Tower.

When they arrived at the bride's chamber, the merry ladies were standing all around the room. Flowers in bunches and garlands were everywhere. Ginevra, pink with blushes, already lay under the gay bed coverings. You would almost think she had never slept with him before, Conradin reflected. It was just as well. Everyone was supposed to believe that.

Conradin led the Prince into the room and released him. "Claim your bride," he whispered. But though Alrik had been instructed, he still gave one wildly embarrassed look around at the guests in the room before he carefully crawled under the covers beside Ginevra. Some knights burst into raucous laughter at his backwardness, and some ladies tittered behind their hands.

Then Bianca said a blessing over the pair and kissed Ginevra, shedding a few sisterly tears. The other guests added their blessings and good wishes and filed out. Some of the men were still snickering. An Italian bridegroom would have disrobed at least partially before lying down, but this custom had not been forced on the shy foreigner.

The chamber door was closed and three of Conradin's knights began their watch outside. Conradin feared someone might attack Alrik, knowing he did not have his silver rod that night.

Natheless was there too. She looked immeasurably weary. How did she feel about the man behind the door? Conradin wondered suddenly, feeling a surge of sympathy. He went up to her and took her hand. Among Italians this was a conventional gesture of friendship, but it meant more to the Pelezitereans, and the Princess had objected, the first time Conradin had tried it. This time she did not pull away. She must have learned. "How goes it with you, *Madònna?*" he asked.

She responded with a rudimentary smile. "I am well, Sire. And glad this is over."

"You will retire now?"

"What else? The others are waiting for me."

"I will accompany you to the Silver Tower," he offered.

"What need?" she asked. But she did not stop him.

"Pray do not be mournful," he whispered as they walked through the quiet halls. "God will send you a better husband."

She laughed rather unhappily. "He needn't hurry. For the present I can do without one."

At the door of the castle she said, "Sire, if you come farther, you expose yourself to danger. Pray return now. I am safe with my silver rod."

He did not quite dare kiss her then, though they were alone and she seemed less remote than usual. Instead he pressed her hand and bade her good night.

Natheless walked alone over the grass, feeling oddly touched by Conradin's concern. She shouldn't be, she knew. He was only trying to weaken her loyalty to the Prime Directive. "But I can't be suspicious of everyone, all the time," she thought wearily. It had been quite a night's work, but well done. Good relations between the Pelezitereans and their informants had been restored. Reinforcements had been obtained and the long watch for Jimmik Centauri would begin again. And what would happen to the planet now? Could they save the culture? Every moment they remained, it changed a little. That could not be helped. The Archon's doubting words returned to her. She had been shocked to hear him admit the chance of the mission failing. "Life will go on," he had said. The notion was strangely exhilarating. There were more than two alternatives for the planet; there was a whole range of possibilities. Even when people wouldn't do what they should, they would always be doing something or other. Natheless wondered why the thought suddenly seemed profound. "I must be just too tired," she speculated.

She might well be tired. She felt she had lived enough for three lifetimes in the last two weeks. Life might go on, but not for her, not now, not until she had slept at least ten hours. She continued on her way across the courtyard to the Lander.

Notes

Although this is not strictly a historical work, a few acknowledgments seem in order. The letter that Conradin thinks of on page 99, written by Frederick II to his son Conrad, is mentioned in most biographies of Frederick II, but in this case I quoted it directly from page 319 of E. O. Lorimer's translation of Ernst Kantorowicz's biography of Frederick II (New York, 1931). The poem on pages 123–126 is a partial, loose translation of a poem by Rinaldo d'Aquino, *"Già mai non mi conforto,"*—one of the most frequently translated poems of the period. The poem on pages 88–89 is not a direct translation of any poem I have seen, but it and its interpretation were inspired by Dante Gabriel Rossetti's translation and commentary on a poem of Frederick II, found in Rossetti's work, *Dante and His Circle* (Boston, 1899).

I am of course indebted to many other works and people for details on the historical background of this story, but to acknowledge them all properly and explain the relationship between their facts and theories and my fiction would take a book three times as long as this one and would hardly be worth it. So, regrettably, I am forced to leave the thing undone.

About the Author

Gwenyth Hood grew up in Vermont and began her writing at the age of eleven, an activity that continued through her teen and college years, culminating in a literary prize in her senior year at Wellesley College. She majored there in Medieval and Renaissance Studies and Latin, graduating with honors, and was elected to Phi Beta Kappa. In 1979 she earned her M.A. in Comparative Literature from the University of Michigan, and that same year her historical fiction, *Fior del Verde*, was awarded the highest prize in the novel category of the University's Hopwood Contest. Now a Ph.D. candidate in Comparative Literature at Michigan, Gwenyth Hood lives in West Lafayette, Indiana.